T0334499

THE CLAY SANSKRIT LIBRARY
FOUNDED BY JOHN & JENNIFER CLAY

WWW.CLAYSANSKRITLIBRARY.COM
WWW.NYUPRESS.ORG

First Edition 2007

The Clay Sanskrit Library is co-published by
New York University Press
and the JJC Foundation.

Further information about this volume
and the rest of the Clay Sanskrit Library
is available on the following websites:
www.claysanskritlibrary.com
www.nyupress.org

ISBN: 978-0-8147-5737-6 (cloth : alk. paper)

Artwork by Robert Beer.
Typeset in Adobe Garamond at 10.25 : 12.3+pt.
XML-development by Stuart Brown.
Editorial input from
Tomoyuki Kono & Eszter Somogyi.
Printed in Great Britain by St Edmundsbury Press Ltd,
Bury St Edmunds, Suffolk, on acid-free paper.
Bound by Hunter & Foulis, Edinburgh, Scotland.

MAHĀBHĀRATA
BOOK NINE

ŚALYA
VOLUME TWO

TRANSLATED BY

JUSTIN MEILAND

NEW YORK UNIVERSITY PRESS
JJC FOUNDATION

2007

Library of Congress Cataloging-in-Publication Data
Mahābhārata. Śalyaparvan. Adhyāya 30–65.
English & Sanskrit.
Mahabharata. Book 9, "Śalya." Vol. 2
edited and translated by Justin Meiland.
p. cm. – (The Clay Sanskrit library)
In English with Sanskrit parallel text;
includes translation from Sanskrit.
Includes bibliographical references and index.
ISBN 978-0-8147-5737-6 (cloth : alk. paper)
I. Meiland, J.,
II. Title. III. Series.

CONTENTS

SANSKRIT ALPHABETICAL ORDER

Vowels:	*a ā i ī u ū ṛ ṝ ḷ ḹ e ai o au ṃ ḥ*
Gutturals:	*k kh g gh ṅ*
Palatals:	*c ch j jh ñ*
Retroflex:	*ṭ ṭh ḍ ḍh ṇ*
Dentals:	*t th d dh n*
Labials:	*p ph b bh m*
Semivowels:	*y r l v*
Spirants:	*ś ṣ s h*

GUIDE TO SANSKRIT PRONUNCIATION

a	b*u*t
ā, â	f*a*ther
i	s*i*t
ī, î	f*ee*
u	p*u*t
ū, û	b*oo*
ṛ	vocalic *r*, American p*ur*dy or English p*re*tty
ṝ	lengthened *ṛ*
ḷ	vocalic *l*, ab*le*
e, ê, ē	m*a*de, esp. in Welsh pronunciation
ai	b*i*te
o, ô, ō	r*o*pe, esp. Welsh pronunciation; Italian s*o*lo
au	s*ou*nd
ṃ	*anusvāra* nasalizes the preceding vowel
ḥ	*visarga*, a voiceless aspiration (resembling English *h*), or like Scottish lo*ch*, or an aspiration with a faint echoing of the preceding vowel so that *taiḥ* is pronounced *taih*ⁱ
k	lu*ck*
kh	blo*ckh*ead
g	*g*o
gh	bi*gh*ead
ṅ	a*n*ger
c	*ch*ill
ch	mat*chh*ead
j	*j*og
jh	aspirated *j*, he*dgeh*og
ñ	ca*ny*on
ṭ	retroflex *t*, *t*ry (with the tip of tongue turned up to touch the hard palate)
ṭh	same as the preceding but aspirated
ḍ	retroflex *d* (with the tip of tongue turned up to touch the hard palate)
ḍh	same as the preceding but aspirated
ṇ	retroflex *n* (with the tip

	of tongue turned up to touch the hard palate)
t	French *t*out
th	ten*t h*ook
d	*d*inner
dh	guil*dh*all
n	*n*ow
p	*p*ill
ph	u*ph*eaval
b	*b*efore
bh	a*bh*orrent
m	*m*ind
y	*y*es
r	trilled, resembling the Italian pronunciation of *r*
l	*l*inger
v	*w*ord
ś	*sh*ore
ṣ	retroflex *sh* (with the tip of the tongue turned up to touch the hard palate)
s	hi*ss*
h	*h*ood

CSL PUNCTUATION OF ENGLISH

The acute accent on Sanskrit words when they occur outside of the Sanskrit text itself, marks stress, e.g. Ramáyana. It is not part of traditional Sanskrit orthography, transliteration or transcription, but we supply it here to guide readers in the pronunciation of these unfamiliar words. Since no Sanskrit word is accented on the last syllable it is not necessary to accent disyllables, e.g. Rama.

The second CSL innovation designed to assist the reader in the pronunciation of lengthy unfamiliar words is to insert an unobtrusive middle dot between semantic word breaks in compound names (provided the word break does not fall on a vowel resulting from the fusion of two vowels), e.g. Maha·bhárata, but Ramáyana (not Rama·áyana). Our dot echoes the punctuating middle dot (·) found in the oldest surviving forms of written Indic, the Ashokan inscriptions of the third century BCE.

The deep layering of Sanskrit narrative has also dictated that we use quotation marks only to announce the beginning and end of every direct speech, and not at the beginning of every paragraph.

CSL PUNCTUATION OF SANSKRIT

The Sanskrit text is also punctuated, in accordance with the punctuation of the English translation. In mid-verse, the punctuation will not alter the *sandhi* or the scansion. Proper names are capitalized. Most Sanskrit metres have four "feet" *(pāda):* where possible we print the common *śloka* metre on two lines. In the Sanskrit text, we use French *Guillemets* (e.g. *«kva saṃcicīrṣuḥ?»*) instead of English quotation marks (e.g. "Where are you off to?") to avoid confusion with the apostrophes used for vowel elision in *sandhi*.

Sanskrit presents the learner with a challenge: *sandhi* ("euphonic combination"). *Sandhi* means that when two words are joined in connected speech or writing (which in Sanskrit reflects speech), the last letter (or even letters) of the first word often changes; compare the way we pronounce "the" in "the beginning" and "the end."

In Sanskrit the first letter of the second word may also change; and if both the last letter of the first word and the first letter of the second are vowels, they may fuse. This has a parallel in English: a nasal consonant is inserted between two vowels that would otherwise coalesce: "a pear" and "an apple." Sanskrit vowel fusion may produce ambiguity. The chart at the back of each book gives the full *sandhi* system.

Fortunately it is not necessary to know these changes in order to start reading Sanskrit. For that, what is important is to know the form of the second word without *sandhi* (pre-*sandhi*), so that it can be recognized or looked up in a dictionary. Therefore we are printing Sanskrit with a system of punctuation that will indicate, unambiguously, the original form of the second word, i.e., the form without *sandhi*. Such *sandhi* mostly concerns the fusion of two vowels.

In Sanskrit, vowels may be short or long and are written differently accordingly. We follow the general convention that a vowel with no mark above it is short. Other books mark a long vowel either with a bar called a macron (*ā*) or with a circumflex (*â*). Our system uses the macron, except that for initial vowels in *sandhi* we use a circumflex to indicate that originally the vowel was short, or the shorter of two possibilities (*e* rather than *ai*, *o* rather than *au*).

When we print initial	before *sandhi* that vowel was
â,	*a*
î or *ê*,	*i*
û or *ô*,	*u*
âi,	*e*
âu,	*o*

ā,	*ā* (i.e., the same)
ī,	*ī* (i.e., the same)
ū,	*ū* (i.e., the same)
ē,	*ī*
ō,	*ū*
āi,	*ai*
āu,	*au*

', before *sandhi* there was a vowel *a*

FURTHER HELP WITH VOWEL SANDHI

When a final short vowel (*a, i* or *u*) has merged into a following vowel, we print ' at the end of the word, and when a final long vowel (*ā, ī* or *ū*) has merged into a following vowel we print " at the end of the word. The vast majority of these cases will concern a final *a* or *ā*.

Examples:

What before *sandhi* was *atra asti* is represented as *atr' âsti*

atra āste	*atr' āste*
kanyā asti	*kany" âsti*
kanyā āste	*kany" āste*
atra iti	*atr' êti*
kanyā iti	*kany" êti*
kanyā īpsitā	*kany" ēpsitā*

Finally, three other points concerning the initial letter of the second word:

(1) A word that before *sandhi* begins with *ṛ* (vowel), after *sandhi* begins with *r* followed by a consonant: *yatha" rtu* represents pre-*sandhi* *yathā ṛtu*.

(2) When before *sandhi* the previous word ends in *t* and the following word begins with *ś*, after *sandhi* the last letter of the previous word is *c* and the following word begins with *ch*: *syāc chāstravit* represents pre-*sandhi syāt śāstravit*.

(3) Where a word begins with *h* and the previous word ends with a double consonant, this is our simplified spelling to show the pre-*sandhi*

form: *tad hasati* is commonly written as *tad dhasati*, but we write *tadd hasati* so that the original initial letter is obvious.

COMPOUNDS

We also punctuate the division of compounds (*samāsa*), simply by inserting a thin vertical line between words. There are words where the decision whether to regard them as compounds is arbitrary. Our principle has been to try to guide readers to the correct dictionary entries.

EXAMPLE

Where the Deva·nágari script reads:

कुम्भस्थली रक्षतु वो विकीर्णसिन्दूररेणुर्द्विरदाननस्य ।
प्रशान्तये विघ्नतमश्छटानां निष्ठ्यूतबालातपपल्लवेव ॥

Others would print:

kumbhasthalī rakṣatu vo vikīrṇasindūrareṇur dviradānanasya /
praśāntaye vighnatamaśchaṭānāṃ niṣṭhyūtabālātapapallaveva //

We print:

kumbha|sthalī rakṣatu vo vikīrṇa|sindūra|reṇur dvirad'|ānanasya
praśāntaye vighna|tamaś|chaṭānāṃ niṣṭhyūta|bāl'|ātapa|pallav" êva.

And in English:

"May Ganésha's domed forehead protect you! Streaked with vermilion dust, it seems to be emitting the spreading rays of the rising sun to pacify the teeming darkness of obstructions."

"Nava·sáhasanka and the Serpent Princess" I.3 by Padma·gupta

INTRODUCTION

THE MAIN EVENT of this, the second half of 'Shalya' (*Śalya/parvan*), is the decisive mace battle that occurs between two sworn enemies, Bhima and Dur·yódhana, at the end of the great war of the Bharatas. The self-contained nature of the section is suggested by the fact that some manuscripts and editions treat it as a separate book (*parvan*) called the 'Book of the Mace' (*Gadā/parvan*).[1] Conspicuous for the poignant and ambiguous manner in which the text portrays the slaughter of the Káurava king through "unlawful means" (58.19), the volume also contains a lengthy passage describing the merits of worshipping at pilgrimage sites on the Sarásvati river.

The Story So Far

For readers unfamiliar with the first volume of 'Shalya,' it would be useful to summarize the events leading up to the second half of the book. The focus of the 'Maha·bhárata' centers around a dynastic power struggle between two groups of cousins, the Káuravas and the Pándavas. The Pándavas are forced to spend thirteen years in exile after the eldest of the five Pándava brothers, Yudhi·shthira, loses his kingdom in a gambling match to Dur·yódhana, the eldest of Dhrita·rashtra's sons. Not only do the Pándavas lose their kingdom but their wife, Dráupadi, is also humiliated when she is dragged into an assembly hall during her menstruation period and when Dur·yódhana's brother, Duhshásana, attempts to disrobe her in front of the royal court. Dur·yódhana's refusal to make peace with the Pándavas after their exile has ended leads to a war on the plains of Kuru·kshetra.

Following the advice of the Mádhava hero Krishna, who acts as the charioteer of the Pándava warrior Árjuna, the Pándavas kill four successive generals of the Káurava army. While the first three generals are killed through tactics that conflict with the rules of combat and that are sensitively explored by the text for the moral dilemmas they pose, the fourth general, Shalya, is the only leader to be honorably killed in a duel that accords with the warrior code. At Shalya's death, the remainder of the already depleted Káurava army is destroyed, leaving only four warriors alive: Krita·varman, Kripa, Ashva·tthaman, and Dur·yódhana. The first volume of 'Shalya' concludes with Dur·yódhana fleeing the battlefield in order to take refuge in a lake.

Dur·yódhana's Defeat

Dur·yódhana is far from what one might describe as a model of good kingship. Impetuous and headstrong, he is in many ways an example of reckless government and irresponsible leadership, culpable for the deaths of his allies and kinsmen. In particular, one of his major faults, of which he and other characters in the epic are frequently reminded, is that he repeatedly rejects the advice of sages, counsellors, and elders (61.48, 63.44):

> *You never listened to the teachings of Brihas·pati and Úshanas. You never honored the elderly or listened to beneficial words. [. . .] Even though Bhishma, Soma·datta, Báhlika, Kripa, Drona, Drona's son, and wise Vídura all constantly entreated you to make peace, you did not follow their advice.*

From his childhood, Dur·yódhana is guilty of committing a number of wrongdoings against the Pándavas and at different stages in the epic, including this particular volume, various characters accuse him of crimes that even his closest family members condemn. One crime that is constantly brought up is Dráupadi's humiliation in the assembly hall; her desire for vengeance is a major factor motivating the need for Dur·yódhana's downfall.[2] But, although significant, this is only one among a whole catalog of misdeeds that the Pándavas feel more than justifies the death of their enemy, who is branded as a "clan destroyer" (33.48). Yudhi·shthira, for example, accuses Dur·yódhana thus (31.66ff.):

> *You made special efforts to burn us, use snakes and poisons against us, and drown us too. By stealing our kingdom, speaking abusive words, and maltreating Dráupadi, you have wronged us, O king. For this reason you cannot live, you criminal.*[3]

Dur·yódhana's transgressions, coupled with his reckless disregard for good advice and the course of fate, lead to the Káurava hero being described with words such as "evil" (*pāpa*), "foolish" (*dur/mati*), "dim-witted" (*mand'/ātman*) and "villainous" (*duṣṭ'/ātman*).

However, for all Dur·yódhana's manifest faults, there is also a certain nobility—based on his tenacious subscription to a warrior code, in which the quest for power and the glory of conquering one's foes are paramount—that is expressed in the Káurava's stubborn refusal to submit to his enemies (even if their demands are fair) and it would be simplistic to cast Dur·yódhana purely as a villain. He possesses several heroic qualities, particularly in terms of his strength and martial valor, that result in numerous eulogies of the Káurava king. He is, for example, described thus when he emerges from the lake to fight Bhima (32.39ff.):

> *When they saw Dur·yódhana brandishing his mace and looking like a peaked mountain or like trident-bearing Shiva when enraged with creatures—how that Bhárata shone like the blazing sun as he wielded his mace!—when they saw the mighty-armed enemy-tamer rise out of the water, mace in hand, every living being thought that he resembled staff-bearing Death.*

Indeed, Dur·yódhana's hotblooded temperament and distinguished ability as a warrior echo Bhima's character in many ways, thus making the two heroes suitable opponents for the duel forming the main event of this volume.[4] Krishna himself points out (33.2ff.) that no one except Bhima can match Dur·yódhana in a fight and he further admits (33.8ff.) that Dur·yódhana's superior skill outweighs Bhima's superior physical strength.

One of Dur·yódhana's main concerns as a kshatriya warrior is to attain the glory of dying in battle and thereby reach heaven. It is therefore all the more remarkable that when we meet Dur·yódhana at the beginning of this volume, he is hiding in a lake and avoiding the Pándavas. This is the king's lowest point in the epic. Not only does his reluctance to fight disappoint his allies, but he also lays himself open to the ridicule of his enemies. Yudhi·shthira, for example, berates him thus (31.20ff.):

Remember your clan and your birth! How can you boast of a birth in the Káurava lineage if you enter water and abide there, fearful of battle? [. . .] How is it, my friend, that you lie in a lake when you have caused the deaths of your relatives, friends, uncles, and kinsmen? Although arrogant about your heroism, you are no hero.

Although Dur·yódhana gives various excuses for his actions—with words that suggest more a sense of shame than truth[5]—he ultimately responds to Yudhi·shthira's demands to fight and emerges from the water a hero again. Ironically, however, while Yudhi·shthira appeals to the warrior code in order to convince Dur·yódhana to re-engage in battle, it is only by transgressing the warrior code that Bhima is finally able to fell his enemy. This he achieves by breaking Dur·yódhana's thighs (on Krishna's advice), an act that violates the rules of combat. Bala·rama, known for his impartiality toward the Káuravas and Pándavas and a teacher of both Dur·yódhana and Bhima, is incensed when he sees this dishonorable deed (60.4ff.):

Shame on you, Bhima! Shame on you! It is shameful to strike an opponent below the navel in honorable combat. I have never seen an action like Vrikódara's before in a mace contest. The Teachings state that one should never strike below the navel. This fool does not know the Teachings and acts according to his own will!

Nor does the text restrain itself from problematizing the moral implications of defeating the Káurava king in this way. Krishna himself repeatedly admits that Dur·yódhana cannot be conquered justly (*dharma*) and that the Pándavas must resort to deceit (*māyā*) and unlawful means (*a/nyā-ya*) if they are to win.[6] Furthermore, when Dur·yódhana is felled, the numerous bad omens that appear (58.48ff.) accentuate the transgressive nature of Bhima's deed, leaving the Pándava troops "bewildered" (58.59). Support for Dur·yódhana from the surrounding environment is further expressed when Dur·yódhana criticizes Krishna for his immoral slaughter of several Káurava allies and eulogizes his own achievements (61.27ff., 61.50ff.), whereupon a shower of flowers falls from the sky and deities voice their approval. At this juncture, Krishna's own men are said to feel shame (61.57ff.):

> *When they saw these miracles and witnessed the honor being done to Dur·yódhana, the men who were headed by Vasudéva were ashamed. When they heard how Bhishma, Drona, Karna and Bhuri·shravas had been immorally killed, they were sorrowful and stricken with grief.*

Nor do the crimes committed against Dur·yódhana cease with the breaking of his thighs. In his rage, Bhima also rubs the Káurava's head with his foot, an act of which Krishna himself disapproves (60.30–1). Bala·rama, who is established by the narrative as an impartial judge of the duel, is so outraged by these actions that he even attempts to attack Bhima. Although restrained by his brother Krishna, Rama remains unpersuaded by what the narrator describes as Krishna's "fraudulent morality" (60.23) and instead turns his back on the scene, condemning Bhima's victory thus (60.24ff.):

> *The Pándava will be known in the world as a crooked fighter because he has slain righteous King Su·yódhana*

through unjust means. But righteous Dur·yódhana—the royal son of Dhrita·rashtra and lord of men—will attain the eternal realm because he was killed as a fair fighter.

Both Krishna and Yudhi·shthira (59.21ff., 61.39ff.) cite Dur·yódhana's own immoral behavior as the fundamental cause of the sufferings of the war and as a justification for his present misfortune.[7]

It is because of your own wrongdoing—your greed, madness and stupidity—that you suffer this terrible misfortune, descendant of Bharata. You have arrived at your own destruction after causing the deaths of your friends, brothers, fathers, sons, grandchildren and others. (59.23ff.)

Ultimately, however, the primary justification used for both Bhima's immoral act and other tactics employed throughout the war is simply that the goal of victory validates the means—the Pándavas need to resort to such unlawful methods if they are to win.[8] Krishna's almost Machiavellian outlook is expressed when he addresses the Pándavas with the following words (61.60ff.):

If you had fought fairly in battle, you could never have killed swift-weaponed Dur·yódhana or all these great and courageous warriors. This king could never have been killed through just means, nor could all the great archers and great warriors that were led by Bhishma. In my desire to benefit you, I have killed every one of these men in battle by using various ploys and repeated deception.

Although the Pándavas have several moral arguments in their favor, the decisive reason for their victory is simply that they have Krishna and fate on their side.[9] Furthermore, on the theological level of the text, Krishna is identified with the god Vishnu and it is thus devotion to Vishnu that has overridden the old kshatriya code. One of the remarkable aspects of Dur·yódhana's character is that he continues to defy Krishna, even at his death (65.28):[10]

> *Although I am aware of the might of infinitely powerful Krishna, he has not toppled me from practicing the kshatriya law properly. I have fulfilled that law. I am not at all to be mourned.*

This defiance continues through to the end of the book (Canto 65) when Dur·yódhana consecrates Ashva·tthaman as the fifth general of the Káuravas, an act that leads to the terrible massacre of the next book, 'The Dead of the Night' (*Sauptika/parvan*).

While there is an element of humiliation in Dur·yódhana's final moments, as the Pándavas abandon their crippled enemy on the ground bewailing the maltreatment he has received, there is also a degree of poignant pathos as this once great warrior is left to die alone and apart from his loved ones. This pathos is mixed with a tone of solemnity and respect as the king sings several swansongs (61.50ff., 64.18ff., 65.24ff.), in which he lists the virtuous deeds he has performed as a kshatriya, repeatedly voicing the refrain: "Who has a better end than I?" While the claims Dur·yódhana makes may at times be questionable and while he conveniently omits to mention his own responsibilty in causing the deaths of his allies and relatives, there is, one senses, a gravitas to these passages that invests the hero with due honor at his final hour.[11]

The *Tīrtha* Pilgrimage

Although the mace battle is the most significant event in this volume regarding the "main narrative" represented by the war between the Káuravas and the Pándavas, the majority of the text (Cantos 35–54) comprises an account of Bala·rama's pilgrimage of the sacred sites (*tīrtha*s) along the Sarásvati river. The structure of the second half of 'Shalya' therefore consists of the mace battle at either end of the volume and the pilgrimage account placed in between. This circular framework is reinforced by the fact that some verses are repeated almost verbatim before and after the Sarásvati section.[12]

Devotional worship at *tīrtha*s plays a significant role in Hindu thought. A *tīrtha* is a sacred site, often located beside a body of water, where devotees can make merit by performing various religious acts, such as offering donations, bathing, fasting, or even giving up one's body.[13] Often such sites are associated with the deed of a particular deity or an important human being, and the majority of the account of Bala·rama's pilgrimage describes the various great feats that have been performed at different sites along the Sarásvati river. These range from the performance of a sacrifice or an act of asceticism to the consecration of Kumára as general of the gods. They also include the feats of various female ascetics,[14] one of whom surpasses her fellow male ascetics in her practice of austerities and another of whom wins a place alongside Indra in heaven (Canto 48). Mention is also frequently made of the benefits that accrue from bathing or performing other religious practices at these sites. Shiva, for example, describes the fruits of worshipping him at the *tīrtha* of Sapta·sarásvata (38.51):

> *Whoever worships me at this* tirtha *of Sapta·sarásvata will have no difficulty in gaining their desires either in this world or the next. Without doubt, they will reach the world of Sarásvati.*

The apparent dislocation of the Sarásvati account from the main narrative of the war may tempt scholars to view the section as a later addition. However, there are important ways in which the passage can be considered to relate to the war and to the mace battle that brackets it.

Bala·rama's decision to embark on his journey is motivated by an argument he has with Krishna, in which he unsuccessfully attempts to persuade his brother not to take sides in the war. Departing just before the battle begins, Bala·rama's pilgrimage thus occurs in tandem with the events of the war and his serene acts of worship at the *tīrtha*s stand in marked contrast to the horrors committed at Kuru·kshetra. In an important sense, therefore, the *tīrtha* pilgrimage can be seen as providing a type of purification for the terrible events of the war. This is particularly significant when one considers the passage in which Kuru·kshetra is praised as a site where men who give up their lives in battle directly enter heaven (Canto 53). Not only does this serve to purify the deaths of those who have died in battle so far, it also particularly relates to Dur·yódhana and his imminent slaughter in the mace contest. Hence the significance of Bala·rama's words when he directs the warriors to fight their duel at Kuru·kshetra (or Samánta·pánchaka) (55.6ff.):

> *Best of kings, I have heard seers say that Kuru·kshetra is an extremely sacred and pure place that leads to heaven and is frequented by gods, seers and great-spirited brahmins. Those who give up their bodies in battle there will forever live with Shakra in heaven, my lord. Let us therefore quickly go to Samánta·pánchaka, Your Majesty. In the realm of the gods, Samánta·pánchaka is famed as the northern altar of Praja·pati.*

In addition to securing Dur·yódhana's place in heaven, the *tīrtha* passage also establishes Bala·rama as a man of religious virtue and devotion, thus giving heightened significance to his outrage at the dishonorable way in which the Káurava king is slain. As someone who has not witnessed any of the horrors of the war, his presence at the mace battle serves as a stark reminder of the losses that have occurred as a result of the atrocities. While joyfully welcomed to the mace contest by both sides, these courtesies are but shortlived, belonging to a world previous to the battle, and Bala·rama is quick to leave the scene in disgust, turning his back on the victory of the Pándavas.

The Sanskrit Text and the Translation

As in the first volume of 'Shalya,' I have used Kinjawadekar's edition of the "vulgate" established by Nila·kantha as the main text for my translation and I have also referred to variants found in two nineteenth-century Bombay editions of Nila·kantha, one of which (Edition B) is extremely close to KINJAWADEKAR. For problematic passages, I have occasionally made use of Nila·kantha variants listed under Dn in the apparatus of the Critical Edition (CE). A full list of all variants from these three Nila·kantha editions and any emendations can be found on the CSL website.

The frequency of epithets in epic literature poses a problem for translators, as they can sometimes threaten to break the flow of sentences in English. Since this translation aims to remain close to the Sanskrit, I have attempted to translate all epithets when they occur but have occasionally omitted them when there is more than one common epithet in a sentence or if they appear to hinder the translation too greatly.

Where possible, I cite CSL volumes when making references to other sections of the 'Maha·bhárata.' However, since several volumes are in the process of being translated and since verse numbers cannot be predicted in advance, I have sometimes had to refer to the Critical Edition, with the intention that this will be rectified in the future.

NOTES

1 See for example edition A, which treats the section as a separate *parvan*. Editions B and K treat the section as a sub-*parvan* of the *Śalya/parvan*.

2 The power of female wrath is an important theme in the epic. Consider, for example, the fear that Yudhi·shthira expresses at Gandhári's potential anger when she hears of her sons' slaughter: 63.8ff.

3 For other passages, see: 33.41ff., 56.20ff., 59.4ff., 61.39ff.

4 See Cantos 55–57 for numerous verses comparing the two heroes.

5 See for example 31.37, where Dur·yódhana claims that he has retreated simply because he is weary. Dur·yódhana's exchange with Yudhi·shthira is also full of cutting sarcasm; see for example 31.50ff., in which Dur·yódhana tells Yudhi·shthira to enjoy the earth now that it has been destroyed.

6 See particularly 58.3ff. and 61.60ff. Krishna is also against the very existence of the duel, accusing Yudhi·shthira of gross irresponsibility in offering Dur·yódhana the kingdom if he beats his opponent and comparing his misjudgment to the recklessness he showed in gambling away his kingdom in the assembly hall (33.2ff.).

7 Fate is also referred to as a factor. See, for example, 59.25, 63.46.

8 Krishna seeks some warrant for his actions by citing the gods' use of deceit in defeating demons in the past (31.8ff., 58.5, 61.67). However, although demons are frequently associated with chaos, issues of morality are often not of foremost importance in these battles and, in epic and Vedic literature at least, the conflict between the gods and demons is often an amoral power struggle based around control over sacrifice.

9 For an illuminating study on the role of Krishna in the 'Maha·bhárata,' see Hiltebeitel 1990.

10 See Gitomer 1992 for Dur·yódhana's relationship with Krishna in both Sanskrit epic and drama.

11 Dur·yódhana does not actually die until Canto 9 of the *Sauptika/parvan*, where we are told that he attains heaven after learning of Ashva·tthaman's gruesome massacre of the Pándava troops.

12 Compare 33.30ff. and 56.16ff.

13 *Tīrtha* is a difficult word to translate. Literally meaning "crossing," a *tīrtha* enables devotees to "cross over" to the other world. Throughout the volume, I have sometimes translated the word as "sacred site" and sometimes let it stand as *tīrtha*. Many *tīrtha*s are found by rivers, where steps enable devotees to bathe in and sip the sacred water. Another lengthy passage on *tīrtha*s is found in MBh CE III.80–153. See VASSILKOV 2000 for a discussion of pilgrimage and the 'Maha·bhárata.'

14 Cantos 48, 52, and 54.6–8.

Bibliography

THE MAHA·BHÁRATA IN SANSKRIT

The Mahābhāratam with the Bharata Bhawadeepa Commentary of Nīlakaṇṭha. Edited by RAMACHANDRASHASTRI KINJAWADEKAR. 1929–36. 7 vols. Poona: Chitrashala Press. (Edition K).

The Mahābhārata with Nīlakaṇṭha's commentary. Edited by BALAKRISHNA KARBELKAR *et al.* 1862. 8 vols. Bombay: Bapusadashiva Press. (Edition A).

The Mahābhārata with Nīlakaṇṭha's commentary. Edited by A. KHADILKAR. 1862–3. 8 vols. Bombay: Ganapati Krishnaji's Press. (Edition B).

The Mahābhārata. Critically edited by V.K. SUKTHANKAR, S.K. BELVALKAR, P.L. VAIDYA *et al.* 1933–66. 19 vols. Poona: Bhandarkar Oriental Research Institute. (MBh CE).

THE MAHA·BHÁRATA IN TRANSLATION

GANGULI, KISARI MOHAN (trans.) [early editions ascribed to the publisher, P.C. ROY]. 1884–99. *The Mahabharata of Krishna-Dwaipayana Vyasa.* 12 vols. Calcutta: Bharata Press.

VAN BUITENEN, J.A.B. (trans. and ed.). 1973–78. *The Mahābhārata* [Books 1–5]. 3 vols. Chicago: Chicago University Press.

SECONDARY SOURCES

(Either used in the Introduction and Notes, or works that contribute to understanding this part of the 'Maha·bhárata')

BROCKINGTON, JOHN. 1998. *The Sanskrit Epics*. Leiden: Brill.

DONIGER, WENDY and SMITH, BRIAN K. (trans.). 1991. *The Laws of Manu*. New Delhi: Penguin Books India.

GITOMER, DAVID. 1992. 'King Duryodhana: The *Mahābhārata* Discourse of Sinning and Virtue in Epic and Drama.' *Journal of American Oriental Studies* 112. 222–232.

HILTEBEITEL, ALF. 1990. *The Ritual of Battle: Krishna in the Mahābhārata*. Albany: State University of New York Press.

MONIER-WILLIAMS, MONIER. 1899. *A Sanskrit-English Dictionary*. Oxford: Oxford University Press.

OBERLIES, THOMAS. 2003. *A Grammar of Epic Sanskrit*. Berlin: Walter de Gruyter.

SØRENSEN, SØREN. 1904–25. *An Index to the Names in the Mahābhārata*. London: Williams and Norgate.

VASSILKOV, YAROSLAV. 2000. 'Indian Practice of Pilgrimage and the Growth of the *Mahābhārata* in the Light of New Epigraphical Sources. Stages and Traditions: Temporal and Historical Frameworks in Epic and Puranic Literature.' Ed. M. Brockington. Zagreb: Academia Scientiarum et Artium Croatica. 133–156.

30–33
DUR·YÓDHANA CHALLENGED

DHṚTARĀṢṬRA uvāca:

30.1 HATEṢU SARVA|SAINYEṢU Pāṇḍu|putrai raṇ'|âjire
mama sainy'|âvaśiṣṭās te kim akurvata Sañjaya,
Kṛtavarmā Kṛpaś c' âiva Droṇa|putraś ca vīryavān?
Duryodhanaś ca mand'|ātmā rājā kim akarot tadā?

SAÑJAYA uvāca:

saṃprādravatsu dāreṣu kṣatriyāṇāṃ mah"|ātmanām
vidrute śibire śūnye bhṛś'|ôdvignās trayo rathāḥ.
niśamya Pāṇḍu|putrāṇāṃ tadā vai jayināṃ svanam,
vidrutaṃ śibiraṃ dṛṣṭvā sāy'|âhne rāja|gṛddhinaḥ
sthānaṃ n' ârocayaṃs tatra. tatas te hradam abhyayuḥ.
30.5 Yudhiṣṭhiro 'pi dharm'|ātmā bhrātṛbhiḥ sahito raṇe
hṛṣṭaḥ paryacarad rājan Duryodhana|vadh'|ēpsayā.
mārgamāṇās tu saṃkruddhās tava putraṃ jay'|âiṣiṇaḥ,
yatnato 'nveṣamāṇās te n' âiv' âpaśyañ jan'|âdhipam.
sa hi tīvreṇa vegena gadā|pāṇir apākramat
taṃ hradaṃ prāviśac c' âpi viṣṭabhy' āpaḥ sva|māyayā.
yadā tu Pāṇḍavāḥ sarve su|pariśrānta|vāhanāḥ
tataḥ sva|śibiraṃ prāpya vyatiṣṭhanta sa|sainikāḥ.
tataḥ Kṛpaś ca Drauṇiś ca Kṛtavarmā ca Sātvataḥ,
sanniviṣṭeṣu Pārtheṣu prayātās taṃ hradaṃ śanaiḥ.
30.10 te taṃ hradaṃ samāsādya yatra śete jan'|âdhipaḥ
abhyabhāṣanta dur|dharṣaṃ rājānaṃ suptam ambhasi:

DHRITA·RASHTRA said:

WHEN ALL THE soldiers had been killed by Pandu's sons on the battlefield, what did my surviving troops do, Sánjaya, namely Krita·varman, Kripa, and the fierce son of Drona? And what did foolish King Dur·yódhana* do? 30.1

SÁNJAYA said:

When the wives of the heroic kshatriyas* were fleeing and the camp was empty and deserted, the three warriors became deeply distressed. It was evening time and on hearing the cheers of Pandu's victorious sons and seeing the abandoned camp, they longed for their king and were unwilling to stay there any longer. They therefore set off for the lake.*

Righteous Yudhi·shthira, however, joyfully rampaged with his brothers on the battlefield, eager to kill Dur·yódhana, Your Majesty. In their desire for victory, the Pándavas furiously sought after your son and endeavored to track him down but could not see the king anywhere. Bearing his mace, Dur·yódhana had fled with ardent speed and entered the lake after magically freezing its waters. Since their animals were extremely tired, the Pándavas all returned to their camp and rested there with their troops. 30.5

While the Parthas stayed in their camp, Kripa, Krita·varman the Sátvata, and the son of Drona slowly advanced toward the lake. On reaching the lake where the king lay, they addressed the invincible monarch as he slept in the water: 30.10

«rājann uttiṣṭha! yudhyasva sah' âsmābhir Yudhiṣṭhiram!
jitvā vā pṛthivīṃ bhuṅkṣva hato vā svargam āpnuhi!
teṣām api balaṃ sarvaṃ hataṃ Duryodhana tvayā.
pratividdhāś ca bhūyiṣṭhaṃ ye śiṣṭās tatra sainikāḥ
na te vegaṃ viṣahituṃ śaktās tava viśāṃ pate
asmābhir api guptasya. tasmād uttiṣṭha Bhārata!»

DURYODHANA uvāca:

diṣṭyā paśyāmi vo muktān īdṛśāt puruṣa|kṣayāt
Pāṇḍu|Kaurava|saṃmardāj jīvamānān nara'|ṛṣabhān!
vijeṣyāmo vayaṃ sarve viśrāntā vigata|klamāḥ.
bhavantaś ca pariśrāntā vayaṃ ca bhṛśa|vikṣatāḥ.
udīrṇaṃ ca balaṃ teṣāṃ. tena yuddhaṃ na rocaye.
30.15 na tv etad adbhutaṃ vīrā yad vo mahad idaṃ manaḥ.
asmāsu ca parā bhaktir. na tu kālaḥ parākrame.
viśramy' âikāṃ niśām adya bhavadbhiḥ sahito raṇe
pratiyotsyāmy ahaṃ śatrūñ śvo. na me 'sty atra saṃśayaḥ.

SAÑJAYA uvāca:

evam ukto 'bravīd Drauṇī rājānaṃ yuddha|dur|madam:
«uttiṣṭha rājan! bhadraṃ te vijeṣyāmo vayaṃ parān!
iṣṭā|pūrtena dānena satyena ca jayena ca
śape rājan yathā hy adya nihaniṣyāmi Somakān!
mā sma yajña|kṛtāṃ prītim āpnuyāṃ saj|jan'|ôcitām
yad' îmāṃ rajanīṃ vyuṣṭāṃ na hi hanmi parān raṇe!

"Rise, Your Majesty! Fight with us against Yudhi·shthira! Either conquer and enjoy the earth or die and attain heaven! You have destroyed their entire army, Dur·yódhana. The remainder of their troops are mostly wounded and are unable to withstand your power, especially if you are protected by us, lord of the people. Rise, therefore, descendent of Bharata!"

DUR·YÓDHANA said:

How splendid to see that you bull-like men are alive and that you have escaped from this war between the Pandus and Káuravas, this massacre of human beings! After we have all rested and dispelled our fatigue, we will achieve victory. You are tired and I am badly wounded. Their army is stirred up and I am not keen to fight against it.

It is not surprising that you have such lofty thoughts, O heroes. You have shown the highest devotion toward me. But this is not the time for attack. Today I will rest for one night and tomorrow I will fight back against the enemy, accompanied by you in battle. Of this I have no doubt. 30.15

SÁNJAYA said:

In response, the son of Drona said these words to King Dur·yódhana, who is difficult to defeat in battle:

"Rise, Your Majesty! Fortune be with you, we will conquer the enemy!

By my sacrificial store* and gifts, and by truth and victory, I swear that I will vanquish the Sómakas today, Your Majesty! If I have not slaughtered the enemy in battle after

30.20 n' â|hatvā sarva|Pāñcālān vimokṣye kavacaṃ vibho!
iti satyaṃ bravīmy etat tan me śṛṇu jan'|âdhipa.»

teṣu saṃbhāṣamāṇeṣu vyādhās taṃ deśam āyayuḥ
māṃsa|bhāra|pariśrāntāḥ pānīy'|ârthaṃ yad|ṛcchayā.
te hi nityaṃ mahā|rāja Bhīmasenasya lubdhakāḥ
māṃsa|bhārān upājahrur bhaktyā paramayā vibho.
te tatra dhiṣṭhitās teṣāṃ sarvaṃ tad vacanaṃ rahaḥ
Duryodhana|vacaś c' âiva śuśruvuḥ saṃgatā mithaḥ:
te 'pi sarve mah"|êṣv|āsā a|yuddh'|ârthini Kaurave
nirbandhaṃ paramaṃ cakrus tadā vai yuddha|kāṅkṣiṇaḥ.

30.25 tāṃs tathā samudīkṣy' âtha Kauravāṇāṃ mahā|rathān
a|yuddha|manasaṃ c' âiva rājānaṃ sthitam ambhasi,
teṣāṃ śrutvā ca saṃvādaṃ rājñaś ca salile sataḥ,
vyādh" âbhyajānan* rāj'|êndra salila|sthaṃ Suyodhanam.
te pūrvaṃ Pāṇḍu|putreṇa pṛṣṭā hy āsan sutaṃ tava
yad|ṛcch" ôpagatās tatra rājānaṃ parimārgitāḥ.

tatas te Pāṇḍu|putrasya smṛtvā tad bhāṣitaṃ tadā
anyonyam abruvan rājan mṛga|vyādhāḥ śanair iva:

«Duryodhanaṃ khyāpayāmo dhanaṃ dāsyati Pāṇḍavaḥ.
su|vyaktam iha naḥ khyāto hrade Duryodhano nṛpaḥ.

30.30 tasmād gacchāmahe sarve yatra rājā Yudhiṣṭhiraḥ
ākhyātuṃ salile suptaṃ Duryodhanam a|marṣaṇam.

this night has passed, then may I not enjoy the bliss that comes from sacrifices and that is due to good men.

I will not take off my armor until I have destroyed all the Panchálas, my lord! Listen, ruler of people, to this truth that I speak." 30.20

While the men were talking to each other, some hunters who were tired from carrying their loads of meat happened to arrive in the area in order to drink water. These hunters regularly brought loads of meat to Bhima·sena in their deep devotion to him, great king. Standing at that spot and gathered together in secret, they heard the entire private conversation of those warriors, including Dur·yódhana's words. They listened as the great archers, who were eager for war, all strongly argued against the Káurava king, who was unwilling to fight.

When the hunters observed the great warriors of the Káuravas and saw the king lying in the water with no inclination for war, and when they heard the conversation between the men and the water-residing king, they discovered that Su·yódhana was hiding in the lake, Your Majesty. The son of Pandu had earlier asked them about your son and, by chance, they had now come to that place and tracked down the king. 30.25

Remembering the words of Pandu's son, Your Majesty, the animal hunters quietly said to each other:

"The Pándava will give us money if we tell him about Dur·yódhana. It is very clear to us that famous King Dur·yódhana is in this lake. Let us therefore all go to King Yudhi·shthira and inform him that intolerant Dur·yódhana sleeps 30.30

Dhṛtarāṣṭr'|ātma|jaṃ tasmai Bhīmasenāya dhīmate
śayānaṃ salile sarve kathayāmo dhanur|bhṛte.
sa no dāsyati su|prīto dhanāni bahulāny uta.
kiṃ no māṃsena śuṣkeṇa parikliṣṭena śoṣiṇā?»
evam uktvā tu te vyādhāḥ saṃprahṛṣṭā dhan'|ârthinaḥ
māṃsa|bhārān upādāya prayayuḥ śibiraṃ prati.
Pāṇḍav" âpi mahā|rāja labdha|lakṣāḥ prahāriṇaḥ
a|paśyamānāḥ samare Duryodhanam avasthitam,
30.35 nikṛtes tasya pāpasya te pāraṃ gaman'|ēpsavaḥ
cārān saṃpreṣayām āsuḥ samantāt tad raṇ'|âjire.
āgamya tu tataḥ sarve naṣṭaṃ Duryodhanaṃ nṛpam
nyavedayanta sahitā Dharma|rājasya sainikāḥ.
teṣāṃ tad vacanaṃ śrutvā cārāṇāṃ Bharata'|rṣabha
cintām abhyagamat tīvrāṃ niśaśvāsa ca pārthivaḥ.
atha sthitānāṃ Pāṇḍūnāṃ dīnānāṃ Bharata'|rṣabha
tasmād deśād apakramya tvaritā lubdhakā vibho
ājagmuḥ śibiraṃ hṛṣṭā dṛṣṭvā Duryodhanaṃ nṛpam.
vāryamāṇāḥ praviṣṭāś ca Bhīmasenasya paśyataḥ.
te tu Pāṇḍavam āsādya Bhīmasenaṃ mahā|balam
tasmai tat sarvam ācakhyur yad vṛttaṃ yac ca vai śrutam.
30.40 tato Vṛkodaro rājan dattvā teṣāṃ dhanaṃ bahu,
Dharma|rājāya tat sarvam ācacakṣe paran|tapaḥ:
«asau Duryodhano rājan vijñāto mama lubdhakaiḥ
saṃstabhya salilaṃ śete yasy' ârthe paritapyase.»

in this water. We should also all tell the wise archer Bhima·sena that Dhrita·rashtra's son lies in this lake. He will be very pleased and give us much wealth. What need have we for this dried meat that is withered and parched?"

Saying these words, the hunters joyfully took up their loads of meat and set off for the camp, eager for wealth.

Meanwhile, the conquering Pándavas, who always hit their marks, were unable to see Dur·yódhana on the battlefield, Your Majesty. Eager to cease the depravity of that villain, they dispatched scouts all over the battlefield. But when the soldiers returned, they all jointly informed the King of Righteousness that King Dur·yódhana had disappeared. On hearing the scouts' words, the king became filled with great anxiety and sighed, bull of the Bharatas. 30.35

While the Pandus were in this downcast state, the hunters swiftly departed from the lake and arrived at the camp, joyful that they had seen King Dur·yódhana, bull of the Bharatas. Although prohibited from doing so, they entered the camp, with Bhima·sena watching all the while. They then approached Bhima·sena, the mighty Pándava, and informed him of everything that had happened and everything that they had heard.

Enemy-scorching Vrikódara then paid the hunters handsomely and told the King of Righteousness all the news: 30.40

"Dur·yódhana—the cause of your distress—has been spotted by my hunters, Your Majesty. He is lying in water that he has frozen."

tad vaco Bhīmasenasya priyaṃ śrutvā viśāṃ pate
Ajātaśatruḥ Kaunteyo hṛṣṭo 'bhūt saha sodaraiḥ.
taṃ ca śrutvā mah"|êṣv|āsaṃ praviṣṭaṃ salila|hrade,
kṣipram eva tato 'gacchan puras|kṛtya Janārdanam.
tataḥ kila|kilā|śabdaḥ prādur āsīd viśāṃ pate
Pāṇḍavānāṃ prahṛṣṭānāṃ Pañcālānāṃ ca sarvaśaḥ.
30.45 siṃha|nādāṃs tataś cakruḥ kṣveḍāṃś ca Bharata'|rṣabha
tvaritāḥ kṣatriyā rājañ jagmur Dvaipāyanaṃ hradam.
«jñātaḥ pāpo Dhārtarāṣṭro dṛṣṭaś c' êty» a|sakṛd raṇe
prākrośan Somakās tatra hṛṣṭa|rūpāḥ samantataḥ.
teṣām āśu prayātānāṃ rathānāṃ tatra veginām
babhūva tumulaḥ śabdo diva|spṛk pṛthivī|pate.
Duryodhanaṃ parīpsantas tatra tatra Yudhiṣṭhiram
anvayus tvaritās te vai rājānaṃ śrānta|vāhanāḥ,
Arjuno Bhīmasenaś ca Mādrī|putrau ca Pāṇḍavau
Dhṛṣṭadyumnaś ca Pāñcālyaḥ Śikhaṇḍī cāpa|rājitaḥ
30.50 Uttamaujā Yudhāmanyuḥ Sātyakiś ca mahā|rathaḥ
Pañcālānāṃ ca ye śiṣṭā Draupadeyāś ca Bhārata
hayāś ca sarve nāgāś ca śataśaś ca padātayaḥ.
tataḥ prāpto mahā|rāja Dharma|rājaḥ pratāpavān
Dvaipāyanaṃ hradaṃ ghoraṃ yatra Duryodhano 'bhavat.
śīt'|â|mala|jalaṃ hṛdyaṃ dvitīyam iva sāgaram
māyayā salilaṃ stabhya yatr' âbhūt te sthitaḥ sutaḥ.
atyadbhutena vidhinā daiva|yogena Bhārata
salil'|ântar|gataḥ śete dur|darśaḥ kasya cit prabho
mānuṣasya manuṣy'|êndra gadā|hasto jan'|âdhipaḥ.

Ajáta·shatru, the son of Kunti, was delighted when he heard Bhima·sena's welcome words, as were his brothers, lord of the people. On hearing that the great archer had entered the lake, they quickly departed, with Janárdana in front of them.

In their joy, the Pándavas and Panchálas then cheered on all sides, lord of the people. After shouting and making lion-roars, the warriors quickly set off for the Dvaipáyana lake, bull of the Bharatas. 30.45

All over the battlefield the jubilant Sómakas repeatedly shouted: "The evil son of Dhrita·rashtra has been found and seen!" As the men rapidly advanced forward, their swift chariots made a cacophony of noise that penetrated the heavens, lord of the people. In their eagerness to find Dur·yódhana, Árjuna, Bhima·sena, the two Pándava sons of Madri, the Panchála prince Dhrishta·dyumna, Shikhándin, who is radiant with his bow, Uttamáujas, Yudha·manyu, the great warrior Sátyaki, the surviving Panchálas, and the sons of Dráupadi—as well as all their horses, elephants, and hundreds of infantrymen—swiftly followed King Yudhi·shthira here and there, even though their animals were tired, descendant of Bharata. 30.50

The mighty King of Righteousness then reached the terrible lake of Dvaipáyana, where Dur·yódhana was situated. It was in that charming lake—which had cool and clean water and which resembled a second ocean—that your son rested after magically freezing its waters. Through some miraculous ordinance or divine application, the king lay hidden in the water, mace in hand, invisible to any human, descendant of Bharata.

tato Duryodhano rājā salil'|ântar|gato vasan
śuśruve tumulaṃ śabdaṃ jalad'|ôpama|niḥsvanam.

30.55 Yudhiṣṭhiraś ca rāj'|êndra taṃ hradaṃ saha sodaraiḥ
ājagāma mahā|rāja tava putra|vadhāya vai,
mahatā śaṅkha|nādena ratha|nemi|svanena ca
ūrdhvaṃ dhunvan mahā|reṇuṃ kampayaṃś c' âpi medinīm.

Yaudhiṣṭhirasya sainyasya śrutvā śabdaṃ mahā|rathāḥ
Kṛtavarmā Kṛpo Drauṇī rājānam idam abruvan:
«ime hy āyānti saṃhṛṣṭāḥ Pāṇḍavā jita|kāśinaḥ.
apayāsyāmahe tāvad anujānātu no bhavān.»

Duryodhanas tu tac chrutvā
teṣāṃ tatra tarasvinām
«tath" êty» uktvā hradaṃ taṃ vai
māyay" âstambhayat prabho.

30.60 te tv anujñāpya rājānaṃ bhṛśaṃ śoka|parāyaṇāḥ
jagmur dūre mahā|rāja Kṛpa|prabhṛtayo rathāḥ.
te gatvā dūram adhvānaṃ nyagrodhaṃ prekṣya māriṣa
nyaviśanta bhṛśaṃ śrāntāś cintayanto nṛpaṃ prati:

«viṣṭabhya salilaṃ supto Dhārtarāṣṭro mahā|balaḥ
Pāṇḍavāś c' âpi saṃprāptās taṃ deśaṃ yuddham īpsavaḥ.
kathaṃ nu yuddhaṃ bhavitā? kathaṃ rājā bhaviṣyati?
kathaṃ nu Pāṇḍavā rājan pratipatsyanti Kauravam?»

ity evaṃ cintayānās tu rathebhyo 'śvān vimucya te
tatr' āsāṃ cakrire rājan Kṛpa|prabhṛtayo rathāḥ.

From within the lake, King Dur·yódhana heard this tumultuous noise that rumbled like a thundercloud. Swirling up a mass of dust and making the earth tremble with the blare of his conches and the rumble of his chariot wheels, Yudhi·shthira then arrived at the lake with his brothers in order to kill your son, great king. 30.55

On hearing the noise of Yudhi·shthira's army, the mighty warriors Krita·varman, Kripa, and the son of Drona said to the king:

"Here come the joyful, conquering Pándavas. Please give us leave to depart!"

Hearing the words of those mighty men, Dur·yódhana consented to their request and magically froze the lake, my lord. After gaining the king's permission, Kripa and the other warriors traveled far away, filled with deep grief, great king. After they had gone a long distance, the exhausted men spotted a banyan tree and set up camp, brooding over their king: 30.60

"The mighty son of Dhrita·rashtra sleeps in frozen water and the Pándavas have arrived at that site, seeking warfare. How will the battle turn out? What will happen to the king? How will the Pándavas behave toward the Káurava, O king?"*

Thinking this, Kripa and the other warriors released the horses from their chariots and rested at that site, Your Majesty.

SAÑJAYA uvāca:

31.1 TATAS TEṢV apayāteṣu ratheṣu triṣu Pāṇḍavāḥ
tam̩ hradam̩ pratyapadyanta yatra Duryodhano 'bhavat.
āsādya ca Kuru|śreṣṭha tadā Dvaipāyanam̩ hradam,
stambhitam̩ Dhārtarāṣṭreṇa dr̩ṣṭvā tam̩ salil'|āśayam,
Vāsudevam idam̩ vākyam abravīt Kuru|nandanaḥ:
«paśy' êmām̩ Dhārtarāṣṭreṇa māyām apsu prayojitām.
viṣṭabhya salilam̩ śete n' âsya mānuṣato bhayam.
daivīm̩ māyām imām̩ kr̩tvā salil'|ântar|gato hy ayam
nikr̩tyā nikr̩ti|prajño. na me jīvan vimokṣyate!
31.5 yady asya samare sāhyam̩ kurute vajra|bhr̩t svayam
tath" âpy enam̩ hatam̩ yuddhe lokā drakṣyanti Mādhava.»

VĀSUDEVA uvāca:

māyāvina imām̩ māyām̩ māyayā jahi Bhārata.
māyāvī māyayā vadhyaḥ! satyam etad Yudhiṣṭhira.
kriy"|âbhyupāyair bahubhir māyām apsu prayojya ca
jahi tvam̩ Bharata|śreṣṭha māy"|ātmānam̩ Suyodhanam.
kriy"|âbhyupāyair Indreṇa nihatā daitya|dānavāḥ.
kriy"|âbhyupāyair bahubhir Balir baddho mah"|ātmanā.
kriy"|âbhyupāyaiḥ bahubhir Hiraṇyākṣo mah"|âsuraḥ
Hiraṇyakaśipuś c' âiva kriyay" âiva niṣūditau.
Vr̩traś ca nihato rājan kriyay" âiva. na sam̩śayaḥ.

SÁNJAYA said:

AFTER THE THREE warriors had departed, the Pándavas arrived at the lake where Dur·yódhana lay. Approaching the Dvaipáyana lake, Yudhi·shthira, that delight of the Kurus, saw that the body of water had been frozen by the son of Dhrita·rashtra and said these words to Vasudéva, best of Kurus: 31.1

"Look at the magic that the son of Dhrita·rashtra has worked on these waters. Here he lies, after hardening the water, and has no fear of any human. By employing such divine magic, this master of base behavior hides in this lake through trickery. But he will not escape me alive! The worlds will see Dur·yódhana slaughtered in battle, Mádhava, even if thunderbolt-wielding Indra himself were to help him fight." 31.5

VASUDÉVA said:

It is through a trick, descendant of Bharata, that you must destroy this magician's magic. A trickster must be killed by a trick! This is the truth, Yudhi·shthira.

Work your own magic on the water and use numerous ploys and devices to destroy Su·yódhana, who himself has a deceitful soul, best of Bharatas.

It was through numerous ploys and devices that Indra killed the *daitya*s and *dánava*s. It was through numerous ploys and devices that great-spirited Vishnu bound Bali.* It was through numerous ploys and devices that the great demon Hiranyáksha was annihilated. And it was through a ruse too that Hiránya·káshipu was killed. Vritra was also slaughtered by strategy.* Of this there is no doubt.

31.10 tathā Pulastya|tanayo Rāvaṇo nāma rākṣasaḥ
Rāmeṇa nihato rājan s'|ânubandhaḥ sah'|ânugaḥ.
kriyayā yogam āsthāya tathā tvam api vikrama.
kriy"|âbhyupāyair nihatau mayā rājan purātanau
Tārakaś ca mahā|daityo Vipracittiś ca vīryavān.
Vātāpir Ilvalaś c' âiva Triśirāś ca tathā vibho
Sund'|Ôpasundāv asurau kriyay" âiva niṣūditau.
kriy"|âbhyupāyair Indreṇa tri|divaṃ bhujyate vibho.
kriyā balavatī rājan. n' ânyat kiñ cid Yudhiṣṭhira.
daityāś ca dānavāś c' âiva rākṣasāḥ pārthivās tathā
kriy"|âbhyupāyair nihatāḥ. kriyāṃ tasmāt samācara!

SAÑJAYA uvāca:

31.15 ity ukto Vāsudevena Pāṇḍavaḥ saṃśita|vrataḥ
jala|sthaṃ taṃ mahā|rāja tava putraṃ mahā|balam
abhyabhāṣata Kaunteyaḥ prahasann iva Bhārata:
«Suyodhana kim|artho 'yam ārambho 'psu kṛtas tvayā
sarvaṃ kṣatraṃ ghātayitvā sva|kulaṃ ca viśāṃ pate?
jal'|āśayaṃ praviṣṭo 'dya vāñchañ jīvitam ātmanaḥ?
uttiṣṭha rājan! yudhyasva sah' âsmābhiḥ Suyodhana!
sa te darpo nara|śreṣṭha sa ca mānaḥ kva te gataḥ
yas tvaṃ saṃstabhya salilaṃ bhīto rājan vyavasthitaḥ?
sarve tvāṃ ‹śūra ity› evaṃ janā jalpanti saṃsadi.
vyarthaṃ tad bhavato manye śauryaṃ salila|śāyinaḥ.

It was by similar means that Rama—along with his companions and followers—killed the demon Rávana, that son of Pulástya.* You too should display your valor by employing strategy. It was through ploys and devices that, in ancient times, I slaughtered the great demon Táraka and mighty Vipra·chitti, Your Majesty.* In a similar fashion, Vatápi, Ílvala, Tri·shiras, and the two demons Sunda and Upasúnda were all killed through strategies, my lord.* It is by using ploys and devices that Indra enjoys heaven, my lord. 31.10

Expedience is powerful, Your Majesty. Nothing else, Yudhi·shthira.

*Daitya*s, *dánava*s, *rákshasa*s and kings have all been destroyed through ploys and devices. It is therefore strategy that you should practice!*

SÁNJAYA said:

After Vasudéva had addressed him this way, the son of Kunti—that Pándava of rigid vows—spoke to your mighty son as he lay in the water, great king. With a smirk he said these words, descendant of Bharata: 31.15

"Su·yódhana, lord of the people, why have you resorted to these waters after annihilating the entire warrior race and your own family? Why have you today entered this lake, longing for your life?

Rise, O king! Fight against us, Su·yódhana! Where has your pride and honor gone, best of men, if you freeze water and retreat there in fear? All the people in the assembly say that you are a hero. But your heroism must, I believe, be false if you are lying in a lake!

31.20 uttiṣṭha rājan yudhyasva! kṣatriyo ’si kul’|ôdbhavaḥ
Kauraveyo viśeṣeṇa. kulaṃ janma ca saṃsmara!
sa kathaṃ Kaurave vaṃśe praśaṃsañ janma c’ ātmanaḥ
yuddhād bhītas tatas toyaṃ praviśya pratitiṣṭhasi?
a|yuddham a|vyavasthānaṃ: n’ âiṣa dharmaḥ sanātanaḥ.
an|ārya|juṣṭam a|svargyaṃ raṇe rājan palāyanam.

kathaṃ pāram a|gatvā hi yuddhe tvaṃ vai jijīviṣuḥ
imān nipatitān dṛṣṭvā putrān bhrātṝn pitṝṃs tathā?
saṃbandhino vayasyāṃś ca mātulān bāndhavāṃs tathā
ghātayitvā kathaṃ tāta hrade tiṣṭhasi sāṃpratam?

31.25 śūra|mānī na śūras tvaṃ. mṛṣā vadasi, Bhārata,
‹śūro ’ham iti› dur|buddhe sarva|lokasya śṛṇvataḥ.
na hi śūrāḥ palāyante śatrūn dṛṣṭvā kathañ cana.
brūhi vā tvaṃ yayā vṛttyā śūra tyajasi saṃgaram.

sa tvam uttiṣṭha yudhyasva! vinīya bhayam ātmanaḥ!
ghātayitvā sarva|sainyaṃ bhrātṝṃś c’ âiva Suyodhana,
n’ êdānīṃ jīvite buddhiḥ kāryā dharma|cikīrṣayā
kṣatra|dharmam upāśritya tvad|vidhena Suyodhana.

yat tu Karṇam upāśritya Śakuniṃ c’ âpi Saubalam
a|martya iva saṃmohāt tvam ātmānaṃ na buddhavān.
tat pāpaṃ su|mahat kṛtvā pratiyudhyasva Bhārata!
kathaṃ hi tvad|vidho mohād rocayeta palāyanam?

31.30 kva te tat pauruṣaṃ yātaṃ? kva ca mānaḥ Suyodhana?
kva ca vikrāntatā yātā? kva ca visphūrjitaṃ mahat?
kva te kṛt’|âstratā yātā? kiñ ca śeṣe jal’|āśaye?

Rise, king, and fight! You are a kshatriya, born of a noble family! In particular you are a Káurava. Remember your clan and your birth! How can you boast of a birth in the Káurava lineage if you enter water and abide there, fearful of battle? Refusal to fight and lack of resilience: this is not the eternal law. Flight on the battlefield does not become one who is noble and does not lead to heaven, Your Majesty. 31.20

How is it that when you have seen your sons, brothers and ancestors slaughtered, you still desire to live and have not reached the further shore in this war? How is it, my friend, that you lie in a lake when you have caused the deaths of your relatives, friends, uncles, and kinsmen?

Although arrogant about your heroism, you are no hero. Your words are false, wicked Bhárata, when you say with the entire world as your audience: 'I am a hero!' Under no circumstances should heroes flee when they see their enemy. Or tell us, hero, of the situation that made you abandon battle. 31.25

Rise and fight! Restrain your fear! When you have destroyed your brothers and entire army, a man such as you, who desires to act morally and who adheres to the warrior code, should not now think about life, Su·yódhana.

You thought you were like an immortal when you relied on Karna and Shákuni, the son of Súbala. In your confusion, you did not understand yourself. Having committed this great evil, fight against us, descendant of Bharata! How, out of delusion, can a man such as you choose flight? Where has your manliness gone? Where is your pride, Su·yódhana? Where has your courage gone? Where is your great roar? 31.30

sa tvam uttiṣṭha! yudhyasva kṣatra|dharmeṇa, Bhārata!
asmāṃs tu vā parājitya praśādhi pṛthivīm imām
atha vā nihato 'smābhir bhūmau svapsyasi Bhārata.
eṣa te paramo dharmaḥ sṛṣṭo Dhātrā mah"|ātmanā.
taṃ kuruṣva yathā|tathyaṃ. rājā bhava mahā|ratha!»

SAÑJAYA uvāca:

evam ukto mahā|rāja Dharma|putreṇa dhīmatā
salila|sthas tava suta idaṃ vacanam abravīt:

DURYODHANA uvāca:

31.35 n' âitac citraṃ mahā|rāja yad bhīḥ prāṇinam āviśet.
na ca prāṇa|bhayād bhīto vyapayāto 'smi Bhārata.
a|rathaś c' â|niṣaṅgī ca nihataḥ pārṣṇi|sārathiḥ.
ekaś c' âpy a|gaṇaḥ saṅkhye pratyāśvāsam arocayam.
na prāṇa|hetor na bhayān na viṣādād viśāṃ pate
idam ambhaḥ praviṣṭo 'smi. śramāt tv idam anuṣṭhitam.
tvaṃ c' āśvasihi Kaunteya ye c' âpy anugatās tava.
aham utthāya vaḥ sarvān pratiyotsyāmi saṃyuge.

YUDHIṢṬHIRA uvāca:

āśvastā eva sarve sma ciraṃ tvāṃ mṛgayāmahe.
tad idānīṃ samuttiṣṭha, yudhyasv' êha Suyodhana.
31.40 hatvā vā samare Pārthān sphītaṃ rājyam avāpnuhi,
nihato vā raṇe 'smābhir vīra|lokam avāpsyasi!

Where is your skill in weaponry? Why are you lying in a lake?

Rise and fight according to the warrior code, Bhárata! Either defeat us and rule over this earth or be destroyed by us and sleep on the ground, descendant of Bharata. This is your supreme duty, created by great-spirited Dhatri himself. Act as is proper. Be a king, great warrior!"

SÁNJAYA said:

Addressed in this way by the wise son of Righteousness, your son said these words as he lay in the water, great king.

DUR·YÓDHANA said:

It is not unusual for living beings to be overcome by fear, great king. But I have not retreated out of fear for my life, descendant of Bharata. I had no chariot or quiver and my rear-charioteer had been killed. I was alone and unsupported on the battlefield and I needed to have some rest. It was not out of concern for my life, nor out of fear or despondency that I entered this water, lord of the people. I did it out of weariness. 31.35

You too should rest, son of Kunti, as should those who follow you. I will rise and fight you all in battle.

YUDHI·SHTHIRA said:

We have already rested and have been hunting you for a long time. So rise now, Su·yódhana, and fight on this spot! Either kill the Parthas in battle and acquire this fertile kingdom, or be killed by us on the battlefield and acquire the world of heroes! 31.40

DURYODHANA uvāca:

yad|artham rājyam icchāmi Kurūṇāṃ Kuru|nandana
ta ime nihatāḥ sarve bhrātaro me jan'|ēśvara.
kṣīṇa|ratnāṃ ca pṛthivīṃ hata|kṣatriya|puṅgavām
na hy utsahāmy ahaṃ bhoktuṃ vidhavām iva yoṣitam.
ady' âpi tv aham āśaṃse tvāṃ vijetuṃ Yudhiṣṭhira
bhaṅktvā Pāñcāla|Pāṇḍūnām utsāhaṃ Bharata'|rṣabha.
na tv idānīm ahaṃ manye kāryaṃ yuddhena karhi cit
Droṇe Karṇe ca saṃśānte nihate ca pitāmahe.

31.45 astv idānīm iyaṃ rājan kevalā pṛthivī tava.
a|sahāyo hi ko rājā rājyam icchet praśāsitum.
suhṛdas tādṛśān hitvā putrān bhrātṝn pitṝn api
bhavadbhiś ca hṛte rājye ko nu jīveta mādṛśaḥ?
ahaṃ vanaṃ gamiṣyāmi hy ajinaiḥ prativāsitaḥ.
ratir hi n' âsti me rājye hata|pakṣasya, Bhārata.
hata|bāndhava|bhūyiṣṭhā hat'|âśvā hata|kuñjarā
eṣā te pṛthivī rājan—bhuṅkṣv' âināṃ vigata|jvaraḥ!
vanam eva gamiṣyāmi vasāno mṛga|carmaṇī.
na hi me nirjanasy' âsti jīvite 'dya spṛhā vibho.

31.50 gaccha tvaṃ bhuṅkṣva rāj'|êndra pṛthivīṃ nihat'|ēśvarām
hata|yodhāṃ naṣṭa|ratnāṃ kṣīṇa|vaprāṃ yathā|sukham!

DUR·YÓDHANA said:

Delight of the Kurus and lord of the people, it was for my brothers' sake that I desired the Kurus' kingdom, but they have all been slaughtered. When its jewels are lost and its bull-like warriors killed, I have no desire to enjoy the earth like a man enjoying a widowed woman. However, I do want to defeat you today, Yudhi·shthira, after breaking the strength of the Panchálas and Pandus.

But when Drona and Karna have been quelled and my grandfather Bhishma has been slaughtered, I feel there is no longer any need for war. Let this entire earth now be yours, O king. For what monarch would want to rule over a kingdom without any friends? What man such as I could live when he has left behind such friends, sons, brothers and fathers, and when his kingdom has been taken from him by you? 31.45

I will enter the forest, dressed in antelope-skin. For I can take no pleasure in a kingdom when my allies have been killed, Bhárata. This earth has lost most of its kinsmen and its horses and elephants are dead, Your Majesty—enjoy it carefree! I will enter the forest, clothed in deer-hide. For I no longer have any desire to live when I have no-one around me, my lord.

Go, king of kings, and enjoy this earth at your pleasure—now that its lords are slain, its warriors killed, its jewels lost, and its ramparts destroyed! 31.50

SAÑJAYA uvāca:

Duryodhanaṃ tava sutaṃ salila|sthaṃ mahā|yaśāḥ
śrutvā tu karuṇaṃ vākyam abhāṣata Yudhiṣṭhiraḥ.

YUDHIṢṬHIRA uvāca:

«ārta|pralāpān mā tāta salila|sthaḥ prabhāṣithāḥ!
n' âitan manasi me rājan vāśitaṃ śakuner iva.
yadi v" âpi samarthaḥ syās tvaṃ dānāya Suyodhana
n' âham iccheyam avaniṃ tvayā dattāṃ praśāsitum.
a|dharmeṇa na gṛhṇīyāṃ tvayā dattāṃ mahīm imām.
na hi dharmaḥ smṛto rājan kṣatriyasya pratigrahaḥ.
31.55 tvayā dattāṃ na c' êccheyaṃ pṛthivīm a|khilām aham.
tvāṃ tu yuddhe vinirjitya bhokt" âsmi vasudhām imām.
an|īśvaraś ca pṛthivīṃ kathaṃ tvaṃ dātum icchasi?
tvay" êyaṃ pṛthivī rājan kin na dattā tad" âiva hi
dharmato yācamānānāṃ praśam'|ârthaṃ kulasya naḥ?
Vārṣṇeyaṃ prathamaṃ rājan pratyākhyāya mahā|balam
kim idānīṃ dadāsi tvaṃ? ko hi te citta|vibhramaḥ?
abhiyuktas tu ko rājā dātum icchedd hi medinīm?
na tvam adya mahīṃ dātum īśaḥ Kaurava|nandana
ācchettuṃ vā balād rājan. sa kathaṃ dātum icchasi?
māṃ tu nirjitya saṃgrāme pālay' êmāṃ vasun|dharām!
sūcy'|agreṇ' âpi yad bhūmer api bhidyeta Bhārata
tan|mātram api tan mahyaṃ na dadāti purā bhavān.
31.60 sa kathaṃ pṛthivīm etāṃ pradadāsi viśāṃ pate
sūcy|agraṃ n' âtyajaḥ pūrvaṃ sa kathaṃ tyajasi kṣitim!
evam aiśvaryam āsādya praśāsya pṛthivīm imām

SÁNJAYA said:

On hearing this pitiful speech, glorious Yudhi·shthira addressed your son Dur·yódhana as he lay in the water.

YUDHI·SHTHIRA said:

"Stop spouting these wretched babblings as you lie there in water, my friend! This bird-like warbling has no effect on my mind, O king. Even if you were able to offer me the earth, I would not want to rule over it if it had been given by you, Su·yódhana. I could not unlawfully accept this earth as a gift from you. For it is not the conduct of a kshatriya to accept gifts, O king.*

31.55 I would not want the entire earth if you gave it to me. Instead I will enjoy this earth after I have defeated you in battle. Why do you only want to hand over the earth when you have no power? Why did you not give us the earth previously, Your Majesty, when we rightfully requested it in order to have peace for our clan? If you originally rejected Krishna, the mighty Varshnéya, why do you now offer up the earth?* What is this change of heart? What responsible king would want to give away the earth? You do not have the power to give away the earth today, delight of the Káuravas, nor to tear it from us by force. Why do you want to give it away? Conquer me in battle and guard this earth instead!

Previously you were unwilling to give me even as much land as could be split by a needle-point, descendant of Bharata! 31.60 How can you now offer this earth, lord of the people, when previously you would not even give a needle-point's worth? What fool would be willing to give his enemy

ko hi mūḍho vyavasyeta śatror dātuṃ vasun|dharām?
tvaṃ tu kevala|maurkhyeṇa vimūḍho n' âvabuddhyase:
pṛthivīṃ dātu|kāmo 'pi jīvitena vimokṣyase.
asmān vā tvaṃ parājitya praśādhi pṛthivīm imām
atha vā nihato 'smābhir vraja lokān an|uttamān.
āvayor jīvato rājan mayi ca tvayi ca dhruvam
saṃśayaḥ sarva|bhūtānāṃ vijaye nau bhaviṣyati.

31.65 jīvitaṃ tava duṣ|prajña mayi saṃprati vartate.
jīvayeyam ahaṃ kāmaṃ. na tu tvaṃ jīvituṃ kṣamaḥ.
dahane hi kṛto yatnas tvay" âsmāsu viśeṣataḥ
āśī|viṣair viṣaiś c' âpi jale c' âpi praveśanaiḥ.
tvayā vinikṛtā rājan rājyasya haraṇena ca
a|priyāṇāṃ ca vacanair Draupadyāḥ karṣaṇena ca.
etasmāt kāraṇāt pāpa jīvitaṃ te na vidyate.
uttiṣṭh' ôttiṣṭha yudhyasva! yuddhe śreyo bhaviṣyati.»

SAÑJAYA uvāca:

evaṃ tu vividhā vāco jaya|yuktāḥ punaḥ punaḥ
kīrtayanti sma te vīrās tatra tatra jan'|âdhipa.

DHṚTARĀṢṬRA uvāca:

32.1 EVAṂ SAṂTARJYAMĀNAS tu mama putro mahī|patiḥ
prakṛtyā manyumān vīraḥ katham āsīt paran|tapaḥ?
na hi saṃtarjanā tena śruta|pūrvā kathañ cana;
rāja|bhāvena mānyaś ca sarva|lokasya so 'bhavat.
yasy' ātapatra|cchāy" âpi svakā bhānos tathā prabhā
khedāy' âiv' âbhimānitvāt sahet s' âivaṃ* kathaṃ giraḥ?

the earth after he has ruled and held sway over it? Confounded by your utter stupidity, you cannot realize this point: even though you are willing to give up the earth, you will not escape with your life!

Either defeat me and rule over this earth or be killed by me and reach the highest realms. If we were alive—both you and I—then all living beings would certainly be unsure as to which one of us is the victor. Your life now depends on me, you fool. I could let you live if I liked. But you are not fit to live. You made special efforts to burn us, use snakes and poisons against us, and drown us too.* By stealing our kingdom, speaking abusive words, and maltreating Dráupadi, you have wronged us, O king. For this reason you cannot live, you criminal. 31.65

Rise, rise, and fight! The good lies in war!"

SÁNJAYA said:

In this way, lord of the people, the Pándava heroes repeatedly proclaimed various speeches here and there, intent as they were on victory.*

DHRITA·RASHTRA said:

WHEN MY SON, the lord of the earth, was berated in this way, how did the enemy-tamer react, hero that he is and wrathful by nature? For he has never previously heard any criticism; instead the whole world has honored him for his royalty. How could he endure such words when even the shade of his parasol or the brightness of the sun used to pain him in his pride? 32.1

iyaṃ ca pṛthivī sarvā sa|mlecch'|āṭavikā bhṛśam
prasādād dhriyate yasya pratyakṣaṃ tava Sañjaya,
32.5 sa tathā tarjyamānas tu Pāṇḍu|putrair viśeṣataḥ
vihīnaś ca svakair bhṛtyair nirjane c' āvṛto bhṛśam
sa śrutvā kaṭukā vāco jaya|yuktāḥ punaḥ punaḥ
kim abravīt Pāṇḍaveyāṃs? tan mam' ācakṣva Sañjaya.

SAÑJAYA uvāca:

tarjyamānas tadā rājann udaka|sthas tav' ātma|jaḥ
Yudhiṣṭhireṇa rāj'|êndra bhrātṛbhiḥ sahitena ha,
śrutvā sa kaṭukā vāco viṣama|stho nar'|âdhipaḥ
dīrgham uṣṇaṃ ca niḥśvasya salila|sthaḥ punaḥ punaḥ,
salil'|ântar|gato rājā dhunvan hastau punaḥ punaḥ
manaś cakāra yuddhāya rājānaṃ c' âbhyabhāṣata:
32.10 «yūyaṃ sa|suhṛdaḥ Pārthāḥ sarve sa|ratha|vāhanāḥ.
aham ekaḥ paridyūno viratho hata|vāhanaḥ.
ātta|śastrai rath'|ôpetair bahubhiḥ parivāritaḥ
katham ekaḥ padātiḥ sann a|śastro yoddhum utsahe?
ek'|âikena tu māṃ yūyaṃ yodhayadhvaṃ Yudhiṣṭhira.
na hy eko bahubhir vīrair nyāyyo yodhayituṃ yudhi—
viśeṣato vikavacaḥ śrāntaś c' āpat samāśritaḥ
bhṛśaṃ vikṣata|gātraś ca śrānta|vāhana|sainikaḥ.

You yourself have witnessed, Sánjaya, how this entire earth, with all its barbarians and foresters, is supported by Dur·yódhana's grace. What then did Dur·yódhana say to the Pándavas when, deprived of all his servants and completely surrounded in that peopleless place, he was reviled in this way—and particularly by the sons of Pandu—repeatedly hearing their cruel and triumphant words? Tell me this, Sánjaya. 32.5

SÁNJAYA said:

Your Majesty, when Yudhi·shthira and his brothers abused your son in this way as he lay in the water, and when that ruler of men heard their vicious words while in that dire situation, he repeatedly breathed out long and hot sighs. Shaking his hands repeatedly as he lay in the water, the king set his heart on battle and replied to King Yudhi·shthira with these words:

"You Parthas still all have your friends, as well as your chariots and animals. I am alone and wretched and have no chariot or animals. How can a man, who is alone and on foot, wage war if he has no weapons and is surrounded by many troops who are equipped with arms and chariots? You should fight me one against one, Yudhi·shthira. For it is not right for one man to fight many heroes in battle—especially if he is armorless, exhausted, and fallen on misfortune, and if his limbs are severely mangled and his troops and animals fatigued. 32.10

na me tvatto bhayaṃ rājan na ca Pārthād Vṛkodarāt,
Phālgunād Vāsudevād vā Pañcālebhyo 'tha vā punaḥ,
32.15 yamābhyāṃ Yuyudhānād vā ye c' ânye tava sainikāḥ.
ekaḥ sarvān ahaṃ kruddho vārayiṣye yudhi sthitaḥ.
dharma|mūlā satāṃ kīrtir manuṣyāṇāṃ jan'|âdhipa.
dharmaṃ c' âiv' êha kīrtiṃ ca pālayan prabravīmy aham.
aham utthāya sarvān vai pratiyotsyāmi saṃyuge
anugamy' āgatān sarvān ṛtūn saṃvatsaro yathā.
adya vaḥ sa|rathān s'|âśvān a|śastro viratho 'pi san
nakṣatrāṇ' îva sarvāṇi savitā rātri|saṃkṣaye
tejasā nāśayiṣyāmi sthirī|bhavata Pāṇḍavāḥ.
ady' ānṛṇyaṃ gamiṣyāmi kṣatriyāṇāṃ yaśasvinām
Bāhlīka|Droṇa|Bhīṣmāṇāṃ Karṇasya ca mah"|ātmanaḥ,
32.20 Jayadrathasya śūrasya Bhagadattasya c' ôbhayoḥ
Madra|rājasya Śalyasya Bhūriśravasa eva ca,
putrāṇāṃ Bharata|śreṣṭha Śakuneḥ Saubalasya ca,
mitrāṇāṃ suhṛdāṃ c' âiva bāndhavānāṃ tath" âiva ca.
ānṛṇyam adya gacchāmi hatvā tvāṃ bhrātṛbhiḥ saha.»
etāvad uktvā vacanaṃ virarāma jan'|âdhipaḥ.

YUDHIṢṬHIRA uvāca:

diṣṭyā tvam api jānīṣe kṣatra|dharmaṃ Suyodhana!
diṣṭyā te vartate buddhir yuddhāy' âiva mahā|bhuja!
diṣṭyā śūro 'si Kauravya! diṣṭyā jānāsi saṃgaram
yas tvam eko hi naḥ sarvān saṃgare yoddhum icchasi!

I am not afraid of you, O king, nor of the Partha Vrikódara, nor Phálguna, Vasudéva, the Panchálas, the twin brothers, Yuyudhána, or your other troops. Standing alone in battle, I will ward you all off in my rage. 32.15

For humans that are good, it is righteousness that forms the foundation of fame, lord of men. I speak as someone who guards both righteousness and fame in this world. I will rise up and fight you all in battle, confronting you all as you approach me, just as the year confronts the seasons. Just as the sun destroys all the stars at the end of the night with its brilliance, so I will destroy you Pándavas with my ardor on this day, even though you are strong and have chariots and horses, while I have neither weapons nor chariot.

Today I will remove my debt to the glorious warriors Bahlíka, Drona, and Bhishma, and to great-sprited Karna, heroic Jayad·ratha, Bhaga·datta, Shalya the king of the Madras, Bhuri·shravas, my sons, Shákuni the son of Súbala, and my friends, companions, and relatives too, best of Bharatas. By killing you and your brothers, I will remove my debts on this day." 32.20

With these words, the lord of the people fell silent.

YUDHI·SHTHIRA said:

How splendid that even you know the warrior code, Su·yódhana! How splendid that your mind is concerned with battle, mighty-armed warrior! How splendid that you are a hero, Káurava! How splendid that you are knowledgeable in warfare and are eager to fight all of us alone in battle!

32.25 eka ekena saṃgamya yat te saṃmatam āyudham
tat tvam ādāya yudhyasva! prekṣakās te vayaṃ sthitāḥ.
svayam iṣṭaṃ ca te kāmaṃ vīra bhūyo dadāmy aham:
hatv" âikaṃ bhavato rājyaṃ hato vā svargam āpnuhi!

DURYODHANA uvāca:

ekaś ced yoddhum ākrande śūro 'dya mama dīyatām!
āyudhānām iyaṃ c' âpi vṛtā tvat|saṃmate gadā.
hant' âikaṃ bhavatām ekaḥ śakyaṃ māṃ yo 'bhimanyate
padātir gadayā saṅkhye sa yudhyatu mayā saha!
vṛttāni ratha|yuddhāni vicitrāṇi pade pade.
idam ekaṃ gadā|yuddhaṃ bhavatv ady' âdbhutaṃ mahat.
32.30 astrāṇām api paryāyaṃ kartum icchanti mānavāḥ;
yuddhānām api paryāyo bhavatv anumate tava.
gadayā tvāṃ mahā|bāho vijeṣyāmi sah'|ânujam
Pañcālān Sṛñjayāṃś c' âiva ye c' ânye tava sainikāḥ.
na hi me saṃbhramo jātu Śakrād api Yudhiṣṭhira.

Confronting us one against one, choose whatever weapon you like and fight! We will stand here and watch you. 32.25

Furthermore, hero, I will grant you the wish that you yourself have desired: if you kill one of us then the kingdom is yours, but if you are killed then attain heaven!

DUR·YÓDHANA said:

As long as he is alone, then give me a hero to fight in battle today! With your consent, I choose this mace as my weapon. Come! Whichever one of you considers me his equal—one man against the other—let him fight against me on foot with a mace in battle!

There have, on various occasions, been different chariot contests. Let there now be a huge and extraordinary mace contest. Men often desire to change their weapons; with your permission, let there be such a change. With my mace, I will triumph over you and your brothers, mighty-armed hero, as well as over the Panchálas, Srínjayas, and other troops. I never waver, Yudhi·shthira, not even in the face of Shakra. 32.30

YUDHIṢṬHIRA uvāca:

uttiṣṭh' ôttiṣṭha Gāndhāre! māṃ yodhaya Suyodhana
eka ekena saṃgamya saṃyuge gadayā balī!
puruṣo bhava Gāndhāre, yudhyasva su|samāhitaḥ!
adya te jīvitaṃ n' âsti yad' Îndro 'pi tav' āśrayaḥ!

SAÑJAYA uvāca:

etat sa nara|śārdūlo n' âmṛṣyata tav' ātma|jaḥ
salil'|ântar|gataḥ śvabhre mahā|nāga iva śvasan.
32.35 tath" âsau vāk|pratodena tudyamānaḥ punaḥ punaḥ
vaco na mamṛṣe rājann uttam'|âśvaḥ kaśām iva.
saṃkṣobhya salilaṃ vegād gadām ādāya vīryavān
adri|sāra|mayīṃ gurvīṃ kāñcan'|âṅgada|bhūṣaṇām
antar|jalāt samuttasthau nāg'|êndra iva niḥśvasan.
sa bhittvā stambhitaṃ toyaṃ skandhe kṛtv" āyasīṃ gadām
udatiṣṭhata putras te pratapan raśmivān iva.
tataḥ śaiky'|āyasīṃ gurvīṃ jātarūpa|pariṣkṛtām
gadāṃ parāmṛśad dhīmān Dhārtarāṣṭro mahā|balaḥ.

gadā|hastaṃ tu taṃ dṛṣṭvā sa|śṛṅgam iva parvatam
prajānām iva saṃkruddhaṃ śūla|pāṇim iva sthitam—
sa|gado Bhārato bhāti pratapan bhāskaro yathā!—
32.40 tam uttīrṇaṃ mahā|bāhuṃ gadā|hastam arin|damam
menire sarva|bhūtāni daṇḍa|pāṇim iv' ântakam.

YUDHI·SHTHIRA said:

Rise, rise, son of Gandhári! Fight against me, Su·yódhana, one mighty man clashing against the other with a mace in battle. Be a man, son of Gandhári, and fight with zeal! Today you will lose your life, even if Indra himself were to support you!

SÁNJAYA said:

Your son—that tiger of a man—could not bear these words as he lay in the water like a great hissing snake in its hole. Repeatedly stung by Yudhi·shthira's goading speech, 32.35 he could not endure these words, Your Majesty, just as a fine horse cannot bear a whip. Ruffling the waters with his movement and taking up his heavy mace—which was made of iron and adorned with gold bangles—mighty Dur·yódhana rose from the depths of the water, hissing like a king of snakes. Placing the iron mace on his shoulder, your son burst through the frozen water and rose up like the blazing sun. The wise and powerful son of Dhrita·rashtra then seized hold of his slinged iron mace, which was heavy and embellished with gold.

When they saw Dur·yódhana brandishing his mace and looking like a peaked mountain or like trident-bearing Shiva when enraged with creatures—how that Bhárata shone like the blazing sun as he wielded his mace!—when they saw 32.40 the mighty-armed enemy-tamer rise out of the water, mace in hand, every living being thought that he resembled staff-bearing Death.

vajra|hastam yathā Śakraṃ śūla|hastaṃ yathā Haram
dadṛśuḥ sarva|Pañcālāḥ putraṃ tava jan'|âdhipa.
tam uttīrṇaṃ tu saṃprekṣya samahṛṣyanta sarvaśaḥ
Pañcālāḥ Pāṇḍaveyāś ca te 'nyonyasya talān daduḥ.
avahāsaṃ tu taṃ matvā putro Duryodhanas tava
udvṛtya nayane kruddho didhakṣur iva Pāṇḍavān
tri|śikhāṃ bhru|kuṭīṃ kṛtvā saṃdaṣṭa|daśana|cchadaḥ
pratyuvāca tatas tān vai Pāṇḍavān saha|Keśavān.

DURYODHANA uvāca:

32.45 asy' âvahāsasya phalaṃ pratibhokṣyatha Pāṇḍavāḥ!
gamiṣyatha hatāḥ sadyaḥ sa|Pañcālā Yama|kṣayam!

SAÑJAYA uvāca:

utthitaś ca jalāt tasmāt putro Duryodhanas tava
atiṣṭhata gadā|pāṇī rudhireṇa samukṣitaḥ.
tasya śoṇita|digdhasya salilena samukṣitam
śarīraṃ sma tadā bhāti sravann iva mahī|dharaḥ.
tam udyata|gadaṃ vīraṃ menire tatra Pāṇḍavāḥ
Vaivasvatam iva kruddhaṃ Kinkar'|ôdyata|pāṇinam.
sa megha|ninado harṣān nadann iva ca go|vṛṣaḥ
ājuhāva tataḥ Pārthān gadayā yudhi vīryavān.

DURYODHANA uvāca:

32.50 ek'|âikena ca māṃ yūyam āsīdata Yudhiṣṭhira.
na hy eko bahubhir nyāyyo vīro yodhayituṃ yudhi,
nyasta|varmā viśeṣeṇa śrāntaś c' âpsu pariplutaḥ
bhṛśaṃ vikṣata|gātraś ca hata|vāhana|sainikaḥ.

All the Panchálas considered your son to be like thunderbolt-wielding Shakra or trident-wielding Hara, lord of men. Even so, when they saw Dur·yódhana emerge, the Panchálas and Pándavas all started to rejoice and slapped each other's hands.* Viewing this as an insult, your son Dur·yódhana rolled his eyes in anger, as if about to incinerate the Pándavas. Furrowing his brow into three lines and biting his lips, he addressed the Pándavas and Késhava with these words.

DUR·YÓDHANA said:

You will taste the fruit of this insult, Pándavas! You and the Panchálas will die this very day and enter the house of Yama. 32.45

SÁNJAYA said:

Rising out of the water, your son Dur·yódhana stood there, grasping his mace and drenched in blood. Soaked with water, the body of that blood-smeared hero glistened like a mountain shedding streams. The Pándavas considered the mace-bearing hero to be like Yama, the angry son of Vivásvat, when he wields his raised Kínkara rod. Roaring joyfully like a bull, and with the rumble of a thundercloud, mighty Dur·yódhana then challenged the Parthas with his mace to fight in battle.

DUR·YÓDHANA said:

Attack me one against one, Yudhi·shthira. For it is not right for one hero to fight many in battle, especially if he is armorless, exhausted, and has been submerged in water, and if his limbs are severely wounded and his soldiers and 32.50

avaśyam eva yoddhavyaṃ sarvair eva mayā saha.
yuktaṃ tv a|yuktam ity etad vetsi tvaṃ c' âiva sarvadā.

YUDHIṢṬHIRA uvāca:

mā bhūd iyaṃ tava prajñā katham evaṃ Suyodhana
yad" Âbhimanyuṃ bahavo jaghnur yudhi mahā|rathāḥ?
kṣatra|dharmaṃ bhṛśaṃ krūraṃ nirapekṣaṃ su|nirghṛṇam;
anyathā tu kathaṃ hanyur Abhimanyuṃ tathā|gatam?
32.55 sarve bhavanto dharma|jñāḥ. sarve śūrās tanu|tyajaḥ.
nyāyena yudhyatāṃ proktā Śakra|loka|gatiḥ parā.
yady ekas tu na hantavyo bahubhir dharma eva tu
tad" Âbhimanyuṃ bahavo nijaghnus tvan|mate katham?
sarvo vimṛśate jantuḥ kṛcchra|stho dharma|darśanam;
pada|sthaḥ pihitaṃ dvāraṃ para|lokasya paśyati.
āmuñca kavacaṃ vīra mūrdha|jān yamayasva ca!
yac c' ânyad api te n' âsti tad apy ādatsva Bhārata.
imam ekaṃ ca te kāmaṃ vīra bhūyo dadāmy aham:
pañcānāṃ Pāṇḍaveyānāṃ yena tvaṃ yoddhum icchasi
taṃ hatvā vai bhavān rājā; hato vā svargam āpnuhi!
ṛte ca jīvitād vīra yuddhe kiṃ kurma te priyam?

SAÑJAYA uvāca:

32.60 tatas tava suto rājan varma jagrāha kāñcanam
vicitraṃ ca śiras|trāṇaṃ jāmbūnada|pariṣkṛtam.
so 'vabaddha|śiras|trāṇaḥ śubha|kāñcana|varma|bhṛt
rarāja rājan putras te kāñcanaḥ śaila|rāḍ iva.
saṃnaddhaḥ sa|gado rājan sajjaḥ saṃgrāma|mūrdhani

animals dead. I must certainly fight all of you. You yourself know in every way what is proper and improper.

YUDHI·SHTHIRA said:

How is it, Su·yódhana, that you did not have this wisdom previously when several great warriors fought against Abhimányu in battle? The warrior code must be extremely cruel, indifferent, and merciless; otherwise how could they have killed Abhimányu when he was in that plight? All of you knew what was right. All of you were heroes who were willing to sacrifice their bodies. The realm of Shakra has been proclaimed as the supreme destiny for those who fight lawfully. If it is right that one warrior should not be killed by many, then how is it that, on your command, many men killed Abhimányu?* Everyone turns to morality when they are in a difficult situation; left standing on their feet, they see the door to the other world closed. 32.55

Put on your armor, hero, and bind your hair! And take up whatever else you lack, descendant of Bharata! Furthermore, I grant you this single wish, hero: if you kill the one man that you choose to fight among the five Pándavas, then you will be king; otherwise, die and attain heaven! What other kindness can we give you in battle, hero—except your life?

SÁNJAYA said:

Your son then put on his golden armor, Your Majesty, and donned a glistening helmet that was adorned with gold. Tying on his helmet and wearing this glorious gold armor, your son looked as radiant as the golden king of the mountains, Your Majesty.* Clad in armor and wielding his mace, 32.60

abravīt Pāṇḍavān sarvān putro Duryodhanas tava:
«bhrātṝṇāṃ bhavatām eko yudhyatāṃ gadayā mayā!
Sahadevena vā yotsye Bhīmena Nakulena vā
athavā Phālgunen' âdya tvayā vā, Bharata'|rṣabha!
yotsye 'haṃ saṃgaraṃ prāpya vijeṣye ca raṇ'|âjire!
aham adya gamiṣyāmi vairasy' ântaṃ su|dur|gamam
gadayā puruṣa|vyāghra hema|paṭṭa|nibaddhayā.

32.65 gadā|yuddhe na me kaś cit sadṛśo 'st' îti cintaye.
gadayā vo haniṣyāmi sarvān eva samāgatān.
na me samarthāḥ sarve vai yoddhuṃ nyāyena ke cana.
na yuktam ātmanā vaktum evaṃ garv'|ôddhataṃ vacaḥ.
athavā sa|phalaṃ hy etat kariṣye bhavatāṃ puraḥ!
asmin muhūrte satyaṃ vā mithyā v" âitad bhaviṣyati.
gṛhṇātu ca gadāṃ yo vai yotsyate 'dya mayā saha!»

SAÑJAYA uvāca:

33.1 EVAṂ DURYODHANE rājan garjamāne muhur muhuḥ
Yudhiṣṭhirasya saṃkruddho Vāsudevo 'bravīd idam:
«yadi nāma hy ayaṃ yuddhe varayet tvāṃ Yudhiṣṭhira
Arjunaṃ Nakulaṃ c' âiva Sahadevam ath' âpi vā—
kim idaṃ sāhasaṃ rājaṃs tvayā vyāhṛtam īdṛśam
‹ekam eva nihaty' ājau bhava rājā Kuruṣv› iti?—
na samarthān ahaṃ manye gadā|hastasya saṃyuge.

your armed son Dur·yódhana addressed all the Pándavas at the front of the battlefield:

"Let one of you brothers fight me with your mace! Today I will fight against Saha·deva, Bhima, Nákula, Phálguna, or you, bull-like Bhárata! Entering battle, I will fight and be victorious on the battlefield! With my mace, which is bound in gold cloth, I will today attain the goal of heroism that is so difficult to achieve, tiger among men.

There is, I believe, no-one that can equal me in a mace contest. With my mace, I will kill every one of you that has gathered here. None of you has the ability to fight against me fairly. 32.65

But it is not right for me to utter such pride-swollen words. Instead I will fulfill them in front of you! This is the moment when my words will turn out to be true or false. Let that man who will fight against me today take up his mace!"

SÁNJAYA said:

As DUR·YÓDHANA roared repeatedly in this way, Vasudéva angrily addressed Yudhi·shthira, Your Majesty, saying: 33.1

"Yudhi·shthira, if this man chooses to fight either you, Árjuna, Nákula, or Saha·deva in battle—why, Your Majesty, did you rashly tell Dur·yódhana that he would be king of the Kurus if he killed only one of you in battle?—if this is his choice, then I do not think any of you are a match for him when he wields his mace in war.

etena hi kṛtā yogyā varṣāṇ' îha trayodaśa
āyase puruṣe rājan Bhīmasena|jighāṃsayā.
33.5 kathaṃ nāma bhavet kāryam asmābhir Bharata'|rṣabha?
sāhasaṃ kṛtavāṃs tvaṃ tu hy anukrośān nṛp'|ôttama.
n' ânyam asy' ânupaśyāmi pratiyoddhāram āhave
ṛte Vṛkodarāt Pārthāt. sa ca n' âtikṛta|śramaḥ.
tad idaṃ dyūtam ārabdhaṃ punar eva yathā purā
viṣamaṃ Śakuneś c' âiva tava c' âiva viśāṃ pate.
balī Bhīmaḥ samarthaś ca. kṛtī rājā Suyodhanaḥ.
balavān vā kṛtī v" êti kṛtī rājan viśiṣyate.
so 'yaṃ rājaṃs tvayā śatruḥ same pathi niveśitaḥ
nyastaś c' ātmā su|viṣame kṛcchram āpāditā vayam.
33.10 ko nu sarvān vinirjitya śatrūn ekena vairiṇā
kṛcchra|prāptena ca tathā hārayed rājyam āgatam,
paṇitvā c' âika|pāṇena rocayed evam āhavam?
na hi paśyāmi taṃ loke yo 'dya Duryodhanaṃ raṇe
gadā|hastaṃ vijetuṃ vai śaktaḥ syād a|maro 'pi hi.
na tvaṃ Bhīmo na Nakulaḥ Sahadevo 'tha Phālgunaḥ
jetuṃ nyāyena śakto vai. kṛtī rājā Suyodhanaḥ.
sa kathaṃ vadase śatruṃ ‹yudhyasva gaday" êti› hi
‹ekaṃ ca no nihaty' ājau bhava rāj" êti› Bhārata?
Vṛkodaraṃ samāsādya saṃśayo vai jaye hi naḥ
nyāyato yudhyamānānāṃ. kṛtī hy eṣa mahā|balaḥ.

For thirteen years, Your Majesty, he has practiced on an iron figure in his desire to kill Bhima·sena. How can we achieve our goal, bull of the Bharatas? It was out of compassion that you acted so recklessly, best of kings.* 33.5

Except for Vrikódara, the son of Pritha, I see no-one else who can fight Dur·yódhana in battle. And Vrikódara is not overly tired.

Once again you have undertaken a gambling match, just as before when you played Shákuni in that unfair game, lord of the people.*

Bhima is mighty and powerful. But King Su·yódhana is skillful. Between a powerful and a skillful man, the skillful one succeeds, Your Majesty. You have placed this enemy on an even ground, Your Majesty, but you have placed yourself on an extremely uneven ground and exposed us to danger.

Who would conquer all his enemies and then allow a single foe—and one in a dire situation—to seize his kingdom when it is already in his grasp? Who would so favor his enemy by gambling a war on a single stake? 33.10

I do not see anyone today in the world who can conquer Dur·yódhana when he wields his mace in battle, not even a god. Neither you, Bhima, Nákula, Saha·deva, nor Phálguna can conquer him through fair means. King Su·yódhana is skillful. How, descendant of Bharata, could you say to your enemy: 'Fight with your mace!' and 'Kill one of us in battle and become king'? Even if Dur·yódhana battles against Vrikódara, our victory will be doubtful if we fight fairly. For that mighty man is skillful.

33.15 ‹ekaṃ v" âsmān nihatya tvaṃ bhava rāj" êti› vai punaḥ
nūnaṃ na rājya|bhāg" êṣā Pāṇḍoḥ Kuntyāś ca santatiḥ
atyanta|vana|vāsāya sṛṣṭā bhaikṣyāya vā punaḥ!»

BHĪMASENA uvāca:

Madhu|sūdana mā kārṣīr viṣādaṃ Yadu|nandana!
adya pāraṃ gamiṣyāmi vairasya bhṛśa|dur|gamam.
ahaṃ Suyodhanaṃ saṅkhye haniṣyāmi. na saṃśayaḥ.
vijayo vai dhruvaḥ Kṛṣṇa Dharma|rājasya dṛśyate!
adhyardhena guṇen' êyaṃ gadā gurutarī mama.
na tathā Dhārtarāṣṭrasya mā kārṣīr Mādhava vyathām.
aham enaṃ hi gadayā saṃyuge yoddhum utsahe.
bhavantaḥ prekṣakāḥ sarve mama santu Janārdana!
33.20 s'|â|marān api lokāṃs trīn nānā|śastra|dharān yudhi
yodhayeyaṃ raṇe Kṛṣṇa—kim ut' âdya Suyodhanam?

SAÑJAYA uvāca:

tathā saṃbhāṣamāṇaṃ tu Vāsudevo Vṛkodaram
hṛṣṭaḥ saṃpūjayām āsa vacanaṃ c' êdam abravīt:
«tvām āśritya mahā|bāho Dharma|rājo Yudhiṣṭhiraḥ
nihat'|āriḥ svakāṃ dīptāṃ śriyaṃ prāpto. na saṃśayaḥ.
tvayā vinihatāḥ sarve Dhṛtarāṣṭra|sutā raṇe.
rājāno rāja|putrāś ca nāgāś ca vinipātitāḥ.
Kaliṅgā Māgadhāḥ prācyā Gāndhārāḥ Kuravas tathā
tvām āsādya mahā|yuddhe nihatāḥ Pāṇḍu|nandana.

Because you repeatedly gave Dur·yódhana the option to kill one of us and become king, Pandu and Kunti's lineage will surely never have its share of the kingdom. Instead it is surely destined once more for mendicancy and an endless life in the forest!" 33.15

BHIMA·SENA said:

Destroyer of Madhu, delight of the Yadus, do not despair! Today I will end this hostility, extremely difficult though that may be. I will kill Su·yódhana in battle. Have no doubt. Victory for the King of Righteousness will surely be seen, Krishna!

My mace is one and a half times heavier than his. Do not be so alarmed by Dhrita·rashtra's son, Mádhava. I am able to fight him in battle with my mace. Let all of you be my witnesses, Janárdana! I could fight the three worlds in battle with all their gods, even if they were armed with various weapons—what then of Su·yódhana on this day, Krishna? 33.20

SÁNJAYA said:

Vasudéva joyfully honored Vrikódara when he spoke this way and addressed him with these words:

"It is by relying on you, mighty-armed hero, that Yudhi·shthira, the King of Righteousness, has slaughtered his enemies and acquired his blazing glory! Of this there is no doubt. You have killed all of Dhrita·rashtra's sons in battle. Kings, princes, and elephants have been slain by you! In this great battle, delight of Pandu, you have attacked and slaughtered the Kalíngas, Mágadhas, easterners, Gandháras, and Kurus.

33.25 hatvā Duryodhanaṃ c' âpi prayacch' ôrvīṃ sa|sāgarām
Dharma|rājāya Kaunteya yathā Viṣṇuḥ Śacī|pateḥ!
tvāṃ ca prāpya raṇe pāpo Dhārtarāṣṭro vinaṅkṣyati.
tvam asya sakthinī bhaṅktvā pratijñāṃ pālayiṣyasi.
yatnena tu sadā Pārtha yoddhavyo Dhṛtarāṣṭra|jaḥ
kṛtī ca balavāṃś c' âiva yuddha|śauṇḍaś ca nityadā.»
tatas tu Sātyakī rājan pūjayām āsa Pāṇḍavam
Pañcālāḥ Pāṇḍaveyāś ca Dharma|rāja|puro|gamāḥ
tad vaco Bhīmasenasya sarva ev' âbhyapūjayan.
tato bhīma|balo Bhīmo Yudhiṣṭhiram ath' âbravīt
Sṛñjayaiḥ saha tiṣṭhantaṃ tapantam iva bhāskaram:
33.30 «aham etena saṃgamya saṃyuge yoddhum utsahe.
na hi śakto raṇe jetuṃ mām eṣaḥ puruṣ'|âdhamaḥ.
adya krodhaṃ vimokṣyāmi nihitaṃ hṛdaye bhṛśam
Suyodhane Dhārtarāṣṭre Khāṇḍave 'gnim iv' Ârjunaḥ.
śalyam ady' ôddhariṣyāmi tava Pāṇḍava hṛc|chayam
nihatya gadayā pāpam. adya rājan sukhī bhava!
adya kīrti|mayīṃ mālāṃ pratimokṣye tav' ân|agha.
prāṇāñ śriyaṃ ca rājyaṃ ca mokṣyate 'dya Suyodhanaḥ!
rājā ca Dhṛtarāṣṭro 'dya śrutvā putraṃ mayā hatam
smariṣyaty a|śubhaṃ karma yat tac Chakuni|buddhi|jam!»

Kill Dur·yódhana, O son of Kunti, and hand over the earth with its oceans to the King of Righteousness, just as Vishnu once did for the husband of Shachi!* 33.25

The evil son of Dhrita·rashtra will be destroyed when he confronts you in battle. You will keep your vow by breaking his thighs.

But you should always be careful when you fight the son of Dhrita·rashtra, O Partha. He is skillful and strong and forever drunk with war."

Sátyaki then applauded the Pándava, Your Majesty, and every one of the Panchálas and Pándavas headed by the King of Righteousness also applauded Bhima·sena's words. Bhima—who possessed terrifying might—then addressed Yudhi·shthira, who stood among the Srínjayas blazing like the sun:

"I am able to confront Dur·yódhana in battle and fight him. For this lowest of men cannot conquer me on the battlefield. 33.30

Against Su·yódhana, the son of Dhrita·rashtra, I will today release the anger that has lain deep in my heart, just as Árjuna released fire in the Khándava forest.* By killing this sinner with my mace, I will today remove the barb that lies in your heart, Pándava. Be happy on this day, Your Majesty! On this day, faultless king, I will place a garland of fame around your neck. On this day Su·yódhana will give up his life, glory and kingdom! On this day King Dhrita·rashtra will learn that I have killed his son and he will remember the impure deed that sprang from Shákuni's mind!"*

33.35 ity uktvā Bharata|śreṣṭho gadām udyamya vīryavān
udatiṣṭhata yuddhāya Śakro Vṛtram iv' āhvayan.
tad" āhvānam a|mṛśyan vai tava putro 'tivīryavān
pratyupasthita ev' āśu matto mattam iva dvipam.
gadā|hastaṃ tava sutaṃ yuddhāya samupasthitam
dadṛśuḥ Pāṇḍavāḥ sarve Kailāsam iva sṛṅgiṇam.
tam ekākinam āsādya Dhārtarāṣṭraṃ mahā|balam
viyūtham iva mātaṅgaṃ samahṛṣyanta Pāṇḍavāḥ.

na saṃbhramo na ca bhayaṃ na ca glānir na ca vyathā
āsīd Duryodhanasy' âpi. sthitaḥ siṃha iv' āhave.
33.40 samudyata|gadaṃ dṛṣṭvā Kailāsam iva śṛṅgiṇam
Bhīmasenas tadā rājan Duryodhanam ath' âbravīt:

«rājñ" âpi Dhṛtarāṣṭreṇa tvayā c' âsmāsu yat kṛtam
smara tad duṣ|kṛtaṃ karma yad bhūtaṃ Vāraṇāvate,
Draupadī ca parikliṣṭā sabhā|madhye rajasvalā
dyūte yad vijito rājā Śakuner buddhi|niścayāt,
yāni c' ânyāni duṣṭ'|ātman pāpāni kṛtavān asi
an|āgaḥsu ca Pārtheṣu tasya paśya mahat phalam.

tvat|kṛte nihataḥ śete śara|talpe mahā|yaśāḥ
Gāṅgeyo Bharata|śreṣṭhaḥ sarveṣāṃ naḥ pitāmahaḥ.
33.45 hato Droṇaś ca Karṇaś ca hataḥ Śalyaḥ pratāpavān
vairasya c' ādi|kart" âsau Śakunir nihato raṇe.
bhrātaras te hatāḥ śūrāḥ putrāś ca saha|sainikāḥ
rājānaś ca hatāḥ śūrāḥ samareṣv a|nivartinaḥ.

Saying these words and brandishing his mace, the mighty champion of the Bharatas stood up, challenging Dur·yódhana to fight, just as Shakra once challenged Vritra. Unable to endure the challenge, your extremely fierce son swiftly stood up to confront him, like one frenzied elephant against another. All the Pándavas watched your son as he came forward to fight, mace in hand, resembling the peaked mountain Kailása. Indeed the Pándavas were thrilled when they saw the mighty son of Dhrita·rashtra charge forward on his own, like an elephant separated from its herd. 33.35

There was no hesitation, fear, weariness or alarm in Dur·yódhana. He stood on the battlefield like a lion.

When Bhima·sena saw Dur·yódhana wielding his mace as if he were the peaked mountain Kailása, he addressed him with these words, Your Majesty: 33.40

"Remember the wicked deeds that you and King Dhrita·rashtra committed against us, such as the events that occurred at Varanávata,* or how Dráupadi was wronged in the assembly hall during her menstruation, or how the king was defeated in a gambling match through Shákuni's plan.* See the great fruit of these and other deeds that you committed against the sinless Parthas, you villain.

Because of you, Bhishma, that glorious son of Ganga and best of Bharatas, grandfather to us all, lies dead on a bed of arrows. Drona, Karna, and splendid Shalya have been killed. Shákuni too, the initiator of these hostilities, has been slain in battle. Your heroic brothers are dead, as are your sons and their troops. Heroic kings have been slaughtered, men 33.45

ete c' ânye ca nihatā bahavaḥ kṣatriya'|rṣabhāḥ.
prātikāmī tathā pāpo Draupadyāḥ kleśa|kṛdd hataḥ.
avaśiṣṭas tvam ev' âikaḥ kula|ghno 'dhama|pūruṣaḥ.
tvām apy adya haniṣyāmi gadayā. n' âtra saṃśayaḥ.
adya te 'haṃ raṇe darpaṃ sarvaṃ nāśayitā nṛpa
rājy'|āśāṃ vipulāṃ rājan Pāṇḍaveṣu ca duṣ|kṛtam.

DURYODHANA uvāca:

33.50 «kiṃ katthitena bahunā? yudhyasv' âdya mayā saha!
adya te 'haṃ vineṣyāmi yuddha|śraddhāṃ Vṛkodara!
kiṃ na paśyasi māṃ pāpa gadā|yuddhe vyavasthitam,
Himavac|chikhar'|ākārāṃ pragṛhya mahatīṃ gadām?
gadinaṃ ko 'dya māṃ pāpa hantum utsahate ripuḥ
nyāyato yudhyamānasya deveṣv api Purandaraḥ?
mā vṛthā garja Kaunteya śārad'|âbhram iv' â|jalam.
darśayasva balaṃ yuddhe yāvat tat te 'dya vidyate!»
tasya tad vacanaṃ śrutvā Pāṇḍavāḥ saha|Sṛñjayāḥ
sarve saṃpūjayām āsus tad vaco vijigīṣavaḥ.
33.55 unmattam iva mātaṅgaṃ tala|śabdena mānavāḥ
bhūyaḥ saṃharṣayām āsū rājan Duryodhanaṃ nṛpam.
bṛṃhanti kuñjarās tatra hayā heṣanti c' â|sakṛt.
śastrāṇi saṃpradīpyante Pāṇḍavānāṃ jay'|âiṣiṇām.

SÁNJAYA said:

YOUR MAJESTY, when this fierce battle was imminent and the heroic Pándavas had all sat down, Rama—whose banner is a palm-tree and whose weapon is a plow—arrived at the scene after hearing that a battle between his two pupils was commencing. 34.1

The Pándavas and Késhava felt the greatest joy at seeing Rama. Approaching and embracing him, they honored him in the appropriate manner. After honoring him, Your Majesty, they said: "See your pupils' skill in battle, Rama."

Rama looked at Krishna and the Pándavas, and also at Dur·yódhana the Káurava, who stood there wielding his mace, and said: 34.5

"It has been forty-two days since my departure. I set out under the Pushya constellation and have returned under Shrávana. I am keen to see my pupils fight a mace battle, Mádhava."

Dur·yódhana and Vrikódara then entered the battleground, wielding their maces. Both heroes looked glorious.

King Yudhi·shthira then embraced plow-weaponed Rama and welcomed him by asking after his health in the proper way. Those great archers, the two glorious Krishnas, also greeted plow-weaponed Rama and joyfully embraced him with delight. The two heroic sons of Madri and five sons of Dráupadi likewise stood and greeted the mighty son of Róhini. Brandishing their maces, powerful Bhima·sena and your son also honored Bala the same way. On all sides the kings honored Rama with welcoming words and said to the great-spirited son of Róhini: "Look at this battle, mighty-armed hero!" 34.10

parişvajya tadā Rāmaḥ Pāṇḍavān saha|Sṛñjayān
apṛcchat kuśalaṃ sarvān pārthivāṃś c' â|mit'|âujasaḥ.
tath" âiva te samāsādya papracchus tam an|āmayam.
pratyabhyarcya halī sarvān kṣatriyāṃś ca mah"|ātmanaḥ
kṛtvā kuśala|saṃyuktāṃ saṃvidaṃ ca yathā|vayaḥ,

34.15 Janārdanaṃ Sātyakiṃ ca premṇā sa pariṣasvaje
mūrdhni c' âitāv upāghrāya kuśalaṃ paryapṛcchata.
tau ca taṃ vidhivad rājan pūjayām āsatur gurum
Brahmāṇam iva dev'|ēśam Indr'|Ôpendrau mud"|ânvitau.

tato 'bravīd Dharma|suto Rauhiṇeyam arin|damam:
«idaṃ bhrātror mahā|yuddhaṃ paśya Rām' êti» Bhārata.

teṣāṃ madhye mahā|bāhuḥ śrīmān Keśava|pūrva|jaḥ
nyaviśat parama|prītaḥ pūjyamāno mahā|rathaiḥ.
sa babhau rāja|madhya|stho nīla|vāsāḥ sita|prabhaḥ
div" îva nakṣatra|gaṇaiḥ parikīrṇo niśā|karaḥ.

34.20 tatas tayoḥ saṃnipātas tumulo loma|harṣaṇaḥ
āsīd anta|karo rājan vairasya tava putrayoḥ.

Embracing the Pándavas and Srínjayas, Rama inquired after the health of all the kings, who had limitless strength. They too approached him in the same way and asked after his health. After he had greeted all the heroic warriors and talked to them of their health in accordance with their years, plow-bearing Rama lovingly embraced Janárdana and Sátyaki. Sniffing them on their heads, he asked after their health. Like Indra and Upéndra honoring Brahma, the lord of the gods, they in turn joyfully honored their teacher in the proper manner. 34.15

Then, descendant of Bharata, the son of Righteousness addressed the enemy-taming son of Róhini, saying: "Look at this great battle between brothers, Rama!"

With great joy, the glorious and mighty-armed elder brother of Késhava then sat down in the middle of those heroes, honored by the great warriors. As he sat among those kings, with his blue robes and bright complexion, he shone like the moon in the sky when surrounded by hosts of stars.

A tumultuous and hair-raising encounter then took place between your two sons, Your Majesty, bringing an end to the hostilities. 34.20

35–54
SARÁSVATI'S SACRED SITES

JANAMEJAYA uvāca:

35.1 PŪRVAM EVA YADĀ Rāmas tasmin yuddha upasthite
āmantrya Keśavaṃ yāto Vṛṣṇibhiḥ sahitaḥ prabhuḥ.
«sāhāyyaṃ Dhārtarāṣṭrasya na ca kart" âsmi Keśava
na c' âiva Pāṇḍu|putrāṇāṃ. gamiṣyāmi yath"|āgatam!»
evam uktvā tadā Rāmo yātaḥ kṣatra|nibarhaṇaḥ.
tasya c' āgamanaṃ bhūyo brahmañ śaṃsitum arhasi.
ākhyāhi me vistaraśaḥ kathaṃ Rāma upasthitaḥ
kathaṃ ca dṛṣṭavān yuddhaṃ. kuśalo hy asi sattama.

VAIŚAMPĀYANA uvāca:

Upaplavye niviṣṭeṣu Pāṇḍaveṣu mah"|ātmasu
preṣito Dhṛtarāṣṭrasya samīpaṃ Madhu|sūdanaḥ
śamaṃ prati mahā|bāho hit'|ârthaṃ sarva|dehinām.
35.5 sa gatvā Hāstinapuraṃ Dhṛtarāṣṭraṃ sametya ca
uktavān vacanaṃ tathyaṃ hitaṃ c' âiva viśeṣataḥ.
na ca tat kṛtavān rājā yath"|ākhyātaṃ hi tat purā.
an|avāpya śamaṃ tatra Kṛṣṇaḥ puruṣa|sattamaḥ
āgacchata mahā|bāhur Upaplavyaṃ jan'|âdhipa.
tataḥ pratyāgataḥ Kṛṣṇo Dhārtarāṣṭra|visarjitaḥ
a|kriyāyāṃ nara|vyāghra Pāṇḍavān idam abravīt:
«na kurvanti vaco mahyaṃ Kuravaḥ kāla|noditāḥ.
nirgacchadhvaṃ Pāṇḍaveyāḥ puṣyeṇa sahitā mayā.»
tato vibhajyamāneṣu baleṣu balināṃ varaḥ
provāca bhrātaraṃ Kṛṣṇaṃ Rauhiṇeyo mahā|manāḥ:
35.10 «teṣām api mahā|bāho sāhāyyaṃ Madhu|sūdana
kriyatām iti» tat Kṛṣṇo n' âsya cakre vacas tadā.
tato manyu|parīt'|ātmā jagāma Yadu|nandanaḥ

JANAM·ÉJAYA said:

BEFOREHAND, WHEN the war was impending, Lord Rama had taken leave of Késhava and set off with the Vrishnis. Warrior-destroying Rama had departed with these words: "I am an ally of neither Dhrita·rashtra's son nor the sons of Pandu, Késhava. I will go as I came!" 35.1

Inform me further, brahmin, of Rama's return. Tell me in detail how he arrived and how he saw the contest. For you are skilled in narration, excellent brahmin.

VAISHAMPÁYANA said:

When the heroic Pándavas were staying in Upaplávya, Krishna, the destroyer of Madhu, was sent to Dhrita·rashtra in order to sue for peace for the benefit of all embodied creatures, mighty-armed king.* Traveling to Hástina·pura, he approached Dhrita·rashtra and told him words that were true and of particular benefit. But, as related earlier, the king did not act on Krishna's words. Unable to acquire peace in Hástina·pura, mighty-armed Krishna, that best of men, returned to Upaplávya, Your Majesty. Dismissed by the son of Dhrita·rashtra, Krishna returned and told the Pándavas of his unfulfilled task, tiger-like man: 35.5

"The Kurus have not followed my advice, driven on as they are by Time. Set forth with me under the Pushya constellation, Pándavas."

While the armies were being arrayed, the high-minded son of Róhini, that best of mighty men, then addressed his brother Krishna with these words: "We should be the allies of the Káuravas too, mighty-armed destroyer of Madhu." But Krishna did not follow his words. Enraged, glorious 35.10

tīrtha|yātrāṃ hala|dharaḥ Sarasvatyāṃ mahā|yaśāḥ,
maitra|nakṣatra|yoge sma sahitaḥ sarva|Yādavaiḥ.

āśrayām āsa Bhojas tu Duryodhanam arin|damaḥ,
Yuyudhānena sahito Vāsudevas tu Pāṇḍavān.

Rauhiṇeye gate śūre puṣyeṇa Madhu|sūdanaḥ
Pāṇḍaveyān puraskṛtya yayāv abhimukhaḥ Kurūn.

gacchann eva pathi|sthas tu Rāmaḥ preṣyān uvāca ha:

«saṃbhārāṃs tīrtha|yātrāyāṃ sarv'|ôpakaraṇāni ca
ānayadhvaṃ Dvārakāyām agnīn vai yājakāṃs tathā,

35.15 suvarṇa|rajataṃ c' âiva dhenūr vāsāṃsi vājinaḥ
kuñjarāṃś ca rathāṃś c' âiva khar'|ôṣṭraṃ vāhanāni ca.
kṣipram ānīyatāṃ sarvaṃ tīrtha|hetoḥ paricchadam.
pratisrotaḥ Sarasvatyā gacchadhvaṃ śīghra|gāminaḥ.
ṛtvijaś c' ānayadhvaṃ vai śataśaś ca dvija'|rṣabhān!»

evaṃ saṃdiśya tu preṣyān Baladevo mahā|balaḥ
tīrtha|yātrāṃ yayau rājan Kurūṇāṃ vaiśase tadā.
Sarasvatīṃ pratisrotaḥ samantād abhijagmivān
ṛtvigbhiś ca suhṛdbhiś ca tath" ânyair dvija|sattamaiḥ,
rathair gajais tath" âśvaiś ca preṣyaiś ca Bharata'|rṣabha
go|khar'|ôṣṭra|prayuktaiś ca yānaiś ca bahubhir vṛtaḥ.

Rama, the plow-bearing delight of the Yadus, departed for a pilgrimage of the *tirtha*s on the Sarásvati river.* He left under the conjunction of the Maitra constellation and was accompanied by all the Yádavas.

Krita·varman, that enemy-taming Bhoja, then took the side of Dur·yódhana, while Vasudéva and Yuyudhána took the side of the Pándavas.

After the heroic son of Róhini had departed, Krishna, the destroyer of Madhu, took up position behind the Pándavas and advanced forward to confront the Kurus under the Pushya constellation.

Rama, meanwhile, addressed his servants as he traveled on the road, saying:

"Bring provisions and all the necessary equipment for a pilgrimage of the sacred sites. Bring the fires from Dváraka and the sacrificial priests too. Bring gold, silver, cows, clothes, horses, elephants, vehicles, asses, camels, and draft animals. Quickly bring everything necessary for the *tirtha*s. Proceed swiftly up the Sarásvati. Bring sacrificial priests and hundreds of bull-like brahmins!" 35.15

Instructing his servants this way, powerful Bala·deva set off on his pilgrimage while the Kurus were being slaughtered, Your Majesty. He traveled upstream all along the Sarásvati, accompanied by priests, friends, and other excellent brahmins, as well as by vehicles, elephants, horses, servants, and numerous carriages, to which cows, asses, and camels were yoked, bull of the Bharatas.

35.20 śrāntānāṃ klānta|vapuṣāṃ śiśūnāṃ vipul'|āyuṣām
deśe deśe tu deyāni dānāni vividhāni ca
arcāyai c' ârthināṃ rājan kḷptāni bahuśas tathā.
yo yo yatra dvijo bhojyaṃ bhoktuṃ kāmayate tadā
tasya tasya tu tatr' âivam upajahrus tadā nṛpa.
tatra tatra sthitā rājan Rauhiṇeyasya śāsanāt
bhakṣya|peyasya kurvanti rāśīṃs tatra samantataḥ.
vāsāṃsi ca mah"|ârhāṇi paryaṅk'|āstaraṇāni ca
pūj"|ârthaṃ tatra kḷptāni viprāṇāṃ sukham icchatām.
yatra yaḥ svadate vipraḥ kṣatriyo v" âpi Bhārata
tatra tatra tu tasy' âiva sarvaṃ kḷptam adṛśyata.
yathā|sukhaṃ janaḥ sarvo yāti tiṣṭhati vai tadā.
35.25 yātu|kāmasya yānāni pānāni tṛṣitasya ca
bubhukṣitasya c' ânnāni svādūni Bharata'|rṣabha
upajahrur narās tatra vastrāṇy ābharaṇāni ca.

sa panthāḥ prababhau rājan sarvasy' âiva sukh'|āvahaḥ
svarg'|ôpamas tadā vīra narāṇāṃ tatra gacchatām.
nitya|pramudit'|ôpetaḥ svādu|bhakṣyaḥ śubh'|ânvitaḥ
vipaṇy'|āpaṇa|paṇyānāṃ nānā|jana|śatair vṛtaḥ
nānā|druma|lat"|ôpeto nānā|ratna|vibhūṣitaḥ.

In every place, descendant of Bharata, hordes of diverse and worthy gifts were respectfully given to the weary and the tired, to children and the elderly, and to those who made petitions. Whenever a brahmin wanted something to eat, they gave it to him, Your Majesty. On the orders of Róhini's son, the men formed heaps of food and drink here and there on all sides. Expensive clothes and couch-covers were reverently given to brahmins that sought comfort. In every place, whenever a brahmin or kshatriya relished something, one saw it offered to them in full, descendant of Bharata. Everyone moved and dwelled happily at that time. The men gave vehicles to those who wanted to travel, drink to the thirsty, tasty food to the hungry, and clothes and ornaments too, bull of the Bharatas. 35.20 35.25

The road looked glorious as the men traveled along it, heroic king. Bringing happiness to everyone, it resembled a heaven. Full of constant joy, it was endowed with auspice. It had delicious food and was filled with hundreds of different people in shops, stalls, and booths. It had different trees and vines and was adorned with various jewels.

tato mah''|ātmā niyame sthit'|ātmā
puṇyeṣu tīrtheṣu vasūni rājan
dadau dvijebhyaḥ kratu|dakṣiṇāś ca
Yadu|pravīro hala|bhṛt pratītaḥ.
dogdhrīś ca dhenūś ca sahasraśo vai
su|vāsasaḥ kāñcana|baddha|śṛṅgīḥ
hayāṃś ca nānā|vidha|deśa|jātān
yānāni dāsāṃś ca śubhān dvijebhyaḥ,
35.30 ratnāni muktā|maṇi|vidrumaṃ c' âpy
agryaṃ suvarṇaṃ rajataṃ su|śuddham
ayas|mayaṃ tāmra|mayaṃ ca bhāṇḍaṃ
dadau dvij'|âtipravareṣu Rāmaḥ.
evaṃ sa vittaṃ pradadau mah''|ātmā
Sarasvatī|tīrtha|vareṣu bhūri
yayau krameṇ' â|pratima|prabhāvas
tataḥ Kurukṣetram udāra|vṛttiḥ.

JANAMEJAYA uvāca:

Sārasvatānāṃ tīrthānāṃ guṇ'|ôtpattiṃ vadasva me
phalaṃ ca dvi|padāṃ śreṣṭha karma|nirvṛttim eva ca
yathā|krameṇa bhagavaṃs tīrthānām anupūrvaśaḥ;
brahman Brahma|vidāṃ śreṣṭha paraṃ kautūhalaṃ hi me.

VAIŚAMPĀYANA uvāca:

tīrthānāṃ ca phalaṃ rājan guṇ'|ôtpattiṃ ca sarvaśaḥ
may'' ôcyamānaṃ vai puṇyaṃ śṛṇu rāj'|êndra kṛtsnaśaḥ.
35.35 pūrvaṃ mahā|rāja Yadu|pravīra
ṛtvik|suhṛd|vipra|gaṇaiś ca sārdham
puṇyaṃ Prabhāsaṃ samupājagāma
yatr' ôḍu|rāḍ yakṣmaṇā kliśyamānaḥ.
vimukta|śāpaḥ punar āpya tejaḥ

The plow-bearing hero of the Yadus—who was great-spirited and established in self-restraint—joyfully offered gifts and sacrificial fees to brahmins at the sacred sites, Your Majesty. Rama gave the brahmins thousands of milk cows that were covered with fine cloths and had horns bound with gold. He gave them horses from different countries, as well as vehicles and fine slaves. He gave jewels, pearls and coral to eminent brahmins, as well as gold of excellent quality, very fine silver, and goods made of iron and copper. 35.30

In this way, the mighty hero gave away wealth at the fine sacred sites of the Sarásvati, and in due course that man of unrivaled power and noble conduct arrived at Kuru·kshetra.

JANAM·ÉJAYA said:

Tell me, best of men, how Sarásvati's *tirtha*s came to possess their virtuous qualities. Tell me, in due order and succession, the rewards of these sites and the result of performing rituals there, my lord. For I am extremely curious, brahmin supreme among those who know Brahman.

VAISHAMPÁYANA said:

Listen, king of kings, to a full description of all the rewards of these *tirtha*s and the auspicious origins of their virtues.

Accompanied by troops of sacrificial priests, friends and brahmins, the hero of the Yadus first arrived at the holy site of Prabhása, great king. It was here that the moon was once afflicted with consumption. After it had been released from the curse, the moon again regained its power and illuminated the entire world, king of men. It is because 35.35

sarvaṃ jagad bhāsayate nar'|êndra.
evaṃ tu tīrtha|pravaraṃ pṛthivyāṃ
prabhāsanāt tasya tataḥ Prabhāsaḥ.

JANAMEJAYA uvāca:
kathaṃ tu bhagavān Somo yakṣmaṇā samagṛhyata?
kathaṃ ca tīrtha|pravare tasmiṃś candro nyamajjata?
katham āplutya tasmiṃs tu punar āpyāyitaḥ śaśī?
etan me sarvam ācakṣva vistareṇa mahā|mune!

VAIŚAMPĀYANA uvāca:
Dakṣasya tanayās tāta prādur āsan viśāṃ pate;
sa sapta|viṃśatiṃ kanyā Dakṣaḥ Somāya vai dadau.
35.40 nakṣatra|yoga|niratāḥ saṅkhyān'|ârthaṃ ca t" âbhavan*
patnyo vai tasya rāj'|êndra Somasya śubha|karmaṇaḥ.
tās tu sarvā viśāl'|âkṣyo rūpeṇ' â|pratimā bhuvi.
atyaricyata tāsāṃ tu Rohiṇī rūpa|saṃpadā.
tatas tasyāṃ sa bhagavān prītiṃ cakre niśā|karaḥ.
s" âsya hṛdyā babhūv' âtha tasmāt tāṃ bubhuje sadā.
purā hi Somo rāj'|êndra Rohiṇyām avasat param.
tatas tāḥ kupitāḥ sarvā nakṣatr'|ākhyā mah"|ātmanaḥ.
tā gatvā pitaraṃ prāhuḥ prajā|patim a|tandritāḥ:
«Somo vasati n' âsmāsu. Rohiṇīṃ bhajate sadā.
tā vayaṃ sahitāḥ sarvās tvat|sakāśe praj'|ēśvara
vatsyāmo niyat'|āhārās tapaś|caraṇa|tat|parāḥ.»
35.45 śrutvā tāsāṃ tu vacanaṃ Dakṣaḥ Somam ath' âbravīt:
«samaṃ vartasva bhāryāsu. mā tv" â|dharmo mahān spṛśet.»
tās tu sarv" âbravīd Dakṣo: «gacchadhvaṃ śaśino 'ntikam.
samaṃ vatsyati sarvāsu candramā mama śāsanāt.»

of the moon's illumination that this foremost of *tirthas* on earth is called Prabhása ("Illumination").

JANAM·ÉJAYA said:

How did Lord Soma become afflicted with consumption? Why did the moon bathe in this eminent *tirtha*? How did the moon regain its power after it had bathed there? Tell me all this in detail, great sage!

VAISHAMPÁYANA said:

Daksha had twenty seven daughters, lord of the people, whom he gave to Soma. These virtuous wives of Soma de- 35.40 lighted in the conjunctions of the stars for the purpose of counting. All of them had wide eyes and were unrivaled in beauty on earth. But Róhini excelled them in the perfection of her beauty.

The illustrious moon therefore took delight in Róhini. She became dear to his heart and he always enjoyed her. In those former times, king of kings, Soma spent the night with Róhini to an exceptional degree. As a result all the other wives—who bore the names of the constellations—became angry at their great-spirited husband. Proceeding swiftly to their father, that lord of creatures, they said:

"Soma does not spend the night with us. He always enjoys Róhini instead. Disciplining our diet and intent on austerities, we shall all live with you, lord of creatures."

Hearing their words, Daksha said to Soma: "Behave 35.45 equally toward your wives. Do not be tainted by great sin." Daksha then told all his daughters: "Go to your hare-marked husband.* The moon will obey my command and behave equally toward you all."

visṛṣṭās tās tathā jagmuḥ śīt'|âṃśu|bhavanaṃ tadā.
tath" âpi Somo bhagavān punar eva mahī|pate
Rohiṇīṃ nivasaty eva prīyamāṇo muhur muhuḥ.
tatas tāḥ sahitāḥ sarvā bhūyaḥ pitaram abruvan:
«tava śuśrūṣaṇe yuktā vatsyāmo hi tav' ântike.
Somo vasati n' âsmāsu; n' âkarod vacanaṃ tava.»
tāsāṃ tad vacanaṃ śrutvā Dakṣaḥ Somam ath' âbravīt:
«samaṃ vartasva bhāryāsu. mā tvāṃ śapsye Virocana!»
35.50 an|ādṛtya tu tad vākyaṃ Dakṣasya bhagavāñ śaśī
Rohiṇyā sārdham avasat. tatas tāḥ kupitāḥ punaḥ.
gatvā ca pitaraṃ prāhuḥ praṇamya śirasā tadā:
«Somo vasati n' âsmāsu. tasmān naḥ śaraṇaṃ bhava.
Rohiṇyām eva bhagavān sadā vasati candramāḥ.
na tvad|vaco gaṇayati n' âsmāsu sneham icchati.
tasmān nas trāhi sarvā vai yathā naḥ Soma āviśet!»
tac chrutvā bhagavān kruddho yakṣmāṇaṃ pṛthivī|pate
sasarja roṣāt Somāya. sa c' ôḍu|patim āviśat.
sa yakṣmaṇ" âbhibhūt'|ātm" âkṣīyat' âhar ahaḥ śaśī.
yatnaṃ c' âpy akarod rājan mokṣ'|ârthaṃ tasya yakṣmaṇaḥ
iṣṭv" êṣṭibhir mahā|rāja vividhābhir niśā|karaḥ,
na c' âmucyata śāpād vai kṣayaṃ c' âiv' âbhyagacchata.
35.55 kṣīyamāṇe tataḥ Some oṣadhyo na prajajñire.
nirāsvāda|rasāḥ sarvā hata|vīryāś ca sarvaśaḥ.
oṣadhīnāṃ kṣaye jāte prāṇinām api saṃkṣayaḥ
kṛśāś c' āsan prajāḥ sarvāḥ kṣīyamāṇe niśā|kare.
tato devāḥ samāgamya Somam ūcur mahī|pate:

Thus dismissed, the women returned to the abode of the cool-rayed moon. But again Lord Soma still dwelled with Róhini, taking delight in her repeatedly, Your Majesty. Once again all the women jointly addressed their father, saying: "We will live with you and serve you. Soma does not dwell with us; he has not obeyed your command."

Hearing their words, Daksha said to Soma: "Behave equally toward your wives. Do not let me curse you, Illuminator!"

Taking no heed of Daksha's words, the hare-marked Lord continued to dwell with Róhini. As a result, all the women again became angry. Going to their father, they bowed their heads and said: 35.50

"Soma still does not dwell with us. Please therefore be our refuge. The Lord Moon always dwells with Róhini alone. He does not respect your words and is unwilling to show us affection. Save us so that Soma may accept us all!"

The Lord became enraged upon hearing this, Your Majesty, and in his fury he cast the disease of consumption onto Soma. The disease entered the lord of the stars. Afflicted by it, the hare-marked moon began to wane day by day. That creator of night tried to release himself from the disease by performing various sacrifices but he could not free himself from the curse and continued to deteriorate, great king.

As Soma waned, so the herbs disappeared. All of them lost their flavor, taste, and potency. And when the herbs decayed so did living beings and all creatures became weakened by the waning of the moon. The gods then gathered together, lord of the earth, and said to Soma: 35.55

«kim idaṃ bhavato rūpam īdṛśaṃ na prakāśate?
kāraṇaṃ brūhi naḥ sarvaṃ yen' êdaṃ te mahad bhayam.
śrutvā tu vacanaṃ tvatto vidhāsyāmas tato vayam.»
evam uktaḥ pratyuvāca sarvāṃs tāñ śaśa|lakṣaṇaḥ
śāpasya lakṣaṇaṃ c' âiva yakṣmāṇaṃ ca tath" ātmanaḥ.
35.60 devās tathā vacaḥ śrutvā gatvā Dakṣam ath' âbruvan:
«prasīda bhagavan Some. śāpo 'yaṃ vinivartyatām.
asau hi candramāḥ kṣīṇaḥ kiñcic|cheṣo hi lakṣyate.
kṣayāc c' âiv' âsya dev'|ēśa prajāś c' âiva gatāḥ kṣayam,
vīrudh|auṣadhayaś c' âiva bījāni vividhāni ca.
teṣāṃ kṣaye kṣayo 'smākaṃ. vin" âsmābhir jagac ca kim?
iti jñātvā loka|guro prasādaṃ kartum arhasi.»
evam uktas tato devān prāha vākyaṃ prajā|patiḥ:
«n' âitac chakyaṃ mama vaco vyāvartayitum anyathā.
hetunā tu mahā|bhāgā nivartiṣyati kena cit.
Samaṃ vartatu sarvāsu śaśī bhāryāsu nityaśaḥ.
35.65 Sarasvatyā vare tīrthe unmajjañ śaśa|lakṣaṇaḥ
punar vardhiṣyate devās. tad vai satyaṃ vaco mama.
mās'|ârdhaṃ ca kṣayaṃ Somo nityam eva gamiṣyati
mās'|ârdhaṃ tu sadā vṛddhiṃ. satyam etad vaco mama.
samudraṃ paścimaṃ gatvā Sarasvaty|abdhi|saṃgamam
ārādhayatu dev'|ēśaṃ. tataḥ kāntim avāpsyati.»

"Why does your form not shine? Tell us in full why this great calamity has afflicted you. When we have heard your words, we will arrange matters."

Addressed this way, the hare-marked moon told all the gods about the nature of his curse and about his disease. On hearing his words, the gods went to Daksha and said: 35.60

"Show grace toward Soma, O Lord. Let this curse be withdrawn. The moon has waned and only a small remainder can still be seen. The creatures too are decaying as a result of the dwindling of the moon, lord of the gods. The plants, herbs, and various seeds are also decaying. When they decay, so do we. And what is the world without us? Knowing this, you should, as master of the world, show grace."

Addressed this way, that lord of creatures said to the gods:

"It is impossible for me to retract my words. They must be averted through some cause, blessed gods. The hare-marked moon should always behave equally toward all his wives. If he submerges himself in an excellent *tirtha* on the 35.65 Sarásvati, the hare-marked moon will again grow strong, O gods. These words of mine are the truth. For the first half of every month Soma will always wane but for the second half of every month he will always wax. These words of mine are the truth. Let Soma go to the western ocean, where the sea and the Sarásvati river meet, and let him propitiate the lord of the gods. He will then regain his splendor."

Sarasvatīṃ tataḥ Somaḥ sa jagāma' ṛṣi|śāsanāt,
Prabhāsaṃ prathamaṃ tīrthaṃ Sarasvatyā jagāma ha.
amā|vāsyāṃ mahā|tejās tatr' ônmajjan mahā|dyutiḥ
lokān prabhāsayām āsa śīt'|âṃśutvam avāpa ca.

35.70 devās tu sarve rāj'|êndra Prabhāsaṃ prāpya puṣkalam
Somena sahitā bhūtvā Dakṣasya pramukhe 'bhavan.
tataḥ prajā|patiḥ sarvā visasarj' âtha devatāḥ
Somaṃ ca bhagavān prīto bhūyo vacanam abravīt:

«m" âvamaṃsthāḥ striyaḥ putra mā ca viprān kadā cana.
gaccha yuktaḥ sadā bhūtvā kuru vai śāsanaṃ mama.»

sa visṛṣṭo mahā|rāja jagām' âtha svam ālayam,
prajāś ca muditā bhūtvā punas tasthur yathā purā.

evaṃ te sarvam ākhyātaṃ yathā śapto niśā|karaḥ
Prabhāsaṃ ca yathā tīrthaṃ tīrthānāṃ pravaraṃ mahat.

35.75 amā|vāsyāṃ mahā|rāja nityaśaḥ śaśa|lakṣaṇaḥ
snātvā hy āpyāyate śrīmān Prabhāse tīrtha uttame.
ataś c' âitat prajānanti Prabhāsam iti bhūmi|pa.
prabhāṃ hi paramāṃ lebhe tasminn unmajjya candramāḥ.

tatas tu Camasodbhedam Acyutas tv agamad balī
Camasodbheda ity evaṃ yaṃ janāḥ kathayanty uta.
tatra dattvā ca dānāni viśiṣṭāni hal'|āyudhaḥ
uṣitvā rajanīm ekāṃ snātvā ca vidhivat tadā
Udapānam ath' âgacchat tvarāvān Keśav'|âgra|jaḥ.
ādyaṃ svasty|ayanaṃ c' âiva yatr' âvāpya mahat phalam
snigdhatvād oṣadhīnāṃ ca bhūmeś ca Janamejaya
jānanti siddhā rāj'|êndra naṣṭām api Sarasvatīm.

Following the seer's command, Soma went to the Sarásvati and reached the first *tirtha* on the Sarásvati called Prabhása. Bathing there on a new-moon day, that god of great splendor and radiance illuminated the worlds and regained his cool rays. All the gods, king of kings, also visited excellent Prabhása and afterwards proceeded with Soma to Daksha. Gratified, the illustrious lord of creatures then dismissed all the deities and once again said to Soma: 35.70

"Never show disrespect toward women, my son, nor toward brahmins. Leave and always follow my command diligently."

Dismissed, the god returned to his abode and the creatures again lived joyfully as before, great king.

I have thus told you everything about how the night-maker was cursed and how the great site of Prabhása became the finest of *tirthas*. On every new-moon day, great king, the glorious hare-marked moon bathes in the excellent *tirtha* of Prabhása and becomes strong. It is because of this that they call the place Prabhása, protector of the earth. For the moon attained his supreme splendor (*prabha*) by bathing at this site. 35.75

Mighty Áchyuta then went to Chámasodbhéda, as people call that *tirtha*. After giving fine gifts there, the plow-bearing hero spent one night at that site and bathed in the appropriate manner. The elder brother of Késhava then quickly traveled to Udapána. Even though the Sarásvati is hidden from view, *siddhas* know that the river runs through this area because they have attained excellent auspice and great fruit there and because the herbs and ground are fertile, Janam·éjaya.

VAIŚAMPĀYANA uvāca:

36.1 TASMĀN NADĪ|GATAṂ c' âpi hy Udapānaṃ yaśasvinaḥ
Tritasya ca mahā|rāja jagām' âtha hal'|āyudhaḥ.
tatra dattvā bahu dravyaṃ pūjayitvā tathā dvijān
upaspṛśya ca tatr' âiva prahṛṣṭo musal'|āyudhaḥ.
tatra dharma|paro hy āsīt Tritaḥ sa su|mahā|tapāḥ.
kūpe ca vasatā tena somaḥ pīto mah"|ātmanā.
tatra c' âinaṃ samutsṛjya bhrātarau jagmatur gṛhān.
tatas tau vai śaśāp' âtha Trito brāhmaṇa|sattamaḥ.

JANAMEJAYA uvāca:

36.5 Udapānaṃ kathaṃ brahman? kathaṃ ca su|mahā|tapāḥ?
patitaḥ kiṃ ca saṃtyakto bhrātṛbhyāṃ dvija|sattama?
kūpe kathaṃ ca hitv" âinaṃ bhrātarau jagmatur gṛhān?
kathaṃ ca yājayām āsa? papau somaṃ ca vai katham?
etad ācakṣva me brahman śrotavyaṃ yadi manyase.

VAIŚAMPĀYANA uvāca:

āsan pūrva|yuge rājan munayo bhrātaras trayaḥ:
Ekataś ca Dvitaś c' âiva Tritaś c' āditya|saṃnibhāḥ.
sarve prajā|pati|samāḥ prajāvantas tath" âiva ca;
Brahma|loka|jitāḥ sarve tapasā brahma|vādinaḥ.
teṣāṃ tu tapasā prīto niyamena damena ca
abhavad Gautamo nityaṃ pitā dharma|rataḥ sadā.
36.10 sa tu dīrgheṇa kālena teṣāṃ prītim avāpya ca

VAISHAMPÁYANA said:

PLOW-BEARING RAMA then proceeded to the river-site of Udapána, which is associated with glorious Trita, Your Majesty. After giving away numerous possessions there and worshipping twice-born brahmins, the club-weaponed hero sipped the water and was filled with joy.* 36.1

It was at this site that Trita, a man of great austerities, once showed his devotion to righteousness. This great-spirited ascetic drank *soma* juice while in a pit.* His two brothers had abandoned him there and returned home. Trita, that best of brahmins, then cursed them both.

JANAM·ÉJAYA said:

What of Udapána, brahmin? And what of the great ascetic? Why did he fall in a pit, best of brahmins, abandoned by his brothers? Why did his brothers leave him there and go home? How did Trita perform a sacrifice? And how did he drink *soma*? Tell me this, brahmin, if you think it is worthy of report. 36.5

VAISHAMPÁYANA said:

In a past era, Your Majesty, there lived three ascetics who were brothers: Ékata, Dvita, and Trita.* All of them were as splendid as the sun and all three had children and were equal to Praja·pati, that lord of creatures. Utterers of sacred speech, they had all won the Brahma world through their austerities.

Their father Gáutama, who always delighted in righteousness, was constantly pleased with them because of their austerity, self-restraint, and discipline. After deriving joy from his sons for a long period of time, illustrious Gáutama 36.10

jagāma bhagavān sthānam anurūpam iv' ātmanaḥ.
rājānas tasya ye hy āsan yājyā rājan mah"|ātmanaḥ
te sarve svar|gate tasmiṃs tasya putrān apūjayan.
teṣāṃ tu karmaṇā rājaṃs tathā c' âdhyayanena ca
Tritaḥ sa śreṣṭhatāṃ prāpa yath" âiv' âsya pitā tathā.
tathā sarve mahā|bhāgā munayaḥ puṇya|lakṣaṇāḥ
apūjayan mahā|bhāgaṃ yath" âsya pitaraṃ tathā.
kadā cidd hi tato rājan bhrātarāv Ekata|Dvitau
yajñ'|ârthaṃ cakratuś cintāṃ tathā vitt'|ârtham eva ca.
36.15 tayor buddhiḥ samabhavat Tritaṃ gṛhya paran|tapa:
«yājyān sarvān upādāya pratigṛhya paśūṃs tataḥ
somaṃ pāsyāmahe hṛṣṭāḥ prāpya yajñaṃ mahā|phalam.»
cakruś c' âiva tathā rājan bhrātaras traya eva ca.
tathā te tu parikramya yājyān sarvān paśūn prati,
yājayitvā tato yājyān labdhvā tu su|bahūn paśūn
yājyena karmaṇā tena pratigṛhya vidhānataḥ
prācīṃ diśaṃ mah"|ātmāna ājagmus te maha"|rṣayaḥ.
Tritas teṣāṃ mahā|rāja purastād yāti hṛṣṭavat
Ekataś ca Dvitaś c' âiva pṛṣṭhataḥ kālayan paśūn.
tayoś cintā samabhavad dṛṣṭvā paśu|gaṇaṃ mahat:
«kathaṃ ca syur imā gāva āvābhyāṃ hi vinā Tritam?»
36.20 tāv anyonyaṃ samābhāṣya Ekataś ca Dvitaś ca ha
yad ūcatur mithaḥ pāpau tan nibodha jan'|ēśvara:
«Trito yajñeṣu kuśalas. Trito vedeṣu niṣṭhitaḥ.
anyās tu bahulā gāvas Tritaḥ samupalapsyate.
tad āvāṃ sahitau bhūtvā gāḥ prakālya vrajāvahe.
Trito 'pi gacchatāṃ kāmam āvābhyāṃ vai vinā|kṛtaḥ.»

departed to the state that befitted him. When the great-spirited ascetic had gone to heaven, all the kings who had been Gáutama's sacrificial patrons honored his sons instead. Due to his deeds and study of the Vedas,* Trita attained foremost importance, just as his father had done. Every illustrious and pure ascetic honored that blessed man, just as they had honored his father.

On one occasion the brothers Ékata and Dvita hatched a plan to perform sacrifices and especially to acquire wealth. Their idea, enemy-tamer, was to grab hold of Trita, acquire all his sacrificial patrons, receive animals, and joyfully drink *soma* after attaining a sacrifice of great fruit. And the three brothers did just that, Your Majesty. They visited all the sacrificial patrons in order to acquire animals and, after they had performed sacrifices for their patrons and acquired very many animals, they duly received fees for their sacrifices. 36.15

The great-spirited seers then proceeded east. Trita was happily walking in front of them, while Ékata and Dvita were driving the animals behind, great king. When they looked at that great herd of animals, the two brothers had this thought: "What if we were to own these cows without Trita?"

Listen, lord of the people, to what those two wicked men, Ékata and Dvita, said to each other as they conversed in secret: 36.20

"Trita is skilled in sacrifice. Trita is consummate in the Vedas. Trita will find many other cows. Let us both leave, driving away the cows. Let Trita go where he likes—so long as it is apart from us."

teṣām āgacchatāṃ rātrau pathi|sthānāṃ vṛko 'bhavat.
tatra kūpo 'vidūre 'bhūt Sarasvatyās taṭe mahān.
atha Trito vṛkaṃ dṛṣṭvā pathi tiṣṭhantam agrataḥ
tad|bhayād apasarpan vai tasmin kūpe papāta ha
a|gādhe su|mahā|ghore sarva|bhūta|bhayaṃ|kare.

36.25 Tritas tato mahā|rāja kūpa|stho muni|sattamaḥ
ārta|nādaṃ tataś cakre. tau tu śuśruvatur munī.
taṃ jñātvā patitaṃ kūpe bhrātarāv Ekata|Dvitau
vṛka|trāsāc ca lobhāc ca samutsṛjya prajagmatuḥ.

bhrātṛbhyāṃ paśu|lubdhābhyām utsṛṣṭaḥ sa mahā|tapāḥ
udapāne tadā rājan nirjale pāṃsu|saṃvṛte
Trita ātmānam ālakṣya kūpe vīrut|tṛṇ'|āvṛte
nimagnaṃ Bharata|śreṣṭha narake duṣ|kṛtī yathā.
sa buddhy" âgaṇayat prājño mṛtyor bhīto hy a|soma|paḥ
«somaḥ kathaṃ tu pātavya iha|sthena mayā bhavet.»

36.30 sa evam abhiniścitya tasmin kūpe mahā|tapāḥ
dadarśa vīrudhaṃ tatra lambamānāṃ yad|ṛcchayā.
pāṃsu|graste tataḥ kūpe vicintya salilaṃ muniḥ
agnīn saṃkalpayām āsa hotre c' ātmānam eva ca.
tatas tāṃ vīrudhaṃ somaṃ saṃkalpya su|mahā|tapāḥ
ṛco yajūṃṣi sāmāni manasā cintayan muniḥ.
grāvāṇaḥ śarkarāḥ kṛtvā pracakre 'bhiṣavaṃ nṛpa.

While they were walking at night, a wolf appeared before them on the path. There was a large pit nearby on the bank of the Sarásvati. When Trita saw the wolf on the path ahead, he fell in the pit as he ran away in fear. The pit was deep and terrifying and aroused fear in every creature. Finding 36.25 himself in this pit, Trita—that supreme ascetic—cried out in distress. The two other ascetics heard him. But when they realized that Trita had fallen in the pit, Ékata and Dvita abandoned him in their greed and fear of the wolf and continued on their way, even though they were his brothers.

Deserted by his brothers because of their greed for animals, the great ascetic Trita discerned that he had been plunged into a waterless well that was covered with dirt, creepers, and grass, like a sinner plunged into hell, best of Bharatas. Fearing death because he had not drunk *soma*, the wise ascetic applied his mind to consider how he could drink *soma*, situated as he was in that pit. As he reflected 36.30 on the matter, the great ascetic noticed a shrub that happened to be hanging there. The ascetic imagined that there was water in that dust-enveloped hole and conceptualized that there were fires and that he was a *hotri* priest.* That ascetic of great austerities then conceived of the shrub as a *soma* plant, contemplating as he did so the Rich, Yajush, and Saman verses.* By transforming grit into *soma*-pressing stones, he extracted *soma* juice, Your Majesty.

ājyaṃ ca salilaṃ cakre bhāgāṃś ca tri|div'|âukasām
somasy' âbhiṣavaṃ kṛtvā cakāra vipulaṃ dhvanim.
sa c' āviśad divaṃ rājan punaḥ|śabdas Tritasya vai
samavāpya ca taṃ yajñaṃ yath"|ôktaṃ brahma|vādibhiḥ.

36.35 vartamāne mahā|yajñe Tritasya su|mah"|ātmanaḥ
āvignaṃ tri|divaṃ sarvaṃ kāraṇaṃ ca na buddhyate.
tataḥ su|tumulaṃ śabdaṃ śuśrāv' âtha Bṛhaspatiḥ
śrutvā c' âiv' âbravīt sarvān devān deva|purohitaḥ:

«Tritasya vartate yajñas. tatra gacchāmahe surāḥ.
sa hi kruddhaḥ sṛjed anyān devān api mahā|tapāḥ.»

tac chrutvā vacanaṃ tasya sahitāḥ sarva|devatāḥ
prayayus tatra yatr' âsau Trita|yajñaḥ pravartate.
te tatra gatvā vibudhās taṃ kūpaṃ yatra sa Tritaḥ
dadṛśus taṃ mah"|ātmānaṃ dīkṣitaṃ yajña|karmasu.

36.40 dṛṣṭvā c' âinaṃ mah"|ātmānaṃ śriyā paramayā yutam
ūcuś c' âinaṃ mahā|bhāgaṃ: «prāptā bhāg'|ârthino vayam.»

ath' âbravīd ṛṣir devān: «paśyadhvaṃ māṃ div'|âukasaḥ
asmin pratibhaye kūpe nimagnaṃ naṣṭa|cetasam.»

tatas Trito mahā|rāja bhāgāṃs teṣāṃ yathā|vidhi
mantra|yuktān samadadat. te ca prītās tad" âbhavan.
tato yathā|vidhi prāptān bhāgān prāpya div'|âukasaḥ
prīt'|ātmāno dadus tasmai varān yān manas" êcchati.
sa tu vavre varaṃ devāṃs: «trātum arhatha mām itaḥ
yaś c' êh' ôpaspṛśet kūpe sa soma|pa|gatiṃ labhet.»

After transforming the imagined water into clarified butter, he offered the gods their shares, extracted *soma* juice, and then uttered a vast noise. Trita's repeated shout penetrated the heavens after he completed the sacrifice in the manner prescribed by those who utter sacred speech.

36.35 The whole of heaven shook during mighty-spirited Trita's great sacrifice but the cause was not realized. Brihas·pati then heard Trita's tremendous shout and, on hearing it, the high priest of the gods said to all the deities:

"Trita is performing a sacrifice. Let us go to him, gods. For in his wrath the great ascetic might even emit other deities."

Hearing these words, all the gods assembled and traveled to where Trita's sacrifice was being performed. When they approached Trita, the deities saw that the great-spirited ascetic had become initiated into sacrificial rites. 36.40 Seeing this great-spirited man possessed of the highest glory, they said to the illustrious ascetic: "We have come here to seek our share."

The seer then said to the gods: "Look, deities, at how I have been plunged into this horrific pit and am out of my wits."

Trita then duly gave them their portions, Your Majesty, which were furnished with mantras. The gods were pleased at this and, after they had received their shares in the proper manner, the gratified deities offered Trita whatever boons his heart desired. This was the boon that Trita asked of the gods: "Save me from this pit. And may whoever sips water from this well attain the state of a *soma* drinker."

36.45 tatra c' ôrmimatī rājann utpapāta Sarasvatī.
tay" ôtkṣiptaḥ samuttasthau pūjayaṃs tri|div'|âukasaḥ.
«tath" êti» c' ôktvā vibudhā jagmū rājan yath"|āgatāḥ
Tritaś c' âbhyagamat prītaḥ svam eva nilayaṃ tadā.

kruddhas tu sa samāsādya tāv ṛṣī bhrātarau tadā
uvāca paruṣaṃ vākyaṃ śaśāpa ca mahā|tapāḥ:
«paśu|lubdhau yuvāṃ yasmān mām utsṛjya pradhāvitau
tasmād vṛk'|ākṛtī raudrau daṃṣṭriṇāv abhitaś carau
bhavitārau mayā śaptau pāpen' ânena karmaṇā
prasavaś c' âiva yuvayor golāṅgūla'|rkṣa|vānarāḥ!»
36.50 ity uktena tadā tena kṣaṇād eva viśāṃ pate
tathā|bhūtāv adṛśyetāṃ vacanāt satya|vādinaḥ.

tatr' âpy a|mita|vikrāntaḥ spṛṣṭvā toyaṃ hal'|āyudhaḥ
dattvā ca vividhān dāyān pūjayitvā ca vai dvijān,
Udapānaṃ ca taṃ vīkṣya praśasya ca punaḥ punaḥ,
nadī|gatam a|dīn'|ātmā prāpto Vinaśanaṃ tadā.

VAIŚAMPĀYANA uvāca:

37.1 TATO VINAŚANAṂ rājañ jagām' âtha hal'|āyudhaḥ
Śūdr'|Ābhīrān prati dveṣād yatra naṣṭā Sarasvatī.
tasmāt tu ṛṣayo nityaṃ prāhur Vinaśan' êti ha.

yatr' âpy upaspṛśya Balaḥ Sarasvatyāṃ mahā|balaḥ
Subhūmikaṃ tato 'gacchat Sarasvatyās taṭe vare.
tatra c' âpsarasaḥ śubhrā nitya|kālam a|tandritāḥ
krīḍābhir vimalābhiś ca krīḍanti vimal'|ānanāḥ.
tatra devāḥ sa|gandharvā māsi māsi jan'|ēśvara

Billowing with water, Sarásvati then welled up in the pit, Your Majesty. Lifted by Sarásvati, Trita rose up, worshipping the gods. The gods agreed to Trita's request and then left the same way they had come, while Trita joyfully returned to his own abode, Your Majesty. 36.45

When the great ascetic encountered his brothers, he uttered violent words and furiously cursed the seers, saying: "Because you abandoned me and ran away out of your greed for animals, I will curse you for your criminal act and you will wander around everywhere in the form of fierce wolves with fangs, and your offspring will be monkeys, bears, and apes!"

As soon as he spoke, the brothers took on this form as a result of the truth-speaker's words, lord of the people. 36.50

Plow-bearing Bala·deva—whose courage is boundless—then sipped the water at that site, gave diverse gifts, and worshipped brahmins. After he had seen Udapána and praised it again and again, the spirited hero moved on to the river-site of Vínashana.

VAISHAMPÁYANA said:

PLOW-BEARING Bala·deva then traveled to Vínashana, Your Majesty, where Sarásvati disappeared out of her hatred for the shudras and Abhíras.* It is for this reason that seers always call it Vínashana ("Disappearance"). 37.1

After mighty Bala had sipped the water at this site on the Sarásvati, he went to Subhúmika, which is on Sarásvati's fine bank. There beautiful nymphs with unblemished faces constantly play pure sports without fatigue. Gods and *gandhárvas* go every month to that sacred site, which is

abhigacchanti tat tīrthaṃ puṇyaṃ brāhmaṇa|sevitam.

37.5 tatr' âdṛśyanta gandharvās tath" âiv' âpsarasāṃ gaṇāḥ
sametya sahitā rājan yathā|prāptaṃ yathā|sukham.
tatra modanti devāś ca pitaraś ca sa|vīrudhaḥ
puṇyaiḥ puṣpaiḥ sadā divyaiḥ kīryamāṇāḥ punaḥ punaḥ.
ākrīḍa|bhūmiḥ sā rājaṃs tāsām apsarasāṃ śubhā
«Subhūmik" êti» vikhyātā Sarasvatyās taṭe vare.

tatra snātvā ca dattvā ca vasu viprāya Mādhavaḥ
śrutvā gītaṃ ca tad divyaṃ vāditrāṇāṃ ca niḥsvanam,
chāyāś ca vipulā dṛṣṭvā deva|gandharva|rakṣasām
gandharvāṇāṃ tatas tīrtham āgacchad Rohiṇī|sutaḥ.

37.10 Viśvāvasu|mukhās tatra gandharvās tapas" ânvitāḥ
nṛtya|vāditra|gītaṃ ca kurvanti su|mano|ramam.
tatra dattvā hala|dharo viprebhyo vividhaṃ vasu
aj'|âvikaṃ go|khar'|ôṣṭraṃ su|varṇaṃ rajataṃ tathā,
bhojayitvā dvijān kāmaiḥ saṃtarpya ca mahā|dhanaiḥ
prayayau sahito vipraiḥ stūyamānaś ca Mādhavaḥ.

tasmād gandharva|tīrthāc ca mahā|bāhur arin|damaḥ
Gargasroto mahā|tīrtham ājagām' âika|kuṇḍalī.
tatra Gargeṇa vṛddhena tapasā bhāvit'|ātmanā
kāla|jñāna|gatiś c' âiva jyotiṣāṃ ca vyatikramaḥ,

37.15 utpātā dāruṇāś c' âiva śubhāś ca Janamejaya
Sarasvatyāḥ śubhe tīrthe viditā vai mah"|ātmanā.
tasya nāmnā ca tat tīrthaṃ «Gargasrota iti» smṛtam.

holy and frequented by brahmins, lord of the people. At this site one can see *gandhárvas* and troops of nymphs who have gathered together, enjoying each other's company as they find it, Your Majesty. Gods and ancestors rejoice at this site surrounded by plants and are continuously sprinkled again and again by divine and auspicious flowers. This beautiful spot, where nymphs play sport on the fine bank of the Sarásvati, is known as Subhúmika. 37.5

After the Mádhava had bathed at this site, given wealth to a brahmin, listened to divine song and music, and seen the vast shadows of gods, *gandhárvas*, and *rákshasas*, the son of Róhini proceeded to the *tirtha* of the *gandhárvas*.* There, *gandhárvas* who are headed by Vishva·vasu and invested with ascetic power perform dance, music and song that fill the mind with great delight. After the plow-bearer had given away diverse objects to brahmins, including goats, sheep, cows, mules, camels, gold and silver, and after he had gratified twice-born men with objects of desire and satisfied them with great wealth, the Mádhava continued on his way, praised by the brahmins who accompanied him. 37.10

That mighty-armed enemy-tamer, who wears only one earring, then left the *tirtha* of the *gandhárvas* for the great site of Garga·srotas. It was at this auspicious site on the Sarásvati that the elderly great-spirited ascetic called Garga, whose soul had been purified by asceticism, once attained knowledge of Time and its course, the movement of the stars, and auspicious and inauspicious omens, Janam·éjaya. It is because of his name that the site is remembered as Garga·srotas ("The Stream of Garga"). 37.15

tatra Gargaṃ mahā|bhāgam ṛṣayaḥ su|vratā nṛpa
upāsāṃ cakrire nityaṃ kāla|jñānaṃ prati prabho.
tatra gatvā mahā|rāja Balaḥ śvet'|ânulepanaḥ
vidhivadd hi dhanaṃ dattvā munīnāṃ bhāvit'|ātmanām
ucc'|âvacāṃs tathā bhakṣyān viprebhyo vipradāya saḥ
nīla|vāsās tad" āgacchac Chaṅkha|tīrthaṃ mahā|yaśāḥ.

tatr' âpaśyan mahā|śaṅkhaṃ mahā|Merum iv' ôcchritam
śveta|parvata|saṃkāśam ṛṣi|saṅghair niṣevitam
Sarasvatyās taṭe jātaṃ nagaṃ tāla|dhvajo balī.

37.20 yakṣā vidyā|dharāś c' âiva rākṣasāś c' â|mit'|âujasaḥ
piśācāś c' â|mita|balā yatra siddhāḥ sahasraśaḥ,
te sarve hy aśanaṃ tyaktvā phalaṃ tasya vanas|pateḥ
vrataiś ca niyamaiś c' âiva kāle kāle sma bhuñjate.
prāptaiś ca niyamais tais tair vicarantaḥ pṛthak pṛthak
a|dṛśyamānā manujair vyacaran puruṣa'|rṣabha.
evaṃ khyāto nara|vyāghra loke 'smin sa vanas|patiḥ
tatas tīrthaṃ Sarasvatyāḥ pāvanaṃ loka|viśrutam.

tasmiṃś ca Yadu|śārdūlo dattvā tīrthe payasvinīḥ
tāmr'|âyasāni bhāṇḍāni vastrāṇi vividhāni ca,

37.25 pūjayitvā dvijāṃś c' âiva pūjitaś ca tapo|dhanaiḥ
puṇyaṃ Dvaitavanaṃ rājann ājagāma hal'|āyudhaḥ.
tatra gatvā munīn dṛṣṭvā nānā|veṣa|dharān Balaḥ
āplutya salile c' âpi pūjayām āsa vai dvijān.
tath" âiva dattvā viprebhyaḥ paribhogān su|puṣkalān
tataḥ prāyād Balo rājan dakṣiṇena Sarasvatīm.

Seers of virtuous vows constantly attended illustrious Garga at this site in order to attain knowledge of Time, my lord. Smeared with white ointment, glorious Bala went to that *tirtha*, great king, and duly gave wealth to pure ascetics and various foods to brahmins. After that, he arrived at the sacred site of Shankha, dressed in his blue robes.

There the mighty palm-bannered hero saw the great *shankha* tree that grows on the bank of the Sarásvati. Tall as great Meru and resembling a white mountain, it was frequented by crowds of seers. *Yakshas*, *vidya·dharas*, *rákshasas* 37.20 of boundless strength, *pisháchas* of limitless power, and *siddhas* in their thousands all followed vows and observances and ate the tree's fruit at various prescribed times, having given up their normal food.* Unseen by humans, they moved about separately, wandering around in the performance of their various observances, bull among men. This tree is thus celebrated in the world, tiger-like man, and it is because of it that this pure *tirtha* on the Sarásvati is renowned throughout the world.

When that tiger of the Yadus had given milk cows at this *tirtha*, as well as copper and iron vessels and various kinds of clothes, and when he had honored brahmins and 37.25 been honored by ascetics who were rich in austerities, plow-weaponed Rama arrived at the holy site of Dvaita·vana, Your Majesty. Arriving there, Bala saw ascetics wearing various kinds of robes and, after bathing in the water, he worshipped twice-born men. When he had given away numerous objects of enjoyment to brahmins, he proceeded along the southern bank of the Sarásvati, Your Majesty.

gatvā c' âivaṃ mahā|bāhur n' âtidūre mahā|yaśāḥ
dharm'|ātmā Nāgadhanvānaṃ tīrtham āgamad Acyutaḥ,
yatra pannaga|rājasya Vāsukeḥ sanniveśanam
mahā|dyuter mahā|rāja bahubhiḥ pannagair vṛtam
ṛṣīṇāṃ hi sahasrāṇi tatra nityaṃ catur|daśa.
37.30 yatra devāḥ samāgamya Vāsukiṃ pannag'|ôttamam
sarva|pannaga|rājānam abhyaṣiñcan yathā|vidhi
pannagebhyo bhayaṃ tatra vidyate na sma Paurava.

tatr' âpi vidhivad dattvā viprebhyo ratna|sañcayān
prāyāt prācīṃ diśaṃ tatra tatra tīrthāny anekaśaḥ
sahasra|śata|saṅkhyāni prathitāni pade pade.
āplutya tatra tīrtheṣu yath"|ôktaṃ tatra ca' ṛṣibhiḥ
kṛtv" ôpavāsa|niyamaṃ dattvā dānāni sarvaśaḥ,
abhivādya munīṃs tān vai tatra tīrtha|nivāsinaḥ
uddiṣṭa|mārgaḥ prayayau yatra bhūyaḥ Sarasvatī
prāṇmukhaṃ vai nivavṛte vṛṣṭir vāta|hatā yathā
ṛṣīṇāṃ Naimiṣeyāṇām avekṣ"|ârthaṃ mah"|ātmanāṃ.
37.35 nivṛttāṃ tāṃ saric|chreṣṭhāṃ tatra dṛṣṭvā tu lāṅgalī
babhūva vismito rājan Balaḥ śvet'|ânulepanaḥ.

JANAMEJAYA uvāca:

kasmāt Sarasvatī brahman nivṛttā prāṅmukhī|bhavat?
vyākhyātam etad icchāmi sarvam adhvaryu|sattama.
kasmiṃś cit kāraṇe tatra vismito Yadu|nandanaḥ?
nivṛttā hetunā kena katham eva sarid|varā?

After not too far a journey, glorious and righteous mighty-armed Áchyuta then arrived at the *tirtha* of Naga·dhánvana. Fourteen thousand ascetics constantly dwell at this site where Vásuki, the king of the snakes, resides, possessing great splendor and surrounded by many serpents, Your Majesty. There is no fear of snakes in this place, descendant of Puru. For it was here that the gods once gathered and duly consecrated Vásuki, that excellent serpent, as king of all snakes. 37.30

After duly giving piles of gems to brahmins, Rama then proceeded east, where there are several hundreds and thousands of *tirtha*s scattered extensively in different places. When he had bathed in those sites and taken a vow of fasting in the manner prescribed by seers, he gave away gifts on all sides. After greeting the ascetics who dwelled at these *tirtha*s, he set out once more along the route that had been described to him. Desiring to see the great-spritied ascetics of the Náimisha forest, he traveled to where the Sarásvati bends east, just as rain bends when it is pounded by the wind. Smeared with white paste, plow-bearing Bala became filled with wonder when he saw the supreme river bend at this spot, Your Majesty. 37.35

JANAM·ÉJAYA said:

Why did Sarásvati turn east, Your Majesty? I yearn to have all this explained, best of *adhváryu* priests.* Why did that delight of the Yadus feel wonder at that spot? Why and how did that best of rivers bend?

VAIŚAMPĀYANA uvāca:

pūrvaṃ Kṛta|yuge rājan Naimiṣeyās tapasvinaḥ
vartamāne su|vipule satre dvādaśa|vārṣike
ṛṣayo bahavo rājaṃs tat satram abhipedire.
uṣitvā ca mahā|bhāgās tasmin satre yathā|vidhi
nivṛtte Naimiṣeye vai satre dvādaśa|vārṣike
ājagmur ṛṣayas tatra bahavas tīrtha|kāraṇāt.
37.40 ṛṣīṇāṃ bahulatvāt tu Sarasvatyā viśāṃ pate
tīrthāni nagarāyante kūle vai dakṣiṇe tadā.

Samantapañcakaṃ yāvat tāvat te dvija|sattamāḥ
tīrtha|lobhān nara|vyāghra nadyās tīraṃ samāśritāḥ.
juhvatāṃ tatra teṣāṃ tu munīnāṃ bhāvit'|ātmanām
svādhyāyen' âtimahatā babhūvuḥ pūritā diśaḥ.
agnihotrais tatas teṣāṃ kriyamānair mah"|ātmanām
aśobhata saric|chreṣṭhā dīpyamānaiḥ samantataḥ.

Vālakhilyā mahā|rāja Aśmakuṭṭāś ca tāpasāḥ
Dantolūkhalinaś c' ânye Prasaṅkhyānās tathā pare,
37.45 vāyu|bhakṣā jal'|āhārāḥ parṇa|bhakṣāś ca tāpasāḥ
nānā|niyama|yuktāś ca tathā sthaṇḍila|śāyinaḥ,
āsan vai munayas tatra Sarasvatyāḥ samīpataḥ
śobhayantaḥ saric|chreṣṭhāṃ Gaṅgām iva div'|âukasaḥ.
śataśaś ca samāpetur ṛṣayaḥ satra|yājinaḥ
te 'vakāśaṃ na dadṛśuḥ Sarasvatyā mahā|vratāḥ.
tato yajñ'|ôpavītais te tat tīrthaṃ nirmimāya vai
juhuvuś c' âgnihotrāṃś ca cakruś ca vividhāḥ kriyāḥ.

VAISHAMPÁYANA said:

In the past, Your Majesty, during the Krita era, many ascetic seers in the Náimisha forest attended a huge twelve-year Sattra sacrifice.* When these illustrious seers had attended the sacrifice in the proper manner and the twelve-year Sattra ritual in the Náimisha forest had finished, many of the ascetics returned on a *tirtha* pilgrimage. Because of the large number of seers, the *tirthas* on the southern bank of the Sarásvati looked like cities, lord of the people. 37.40

In their greed for the sacred sites, those supreme brahmins occupied the bank of the river as far as Samánta·pánchaka, tiger among men. The directions became filled with the abundant recitations of the purified ascetics as they offered oblations there. That supreme river glowed on all sides with the blazing Agni·hotra* sacrifices of these great-spirited ascetics.

Valakhílyas* and Ashma·kutta ascetics, Dantolúkhalins and Prasankhyánas, ascetics who eat the wind, ascetics who live off water, and ascetics who eat leaves, ascetics who practice various forms of discipline and ascetics who lie on the bare ground—all these resided in the vicinity of Sarásvati, adorning that best of rivers, just as deities adorn the Ganga. Hundreds of seers gathered there—men of great vows capable of performing the Sattra sacrifice—but they could not find enough room on the Sarásvati. Measuring out their particular *tirtha* with their sacrificial threads, they performed Agni·hotra sacrifices and various different rituals. 37.45

tatas tam ṛṣi|saṅghātaṃ nirāśaṃ cintay" ânvitam
darśayām āsa rāj'|êndra teṣām arthe Sarasvatī.
37.50 tataḥ kuñjān bahūn kṛtvā sā nivṛttā sarid|varā
ṛṣīṇāṃ puṇya|tapasāṃ kāruṇyāj Janamejaya.
tato nivṛtya rāj'|êndra teṣām arthe Sarasvatī
bhūyaḥ pratīcy|abhimukhī prasusrāva sarid|varā.
«a|mogh'|āgamanaṃ kṛtvā teṣāṃ bhūyo vrajāmy aham»
ity adbhutaṃ mahac cakre tadā rājan mahā|nadī.
evaṃ sa kuñjo rājan vai Naimiṣīya iti smṛtaḥ.
Kuru|śreṣṭha Kurukṣetre kuruṣva mahatīṃ kriyām.
tatra kuñjān bahūn dṛṣṭvā nivṛttāṃ ca Sarasvatīm
babhūva vismayas tatra Rāmasy' âtha mah"|ātmanaḥ.
37.55 upaspṛśya tu tatr' âpi
vidhivad Yadu|nandanaḥ
dattvā dāyān dvi|jātibhyo
bhāṇḍāni vividhāni ca
bhakṣyaṃ bhojyaṃ ca vividhaṃ
brāhmaṇebhyaḥ pradāya ca,
tataḥ prāyād Balo rājan pūjyamāno dvi|jātibhiḥ
Sarasvatī|tīrtha|varaṃ nānā|dvija|gaṇ'|āyutam,
badar'|êṅguda|kāśmarya|plakṣ'|âśvattha|bibhītakaiḥ
kaṅkolaiś ca palāśaiś ca karīraiḥ pīlubhis tathā,
Sarasvatī|tīrtha|ruhais tarubhir vividhais tathā
karūṣaka|varaiś c' âiva bilvair āmrātakais tathā,
atimukta|kaṣaṇḍaiś ca pārijātaiś ca śobhitam
kadalī|vana|bhūyiṣṭham dṛṣṭi|kāntaṃ mano|haram,
37.60 vāyv|ambu|phala|parṇ'|âdair Dantolūkhalikair api
tath" Âśmakuṭṭair Vāneyair munibhir bahubhir vṛtam,
svādhyāya|ghoṣa|saṃghuṣṭaṃ mṛga|yūtha|śat'|ākulam

Out of concern for the ascetics, Sarásvati appeared before that crowd of seers, which was desperate and filled with worry. Creating many abodes, that fine river turned her course out of compassion for those seers of pure austerities, Janam·éjaya. After Sarásvati had turned her course for the ascetics, the supreme river again flowed west. Thinking, "I will continue on my way after I have ensured that these ascetics have not arrived in vain," the great river performed this great wonder. 37.50

In this way, this site became remembered as Naimishíya. Perform a great sacrifice at Kuru·kshetra, best of Kurus!

Great-spirited Rama became filled with wonder when he saw the many abodes and how Sarásvati had turned her course. That delight of the Yadus sipped the water there in the prescribed manner, gave gifts and various goods to twice-born men, and offered food and various edibles to brahmins. 37.55

Honored by brahmins, Bala then proceeded to an excellent *tirtha* on the Sarásvati that was full of diverse crowds of brahmins. Captivating and lovely to see, it abounded with *kádali* groves and was adorned with *bádara*, *ínguda*, *kashmárya*, *plaksha*, *ashváttha* and *bibhítaka* trees, as well as *kankólas*, *paláshas*, *karíras*, *pilus* and various trees that grow at the *tirthas* of the Sarásvati, and also fine *karúshakas*, *bilvas*, *amrátakas*, *atimúktas*, *kashándas*, and *parijátas*. It teemed with crowds of ascetics who eat only wind, water, fruits, or leaves, and with Dantolúkhalika, Ashma·kutta, and Vanéya ascetics. Echoing with the hum of recitations and abounding with hundreds of herds of wild animals, it 37.60

ahiṃsrair dharma|paramair nṛbhir atyartha|sevitam.
Saptasārasvataṃ tīrtham ājagāma hal'|āyudhaḥ
yatra Maṅkaṇakaḥ siddhas tapas tepe mahā|muniḥ.

JANAMEJAYA uvāca:

38.1 SAPTASĀRASVATAṂ kasmāt? kaś ca Maṅkaṇako muniḥ?
kathaṃ siddhaḥ sa bhagavān? kaś c' âsya niyamo 'bhavat?
kasya vaṃśe samutpannaḥ? kiṃ c' âdhītaṃ dvij'|ôttama?
etad icchāmy ahaṃ śrotuṃ vidhivad dvija|sattama.

VAIŚAMPĀYANA uvāca:

rājan sapta Sarasvatyo yābhir vyāptam idaṃ jagat.
āhūtā balavadbhir hi tatra tatra Sarasvatī:
Suprabhā Kāñcanākṣī ca Viśālā ca Manoramā
Sarasvatī c' Âughavatī Sureṇur Vimalodakā.

38.5 pitāmahasya mahato vartamāne mahā|makhe
vitate yajña|vāṭe ca saṃsiddheṣu dvi|jātiṣu,
puṇy'|âha|ghoṣair vimalair vedānāṃ ninadais tathā
deveṣu c' âiva vyagreṣu tasmin yajña|vidhau tadā,
tatra c' âiva mahā|rāja dīkṣite prapitāmahe
yajatas tasya satreṇa sarva|kāma|samṛddhinā,
manasā cintitā hy arthā dharm'|ârtha|kuśalais tadā
upatiṣṭhanti rāj'|êndra dvi|jātīṃs tatra tatra ha.
jaguś ca tatra gandharvā nanṛtuś c' âpsaro|gaṇāḥ
vāditrāṇi ca divyāni vādayām āsur añjasā.

38.10 tasya yajñasya saṃpattyā tutuṣur devatā api
vismayaṃ paramaṃ jagmuḥ kim u mānuṣa|yonayaḥ?

vas full of men who practiced non-violence and who were levoted to righteousness.

Plow-weaponed Rama thus arrived at the *tirtha* of Sapta·arásvata. It was at this site that the great perfected ascetic Mánkanaka once practiced austerities.

JANAM·ÉJAYA said:

38.1 WHY WAS THIS place called Sapta·sarásvata? Who was the eer Mánkanaka? How did that illustrious ascetic become erfected? What were his disciplines? In whose lineage was ie born? What did he study, supreme brahmin? I yearn to iear a proper explanation of this, best of brahmins.

VAISHAMPÁYANA said:

There are, Your Majesty, seven Sarásvatis by which this vorld is covered. For the mighty have summoned Sarásvati n various places. They are: Súprabha, Kanchanákshi, Vi-hála, Mano·rama, the Sarásvati called Óghavati, Surénu, ınd Vimalódaka.

38.5 The great Grandfather once performed a large sacrifice. A sacrificial area was prepared and brahmins were grati-ied. Gods became focused on the ritual, influenced by the ecitations of the Vedas and by pure sounds proclaiming an uspicious day. The Grandfather became initiated into the itual and, as a result of performing this sacrifice that fulfills ll desires, brahmins here and there—who were skilled in ighteousness and benefit—attained whatever their minds onceived. *Gandhárvas* sang songs and troops of nymphs

38.10 lanced and spontaneously played divine instruments. Even he gods felt great wonder and were satisfied by the bounty of that sacrifice, how much more humans?

vartamāne tathā yajñe Puṣkara|sthe pitāmahe
abruvann ṛṣayo: «rājan n' âyaṃ yajño mahā|guṇaḥ
na dṛśyate saric|chreṣṭhā yasmād iha Sarasvatī.»
tac chrutvā bhagavān prītaḥ sasmār' âtha Sarasvatīm.
pitāmahena yajatā āhūtā Puṣkareṣu vai
Suprabhā nāma rāj'|êndra nāmnā tatra Sarasvatī.
tāṃ dṛṣṭvā munayas tuṣṭā vega|yuktāṃ Sarasvatīm
pitāmahaṃ mānayantīṃ kratuṃ te bahu menire.
evam eṣā saric|chreṣṭhā Puṣkareṣu Sarasvatī
pitāmah'|ârthaṃ saṃbhūtā tuṣṭy|arthaṃ ca manīṣiṇām.

38.15 Naimiṣe munayo rājan samāgamya samāsate.
tatra citrāḥ kathā hy āsan vedaṃ prati jan'|ēśvara,
yatra te munayo hy āsan nānā|svādhyāya|vedinaḥ.
te samāgamya munayaḥ sasmarur vai Sarasvatīm.
sā tu dhyātā mahā|rāja ṛṣibhiḥ satra|yājibhiḥ
samāgatānāṃ rāj'|êndra sahāy'|ârthaṃ mah"|ātmanām
ājagāma mahā|bhāgā tatra puṇyā Sarasvatī.
Naimiṣe Kāñcanākṣī tu munīnāṃ satra|yājinām
āgatā saritāṃ śreṣṭhā tatra Bhārata pūjitā.

Gayasya yajamānasya Gayeṣv eva mahā|kratum
āhūtā saritāṃ śreṣṭhā Gaya|yajñe Sarasvatī.

38.20 Viśālāṃ tu Gayeṣv āhur ṛṣayaḥ saṃśita|vratāḥ
sarit sā Himavat|pārśvāt prasrutā śīghra|gāminī.

When the Grandfather was performing this sacrifice at Púshkara, some seers said to him: "Your Majesty, this sacrifice cannot be of great distinction, for the supreme river Sarásvati is not seen in this place." Hearing this, the Lord joyfully brought Sarásvati to mind. Summoned to Púshkara by the sacrificing Grandfather, Sarásvati was given the name Súprabha at that spot, king of kings. The ascetics were delighted when they saw Sarásvati swiftly honoring the Grandfather and they esteemed his sacrifice highly. In this way, Sarásvati, that best of rivers, appeared at Púshkara for the sake of the Grandfather and in order to please the wise.

38.15 On another occasion some ascetics once gathered and sat together in Náimisha, Your Majesty. There they had varied discussions about the Vedas, lord of the people, for they were knowledgeable in various studies. After they had assembled, they brought Sarásvati to mind. Reflected upon by the sacrificing seers, auspicious and illustrious Sarásvati arrived at the site in order to assist the great-spirited men who had gathered there, king of kings. In this way Kanchanákshi, that best of rivers, arose at this site in Náimisha, worshipped by the sacrificing ascetics, descendant of Bharata.

Sarásvati, that best of rivers, was also summoned to Gaya's sacrifice when he was performing a great ritual in the region of the Gayas. 38.20 Seers of firm vows gave the name Vishála to the river at Gaya, which flows rapidly down from the Hímavat slopes.

Auddālakes tathā yajñe yajatas tasya Bhārata
samete sarvataḥ sphīte munīnāṃ maṇḍale tadā,
uttare Kosalā|bhāge puṇye rājan mah"|ātmanaḥ
Uddālakena yajatā pūrvaṃ dhyātā Sarasvatī.
ājagāma saric|chreṣṭhā taṃ deśam muni|kāraṇāt
pūjyamānā muni|gaṇair valkal'|âjina|saṃvṛtaiḥ
«Manoram" êti» vikhyātā sā hi tair manasā kṛtā.

Kuroś ca yajamānasya Kurukṣetre mah"|ātmanaḥ
ājagāma mahā|bhāgā saric|chreṣṭhā Sarasvatī.

38.25 Oghavaty api rāj'|êndra Vasiṣṭhena mah"|ātmanā
samāhūtā Kurukṣetre divya|toyā Sarasvatī.

Dakṣeṇa yajatā c' âpi Gaṅgā|dvāre Sarasvatī
Sureṇur iti vikhyātā prasrutā śīghra|gāminī.
Vimalodā bhagavatī Brahmaṇā yajatā punaḥ
samāhūtā yayau tatra puṇye Haimavate girau.

ekī|bhūtās tatas tās tu tasmiṃs tīrthe samāgatāḥ
Saptasārasvataṃ tīrthaṃ tatas tu prathitaṃ bhuvi.
iti sapta Sarasvatyo nāmataḥ parikīrtitāḥ
Saptasārasvataṃ c' âiva tīrthaṃ puṇyaṃ tathā smṛtam.

38.30 śṛṇu Maṅkaṇakasy' âpi kaumāra|brahmacāriṇaḥ
āpagām avagāḍhasya rājan prakrīḍitaṃ mahat.

In bygone days, descendant of Bharata, when Auddálaki was performing a sacrifice and a swelling circle of ascetics had gathered on all sides, Sarásvati was also reflected on by Uddálaka as he sacrificed in the auspicious northern area of Kósala.* Worshipped by groups of sages clothed in bark and deer-skin, that supreme river came to the site because of those ascetics. She became known as Mano·rama ("Delighter of the Mind") because the ascetics produced her with their minds.

Illustrious Sarásvati, that best of rivers, also appeared at Kuru·kshetra when great-spirited Kuru was performing a sacrifice there. Flowing with divine waters, Sarásvati was summoned to Kuru·kshetra by great-spirited Vasíshtha in the form of Óghavati, Your Majesty. 38.25

At the mouth of the Ganga, swift-flowing Sarásvati was also given the name Surénu by Daksha while he was performing a sacrifice. Furthermore, Sarásvati also arrived at the holy Hímavat mountain in the form of divine Vimalóda when she was summoned by Brahma while he was performing a sacrifice.

These seven rivers become one at this *tirtha*, and so the site is renowned on earth as Sapta·sarásvata ("The Site of the Seven Sarásvatis"). These are the rivers proclaimed as the seven Sarásvatis and it is thus that the auspicious *tirtha* is remembered as Sapta·sarásvata.

Listen now, Your Majesty, to the great sport of the young ascetic Mánkanaka when he plunged into this river. 38.30

dṛṣṭvā yad|ṛcchayā tatra striyam ambhasi Bhārata
snāyantīṃ rucir'|âpāṅgīṃ dig|vāsasam a|ninditām
Sarasvatyāṃ mahā|rāja caskande vīryam ambhasi.
tad retaḥ sa tu jagrāha kalaśe vai mahā|tapāḥ
saptadhā pravibhāgaṃ tu kalaśa|sthaṃ jagāma ha.
tatra' ṛṣayaḥ sapta jātā jajñire Marutāṃ gaṇāḥ:
Vāyuvego Vāyubalo Vāyuhā Vāyumaṇḍalaḥ
Vāyujvālo Vāyuretā Vāyucakraś ca vīryavān.
evam ete samutpannā Marutāṃ janayiṣṇavaḥ.

38.35 idam atyadbhutaṃ rājan śṛṇv āścaryataraṃ bhuvi
maha"|rṣeś caritaṃ yādṛk triṣu lokeṣu viśrutam.

purā Maṅkaṇakaḥ siddhaḥ kuś'|âgreṇ' êti naḥ śrutam
kṣataḥ kila kare rājaṃs tasya śāka|raso 'sravat.
sa vai śāka|rasaṃ dṛṣṭvā harṣ'|āviṣṭaḥ pranṛttavān.
tatas tasmin pranṛtte vai sthāvaraṃ jaṅgamaṃ ca yat
pranṛttam ubhayaṃ vīra tejasā tasya mohitam.

Brahm'|ādibhiḥ surai rājan ṛṣibhiś ca tapo|dhanaiḥ
vijñapto vai Mahādeva ṛṣer arthe nar'|âdhipa:
«n' âyaṃ nṛtyed yathā deva tathā tvaṃ kartum arhasi.»
tato devo muniṃ dṛṣṭvā harṣ'|āviṣṭam atīva ha
surāṇāṃ hita|kām'|ârthaṃ Mahādevo 'bhyabhāṣata:

38.40 «bho! bho! brāhmaṇa dharma|jña!
kim|arthaṃ nṛtyate bhavān?
harṣa|sthānaṃ kim|arthaṃ ca
tav' êdam adhikaṃ mune
tapasvino dharma|pathe sthitasya dvija|sattama?»

By chance, descendant of Bharata, Mánkanaka once saw a beautiful-eyed woman bathing in the water, naked and blameless, and his vital seed leaped into the Sarásvati, great king. That man of great austerities put the seed in a jar and the seed became divided into seven parts. From these parts seven ascetics were born, who then generated the troops of the Maruts. They were called: Vayu·vega, Vayu·bala, Váyuhan, Vayu·mándala, Vayu·jvala, Vayu·retas, and mighty Vayu·chakra. It was in this way that the creators of the Maruts were born.

Listen, Your Majesty, to an even more amazing and wondrous deed that was performed by the great ascetic on this earth and is renowned throughout the three worlds. 38.35

It is said that, in bygone times, the perfected ascetic Mánkanaka became wounded in his hand by the tip of a blade of *kusha* grass and that vegetable juice flowed from his hand. On seeing the vegetable juice, Mánkanaka became filled with joy and danced. When he danced, O hero, both moving and unmoving creatures also danced, intoxicated by the ascetic's power.

Gods led by Brahma and seers rich in austerities then informed Maha·deva of the ascetic's deed, lord of men, saying: "Please make this ascetic stop dancing, O god." When divine Maha·deva saw the ascetic so excessively possessed by joy, he addressed him in order to benefit the gods, saying:

"You! You! Brahmin who knows what is right! Why are you dancing? What is the purpose of this excessive joy, sage and best of brahmins? You are an ascetic established on the path of righteousness!" 38.40

ṚṢIR uvāca:

«kiṃ na paśyasi me brahman karāc chāka|rasaṃ srutam?
yaṃ dṛṣṭvā saṃpranṛtto vai harṣeṇa mahatā vibho.»
tam prahasy' âbravīd devo muniṃ rāgeṇa mohitam:
«ahaṃ na vismayaṃ vipra gacchām' îti. prapaśya mām!»
evam uktvā muni|śreṣṭhaṃ Mahā|devena dhīmatā
aṅguly|agreṇa rāj'|êndra sv'|âṅguṣṭhas tāḍito 'bhavat.
tato bhasma kṣatād rājan nirgataṃ hima|saṃnibham.
tad dṛṣṭvā vrīḍito rājan sa muniḥ pādayor gataḥ.
mene devaṃ Mahādevam idaṃ c' ôvāca vismitaḥ:
38.45 «n' ânyaṃ devād ahaṃ manye Rudrāt parataraṃ mahat!
sur'|âsurasya jagato gatis tvam asi śūla|dhṛt.
tvayā sṛṣṭam idaṃ viśvaṃ vadant' îha manīṣiṇaḥ.
tvām eva sarvaṃ viśati punar eva yuga|kṣaye.
devair api na śakyas tvaṃ parijñātuṃ kuto mayā!
tvayi sarve sma dṛśyante bhāvā ye jagati sthitāḥ!
tvām upāsanta vara|daṃ devā Brahm'|ādayo 'n|agha!
sarvas tvam asi devānāṃ kartā kārayitā ca ha.
tvat|prasādāt surāḥ sarve modant' îh' â|kuto|bhayāḥ.»
evaṃ stutvā Mahā|devaṃ sa ṛṣiḥ praṇato 'bhavat:
«yad idaṃ cāpalaṃ deva kṛtam etat smay'|ādikam
tataḥ prasādayāmi tvāṃ tapo me na kṣared iti.»

THE SEER said:

"Do you not see, brahmin,* how vegetable juice flows from my hand? When I saw it, I danced with great joy, my lord."

With a laugh, the god then replied to that ascetic who was confounded by emotion:

"I am not amazed at this, brahmin. Look at me!" Saying these words to the supreme ascetic, wise Maha·deva struck his thumb with the tip of his fingernail and snow-like ash appeared from the wound, king of kings. When he saw this, the ashamed ascetic fell to the god's feet, Your Majesty. Realizing that the god was Maha·deva, Mánkanaka said these words in wonder:

38.45 "I believe that no god is greater than divine Rudra! You are the recourse of the world, with both its gods and demons, trident-holder. Wise men in this world say that you created the universe. It is to you that everything returns at the dissolution of an era. Even the gods are unable to comprehend you, how much less I! All creatures that exist in the world are seen in you! Brahma and the other gods rest in you, faultless boon-giver! You are the complete creator and cause of the gods. Through your grace all the gods rejoice without fear."

Praising Maha·deva in this way, the seer prostrated himself, saying:

"My act was insolent and based on arrogance. I ask for your grace: may my ascetic power not diminish."

38.50 tato devaḥ prīta|manās tam ṛṣiṃ punar abravīt:
«tapas te vardhatāṃ vipra mat|prasādāt sahasradhā!
āśrame c' êha vatsyāmi tvayā sārdham ahaṃ sadā.
Saptasārasvate c' âsmin yo māṃ arciṣyate naraḥ
na tasya dur|labhaṃ kiñ cid bhavit" êha paratra vā.
Sārasvataṃ ca te lokaṃ gamiṣyanti na saṃśayaḥ.»
etan Maṅkaṇakasy' âpi caritaṃ bhūri|tejasaḥ
sa hi putraḥ Sukanyāyām utpanno Mātariśvanā.

VAIŚAMPĀYANA uvāca:

39.1 UṢITVĀ TATRA Rāmas tu saṃpūjy' āśrama|vāsinaḥ
tathā Maṅkaṇake prītiṃ śubhāṃ cakre hal'|āyudhaḥ.
dattvā dānaṃ dvi|jātibhyo rajanīṃ tām upoṣya ca
pūjito muni|saṅghaiś ca prātar utthāya lāṅgalī,
anujñāpya munīn sarvān spṛṣṭvā toyaṃ ca Bhārata
prayayau tvarito Rāmas tīrtha|hetor mahā|balaḥ.
tatas tv Auśanasaṃ tīrtham ājagāma hal'|āyudhaḥ
Kapālamocanaṃ nāma yatra mukto mahā|muniḥ.
39.5 mahatā śirasā rājan grasta|jaṅgho Mahodaraḥ
rākṣasasya mahā|rāja Rāma|kṣiptasya vai purā.
tatra pūrvaṃ tapas taptaṃ Kāvyena su|mah"|ātmanā
yatr' âsya nītir a|khilā prādur bhūtā mah"|ātmanaḥ
yatra|sthaś cintayām āsa daitya|dānava|vigraham.
tat prāpya ca Balo rājaṃs tīrtha|pravaram uttamam
vidhivad vai dadau vittaṃ brāhmaṇānāṃ mah"|ātmanām.

Pleased with the seer, the god replied: 38.50

"Through my grace, may your ascetic power increase a thousandfold, brahmin! I will always dwell with you in this hermitage. Whoever worships me at this *tirtha* of Sapta·sarásvata will have no difficulty in gaining their desires either in this world or the next. Without doubt, they will reach the world of Sarásvati."

These were the deeds of Mánkanaka of mighty spirit. He was the son of Sukánya and Mataríshvan.

VAISHAMPÁYANA said:

AFTER STAYING at this site, plow-weaponed Rama hon- 39.1 ored the ascetics dwelling in the hermitage and took an auspicious joy in Mánkanaka. The plow-bearer then gave gifts to brahmins, spent the night there, and got up in the morning, honored by groups of ascetics. Mighty Rama then took leave of all the ascetics, sipped the water, and swiftly left for the other sacred sites, decendant of Bharata.

Plow-weaponed Rama then arrived at the *tirtha* of Áushanasa, or Kapála·móchana, where a great ascetic acquired release.* For in the past, great king, the mighty head of a 39.5 demon, that had been hurled by Rama, once clamped itself onto the calf of the ascetic Mahódara.

Úshanas, the great-spirited son of Kavi, had previously performed austerities at this site. It was there that the Law appeared to the great-spirited man in its entirety and that he contemplated the gods' battle with the *daitya*s and *dánava*s. Reaching that supreme and most excellent of *tirtha*s, Bala duly distributed wealth to great-spirited brahmins, Your Majesty.

JANAMEJAYA uvāca:

Kapālamocanaṃ brahman kathaṃ yatra mahā|muniḥ
muktaḥ kathaṃ c' âsya śiro lagnaṃ kena ca hetunā?

VAIŚAMPĀYANA uvāca:

purā vai Daṇḍak'|āraṇye Rāghaveṇa mah"|ātmanā
vasatā rāja|śārdūla rākṣasān śamayiṣyatā,
39.10 Janasthāne śiraś chinnaṃ rākṣasasya dur|ātmanaḥ
kṣureṇa śita|dhāreṇa utpapāta mahā|vane.
Mahodarasya tal lagnaṃ jaṅghāyāṃ vai yad|ṛcchayā
vane vicarato rājann asthi bhittv" âsphurat tadā.
sa tena lagnena tadā dvi|jātir na śaśāka ha
abhigantuṃ mahā|prājñas tīrthāny āyatanāni ca.
sa pūtinā visravatā vedan"|ārto mahā|muniḥ
jagāma sarva|tīrthāni pṛthivyām c' êti naḥ śrutam.
sa gatvā saritaḥ sarvāḥ samudrāṃś ca mahā|tapāḥ
kathayām āsa tat sarvam ṛṣīṇāṃ bhāvit'|ātmanām.
39.15 āplutya sarva|tīrtheṣu na ca mokṣam avāptavān.
sa tu śuśrāva vipr'|êndro munīnāṃ vacanaṃ mahat
Sarasvatyās tīrtha|varaṃ khyātam Auśanasaṃ tadā
sarva|pāpa|praśamanaṃ siddhi|kṣetram an|uttamam.
sa tu gatvā tatas tatra tīrtham Auśanasaṃ dvijaḥ
tata Auśanase tīrthe tasy' ôpaspṛśatas tadā
tac chiraś caraṇaṃ muktvā papāt' ântar|jale tadā.
vimuktas tena śirasā paraṃ sukham avāpa ha
sa c' âpy antar|jale mūrdhā jagām' â|darśanaṃ vibho.

JANAM·ÉJAYA said:

How was the great ascetic released at Kapála·móchana, brahmin, and why did the head attach itself to him?

VAISHAMPÁYANA said:

Heroic Rama, the descendant of Raghu, once dwelled in the Dándaka forest, eager to quell demons, tiger-like king. At Jana·sthana, he cut off the head of an evil demon with a sharp-edged, razor-tipped arrow and the head fell in the great forest.* The head happened to attach itself to the calf of Mahódara as he wandered in the forest. Piercing the bone, the head throbbed there, Your Majesty. 39.10

The wise brahmin did not have the strength to visit *tirtha*s and other sites because this head was stuck to him. But although he suffered pain from the putrid, pussing head, it is said that he nonetheless traveled to all the *tirtha*s on earth. That man of great austerities went to every river and ocean and narrated everything to seers of purified souls.

But although he bathed in every sacred site, he could not attain release from the head. That chief of brahmins then heard ascetics speak lofty words about how the finest of *tirtha*s on the Sarásvati was known as Áushanasa and how it could allay every ill and was the unsurpassed field of perfection. So the brahmin went to the *tirtha* of Áushanasa and, upon sipping the water there, the head detached itself from his leg and fell in the river. Released from the head, Mahódara felt the greatest happiness and the head itself disappeared into the water, my lord. 39.15

tataḥ sa viśirā rājan pūt'|ātmā vīta|kalmaṣaḥ
ājagām' āśramaṃ prītaḥ kṛta|kṛtyo Mahodaraḥ.

39.20 so 'tha gatv" āśramaṃ puṇyaṃ vipramukto mahā|tapāḥ
kathayām āsa tat sarvam ṛṣīṇāṃ bhāvit'|ātmanām.
te śrutvā vacanaṃ tasya tatas tīrthasya māna|da
«Kapālamocanam iti» nāma cakruḥ samāgatāḥ.
sa c' âpi tīrtha|pravaraṃ punar gatvā mahān ṛṣiḥ
pītvā payaḥ su|vipulaṃ siddhim āyāt tadā muniḥ.

tatra dattvā bahūn dāyān viprān saṃpūjya Mādhavaḥ
jagāma Vṛṣṇi|pravaro Ruṣaṅgor āśramaṃ tadā.
yatra taptaṃ tapo ghoram Ārṣṭiṣeṇena Bhārata
brāhmaṇyaṃ labdhavāṃs tatra Viśvāmitro mahā|muniḥ.

39.25 sarva|kāma|samṛddhaṃ ca tad" āśrama|padaṃ mahat
munibhir brāhmaṇaiś c' âiva sevitaṃ sarvadā vibho.

tato hala|dharaḥ śrīmān brāhmaṇaiḥ parivāritaḥ
jagāma tatra rāj'|êndra Ruṣaṅgus tanum atyajat.
Ruṣaṅgur brāhmaṇo vṛddhas tapo|nityaś ca Bhārata
deha|nyāse kṛta|manā vicintya bahudhā tadā,
tataḥ sarvān upādāya tanayān vai mahā|tapāḥ
Ruṣaṅgur abravīt: «tatra nayadhvaṃ māṃ Pṛthūdakam.»
vijñāy' âtīta|vayasaṃ Ruṣaṅguṃ te tapo|dhanāḥ
taṃ ca tīrtham upāninyuḥ Sarasvatyās tapo|dhanam.

Freed from the head, Your Majesty, stainless and pure Mahódara joyfully returned to his hermitage, having achieved what had to be achieved. Liberated, that man of great austerities arrived at the hermitage and narrated everything to the purified seers. Hearing his words, the assembled seers named the sacred site Kapála·móchana ("Release from the Skull"). This ascetic and great seer then returned to that supreme *tirtha*, drank its water in abundance, and attained perfection. 39.20

Bala—that Mádhava and best of Vrishnis—then gave many gifts, worshipped brahmins, and traveled to the hermitage of Rushángu. It was at this site that Arshtishéna had practiced terrible ascetic austerities, descendant of Bharata, and that the great ascetic Vishva·mitra had attained brahminhood. Capable of fulfilling every desire, this great hermitage site was constantly frequented by ascetics and brahmins, my lord. 39.25

Surrounded by brahmins, the glorious plow-bearer then went to the place where Rushángu gave up his body, king of kings. Rushángu was an old brahmin who continuously practiced asceticism, descendant of Bharata. When he had determined to cast away his body, he contemplated the matter for a long time and, after gathering all his sons, Rushángu of great austerities said: "Take me to Prithúdaka." Realizing that their father was very old, the austerity-rich seers took Rushángu, whose wealth lay in asceticism, to that sacred site on the Sarásvati.

39.30 sa taiḥ putrais tadā dhīmān ānīto vai Sarasvatīm
puṇyāṃ tīrtha|śat'|ôpetāṃ vipra|saṅghair niṣevitām.
sa tatra vidhinā rājann āplutya su|mahā|tapāḥ
jñātvā tīrtha|guṇāṃś c' âiva prāh' êdam ṛṣi|sattamaḥ
su|prītaḥ puruṣa|vyāghra sarvān putrān upāsataḥ:

«Sarasvaty|uttare tīre yas tyajed ātmanas tanum
Pṛthūdake japya|paro n' âinaṃ śvo|maraṇaṃ tapet.»

tatr' āplutya sa dharm'|ātmā upaspṛśya hal'|āyudhaḥ
dattvā c' âiva bahūn dāyān viprāṇāṃ vipra|vatsalaḥ.

sasarja yatra bhagavāl̃ lokāl̃ loka|pitāmahaḥ
yatr' Ārṣṭiṣeṇaḥ Kauravya brāhmaṇyaṃ saṃśita|vrataḥ
tapasā mahatā rājan prāptavān ṛṣi|sattamaḥ,
39.35 Sindhu|dvīpaś ca rāja'|rṣir Devāpiś ca mahā|tapāḥ
brāhmaṇyaṃ labdhavān yatra Viśvāmitras tathā muniḥ
mahā|tapasvī bhagavān ugra|tejā mahā|tapāḥ
tatr' ājagāma balavān Balabhadraḥ pratāpavān.

JANAMEJAYA uvāca:

40.1 KATHAM ĀRṢṬIṢEṆO bhagavān vipulaṃ taptavāṃs tapaḥ?
Sindhudvīpaḥ kathaṃ c' âpi brāhmaṇyaṃ labdhavāṃs tadā,
Devāpiś ca kathaṃ brahman Viśvāmitraś ca sattama?
tan mam' ācakṣva bhagavan. paraṃ kautūhalaṃ hi me.

Wise Rushángu was thus led by his sons to the Sarásvati river, which is pure, frequented by crowds of brahmins, and has hundreds of sacred sites. After bathing there in the prescribed manner, that best of seers, who had practiced great austerities, joyfully said these words to all his sons as they waited upon him, knowing as he did the virtues of the *tirtha*, tiger among men: 39.30

"Those who, intent on recitation, give up their bodies at Prithúdaka on the northern bank of the Sarásvati will not be afflicted by a future death."*

Righteous, plow-weaponed Bala then bathed at that site, sipped the water, and, in his kindness to brahmins, gave them many gifts.

Mighty and splendid Bala·bhadra then proceeded to the site where the illustrious Grandfather of the universe emitted the worlds and where Arshtishéna, that superb seer of rigid vows, attained brahminhood through great austerities. It was there too that the royal seer Sindhu·dvipa and the great ascetic Devápi* once attained brahminhood, as did the illustrious ascetic Vishva·mitra, who practiced mighty austerities and was invested with fierce power and great asceticism. 39.35

JANAM·ÉJAYA said:

How DID ILLUSTRIOUS Arshtishéna practice abundant austerities? How did Sindhu·dvipa attain brahminhood and how did Devápi and Vishva·mitra attain the same, eminent brahmin? Tell me this, illustrious Vaishampáyana. For I am extremely curious. 40.1

VAIŚAMPĀYANA uvāca:

purā Kṛta|yuge rājann Ārṣṭiṣeṇo dvij'|ôttamaḥ
vasan guru|kule nityaṃ nityam adhyayane rataḥ.
tasya rājan guru|kule vasato nityam eva ca
samāptiṃ n' âgamad vidyā n' âpi vedā viśāṃ pate.

40.5 sa nirviṇṇas tato rājaṃs tapas tepe mahā|tapāḥ
tato vai tapasā tena prāpya vedān an|uttamān.
sa vidvān veda|yuktaś ca siddhaś c' âpy ṛṣi|sattamaḥ
tatra tīrthe varān prādāt trīn eva su|mahā|tapāḥ:

«asmiṃs tīrthe mahā|nadyā adya|prabhṛti mānavaḥ
āpluto vāji|medhasya phalaṃ prāpsyati puṣkalam.
adya|prabhṛti n' âiv' âtra bhayaṃ vyālād bhaviṣyati
api c' âlpena kālena phalaṃ prāpsyati puṣkalam.»

evam uktvā mahā|tejā jagāma tri|divaṃ muniḥ.
evaṃ siddhaḥ sa bhagavān Ārṣṭiṣeṇaḥ pratāpavān.

40.10 tasminn eva tadā tīrthe Sindhudvīpaḥ pratāpavān
Devāpiś ca mahā|rāja brāhmaṇyaṃ prāpatur mahat.

tathā ca Kauśikas tāta tapo|nityo jit'|êndriyaḥ
tapasā vai su|taptena brāhmaṇatvam avāptavān.

VAISHAMPÁYANA said:

In the past, Your Majesty, during the Krita era, Arshti·shéna, that best of brahmins, continuously delighted in study while permanently dwelling in his teacher's house. But although he permanently lived in his teacher's house, he could not master the sciences or the Vedas, lord of the people. In his despondency, Your Majesty, that man of great austerities practiced asceticism and, through his asceticism, acquired the unsurpassed Vedas. When that wise and eminent seer of great austerities had become furnished with the Vedas and attained perfection, he bestowed three boons at this sacred site: 40.5

"From this day forward, those who bathe at this *tirtha* on the great river will acquire the abundant fruit of a horse sacrifice. From this day forward, there will be no danger from snakes here and people will gain great fruit in a short period of time."

Saying these words, that ascetic of great power went to heaven. It was thus that illustrious and glorious Arshtishéna attained perfection.

At the same site, Your Majesty, glorious Sindhu·dvipa and Devápi attained the great state of brahminhood. 40.10

After he had practiced continuous austerities and conquered his senses, Vishva·mitra, the grandson of Kúshika, likewise attained brahminhood through asceticism of great heat. This is how it occurred.

Gādhir nāma mahān āsīt kṣatriyaḥ prathito bhuvi.
tasya putro 'bhavad rājan Viśvāmitraḥ pratāpavān.
sa rājā Kauśikas tāta mahā|yogy abhavat kila.
sa putram abhiṣicy' âtha Viśvāmitraṃ mahā|tapāḥ,
deha|nyāse manaś cakre. tam ūcuḥ praṇatāḥ prajāḥ:
«na gantavyaṃ mahā|prājña! trāhi c' âsmān mahā|bhayāt!»
40.15 evam uktaḥ pratyuvāca tato Gādhiḥ prajās tadā:
«viśvasya jagato goptā bhaviṣyati suto mama.»
ity uktvā tu tato Gādhir Viśvāmitraṃ niveśya ca
jagāma tridivaṃ rājan. Viśvāmitro 'bhavan nṛpaḥ
na sa śaknoti pṛthivīṃ yatnavān api rakṣitum.
tataḥ śuśrāva rājā sa rākṣasebhyo mahā|bhayam
niryayau nagarāc c' âpi catur|aṅga|bal'|ânvitaḥ.
sa gatvā dūram adhvānaṃ Vasiṣṭh'|āśramam abhyayāt.
tasya te sainikā rājaṃś cakrus tatr' â|nayān bahūn.
tatas tu bhagavān vipro Vasiṣṭho ''śramam* abhyayāt
dadṛśe 'tha tataḥ sarvaṃ bhajyamānaṃ mahā|vanam.
40.20 tasya kruddho mahā|rāja Vasiṣṭho muni|sattamaḥ
«sṛjasva Śabarān ghorān! iti» svāṃ gām uvāca ha.
tath'' ôktā s'' âsṛjad dhenuḥ puruṣān ghora|darśanān.
te tu tad balam āsādya babhañjuḥ sarvato|diśam.
tac chrutvā vidrutaṃ sainyaṃ Viśvāmitras tu Gādhi|jaḥ
tapaḥ paraṃ manyamānas tapasy eva mano dadhe.
so 'smiṃs tīrtha|vare rājan Sarasvatyāḥ samāhitaḥ
niyamaiś c' ôpavāsaiś ca karṣayan deham ātmanaḥ.
jal'|āhāro vāyu|bhakṣaḥ parṇ'|āhāraś ca so 'bhavat
tathā sthaṇḍila|śāyī ca ye c' ânye niyamāḥ pṛthak.

There was a great kshatriya called Gadhin, who was renowned throughout the earth. His son was glorious Vishva·mitra, Your Majesty. They say that King Gadhin, the son of Kúshika, became a great *yogin*. That man of great austerities consecrated his son Vishva·mitra as king and resolved to cast away his body. His people prostrated themselves before him and said: "Do not leave us, wise king! Protect us from great danger!" In response, Gadhin replied: 40.15 "My son will be the protector of the entire world."

Saying this, Gadhin installed Vishva·mitra on the throne and went to heaven, Your Majesty. Vishva·mitra thus became king but was unable to protect the earth, despite his efforts. King Vishva·mitra then heard that there was a great danger from demons and so he departed from the city with a fourfold army. After he had traveled a long way, he arrived at the hermitage of Vasíshtha.* His soldiers committed many immoral deeds there, Your Majesty. The illustrious brahmin Vasíshtha then returned to his hermitage and saw that the great forest was completely destroyed. Vasíshtha, that 40.20 supreme ascetic, became enraged and said to his cow: "Release the terrifying Shábaras!" Instructed this way, the cow emitted men of terrifying appearance, who attacked and destroyed Vishva·mitra's army in every direction.

On hearing that his army had been routed, Vishva·mitra, the son of Gadhin, considered asceticism to be the highest asset and therefore set his mind on ascetic practice. Torturing his body with disciplines and fasts, he meditated at this excellent *tirtha* on the Sarásvati, Your Majesty. His food was water, wind, and leaves, and he slept on the ground and practiced various other disciplines.

40.25 a|sakṛt tasya devās tu vrata|vighnaṃ pracakrire,
na c' âsya niyamād buddhir apayāti mah"|ātmanaḥ.
tataḥ pareṇa yatnena taptvā bahu|vidhaṃ tapaḥ
tejasā bhāskar'|ākāro Gādhi|jaḥ samapadyata.
tapasā tu tathā yuktaṃ Viśvāmitraṃ pitāmahaḥ
amanyata mahā|tejā vara|do varam asya tat.
sa tu vavre varaṃ rājan, «syām ahaṃ brāhmaṇas tv iti.»
«tath" êti» c' âbravīd Brahmā sarva|loka|pitāmahaḥ.
sa labdhvā tapas" ôgreṇa brāhmaṇatvaṃ mahā|yaśāḥ
vicacāra mahīṃ kṛtsnāṃ kṛta|kāmaḥ sur'|ôpamaḥ.

40.30 tasmiṃs tīrtha|vare Rāmaḥ pradāya vividhaṃ vasu
payasvinīs tathā dhenūr yānāni śayanāni ca,
atha vastrāṇy alaṃkāraṃ bhakṣyaṃ peyaṃ ca śobhanam
adadan mudito rājan pūjayitvā dvij'|ôttamān.

yayau rājaṃs tato Rāmo Bakasy' āśramam antikāt
yatra tepe tapas tīvraṃ Dālbhyo Baka iti śrutiḥ.

VAIŚAMPĀYANA uvāca:

41.1 BRAHMA|YONER Avākīrṇaṃ jagāma Yadu|nandanaḥ
yatra Dālbhyo Bako rājann āśrama|stho mahā|tapāḥ
juhāva Dhṛtarāṣṭrasya rāṣṭraṃ Vaicitravīryiṇaḥ.

tapasā ghora|rūpeṇa karṣayan deham ātmanaḥ
krodhena mahat" āviṣṭo dharm'|ātmā vai pratāpavān.
purā hi Naimiṣīyāṇāṃ satre dvādaśa|vārṣike
vṛtte viśvajito 'nte vai Pañcālān ṛṣayo 'gaman.
tatr' ēśvaram ayācanta dakṣiṇ"|ârthaṃ manasviṇaḥ

The gods repeatedly tried to obstruct his vows, but the mind of the great-spirited man did not leave his discipline. After practicing many kinds of asceticism with extreme effort, the son of Gadhin became like the sun in his radiant energy. When he had acquired this ascetic power, the powerful, boon-giving Grandfather resolved to give Vishva·mitra a wish. Vishva·mitra chose the boon of becoming a brahmin and Brahma, the Grandfather of all the worlds, consented. After glorious and god-like Vishva·mitra had attained brahminhood through fierce asceticism, he wandered the entire earth, his desires fulfilled. 40.25

Rama offered diverse wealth at this excellent *tirtha*, along with milk cows, vehicles and beds. After worshipping eminent brahmins, he also joyfully gave away clothes, ornaments, food, and fine drink, Your Majesty. 40.30

Rama then proceeded to the hermitage of Baka, Your Majesty, where it is said that Dalbhya Baka once performed severe austerities.

VAISHAMPÁYANA said:

FROM BRAHMA·YONI the delight of the Yadus then traveled to Avakírna. It was here, Your Majesty, that the great ascetic Baka Dalbhya once made a sacrifice of the kingdom of Dhrita·rashtra, the son of Vichítra·virya, while dwelling at his hermitage.* 41.1

Tormenting his body with gruesome austerities, that glorious and righteous man had become filled with great wrath. For, in the past, during the twelve-year sacrifice of the Naimishíya ascetics, some seers had traveled to the Panchála realm after the Víshvajit ritual had concluded.* There the

bal'|ânvitān vatsatarān nirvyādhīn eka|viṃśatim.
41.5 tān abravīd Bako Dālbhyo: «vibhajadhvaṃ paśūn iti.
paśūn etān ahaṃ tyaktvā bhikṣiṣye rāja|sattamam.»
evam uktvā tato rājan ṛṣīn sarvān pratāpavān
jagāma Dhṛtarāṣṭrasya bhavanaṃ brāhmaṇ'|ôttamaḥ.
sa samīpa|gato bhūtvā Dhṛtarāṣṭraṃ jan'|ēśvaram
ayācata paśūn Dālbhyaḥ. sa c' âinaṃ ruṣito 'bravīt
yad|ṛcchayā mṛtā dṛṣṭvā gās tadā nṛpa|sattamaḥ:
«etān paśūn naya kṣipraṃ brahma|bandho yad' îcchasi.»
ṛṣis tathā vacaḥ śrutvā cintayām āsa dharma|vit:
«aho bata nṛśaṃsaṃ vai vākyam ukto 'smi saṃsadi!»
41.10 cintayitvā muhūrtena roṣ'|āviṣṭo dvij'|ôttamaḥ
matiṃ cakre vināśāya Dhṛtarāṣṭrasya bhū|pateḥ.
sa t' ûtkṛtya mṛtānāṃ vai māṃsāni muni|sattamaḥ
juhāva Dhṛtarāṣṭrasya rāṣṭraṃ nara|pateḥ purā.
Avākīrṇe Sarasvatyās tīrthe prajvālya pāvakam
Bako Dālbhyo mahā|rāja niyamaṃ paramaṃ sthitaḥ
sa tair eva juhāv' âsya rāṣṭraṃ māṃsair mahā|tapāḥ.
tasmiṃs tu vidhivat satre saṃpravṛtte su|dāruṇe
akṣīyata tato rāṣṭraṃ Dhṛtarāṣṭrasya pārthiva.
tataḥ prakṣīyamāṇaṃ tad rājyaṃ tasya mahī|pateḥ
chidyamānaṃ yath" ân|antaṃ vanaṃ paraśunā vibho
babhūv' āpad|gataṃ tac ca vyavakīrṇam a|cetanam.
41.15 dṛṣṭvā tath" âvakīrṇaṃ tu rāṣṭraṃ sa manuj'|âdhipaḥ

wise men asked the king for twenty-one strong and healthy calves as a sacrificial fee. But Baka Dalbhya said to them: 41.5 "Share the animals! I will give them up and instead beg for alms from the highest of kings."

Saying this to all the seers, the glorious and excellent brahmin went to the palace of Dhrita·rashtra, Your Majesty. Approaching Dhrita·rashtra, Dalbhya asked that lord of the people for animals. But the supreme king became furious and, on happening to see some dead cows, replied: "Quickly take these animals, if you so wish, kinsman of Brahma!" Hearing these words, the seer, who was knowledgeable in righteousness, reflected: "O! I have been addressed with base words in the assembly!"

After brooding a while, that supreme brahmin became 41.10 possessed by anger and considered how to destroy King Dhrita·rashtra. Cutting up the flesh of the dead cows, that best of ascetics made a sacrificial offering of King Dhrita·rashtra's realm in those bygone days. After lighting a fire at the *tirtha* of Avakírna on the Sarásvati river, the great ascetic Baka Dalbhya, who practiced the highest discipline, sacrificed Dhrita·rashtra's kingdom with those pieces of flesh, great king.

When the terrible ritual had commenced with due rites, the kingdom of Dhrita·rashtra began to perish, Your Majesty. Just as a limitless forest is cut down by an axe, so the monarch's perishing kingdom fell upon ruin, dwindled away, and became lifeless. When he saw his kingdom 41.15 wasting away, that lord of men became despondent, Your Majesty, and brooded over the matter. Helped by brahmins, Dhrita·rashtra tried to rescue his kingdom in those days of

babhūva dur|manā rājaṃś cintayām āsa ca prabhuḥ.
mokṣ'|ârtham akarod yatnaṃ brāhmaṇaiḥ sahitaḥ purā
na ca śreyo 'dhyagacchat tu kṣīyate rāṣṭram eva ca.

yadā sa pārthivaḥ khinnas te ca viprās tad" ân|agha
yadā c' âpi na śaknoti rāṣṭraṃ mocayituṃ nṛpa
atha vaiprāśnikāṃs tatra papraccha Janamejaya.

tato vaiprāśnikāḥ prāhuḥ: «paśuṃ viprakṛtas tvayā
māṃsair abhijuhot' îti tava rāṣṭraṃ munir Bakaḥ.
tena te hūyamānasya rāṣṭrasy' âsya kṣayo mahān.
tasy' âitat tapasaḥ karma yena te 'dya layo mahān.
apāṃ kuñje Sarasvatyās taṃ prasādaya pārthiva.»

41.20 Sarasvatīṃ tato gatvā sa rājā Bakam abravīt
nipatya śirasā bhūmau prāñjalir Bharata'|rṣabha:

«prasādaye tvāṃ bhagavann. aparādhaṃ kṣamasva me.
mama dīnasya lubdhasya maurkhyeṇa hata|cetasaḥ.
tvaṃ gatis tvaṃ ca me nāthaḥ. prasādaṃ kartum arhasi!»

taṃ tathā vilapantaṃ tu śok'|ôpahata|cetasam
dṛṣṭvā tasya kṛpā jajñe rāṣṭraṃ tasya vyamocayat.
ṛṣiḥ prasannas tasy' âbhūt saṃrambhaṃ ca vihāya saḥ.
mokṣ'|ârthaṃ tasya rājyasya juhāva punar āhutim.
mokṣayitvā tato rāṣṭraṃ pratigṛhya paśūn bahūn
hṛṣṭ'|ātmā Naimiṣ'|āraṇyaṃ jagāma punar eva saḥ.

41.25 Dhṛtarāṣṭro 'pi dharm'|ātmā sva|stha|cetā mahā|manāḥ
svam eva nagaraṃ rājan pratipede maha"|rddhimat.

old, but he could not acquire any prosperity and the kingdom continued to perish.

Both the king and the brahmins became distressed and, when Dhrita·rashtra could not rescue his kingdom, he asked his counsellors for advice, faultless King Janam·éjaya.

The counsellors answered: "You offended the ascetic Baka with the animal you gave him and so he sacrificed your kingdom with pieces of meat. Your kingdom is suffering great disaster from being sacrificed by him. It is this act of asceticism that is causing your great misfortune today. You should placate him, Your Majesty, at the Bower of the Sarásvati waters."

The king therefore went to Sarásvati, bull of the Bharatas. Cupping his hands in respect and lowering his head to the ground, he addressed Baka, saying: 41.20

"I beg for your grace, illustrious lord. Please forgive my crime. I was a greedy wretch and my mind was destroyed by stupidity. You are my refuge and lord. Please give me your grace!"

When Baka saw the king lamenting and stricken with grief, he felt compassion for him and released his kingdom. The seer renounced his anger and gave the king his grace. He then offered another sacrificial libation in order to free Dhrita·rashtra's kingdom. After he had released the kingdom and received many animals, he joyfully returned to the Náimisha forest. High-minded, righteous Dhrita·rashtra also happily returned to his own city, which abounded with prosperity, Your Majesty. 41.25

tatra tīrthe mahā|rāja Bṛhaspatir udāra|dhīḥ
asurāṇām a|bhāvāya bhavāya ca div'|âukasām
māṃsair abhijuhāv' êṣṭim. akṣīyanta tato 'surāḥ
daivatair api saṃbhagnā jita|kāśibhir āhave.

tatr' âpi vidhivad dattvā brāhmaṇebhyo mahā|yaśāḥ
vājinaḥ kuñjarāṃś c' âiva rathāṃś c' âśvatarī|yutān,
ratnāni ca mah"|ârhāṇi dhanaṃ dhānyaṃ ca puṣkalam
yayau tīrthaṃ mahā|bāhur Yāyātaṃ pṛthivī|pate.

41.30 tatra yajñe Yayāteś ca mahā|rāja Sarasvatī
sarpiḥ payaś ca susrāva Nāhuṣasya mah"|ātmanaḥ.
tatr' êṣṭvā puruṣa|vyāghro Yayātiḥ pṛthivī|patiḥ
akrāmad ūrdhvaṃ mudito lebhe lokāṃś ca puṣkalān.

punas tatra ca rājñas tu Yayāter yajataḥ prabhoḥ
audāryaṃ paramaṃ kṛtvā bhaktiṃ c' ātmani śāśvatīm
dadau kāmān brāhmaṇebhyo yān yān yo manas" êcchati.
yo yatra sthita ev' êha āhūto yajña|saṃstare
tasya tasya saric|chreṣṭhā gṛh'|ādi|śayan'|ādikam
ṣaḍ|rasaṃ bhojanaṃ c' âiva dānaṃ nānā|vidhaṃ tathā.
te manyamānā rājñas tu saṃpradānam an|uttamam
rājānaṃ tuṣṭuvuḥ prītā dattvā c' âiv' āśiṣaḥ śubhāḥ.

41.35 tatra devāḥ sa|gandharvāḥ prītā yajñasya saṃpadā
vismitā mānuṣāś c' āsan dṛṣṭvā tāṃ yajña|saṃpadam.

tatas tāla|ketur mahā|dharma|ketur
mah"|ātmā kṛt'|ātmā mahā|dāna|nityaḥ
Vasiṣṭhāpavāhaṃ mahā|bhīma|vegaṃ
dhṛt'|ātmā jit'|ātmā samabhyājagāma.

At this *tirtha*, great king, wise Brihas·pati also once made a sacrificial offering with flesh in order to destroy demons and preserve the gods. As a result, the demons dwindled away, destroyed by the conquering gods in battle.

After glorious, mighty-armed Rama had duly given away horses, elephants, and mule-yoked chariots to brahmins, as well as costly jewels, wealth, and abundant grain, he traveled to the site of Yayáta, lord of the earth. It was here that Sarásvati emitted ghee and milk at the sacrifice of Yayáti, that heroic son of Náhusha. After he had performed his sacrifice at that spot, Yayáti, that tiger among men and lord of the earth, joyfully ascended upwards and attained many realms.* 41.30

Furthermore, when Yayáti—that king and lord—performed his sacrifice at this site and showed great magnanimity and incessant devotion to Sarásvati, the supreme river provided brahmins with whatever pleasures their hearts desired. She gave houses, beds and other possessions, as well as food of six different tastes and various offerings to whoever stood at this site after being invited to the sacrificial area. Esteeming the unsurpassed offering of the king, the brahmins joyfully bestowed auspicious blessings on him and praised him. Gods and *gandhárvas* were delighted at the riches of the sacrifice and humans were amazed when they saw the bounty of the ritual. 41.35

Great-spirited and perfected Rama, whose banner consists of a palm tree and great righteousness, whose self is steady and conquered, and who constantly offers generous gifts, then proceeded toward Vasíshthápavaha ('The Channel of Vasíshtha'), where the current is strong and fierce.

JANAMEJAYA uvāca:

42.1 VASIṢṬHASY' ÂPAVĀHO 'sau bhīma|vegaḥ kathaṃ nu saḥ?
kim|arthaṃ ca saric|chreṣṭhā tam ṛṣiṃ pratyavāhayat?
katham asy' âbhavad vairaṃ? kāraṇaṃ kiṃ ca tat prabho?
śaṃsa pṛṣṭo mahā|prājña. na hi tṛpyāmi. kathyatām!

VAIŚAMPĀYANA uvāca:

Viśvāmitrasya vipra'|rṣer Vasiṣṭhasya ca Bhārata
bhṛśaṃ vairam abhūd rājaṃs tapaḥ|spardhā|kṛtaṃ mahat.
āśramo vai Vasiṣṭhasya Sthāṇutīrthe 'bhavan mahān
pūrvataḥ pārśvataś c' āsīd Viśvāmitrasya dhīmataḥ.
42.5 yatra Sthāṇur mahā|rāja taptavān paramaṃ tapaḥ
tatr' âsya karma tad ghoraṃ pravadanti manīṣiṇaḥ.
yatr' êṣṭvā bhagavān Sthāṇuḥ pūjayitvā Sarasvatīm
sthāpayām āsa tat tīrthaṃ Sthāṇutīrtham iti prabho.
tatra tīrthe surāḥ Skandam abhyaṣiñcan nar'|âdhipa
saināpatyena mahatā sur'|âri|vinibarhaṇam.
tasmin Sārasvate tīrthe Viśvāmitro mahā|muniḥ
Vasiṣṭhaṃ cālayām āsa tapas" ôgreṇa tac chṛṇu.

Viśvāmitra|Vasiṣṭhau tāv ahany ahani Bhārata
spardhāṃ tapaḥ|kṛtāṃ tīvrāṃ cakratus tau tapo|dhanau.
42.10 tatr' âpy adhika|santāpo Viśvāmitro mahā|muniḥ
dṛṣṭvā tejo Vasiṣṭhasya cintām abhijagāma ha.
tasya buddhir iyaṃ hy āsīd dharma|nityasya Bhārata:

JANAM·ÉJAYA said:

WHY DOES THE Channel of Vasíshtha have a fierce current? Why did that supreme river sweep away the seer? How did this feud arise? What was the cause, my lord? Answer my questions, wise Vaishampáyana. I have not heard enough. Please tell me! 42.1

VAISHAMPÁYANA said:

A fierce enmity arose between Vishva·mitra and the brahmin seer Vasíshtha due to their great rivalry in asceticism, descendant of Bharata. Vasíshtha's great hermitage was situated at the Sthanu·tirtha on the eastern bank and wise Vishva·mitra's hermitage was situated on the western bank.

Wise men relate how Sthanu performed dreadful deeds at this site while engaged in the highest asceticism, great king. The place where illustrious Sthanu performed a sacrifice, honored Sarásvati, and established a *tirtha* is called Sthanu·tirtha, my lord. At this site, lord of men, the gods consecrated Skanda—that destroyer of the gods' enemies—as their supreme general. Hear how the great ascetic Vishva·mitra toppled Vasíshtha with his fierce ascetic power at this sacred site on the Sarásvati. 42.5

Day after day, descendant of Bharata, Vishva·mitra and Vasíshtha—who were both rich in austerities—engaged in a fierce rivalry of asceticism. When the great ascetic Vishva·mitra saw Vasíshtha's power, he was extremely anguished and began to brood. These are the thoughts he had, descendant of Bharata, even though he was dedicated to righteousness: 42.10

«iyaṃ Sarasvatī tūrṇaṃ mat|samīpaṃ tapo|dhanam
ānayiṣyati vegena Vasiṣṭhaṃ tapatāṃ varam.
ih' āgataṃ dvija|śreṣṭhaṃ haniṣyāmi. na saṃśayaḥ.»
evaṃ niścitya bhagavān Viśvāmitro mahā|muniḥ
sasmāra saritāṃ śreṣṭhāṃ krodha|saṃrakta|locanaḥ.
sā dhyātā muninā tena vyākulatvaṃ jagāma ha
jajñe c' âinaṃ mahā|vīryaṃ mahā|kopaṃ ca bhāvinī.
tata enaṃ vepamānā vivarṇā prāñjalis tadā
upatasthe muni|varaṃ Viśvāmitraṃ Sarasvatī
42.15 hata|vīrā yathā nārī s" âbhavad duḥkhitā bhṛśam:
«brūhi kiṃ karavāṇ' îti» provāca muni|sattamam.
tām uvāca muniḥ kruddho: «Vasiṣṭhaṃ śīghram ānaya
yāvad enaṃ nihanmy adya!» tac chrutvā vyathitā nadī.
prāñjaliṃ tu tataḥ kṛtvā puṇḍarīka|nibh'|ēkṣaṇā
prākampata bhṛśaṃ bhītā vāyun" êv' āhatā latā.
tathā|rūpāṃ tu tāṃ dṛṣṭvā munir āha mahā|nadīm:
«a|vicāraṃ Vasiṣṭhaṃ tvam ānaysv' ântikaṃ mama!»
sā tasya vacanaṃ śrutvā jñātvā pāpaṃ cikīrṣitam
Vasiṣṭhasya prabhāvaṃ ca jānanty a|pratimaṃ bhuvi,
42.20 s" âbhigamya Vasiṣṭhaṃ ca idam artham acodayat
yad uktā saritāṃ śreṣṭhā Viśvāmitreṇa dhīmatā.
ubhayoḥ śāpayor bhītā vepamānā punaḥ punaḥ
cintayitvā mahā|śāpam ṛṣi|vitrāsitā bhṛśam.
tāṃ kṛśāṃ ca vivarṇāṃ ca dṛṣṭvā cintā|samanvitām
uvāca rājan dharm'|ātmā Vasiṣṭho dvi|padāṃ varaḥ:

"By the force of its current, the Sarásvati river will swiftly bring to me Vasíshtha, that excellent ascetic who is rich in austerities. When he comes here, I will slay that supreme brahmin. Of this there is no doubt."

Making this resolution, the great and illustrious ascetic Vishva·mitra brought to mind that supreme river, his eyes red with fury. When the ascetic reflected on the noble lady, she was stirred and appeared before that man of great wrath and vigor. Pale and trembling, Sarásvati approached the supreme ascetic Vishva·mitra with her hands cupped in respect. Filled with great anguish, like a woman whose husband has been killed, she said to that best of ascetics: "Tell me what I should do." The enraged ascetic replied: "Bring Vasíshtha to me quickly so that I can kill him this day!" Hearing this, the river became agitated. Cupping her palms in respect, Sarásvati, whose eyes were like lotuses, trembled greatly with fear, like a creeper pounded by the wind. Seeing her in this state, the ascetic said to the great river: "Bring Vasíshtha to me—do not hesitate!" 42.15

Hearing his words, and knowing that Vishva·mitra's design was evil and that Vasíshtha's power was unparalled on earth, that supreme river went to Vasíshtha and informed him of wise Vishva·mitra's words. Trembling repeatedly and fearing curses from both men, she felt a deep terror of the seers as she worried about their mighty curses. 42.20

When righteous Vasíshtha saw how Sarásvati was wretched, pale, and full of worry, that finest of men addressed her with these words, Your Majesty:

VASIṢṬHA uvāca:

«pāhy ātmānaṃ saric|chreṣṭhe vaha māṃ śīghra|gāminī.
Viśvāmitraḥ śapedd hi tvāṃ. mā kṛthās tvaṃ vicāraṇām.»

tasya tad vacanaṃ śrutvā kṛpā|śīlasya sā sarit
cintayām āsa Kauravya kiṃ kṛtvā su|kṛtaṃ bhavet.
42.25 tasyāś cintā samutpannā: «Vasiṣṭho mayy atīva hi
kṛtavān hi dayāṃ nityaṃ. tasya kāryaṃ hitaṃ mayā.»
atha kūle svake rājañ japantam ṛṣi|sattamam
juhvānaṃ Kauśikaṃ prekṣya Sarasvaty abhyacintayat
«idam antaram ity» evaṃ tataḥ sā saritāṃ varā.
kūl'|âpahāram akarot svena vegena sā sarit.
tena kūl'|âpahāreṇa Maitrāvaruṇir auhyata
uhyamānaḥ sa tuṣṭāva tadā rājan Sarasvatīm:

«pitāmahasya sarasaḥ pravṛtt" āsi Sarasvati
vyāptaṃ c' êdaṃ jagat sarvaṃ tav' âiv' âmbhobhir uttamaiḥ.
42.30 tvam ev' ākāśa|gā devi megheṣu sṛjase payaḥ.
sarvāś c' āpas tvam ev' êti tvatto vayam adhīmahi.
Puṣṭir Dyutis tathā Kīrtiḥ Siddhir Buddhir Umā tathā
tvam eva Vāṇī Svāhā tvaṃ. tav' āyattam idaṃ jagat.
tvam eva sarva|bhūteṣu vasas' îha catur|vidhā.»

evaṃ Sarasvatī rājan stūyamānā maha"|rṣiṇā
vegen' ôvāha taṃ vipraṃ Viśvāmitr'|āśramaṃ prati
nyavedayata c' âbhīkṣṇaṃ Viśvāmitrāya taṃ munim.
tam ānītaṃ Sarasvatyā dṛṣṭvā kopa|samanvitaḥ
ath' ânveṣat praharaṇaṃ Vasiṣṭh'|ânta|karaṃ tadā.
taṃ tu kruddham abhiprekṣya brahma|vadhyā|bhayān nadī
apovāha Vasiṣṭhaṃ tu prācīṃ diśam a|tandritā
ubhayoḥ kurvatī vākyaṃ vañcayitvā ca Gādhi|jam.

VASÍSHTHA said:

"Protect yourself, best of rivers, and carry me along swiftly. Otherwise Vishva·mitra will curse you. Do not worry."

Hearing the compassionate ascetic's words, the river began to contemplate the best course of action and had this 42.25 thought, Kaurávya: "Vasíshtha has always shown me compassion. I should act for his welfare." When Sarásvati, that finest of rivers, saw the excellent seer Káushika reciting mantras and performing a sacrifice on her river bank, she thought: "This is my opportunity." By the force of her current, the river tore away her bank, and when the bank was torn away Maitrávaruni was carried along too. As he was carried along, Vasíshtha praised Sarásvati, Your Majesty, saying:

"You arose from the Grandfather's lake, Sarásvati, and this entire world is pervaded by your fine waters.* You travel in 42.30 the sky and emit water into the clouds, goddess. You are all the waters and it is through you that we can study the Vedas. You are Pushti, Dyuti, Kirti, Siddhi, Buddhi and Uma. You are Vani and Svaha.* The universe depends on you. Fourfold, you dwell in all living creatures."

Praised by the great seer in this way, Your Majesty, Sarásvati swiftly carried the brahmin to Vishva·mitra's hermitage and promptly introduced the ascetic to Vishva·mitra. When the wrathful ascetic saw Sarásvati had brought Vasíshtha, he looked for a weapon to kill him. But on seeing his wrath, the river effortlessly carried Vasíshtha eastwards out of fear of brahminicide. She thereby obeyed both men, although she deceived the son of Gadhin.

42.35 tato 'pavāhitaṃ dṛṣṭvā Vasiṣṭham ṛṣi|sattamam
abravīd duḥkha|saṃkruddho Viśvāmitro hy a|marṣaṇaḥ:
«yasmān mā tvaṃ saric|chreṣṭhe vañcayitvā punar gatā
śoṇitaṃ vaha kalyāṇi rakṣo|grāmaṇi|saṃmatam.»
tataḥ Sarasvatī śaptā Viśvāmitreṇa dhīmatā
avahac choṇit'|ônmiśraṃ toyaṃ saṃvatsaraṃ tadā.
atha' rṣayaś ca devāś ca gandharv'|âpsarasas tadā
Sarasvatīṃ tathā dṛṣṭvā babhūvur bhṛśa|duḥkhitāḥ.
evaṃ Vasiṣṭhāpavāho loke khyāto jan'|âdhipa
āgacchac ca punar mārgaṃ svam eva saritāṃ varā.

VAIŚAMPĀYANA uvāca:

43.1 SĀ ŚAPTĀ TENA kruddhena Viśvāmitreṇa dhīmatā
tasmiṃs tīrtha|vare śubhre śoṇitaṃ samupāvahat.
ath' ājagmus tato rājan rākṣasās tatra Bhārata
tatra te śoṇitaṃ sarve pibantaḥ sukham āsate.
tṛptāś ca su|bhṛśaṃ tena sukhitā vigata|jvarāḥ
nṛtyantaś ca hasantaś ca yathā svarga|jitas tathā.
kasya cit tv atha kālasya ṛṣayaḥ su|tapo|dhanāḥ
tīrtha|yātrāṃ samājagmuḥ Sarasvatyāṃ mahī|pate.
43.5 teṣu sarveṣu tīrtheṣu tv āplutya muni|puṅgavāḥ
prāpya prītiṃ parāṃ c' âpi tapo|lubdhā viśāradāḥ
prayayur hi tato rājan yena tīrtham asṛg|vaham.
ath' āgamya mahā|bhāgās tat tīrthaṃ dāruṇaṃ tadā
dṛṣṭvā toyaṃ Sarasvatyāḥ śoṇitena pariplutam
pīyamānaṃ ca rakṣobhir bahubhir nṛpa|sattama.

When Vishva·mitra saw the supreme seer Vasíshtha being carried away, the unforgiving ascetic became furious with disappointment and said: 42.35

"Since you have deceived me, lovely lady, and departed once more, your current will turn into blood fit for demon chiefs."

Cursed by wise Vishva·mitra, Sarásvati then flowed with water mixed with blood for a year. Seers, gods, *gandhárvas*, and nymphs became deeply distressed when they saw Sarásvati in that plight.

In this way, the site of Vasíshthápavaha became celebrated in the world and that supreme river returned to her proper course.

VAISHAMPÁYANA said:

CURSED BY WISE and wrathful Vishva·mitra, Sarásvati flowed with blood at that auspicious and excellent *tirtha*. Demons gathered there, royal descendant of Bharata, and all of them lived happily from drinking the blood in the river. Joyful and fully sated, and with their anxieties dispelled, they danced and laughed as if they had conquered heaven. 43.1

After some time, lord of the earth, some seers, who were very rich in austerities, arrived at the Sarásvati river on a tour of the *tirthas*. After bathing at all the sites, Your Majesty, the wise bull-like ascetics, who were greedy for austerities, attained the highest joy. They then traveled to the *tirtha* where the current flowed with blood. Arriving at that terrible site, the illustrious men saw Sarásvati's water running with blood and being drunk by hordes of demons, best of men. On seeing the demons, those ascetics of rigid vows 43.5

tān dṛṣṭvā rākṣasān rājan munayaḥ saṃśita|vratāḥ
paritrāṇe Sarasvatyāḥ paraṃ yatnaṃ pracakrire.
te tu sarve mahā|bhāgāḥ samāgamya mahā|vratāḥ
āhūya saritāṃ śreṣṭhām idaṃ vacanam abruvan:

«kāraṇaṃ brūhi kalyāṇi kim|arthaṃ te hrado hy ayam
evam ākulatāṃ yātaḥ. śrutv" ādhyāsyāmahe vayam.»

43.10 tataḥ sā sarvam ācaṣṭa yathā|vṛttaṃ pravepatī.
duḥkhitām atha tāṃ dṛṣṭvā ūcus te vai tapo|dhanāḥ:

«kāraṇaṃ śrutam asmābhiḥ śāpaś c' âiva śruto 'n|aghe.
kariṣyāmo vayaṃ yatnaṃ sarva eva tapo|dhanāḥ.»

evam uktvā saric|chreṣṭhām ūcus te 'tha paras|param:
«vimocayāmahe sarve śāpād etāṃ Sarasvatīm.»

te sarve brāhmaṇā rājaṃs tapobhir niyamais tathā
upavāsaiś ca vividhair yamaiḥ kaṣṭa|vratais tathā,
ārādhya paśu|bhartāraṃ Mahā|devaṃ jagat|patim
mokṣayām āsus tāṃ devīṃ saric|chreṣṭhāṃ Sarasvatīm.

43.15 teṣāṃ tu sā prabhāvena prakṛti|sthā Sarasvatī
prasanna|salilā jajñe yathā pūrvaṃ tath" âiva hi.
nirmuktā ca saric|chreṣṭhā vibabhau sā yathā purā.

dṛṣṭvā toyaṃ Sarasvatyā munibhis tais tathā kṛtam
tān eva śaraṇaṃ jagmū rākṣasāḥ kṣudhitās tathā.
kṛtv" âñjaliṃ tato rājan rākṣasāḥ kṣudhay" ârditāḥ
ūcus tān vai munīn sarvān kṛpā|yuktān punaḥ punaḥ:

made a great effort to save Sarásvati. The illustrious men of great vows all gathered together and said these words after summoning that supreme river:

"Tell us why your water has become so troubled, lovely lady. When we have heard the reason, we will consider what to do."

Trembling, she told them everything that had happened. 43.10 On seeing her distressed state, the austerity-rich men replied:

"We have heard the reasons, faultless lady, and we have learned of your curse. We will all endeavor to help you, rich as we are in austerities."

Saying these words to that best of rivers, they talked among themselves thus: "Let us all release Sarásvati from her curse."

After propitiating Maha·deva, that lord of animals and ruler of the world, with austerities and disciplines, as well as various fasts, restraints, and painful vows, the brahmins all liberated that supreme river, the goddess Sarásvati. Through 43.15 their power, Sarásvati returned to her normal state and her waters became clear, just as before. Liberated, that best of rivers looked glorious, just as before.

When they saw the ascetics transform Sarásvati's waters in this way, the famished demons took refuge in the men. Stricken with hunger and cupping their hands in respect, the demons repeatedly said the following words to the compassionate ascetics:

«vayaṃ ca kṣudhitāś c' âiva dharmādd hīnāś ca śāśvatāt.
na ca naḥ kāma|kāro 'yaṃ yad vayaṃ pāpa|kāriṇaḥ.
yuṣmākaṃ c' â|prasādena duṣ|kṛtena ca karmaṇā
yat pāpaṃ vardhate 'smākaṃ yataḥ smo brahma|rākṣasāḥ
yoṣitāṃ c' âiva pāpena yoni|doṣa|kṛtena ca,

43.20 evaṃ hi vaiśya|śūdrāṇāṃ kṣatriyāṇāṃ tath" âiva ca
ye brāhmaṇān pradviṣanti te bhavant' îha rākṣasāḥ.
ācāryam ṛtvijaṃ c' âiva guruṃ vṛddha|janaṃ tathā
prāṇino ye 'vamanyante te bhavant' îha rākṣasāḥ.
tat kurudhvam ih' âsmākaṃ tāraṇaṃ dvija|sattamāḥ!
śaktā bhavantaḥ sarveṣāṃ lokānām api tāraṇe!»

teṣāṃ tu vacanaṃ śrutvā tuṣṭuvus tāṃ mahā|nadīm
mokṣ'|ârthaṃ rakṣasāṃ teṣām ūcuḥ prayata|mānasāḥ:

«kṣataṃ kīṭ'|âvapannaṃ ca yac c' ôcchiṣṭ'|ācitaṃ bhavet
sa|keśam avadhūtaṃ ca rudit'|ôpahataṃ ca yat
ebhiḥ saṃsṛṣṭam annaṃ ca bhāgo 'sau rakṣasām iha.

43.25 tasmāj jñātvā sadā vidvān etān yatnād vivarjayet.
rākṣas'|ânnam asau bhuṅkte yo bhuṅkte hy annam īdṛśam.»

śodhayitvā tatas tīrtham ṛṣayas te tapo|dhanāḥ
mokṣ'|ârthaṃ rākṣasānāṃ ca nadīṃ tāṃ pratyacodayan.
maha"|rṣīṇāṃ mataṃ jñātvā tataḥ sā saritāṃ varā
Aruṇām ānayām āsa svāṃ tanuṃ puruṣa'|rṣabha.
tasyāṃ te rākṣasāḥ snātvā tanūs tyaktvā divaṃ gatāḥ.
Aruṇāyāṃ mahā|rāja brahma|vadhy"|âpahā hi sā.
etam artham abhijñāya deva|rājaḥ śata|kratuḥ
tasmiṃs tīrthe vare snātvā vimuktaḥ pāpmanā kila.

"We were hungry and bereft of the eternal truth. We had o agency when we acted wrongfully. Your grace was absent nd we have acquired bad karma. Our sins have increased s brahmin *rákshasas* and our women suffer the evil that omes from the fault of their wombs.*

43.20 Vaishyas, shudras and kshatriyas who despise brahmins lso become *rákshasas* in this world. And those creatures vho have contempt for teachers, priests, instructors, or old eople also become *rákshasas* in this world. Save us, best of rahmins! You have the ability to save all the worlds!"

Hearing their words, the ascetics praised the great river nd, with pious minds, said the following words in order to elease the *rákshasas*:

"Any food that has been damaged, touched by insects, ejected or heaped together, or that contains hair, or is discarded, or tainted by tears, or consists of a mixture of all hese, will be the portion of *rákshasas* in this world. Knowing 43.25 his, a wise man should always carefully avoid such foods. Whoever eats such food eats the food of a *rákshasa*."

After they had purified the *tirtha*, the seers, who were ich in austerities, urged the river to liberate the demons. Jnderstanding the intention of the great seers, that best of ivers turned her body toward Aruná, bull of men.* The emons bathed in the Aruná river, abandoned their bodies, nd went to heaven. For it is at Aruná that Sarásvati can emove the sin of murdering a brahmin. Indra of a hundred sacrifices, that king of the gods, knew this and became eleased from his sin by bathing at this supreme sacred site.

JANAMEJAYA uvāca:

43.30 kim|artham bhagavāñ Śakro
brahma|vadhyām avāptavān?
katham asmiṃś ca tīrthe vai
āpluty' â|kalmaṣo 'bhavat?

VAIŚAMPĀYANA uvāca:

śṛṇuṣv' âitad upākhyānaṃ yathā|vṛttaṃ jan'|ēśvara
yathā bibheda samayaṃ Namucer Vāsavaḥ purā.
Namucir Vāsavād bhītaḥ sūrya|raśmiṃ samāviśat.
ten' Êndraḥ sakhyam akarot samayaṃ c' êdam abravīt:
«na c' ārdreṇa na śuṣkeṇa na rātrau n' âpi c' âhani
vadhiṣyāmy asura|śreṣṭha. sakhe satyena te śape.»
evaṃ sa kṛtvā samayaṃ dṛṣṭvā nīhāram īśvaraḥ
cicched' âsya śiro rājann apāṃ phenena Vāsavaḥ.
43.35 tac chiro Namuceś chinnaṃ pṛṣṭhataḥ Śakram anviyāt
«bho! bho! mitra|han pāp' êti» bruvāṇaṃ Śakram antikāt.
evaṃ sa śirasā tena codyamānaḥ punaḥ punaḥ
pitā|mahāya saṃtapta etam arthaṃ nyavedayat.
tam abravīl loka|gurur:
«Aruṇāyāṃ yathā|vidhi
iṣṭv" ôpaspṛśa dev'|êndra tīrthe pāpa|bhay'|âpahe.
eṣā puṇya|jalā Śakra kṛtā munibhir eva tu.
nigūḍham asy' āgamanam ih' āsīt pūrvam eva tu.
tato 'bhyety' Âruṇāṃ devīṃ plāvayām āsa vāriṇā.
Sarasvaty" Âruṇāyāś ca puṇyo 'yaṃ saṃgamo mahān.
43.40 iha tvaṃ yaja dev'|êndra. dada dānāny anekaśaḥ.
atr' āplutya su|ghorāt tvaṃ pātakād vipra mokṣyase.»

JANAM·ÉJAYA said:

Why did Lord Shakra murder a brahmin? How did he become liberated from his stain by bathing at this sacred site? 43.30

VAISHAMPÁYANA said:

Listen to the story of how Vásava broke his pact with Námuchi in the past, lord of the people.

Námuchi once entered a ray of the sun because of his fear of Vásava. Indra, however, befriended Námuchi and made this pact:

"Best of demons, I shall not slay you with anything wet or dry, and neither at night nor in the daytime. I swear this to you by the truth, my friend."

After he had made this agreement, Lord Vásava caught sight of some mist and cut off Námuchi's head with the foamy water.* Námuchi's sliced off head followed close behind Shakra, shouting: "You! You! Evil slayer of friends!" 43.35 Harrassed again and again by the head, tormented Indra informed the Grandfather of the matter and the teacher of the world said to him:

"Perform a sacrifice with due rites at Aruná, king of the gods, and sip the water at that *tirtha* since it removes the danger of sin. This river has had its waters purified by ascetics, Shakra. Her arrival here was previously concealed but Sarásvati then appeared at divine Aruná and flooded it with her waters. This great confluence between Sarásvati and Aruná is sacred. Perform a sacrifice here, king of the gods. Give many gifts. By bathing here, you will be freed from your terrible sin, wise Indra." 43.40

ity uktaḥ sa Sarasvatyāḥ kuñje vai Janamejaya
iṣṭvā yathāvad Bala|bhid Aruṇāyām upāspṛśat.
sa muktaḥ pāpmanā tena brahma|vadhyā|kṛtena ca
jagāma saṃhṛṣṭa|manās tri|divaṃ tri|daś'|ēśvaraḥ.
śiras tac c' âpi Namuces tatr' âiv' āplutya Bhārata
lokān kāma|dughān prāptam a|kṣayān rāja|sattama.

VAIŚAMPĀYANA uvāca:

tatr' âpy upaspṛśya Balo mah"|ātmā
dattvā ca dānāni pṛthag|vidhāni
avāpya dharmaṃ param'|ârtha|karmā
jagāma Somasya mahat su|tīrtham,

43.45 yatr' âyajad rāja|sūyena Somaḥ
s'|âkṣāt purā vidhivat pārthiv'|êndra
Atrir dhīmān vipra|mukhyo babhūva
hotā yasmin kratu|mukhye mah"|ātmā,
yasy' ânte 'bhūt su|mahad dānavānāṃ
daiteyānāṃ rākṣasānāṃ ca devaiḥ
yasmin yuddhaṃ Tārak'|ākhyaṃ su|tīvraṃ
yatra Skandas Tārak'|ākhyaṃ jaghāna,
saināpatyaṃ labdhavān devatānāṃ
Mahāseno yatra daity'|ânta|kartā
s'|âkṣāc c' âivaṃ nyavasat Kārttikeyaḥ
sadā Kumāro yatra sa plakṣa|rājaḥ.

Addressed in this way, Janam·éjaya, the slayer of Bala duly performed a sacrifice at the Bower of Sarásvati and sipped the water in the Aruná river. Released from the sin of slaying a brahmin, the lord of the thirty gods joyfully returned to heaven. Námuchi's head also plunged into the water, descendant of Bharata, and attained worlds that are deathless and that grant all desires.

VAISHAMPÁYANA said:

After great-spirited Bala had sipped the water at this site, he gave many kinds of gifts and attained merit. That man, whose actions have the highest purpose, then went to the fine and great *tirtha* of Soma. It was here, king of kings, that Soma himself once duly performed the Raja·suya sacrifice.* Wise and great-spirited Atri—that chief among brahmins—had been the *hotri* priest in that eminent sacrifice. At the end of the sacrifice, there was a huge battle between the gods and the *dánava*s, *daitéya*s and *rákshasa*s. This terrible battle was called Táraka because Skanda killed a demon called Táraka. It was here too that demon-slaying Maha·sena acquired generalship over the gods, and thus Kumára, or Karttikéya, always dwells in person where the King of Figs stands.

43.45

JANAMEJAYA uvāca:

44.1 SARASVATYĀḤ prabhāvo 'yam uktas te dvija|sattama.
Kumārasy' âbhiṣekaṃ tu brahman vyākhyātum arhasi.
yasmin deśe ca kāle ca yathā ca vadatāṃ vara
yaiś c' âbhiṣikto bhagavān vidhinā yena ca prabhuḥ,
Skando yathā ca daityānām akarot kadanaṃ mahat
tathā me sarvam ācakṣva. paraṃ kautūhalaṃ hi me.

VAIŚAMPĀYANA uvāca:

Kuru|vaṃśasya sadṛśam kautūhalam idaṃ tava.
harṣam utpādayaty eva vaco me Janamejaya.
44.5 hanta te kathayiṣyāmi śṛṇvānasya nar'|âdhipa
abhiṣekaṃ Kumārasya prabhāvaṃ ca mah"|ātmanaḥ.
tejo Māheśvaraṃ skannam agnau prapatitaṃ purā.
tat sarva|bhakṣo bhagavān n' âśakad dagdhum a|kṣayam.
ten' āsīdati tejasvī dīptimān havya|vāhanaḥ
na c' âiva dhārayām āsa garbhaṃ tejo|mayaṃ tadā.
sa Gaṅgām abhisaṃgamya niyogād Brahmaṇaḥ prabhuḥ
garbham āhitavān divyaṃ bhāskar'|ôpama|tejasam.
atha Gaṅg" âpi taṃ garbham a|sahantī vidhāraṇe
utsasarja girau ramye Himavaty a|mar'|ârcite.
sa tatra vavṛdhe lokān āvṛtya jvalan'|ātma|jaḥ.
44.10 dadṛśur jvalan'|ākāraṃ taṃ garbham atha Kṛttikāḥ
śara|stambe mah"|ātmānam anal'|ātma|jam īśvaram.
«mam' âyam! iti» tāḥ sarvāḥ putr'|ârthinyo 'bhicukruśuḥ.
tāsāṃ viditvā bhāvaṃ taṃ mātṝṇāṃ bhagavān prabhuḥ
prasnutānāṃ payaḥ ṣaḍbhir vadanair apibat tadā.

JANAM·ÉJAYA said:

YOU HAVE DESCRIBED the power of Sarásvati, best of twice-born brahmins. But you should describe the consecration of Kumára, brahmin. The place, the time, and the means; who consecrated the illustrious Lord and with what rite; and how Skanda massacred the *daityas*. Tell me everything, supreme narrator. For I have the greatest curiosity. 44.1

VAISHAMPÁYANA said:

Your curiosity suits one belonging to the Kuru lineage. My words will fill you with joy, Janam·éjaya. If you are listening, lord of men, I will describe great-spirited Kumára's consecration and his power. 44.5

In the past, Mahéshvara's vital seed was spilled and fell into a fire. Lord Agni, who consumes everything, was unable to incinerate the indestructible object. That bearer of oblations became splendid and powerful as a result, but was unable to support that embryo of radiant energy. Under the instruction of Brahma, Lord Agni went to Ganga and deposited in her the divine embryo, which was radiant as the sun. Unable to support the embryo, Ganga emitted it into the glorious Hímavat mountain, which is worshipped by immortals. Covering the worlds, that son of Fire then grew up in that place.

One day the Kríttikas* caught sight of the embryo—that great-spirited lord and son of Fire—as he lay in a clump of reeds bearing the appearance of a flame. In their desire for a son, all the Kríttikas exclaimed: "It's mine!" Realizing their disposition, the illustrious Lord drank milk from all six breastfeeding mothers by using six mouths. When 44.10

taṃ prabhāvaṃ samālakṣya tasya bālasya Kṛttikāḥ
paraṃ vismayam āpannā devyo divya|vapur|dharāḥ.
yatr' ôtsṛṣṭaḥ sa bhagavān Gaṅgayā giri|mūrdhani
sa śailaḥ kāñcanaḥ sarvaḥ saṃbabhau Kuru|sattama.
vardhatā c' âiva garbheṇa pṛthivī tena rañjitā
ataś ca sarve saṃvṛttā girayaḥ kāñcan'|ākarāḥ.

44.15 Kumāraḥ su|mahā|vīryaḥ Kārttikeya iti smṛtaḥ.
Gāṅgeyaḥ pūrvam abhavan mahā|yoga|bal'|ânvitaḥ.
śamena tapasā c' âiva vīryeṇa ca samanvitaḥ
vavṛdhe 'tīva rāj'|êndra candravat priya|darśanaḥ.
sa tasmin kāñcane divye śara|stambe śriyā vṛtaḥ
stūyamānaḥ sadā śete gandharvair munibhis tathā.
tath" âitam anvanṛtyanta deva|kanyāḥ sahasraśaḥ
divya|vāditra|nṛtya|jñāḥ stuvantyaś cāru|darśanāḥ.
anvāste ca nadī devaṃ Gaṅgā vai saritāṃ varā
dadhāra pṛthivī c' âinaṃ bibhratī rūpam uttamam.

44.20 jāta|karm'|ādikās tatra kriyāś cakre Bṛhaspatiḥ.
Vedaś c' âinaṃ catur|mūrtir upatasthe kṛt'|âñjaliḥ.
Dhanurvedaś catuṣ|pādaḥ śastra|grāmaḥ sa|Saṅgrahaḥ
tatr' âinaṃ samupātiṣṭhat s'|âkṣād Vāṇī ca kevalā.

sa dadarśa mahā|vīryaṃ deva|devam Umā|patim
Śaila|putryā samāsīnaṃ bhūta|saṅgha|śatair vṛtam.
nikāyā bhūta|saṅghānāṃ param'|âdbhuta|darśanāḥ
vikṛtā vikṛt'|ākārā vikṛt'|ābharaṇa|dhvajāḥ,
vyāghra|siṃha'|rkṣa|vadanā biḍāla|makar'|ānanāḥ
vṛṣa|daṃśa|mukhāś c' ânye gaj'|ôṣṭra|vadanās tathā

they saw the power of the child, the divine Kríttikas—who bore heavenly forms—became filled with great wonder. The entire mountain-peak where Ganga emitted the Lord became radiant with gold, best of Kurus. The earth became illuminated by the growing embryo and all the mountains appeared golden.

Mighty Kumára thus became known as Karttikéya. Previously known as Gangéya, he possessed great strength as a result of practicing Yoga. Endowed with serenity, asceticism, and power, he grew up to be extremely handsome, just like the moon, king of kings. He lay in that gold and divine clump of reeds, surrounded by glory and continuously worshipped by *gandhárvas* and ascetics. Thousands of beautiful young goddesses—skilled in divine music and dance—danced before him, praising him. The river Ganga, that best of rivers, served the god and the earth held him, bearing a beautiful form. Brihas·pati performed Kumára's birth-rites and other ceremonies there. The fourfold Veda* attended him with hands cupped in respect. The 'Dhanur·veda,' with its four sections and collection of weapons, waited upon him at that site, together with the *sángraha*.* Speech also waited upon him alone and in person. 44.15 44.20

Kumára saw the husband of Uma, that mighty god of gods, sitting together with Mount Hímavat's daughter and surrounded by hundreds of hordes of spirits. These troops of ghostly hordes had wondrous appearances. Transforming themselves, their forms changed and their ornaments and banners changed too. They had the faces of tigers, lions, bears, cats, and *mákaras*.* Some had the mouths of cats, while others had the faces of elephants or camels. Some

ulūka|vadanāḥ ke cid gṛdhra|gomāyu|darśanāḥ,
44.25 krauñca|pārāvata|nibhair vadanai rāṅkavair api
śvā|vic|chalyaka|godhānāṃ aj'|âiḍaka|gavāṃ tathā
sadṛśāni vapūṃṣy anye tatra tatra vyadhārayan.
ke cic chail'|âmbuda|prakhyāś cakr'|ôdyata|gad"|āyudhāḥ
ke cid añjana|puñj'|ābhāḥ ke cic chvet'|âcala|prabhāḥ.

sapta mātṛ|gaṇāś c' âiva samājagmur viśāṃ pate
sādhyā Viśve 'tha Maruto Vasavaḥ Pitaras tathā,
Rudr'|ādityās tathā siddhā bhujagā dānavāḥ khagāḥ
Brahmā svayaṃ|bhūr bhagavān sa|putraḥ saha Viṣṇunā.
Śakras tath" âbhyayād draṣṭuṃ kumāra|varam a|cyutam
Nārada|pramukhāś c' âpi deva|gandharva|sattamāḥ.
44.30 deva'|rṣayaś ca siddhāś ca Bṛhaspati|puro|gamāḥ
pitaro jagataḥ śreṣṭhā devānām api devatāḥ
te 'pi tatra samājagmur Yāmā Dhāmāś ca sarvaśaḥ.

sa tu bālo 'pi balavān mahā|yoga|bal'|ânvitaḥ
abhyājagāma dev'|ēśaṃ śūla|hastaṃ pinākinam.
tam āvrajantam ālakṣya Śivasy' āsīn mano|gatam
yugapac Shaila|putryāś ca Gaṅgāyāḥ Pāvakasya ca:
«kaṃ nu pūrvam ayaṃ bālo gauravād abhyupaiṣyati?
api mām iti?» sarveṣāṃ teṣām āsīn mano|gatam.

teṣām etam abhiprāyaṃ caturṇām upalakṣya saḥ
yugapad yogam āsthāya sasarja vividhās tanūḥ.
44.35 tato 'bhavac catur|mūrtiḥ kṣaṇena bhagavān prabhuḥ.
tasya Śākho Viśākhaś ca Naigameyaś ca pṛṣṭhataḥ.
evaṃ sa kṛtvā hy ātmānaṃ caturdhā bhagavān prabhuḥ
yato Rudras tataḥ Skando jagām' âdbhuta|darśanaḥ,

had the faces of owls, others the appearances of vultures or jackals. Here and there, others had bodies that resembled porcupines,* iguanas, goats, sheep, or cows, and faces that looked like curlews, pigeons, or ranku deer. Some looked like mountains or clouds, some were armed with discuses or raised maces, some resembled masses of collyrium, while others had the appearance of white mountains. 44.25

The seven groups of mothers also gathered there, lord of the people, as did the *sadhyas*, Vishvas, Maruts, Vasus, Ancestors, Rudras, *adítyas*, *siddhas*, snakes, *dánavas*, birds, self-created Lord Brahma, the son of Brahma, and Vishnu. Shakra too went to see that fine and imperishable child, along with eminent gods and *gandhárvas* who were led by Nárada. The gods and seers, as well as the *siddhas* who were led by Brihas·pati, the fathers of the universe, and the most eminent deities all gathered there, along with the Yámas and Dhamas.* 44.30

Although a mere child, mighty Kumára, who possessed great powers from yogic discipline, approached trident-bearing Shiva, that lord of the gods. When they saw him approaching, Shiva, Mount Hímavat's daughter, Ganga, and Fire all had the same simultaneous thought: "Whom will the child first approach out of respect? Will it be me?"

Observing the thoughts of the four gods, Kumára applied his yogic power and emitted several bodies at the same time. In an instant the illustrious Lord had four aspects. Those that stood behind him were Shakha, Vishákha, and Naigaméya. After the illustrious Lord had thus divided himself into four, Skanda—a wonder to behold—approached Rudra, while Vishákha approached the divine daughter of 44.35

Viśākhas tu yayau yena devī giri|var'|ātma|jā
Śākho yayau ca bhagavān Vāyu|mūrtir Vibhāvasum
Naigameyo 'gamad Gaṅgāṃ kumāraḥ pāvaka|prabhaḥ.
sarve bhāsura|dehās te catvāraḥ sama|rūpiṇaḥ
tān samabhyayur a|vyagrās. tad adbhutam iv' âbhavat.
hā|hā|kāro mahān āsīd deva|dānava|rakṣasām
tad dṛṣṭvā mahad āścaryam adbhutaṃ loma|harṣaṇam.
44.40 tato Rudraś ca devī ca Pāvakaś ca Pitāmaham
Gaṅgayā sahitāḥ sarve praṇipetur jagat|patim.
praṇipatya tatas te tu vidhivad rāja|puṃ|gava
idam ūcur vaco rājan Kārttikeya|priy'|ēpsayā:
«asya bālasya bhagavann ādhipatyaṃ yath"|ēpsitam
asmat|priy'|ârthaṃ dev'|ēśa sadṛśaṃ dātum arhasi.»
tataḥ sa bhagavān dhīmān sarva|loka|pitā|mahaḥ
manasā cintayām āsa «kim ayaṃ labhatām iti.»
aiśvaryāṇi ca sarvāṇi deva|gandharva|rakṣasām
bhūta|yakṣa|vihaṃgānāṃ pannagānāṃ ca sarvaśaḥ
44.45 pūrvam ev' ādideś' âsau nikāyeṣu mah"|ātmanām
samarthaṃ ca tam aiśvarye mahā|matir amanyata.
tato muhūrtaṃ sa dhyātvā devānāṃ śreyasi sthitaḥ
saināpatyaṃ dadau tasmai sarva|bhūteṣu Bhārata.
sarva|deva|nikāyānāṃ ye rājānaḥ pariśrutāḥ
tān sarvān vyādideś' âsmai sarva|bhūta|pitā|mahaḥ.
tataḥ Kumāram ādāya devā Brahma|puro|gamāḥ
abhiṣek'|ârtham ājagmuḥ śail'|êndraṃ sahitās tataḥ,
puṇyāṃ Haimavatīṃ devīṃ saric|chreṣṭhāṃ Sarasvatīm
Samantapañcake yā vai triṣu lokeṣu viśrutā.

supreme Mount Hímavat, illustrious Shakha approached Vibha·vasu in the form of Vayu, and Naigaméya—that child of fiery radiance—approached Ganga. These four radiant forms all calmly approached the gods, bearing equal appearances. It was like a miracle.

The gods, *dánavas*, and *rákshasas* all cheered loudly when they saw that great and wonderful hair-raising miracle. Rudra, the goddess Uma, Fire, and Ganga all bowed before the Grandfather, that lord of the world. After duly bowing, bull among kings, they said these words in their desire to favor Karttikéya: 44.40

"Lord and ruler of the gods, as a kindness to us please offer this child some suitable and desirable power."

That wise Lord, the Grandfather of the entire world, then pondered what the child should receive. He had previously designated among troops of great-spirited beings every sovereignty over the gods, *gandhárvas*, and *rákshasas*, as well as over all spirits, *yakshas*, birds, and snakes. And wise Brahma considered that Kumára too was capable of sovereignty. After considering the matter for a while, Brahma, who was concerned with the good of the gods, gave Kumára generalship over all creatures, descendant of Bharata. The Grandfather of every creature therefore allocated him all the gods who were celebrated as rulers over all troops of deities. 44.45

Taking Kumára with them, the gods, who were led by Brahma, then went to the king of the mountains in order to consecrate the child. Approaching auspicious and divine Sarásvati, that supreme river whose source lies in the Hímavat, they went to the site of Samánta·pánchaka,

44.50 tatra tīre Sarasvatyāḥ puṇye sarva|guṇ'|ânvite
niṣedur deva|gandharvāḥ sarve saṃpūrṇa|mānasāḥ.

VAIŚAMPĀYANA uvāca:

45.1 TATO 'BHIṢEKA|saṃbhārān sarvān saṃbhṛtya śāstrataḥ
Bṛhaspatiḥ samiddhe 'gnau juhāv' âgniṃ yathā|vidhi.
tato Himavatā datte maṇi|pravara|śobhite
divya|ratn'|ācite puṇye niṣaṇṇaḥ param'|āsane.
sarva|maṅgala|saṃbhārair vidhi|mantra|puras|kṛtam
ābhiṣecanikaṃ dravyaṃ gṛhītvā devatā|gaṇāḥ,
Indra|Viṣṇū mahā|vīryau sūryā|candramasau tathā
Dhātā c' âiva Vidhātā ca tathā c' âiv' ânil'|ânalau,
45.5 Pūṣṇā Bhagen' Âryamṇā ca Aṃśena* ca Vivasvatā
Rudraś ca sahito dhīmān Mitreṇa Varuṇena ca,
Rudrair Vasubhir ādityair Aśvibhyāṃ ca vṛtaḥ prabhuḥ
Viśvedevair Marudbhiś ca sādhyaiś ca Pitṛbhiḥ saha,
gandharvair apsarobhiś ca yakṣa|rākṣasa|pannagaiḥ
deva'|rṣibhir a|saṅkhyātais tathā brahma'|rṣibhis tathā,
Vaikhānasair Vālakhilyair vāyv|āhārair marīci|paiḥ
Bhṛgubhiś c' Âṅgirobhiś ca Yatibhiś ca mah"|ātmabhiḥ
sarvair vidyā|dharaiḥ puṇyair yoga|siddhais tathā vṛtaḥ,
Pitāmahaḥ Pulastyaś ca Pulahaś ca mahā|tapāḥ
Aṅgirāḥ Kaśyapo 'triś ca Marīcir Bhṛgur eva ca
Kratur Haraḥ Pracetāś ca Manur Dakṣas tath" âiva ca,

which is renowned throughout the three worlds. Their desires fulfilled, the gods and *gandhárvas* all took their seats on Sarásvati's holy bank, which is endowed with every virtue. 44.50

VAISHAMPÁYANA said:

AFTER GATHERING all the items that are prescribed by the Teachings as necessary for a consecration, Brihas·pati performed an oblation in a kindled fire in the proper manner. He then sat down in a fine chair offered by Hímavat. The chair was covered with divine jewels and glistened with excellent gems. Hosts of gods brought consecration objects that were invested with rites and mantras and accompanied by every kind of auspicious item. Mighty Indra and Vishnu also came and gathered there, as did the Sun and Moon, Dhatri and Vidhátri, and the Wind and Fire. 45.1

Wise Rudra was also there, accompanied by Pushan, Bhaga, Áryaman, Ansha, Vivásvat, Mitra and Váruna.* The lord was surrounded by the Rudras, Vasus, *adítyas*, Ashvins, Vishve·devas, Maruts, *sadhyas*, and Ancestors, as well as by *gandhárvas*, nymphs, *yakshas*, *rákshasas*, snakes, countless gods and seers, and brahmin ascetics. He was also surrounded by Vaikhánasa ascetics, Valakhílya ascetics, ascetics who eat the wind and who drink the rays of the sun, by descendants of Bhrigu and Ángiras, by great-spirited Yatis, all the *vidya·dharas*, and those pure beings who have attained perfection through Yoga. 45.5

The Grandfather was also there, as was Pulástya, Púlaha of great austerities, Ángiras, Káshyapa, Atri, Maríchi, Bhrigu, Kratu, Hara, Prachétas, Manu, and Daksha. The seasons also gathered there, lord of the people, as did the 45.10

45.10 ṛtavaś ca grahāś c' âiva jyotīṃṣi ca viśāṃ pate
mūrtimatyaś ca sarito vedāś c' âiva sanātanāḥ,
samudrāś ca hradāś c' âiva tīrthāni vividhāni ca
pṛthivī dyaur diśaś c' âiva pādapāś ca jan'|âdhipa,
Aditir deva|mātā ca Hrīḥ Śrīḥ Svāhā Sarasvatī
Umā Śacī Sinīvālī tathā c' Ânumatiḥ Kuhūḥ
Rākā ca Dhiṣaṇā c' âiva patnyaś c' ânyā div'|âukasām,
Himavāṃś c' âiva Vindhyaś ca Meruś c' âneka|śṛṅgavān
Airāvataḥ s'|ânucaraḥ Kalāḥ Kāṣṭhās tath" âiva ca
Mās'|ârdhamāsā Ṛtavas tathā Rātry|Ahanī nṛpa,
Uccaiḥśravā haya|śreṣṭho nāga|rājaś ca Vāsukiḥ
Aruṇo Garuḍaś c' âiva Vṛkṣāś c' Auṣadhibhiḥ saha
Dharmaś ca bhagavān devaḥ samājagmur hi saṃgatāḥ.
45.15 Kālo Yamaś ca Mṛtyuś ca Yamasy' ânucarāś ca ye
bahulatvāc ca n' ôktā ye vividhā devatā|gaṇāḥ
te Kumār'|âbhiṣek'|ârthaṃ samājagmus tatas tataḥ.

jagṛhus te tadā rājan sarva eva div'|âukasaḥ
ābhiṣecanikaṃ bhāṇḍaṃ maṅgalāni ca sarvaśaḥ.
divya|saṃbhāra|saṃyuktaiḥ kalaśaiḥ kāñcanair nṛpa
Sarasvatībhiḥ puṇyābhir divya|toyābhir eva tu,
abhyaṣiñcan Kumāraṃ vai saṃprahṛṣṭā div'|âukasaḥ
senā|patiṃ mah"|ātmānam asurāṇāṃ bhayaṅ|karam.
purā yathā mahā|rāja Varuṇaṃ vai jal'|ēśvaram
tath" âbhyaṣiñcad bhagavān sarva|loka|pitā|mahaḥ
Kaśyapaś ca mahā|tejā ye c' ânye loka|kīrtitāḥ.

planets, the stars, the rivers in embodied form, the eternal Vedas, the oceans, the lakes, the different *tirthas*, the earth, the sky, the directions, and the trees, protector of the people. Áditi, mother of the *adítya* gods, was also there, as was Hri, Shri, Svaha, Sarásvati, Uma, Shachi, Siniváli, Ánumati, Kuhu, Raka, Dhíshana, and the other wives of the gods. Hímavat was there too, along with Vindhya and many-peaked Meru, as was Airávata and his attendants, and also the Kalás, Kashthas, Months, Fortnights, Seasons, Night and Day, Your Majesty.* Ucchaih·shravas, that best of horses, Vásuki, the king of the *nagas*, Áruna, Gáruda, the Trees, the Herbs, and Dharma, that divine Lord, also came and gathered there. Kala, Yama, Death, Yama's attendants, and various hosts of gods that cannot be described because of their large numbers also assembled there for Kumára's consecration.

45.15

Every one of the gods carried objects of consecration along with all kinds of auspicious items. Using golden jars that contained divine articles, the gods joyfully sprinkled Kumára with Sarásvati's pure and divine waters and consecrated him as their general, a hero to terrorize demons. Just as they had once consecrated Váruna, that lord of the waters, in the past, so the illustrious Grandfather of the entire world, as well as splendid Káshyapa and the other beings who were renowned throughout the world, consecrated Kumára, Your Majesty.

45.20 tasmai Brahmā dadau prīto balino vāta|raṃhasaḥ
kāma|vīrya|dharān siddhān mahā|pāriṣadān prabhuḥ:
Nandisenaṃ Lohitākṣaṃ Ghaṇṭākarṇaṃ ca saṃmatam
caturtham asy' ânucaraṃ khyātaṃ Kumudamālinam.
tatra Sthāṇuṃ mahā|tejā mahā|pāriṣadaṃ prabhuḥ
māyā|śata|dharaṃ kāmaṃ kāma|vīrya|bal'|ânvitam
dadau Skandāya rāj'|êndra sur'|âri|vinibarhaṇam.
sa hi dev'|âsure yuddhe daityānāṃ bhīma|karmaṇām
jaghāna dorbhyāṃ saṃkruddhaḥ prayutāni catur|daśa.

tathā devā dadus tasmai senāṃ nairṛta|saṃkulām
deva|śatru|kṣaya|karīm a|jayyāṃ viśva|rūpiṇīm.
45.25 jaya|śabdaṃ tathā cakrur devāḥ sarve sa|Vāsavāḥ
gandharvā yakṣa|rakṣāṃsi munayaḥ pitaras tathā.

tataḥ prādād anucarau Yamaḥ Kāl'|ôpamāv ubhau
Unmāthaś ca Pramāthaś ca mahā|vīryau mahā|dyutī.
Subhrājo Bhāskaraś c' âiva yau tau Sūry'|ânuyāyinau
tau Sūryaḥ Kārttikeyāya dadau prītaḥ pratāpavān.
Kailāsa|śṛṅga|saṃkāśau śveta|māly'|ânulepanau
Somo 'py anucarau prādān Maṇiṃ Sumaṇim eva ca.
Jvālā|Jihvaṃ tathā jyotir ātma|jāya hut'|âśanaḥ
dadāv anucarau śūrau para|sainya|pramāthinau.

Lord Brahma then joyfully gave Kumára four great attendants who were mighty and swift as the wind, and who had attained perfection and wielded whatever power they desired. They were: Nandi·sena, Lohitáksha, the attendant known as Ghantákarna, and a fourth called Kúmuda·malin. The glorious lord also gave Skanda Sthanu as a great attendant, king of kings. Able to produce a hundred illusions at will, Sthanu could wield any power and strength he desired and crushed the enemies of the gods. In a battle between the gods and demons, wrathful Sthanu slew fourteen million terrifying *daitya*s with his arms. 45.20

In this way, the gods gave Kumára a diverse and invincible army, which abounded with *náirrita*s and brought destruction to the enemies of the gods. All the gods and Vásava, as well as the *gandhárva*s, *yaksha*s, *rákshasa*s, ascetics and ancestors then cried out a shout of victory. 45.25

Yama then gave Kumára two attendants—Unmátha and Pramátha—who were endowed with great might and splendor and who resembled Time. The brilliant Sun also joyfully gave Karttikéya two of his followers: Subhrája and Bháskara. The Moon too gave him two attendants—Mani and Súmani—who looked like the peaks of Mount Kailása and who wore white garlands and ointments. In the same way, oblation-consuming Fire also gave two heroic attendants to his son, Jvala and Jihva, who crushed enemy troops.

45.30 Parighaṃ ca Vaṭaṃ c' âiva Bhīmaṃ ca su|mahā|balam
Dahatiṃ Dahanaṃ c' âiva pracaṇḍau vīrya|saṃmatau
Aṃśo 'py anucarān pañca dadau Skandāya dhīmate.
Utkrośaṃ Pañcakaṃ c' âiva vajra|daṇḍa|dharāv ubhau
dadāv anala|putrāya Vāsavaḥ para|vīra|hā;
tau hi śatrūn Mahendrasya jaghnatuḥ samare bahūn.
Cakraṃ Vikramakaṃ c' âiva Saṅkramaṃ ca mahā|balam
Skandāya trīn anucarān dadau Viṣṇur mahā|yaśāḥ.
Vardhanaṃ Nandanaṃ c' âiva sarva|vidyā|viśāradau
Skandāya dadatuḥ prītāv Aśvinau bhiṣajāṃ varau.
Kundaṃ ca Kusumaṃ c' âiva Kumudaṃ ca mahā|yaśāḥ
Ḍambar'|Āḍambarau c' âiva dadau Dhātā mah"|ātmane.
45.35 Cakr'|Ânucakrau balinau megha|cakrau bal'|ôtkaṭau
dadau Tvaṣṭā mahā|māyau Skandāy' ânucarāv ubhau.

Suvrataṃ Satyasandhaṃ ca dadau Mitro mah"|ātmane
Kumārāya mah"|ātmānau tapo|vidyā|dharau prabhuḥ.
su|darśanīyau vara|dau triṣu lokeṣu viśrutau
Suvrataṃ ca mah"|ātmānaṃ Śubhakarmāṇam eva ca
Kārttikeyāya saṃprādād Vidhātā loka|viśrutau.
Pāṇītakaṃ Kālikaṃ ca mahā|māyāvināv ubhau
Pūṣā ca pārṣadau prādāt Kārttikeyāya Bhārata.
Balaṃ c' Âtibalaṃ c' âiva mahā|vaktrau mahā|balau
pradadau Kārttikeyāya Vāyur Bharata|sattama.
45.40 Yamaṃ c' Âtiyamaṃ c' âiva timi|vaktrau mahā|balau
pradadau Kārttikeyāya Varuṇaḥ satya|saṃgaraḥ.

Ansha gave wise Skanda five attendants: Párigha, Vata, and mighty Bhima, as well as Dáhati and Dáhana, both of whom were fierce and renowned for their power. Vásava—that slayer of enemy heroes—gave the son of Fire Utkrósha and Pánchaka, who both wielded a thunderbolt and club and had killed many of Mahéndra's enemies in battle. Glorious Vishnu gave Skanda three attendants: Chakra, Víkramaka and mighty Sánkrama. Those supreme physicians, the Ashvins, joyfully gave Skanda Várdhana and Nándana, who were expert in every science. Glorious Dhatri gave Kunda, Kúsuma, Kúmuda, Dámbara and Adámbara to heroic Kumára. Tvashtri gave Skanda two mighty attendants, Chakra and Anuchákra, who wielded great magic powers, brandished cloud-discuses, and were superior in strength. 45.30 45.35

Lord Mitra gave great-spirited Kumára Súvrata and Satya·sandha, heroes that wielded knowledge and ascetic power. Vidhátri gave Karttikéya heroic Súvrata and also Shubha·karman—handsome boon-givers who were renowned in the three worlds and famous throughout the universe. Pushan gave Karttikéya two companions, descendant of Bharata: Panítaka and Kálika, both of whom wielded great magic powers. The Wind gave Karttikéya Bala and Átibala, who had large mouths and great strength, best of Bharatas. Váruna, who is true to his promises, gave Karttikéya Yama and Átiyama, who were powerful and had the mouths of whales. 45.40

Suvarcasaṃ mah"|ātmānaṃ tath" âiv' âpy Ativarcasam
Himavān pradadau rājan hut'|âśana|sutāya vai.
Kāñcanaṃ ca mah"|ātmānaṃ Meghamālinam eva ca
dadāv anucarau Merur agni|putrāya Bhārata.
Sthiraṃ c' Âtisthiraṃ c' âiva Merur ev' âparau dadau
mah"|ātmā tv agni|putrāya mahā|bala|parākramau.
Ucchṛṅgaṃ c' Âtiśṛṅgaṃ ca mahā|pāṣāṇa|yodhinau
pradadāv agni|putrāya Vindhyaḥ pāriṣadāv ubhau.

45.45 Saṅgrahaṃ Vigrahaṃ c' âiva Samudro 'pi gadā|dharau
pradadāv agni|putrāya mahā|pāriṣadāv ubhau.
Unmādaṃ Śaṅkukarṇaṃ ca Puṣpadantaṃ tath" âiva ca
pradadāv agni|putrāya Pārvatī śubha|darśanā.
Jayaṃ Mahājayaṃ c' âiva nāgau jvalana|sūnave
pradadau puruṣa|vyāghra Vāsukiḥ pannag'|ēśvaraḥ.
evaṃ sādhyāś ca Rudrāś ca Vasavaḥ Pitaras tathā
Sāgarāḥ Saritaś c' âiva Girayaś ca mahā|balāḥ,
daduḥ senā|gaṇ'|âdhyakṣāñ śūla|paṭṭiśa|dhāriṇaḥ
divya|praharaṇ'|ôpetān nānā|veṣa|vibhūṣitān.

45.50 śṛṇu nāmāni c' âpy eṣāṃ ye 'nye Skandasya sainikāḥ
vividh'|āyudha|saṃpannāś citr'|ābharaṇa|bhūṣitāḥ:
Śaṅkukarṇo Nikumbhaś ca Padmaḥ Kumuda eva ca
Ananto Dvādaśabhujas tathā Kṛṣṇ'|Ôpakṛṣṇakau,
Ghrāṇaśravāḥ Kapiskandhaḥ Kāñcanākṣo Jalandhamaḥ
Akṣaḥ Santarjano rājan Kunadīkas Tamobhrakṛt,
Ekākṣo Dvādaśākṣaś ca tath" âiv' Âikajaṭaḥ prabhuḥ
Sahasrabāhur Vikaṭo Vyāghrākṣaḥ Kṣitikampanaḥ,
Puṇyanāmā Sunāmā ca Sucakraḥ Priyadarśanaḥ
Pariśrutaḥ Kokanadaḥ Priyamālyānulepanaḥ;

Hímavat gave great-spirited Suvárchasa and Ativárchasa to the son of oblation-consuming Fire, Your Majesty. Meru gave the son of Fire two attendants: heroic Kánchana and Megha·malin, descendant of Bharata. Great-spirited Meru also gave another two attendants to the son of Fire: Sthira and Atísthira, both of whom possessed great strength and courage. Vindhya gave the son of Fire two attendants: Uc-chrínga and Atishrínga, who both fought with huge stones. The Ocean also gave the son of Fire two great attendants, Sángraha and Vígraha, who both wielded maces. Párvati, who is auspicious to see, gave Unmáda, Shanku·karna and Pushpa·danta to the son of Fire. Vásuki, that lord of snakes, gave the son of Fire two *naga*s: Jaya and Maha·jaya, O tiger among men. And in the same way, the *sadhya*s, Rudras, Vasus, Ancestors, Seas, Rivers, and mighty Mountains gave Kumára army commanders who wielded pikes, spears and divine weapons and who were adorned with various clothes. 45.45

Listen now to the names of Skanda's other troops, who brandished various weapons and were adorned with different ornaments. They were:* Shanku·karna, Nikúmbha, Padma, Kúmuda, Anánta, Dvádasha·bhuja, Krishna, and Up-akríshnaka; Ghrana·shravas, Kapi·skandha, Kanchanáksha, Jalándhama, Aksha, Santárjana, Kunadíka, and Tamóbhra-krit, Your Majesty; Ekáksha, Dvadasháksha, lord Eka·jata, Sahásra·bahu, Víkata, Vyaghráksha, and Kshiti·kámpana; Punya·naman, Sunáman, Suchákra, Priya·dárshana, Parí-shruta, Kókanada, and Priya·mályanulépana; 45.50

45.55 Ajodaro Gajaśirāḥ Skandhākṣaḥ Śatalocanaḥ
Jvālājihvaḥ Karālākṣaḥ Śitikeśo Jaṭī Hariḥ
Pariśrutaḥ Kokanadaḥ Kṛṣṇakeśo Jaṭādharaḥ,
Caturdaṃṣṭro 'ṣṭajihvaś ca Meghanādaḥ Pṛthuśravāḥ
Vidyutākṣo Dhanurvaktro Jāṭharo Mārutāśanaḥ,
Udārākṣo Rathākṣaś ca Vajranābho Vasuprabhaḥ
Samudravego rāj'|êndra Śailakampī tath" âiva ca,
Vṛṣo Meṣaḥ Pravāhaś ca tathā Nand'|Ôpanandakau
Dhūmraḥ Śvetaḥ Kaliṅgaś ca Siddhārtho Varadas tathā,
Priyakaś c' âiva Nandaś ca Gonandaś ca pratāpavān
Ānandaś ca Pramodaś ca Svastiko Dhruvakas tathā;
45.60 Kṣemavāhaḥ Suvāhaś ca Siddhapātraś ca Bhārata
Govrajaḥ Kanakāpīḍo mahā|pāriṣad'|ēśvaraḥ,
Gāyano Hasanaś c' âiva Bāṇaḥ Khaḍgaś ca vīryavān
Vaitālī Gatitālī ca tathā Kathaka|Vātikau,
Haṃsajaḥ Paṅkadigdhāṅgaḥ Samudronmādanaś ca ha
Raṇotkaṭaḥ Prahāsaś ca Śvetasiddhaś ca Nandanaḥ,
Kālakaṇṭhaḥ Prabhāsaś ca tathā Kumbhāṇḍakodaraḥ
Kālakakṣaḥ Sitaś c' âiva bhūtānāṃ mathanas tathā,
Yajñavāhaḥ Suvāhaś ca Devayājī ca Somapaḥ
Majjanaś ca mahā|tejāḥ Kratha|Krāthau ca Bhārata;
45.65 Tuharaś ca Tuhāraś ca Citradevaś ca vīryavān
Madhuraḥ Suprasādaś ca Kirīṭī ca mahā|balaḥ,
Vatsalo Madhuvarṇaś ca Kalaśodara eva ca
Dharmado Manmathakaraḥ Sūcīvaktraś ca vīryavān,
Śvetavaktraḥ Suvaktraś ca Cāruvaktraś ca Pāṇḍuraḥ
Daṇḍabāhuḥ Subāhuś ca Rajaḥ Kokilakas tathā,
Acalaḥ Kanakākṣaś ca bālānām api yaḥ prabhuḥ
Sañcārakaḥ Kokanado Gṛdhrapatraś ca Jambukaḥ,
Lohājavaktro Javanaḥ Kumbhavaktraś ca Kumbhakaḥ

Ajódara, Gaja·shiras, Skandháksha, Shata·lóchana, Jvala· ihva, Karaláksha, Shiti·kesha, Jatin, Hari, Paríshruta, Kóka- ıada, Krishna·kesha, and Jata·dhara; Chatur·danstra, Ashta· ihva, Megha·nada, Prithu·shravas, Vidyutáksha, Dhanur· ,aktra, Játhara, and Marutáshana; Udaráksha, Ratháksha, Vajra·nabha, Vasu·prabha, Samúdra·vega, and Shaila·kam- ɔin, O king of kings; Vrisha, Mesha, Praváha, Nanda, Upa- ıándaka, Dhumra, Shveta, Kalínga, Siddhártha, and Várada; Príyaka, Nanda, mighty Go·nanda, Anánda, Pra- nóda, Svástika, and Dhrúvaka; Kshema·vaha, Suváha, Siddha·patra, Go·vraja, and Kanakápida, that chief of great ıttendants, descendant of Bharata; Gáyana, Hásana, Bana, ɔowerful Khadga, Vaitálin, Gati·talin, Káthaka, and Vátika; Hánsaja, Panka·digdhánga, Samúdronmádana, Ranótkata, Prahása, Shveta·siddha, and Nándana; Kala·kantha, Pra- ɔhása, Kumbhándakódara, Kala·kaksha, and Sita, that de- troyer of spirits; Yajna·vaha, Suváha, Deva·yajin, Sómapa, ɔowerful Májjana, Kratha, and Krátha,* descendant of Bha- ata; Túhara, Tuhára, mighty Chitra·deva, Mádhura, Supra- áda, and powerful Kirítin; Vátsala, Madhu·varna, Kala- hódara, Dhármada, Mánmatha·kara, and mighty Suchi· aktra; Shveta·vaktra, Suváktra, Charu·vaktra, Pándura, Danda·bahu, Subáhu, Raja, and Kókilaka; Áchala, Kana- káksha, that lord of children, Sancháraka, Kókanada, Gridhra·patra, and Jámbuka; Lohája·vaktra, Jávana, Kumbha·vaktra, Kúmbhaka, Svarna·griva, Krishnáujas, Hansa·vaktra, and Chándrabha; Pani·kurchas, Shambúka, Pancha·vaktra, Shíkshaka, Chasha·vaktra, Jambúka, Shaka· aktra, and Kúnjala.

45.55 45.60 45.65 45.70

Svarṇagrīvaś ca Kṛṣṇaujā Haṃsavaktraś ca Candrabhaḥ,
45.70 Pāṇikūrcāś ca Śambūkaḥ Pañcavaktraś ca Śikṣakaḥ
Cāṣavaktraś ca Jambūkaḥ Śākavaktraś ca Kuñjalaḥ.
yoga|yuktā mah"|ātmānaḥ satataṃ brāhmaṇa|priyāḥ
paitāmahā mah"|ātmāno mahā|pāriṣadāś ca ye
yauvana|sthāś ca bālāś ca vṛddhāś ca Janamejaya,
sahasraśaḥ pāriṣadāḥ Kumāram avatasthire.
vaktrair nānā|vidhair ye tu śṛṇu tāñ Janamejaya:
kūrma|kukkuṭa|vaktrāś ca śaś'|ôlūka|mukhās tathā
khar'|ôṣṭra|vadanāś c' âiva varāha|vadanās tathā,
mārjāra|śaśa|vaktrāś ca dīrgha|vaktrāś ca Bhārata
nakul'|ôlūka|vaktrāś ca kāka|vaktrās tathā pare,
45.75 ākhu|babhruka|vaktrāś ca mayūra|vadanās tathā
matsya|meṣ'|ānanāś c' ânye aj'|âvi|mahiṣ'|ānanāḥ,
ṛkṣa|śārdūla|vaktrāś ca dvīpi|siṃh'|ānanās tathā
bhīmā gaj'|ānanāś c' âiva tathā nakra|mukhāś ca ye,
garuḍ'|ānanāḥ kaṅka|mukhā vṛka|kāka|mukhās tathā
go|khar'|ôṣṭra|mukhāś c' ânye vṛṣa|daṃśa|mukhās tathā,
mahā|jaṭhara|pād'|âṅgās tārak'|âkṣāś ca Bhārata
pārāvata|mukhāś c' ânye tathā vṛṣa|mukhāḥ pare,
kokil'|ābh"|ānanāś c' ânye śyena|tittirik'|ānanāḥ
kṛkalāsa|mukhāś c' âiva virajo|'mbara|dhāriṇaḥ;
45.80 vyāla|vaktrāḥ śūla|mukhāś caṇḍa|vaktrāḥ śubh'|ānanāḥ
āśī|viṣāś cīra|dharā go|nāsā|vadanās tathā,
sthūl'|ôdarāḥ kṛś'|âṅgāś ca sthūl'|âṅgāś ca kṛś'|ôdarāḥ
hrasva|grīvā mahā|karṇā nānā|vyāla|vibhūṣaṇāḥ,
gaj'|êndra|carma|vasanās tathā kṛṣṇ'|âjin'|âmbarāḥ
skandhe|mukhā mahā|rāja tath" âpy udarato|mukhāḥ,
pṛṣṭhe|mukhā hanu|mukhās tathā jaṅghā|mukhā api
pārśv'|ānanāś ca bahavo nānā|deśa|mukhās tathā;

Belonging to the Grandfather, these great attendants were disciplined, great-spirited, constantly dear to brahmins, and heroic. Some of the attendants were youths, some were children, and some were old, Janam·éjaya. They stood before Kumára in their thousands.

Hear of the various different faces they bore, Janam·éjaya. They had the faces of tortoises, chickens, hares, owls, asses, camels and boars. Some had the faces of cats or hares, some had long faces, descendant of Bharata, while others had the faces of mongeese, owls, or crows. Some had the faces of mice, rats, peacocks, fish, sheep, goats, ewes, or buffaloes. Some had the faces of bears, tigers, panthers, or lions. Some were terrifying with their elephant faces, while others had the faces of crocodiles. They had *gáruda* faces, heron faces, wolf faces, crow faces, cow faces, ass faces, camel faces, and also cat faces. They had huge stomachs, feet, and limbs, and they had eyes like stars, descendant of Bharata. Some had the faces of pigeons, while others had the faces of bulls. They had faces like cuckoos, or the faces of hawks, partridges, and lizards, and they wore unsullied clothes. 45.75

Some had the faces of snakes, while others had faces like spears; some had fierce faces, while others had auspicious faces. Some wore snakes, while others wore rags, and some had faces with cow snouts. Some had huge stomachs and thin limbs, while others had small stomachs and big limbs. Some had short necks, some had big ears, and some wore different snakes as ornaments. Some were clothed in the skin of elephant kings, while others were clothed in black deer skin. Some had mouths on their shoulders, while others had mouths on their stomachs, great king. Others had mouths 45.80

tathā kīṭa|pataṅgānāṃ sadṛś'|āsyā gaṇ'|ēśvarāḥ
nānā|vyāla|mukhāś c' ânye bahu|bāhu|śiro|dharāḥ,

45.85 nānā|vṛkṣa|bhujāḥ ke cit kaṭi|śīrṣās tathā pare
bhujaṅga|bhoga|vadanā nānā|gulma|nivāsinaḥ,
cīra|saṃvṛta|gātrāś ca nānā|kanaka|vāsasaḥ
nānā|veṣa|dharāś c' âiva nānā|māly'|ânulepanāḥ
nānā|vastra|dharāś c' âiva carma|vāsasa eva ca,
uṣṇīṣiṇo mukuṭinaḥ su|grīvāś ca su|varcasaḥ
kirīṭinaḥ pañca|śikhās tathā kāñcana|mūrdhajāḥ,
tri|śikhā dvi|śikhāś c' âiva tathā sapta|śikhāḥ pare
śikhaṇḍino mukuṭino muṇḍāś ca jaṭilās tathā,
citra|mālā|dharāḥ ke cit ke cid rom'|ānanās tathā
vigrah'|âika|rasā nityam a|jeyāḥ sura|sattamaiḥ,

45.90 kṛṣṇā nirmāṃsa|vaktrāś ca dīrgha|pṛṣṭhās tan'|ûdarāḥ
sthūla|pṛṣṭhā hrasva|pṛṣṭhāḥ pralamb'|ôdara|mehanāḥ,
mahā|bhujā hrasva|bhujā hrasva|gātrāś ca vāmanāḥ
kubjāś ca hrasva|jaṅghāś ca hasti|karṇa|śiro|dharāḥ,
hasti|nāsāḥ kūrma|nāsā vṛka|nāsās tathā pare
dīrgh'|ôṣṭhā dīrgha|jaṅghāś ca vikarālā hy adho|mukhāḥ,
mahā|daṃṣṭrā hrasva|daṃṣṭrāś catur|daṃṣṭrās tathā pare
vāraṇ'|êndra|nibhāś c' ânye bhīmā rājan sahasraśaḥ,

on their backs, cheeks, and calves. Many had faces on their flanks, while others had mouths on different parts of their body.

The leaders of the troops had faces like worms and insects, while others had the faces of various snakes or multiple arms and heads. Some had different tree-like arms, 45.85 some had heads on their hips, some had faces like snake coils, and some had their dwellings in thickets of various kinds. Some had limbs that were covered in rags, some wore various gold clothes, some wore different types of costumes, some had various garlands and unguents, some wore various garments, while others were dressed in skins. Some wore turbans and some crowns. Some had handsome necks, some radiated great splendor, some wore diadems, some had five hair-tufts, and some had hair of gold. Some had three tufts, some two and some seven. Some were crested, some had crowns, some were bald, and some had matted hair. Some wore beautiful garlands and some had hairy faces. Their constant and sole taste was for conflict, and even the best of the gods could not conquer them.

Some were dark, some had fleshless faces, some had long 45.90 backs, and some had tiny stomachs. Some had large backs, some had short backs, some had hanging stomachs and penises. Some had huge arms, some had short arms, and some were dwarves with short limbs. Some were hunchbacked, some had short legs, and some had the ears and heads of elephants. Some had elephant noses, some had tortoise noses, and some had wolf noses. Some had long lips, some had long legs, and some were terrifying with hanging faces. Some had large fangs, some had short fangs,

su|vibhakta|śarīrāś ca dīptimantaḥ sv|alaṃkṛtāḥ
piṅg'|âkṣāḥ śaṅku|karṇāś ca rakta|nāsāś ca Bhārata,

45.95 pṛthu|daṃṣṭrā mahā|daṃṣṭrāḥ sthūl'|âuṣṭhā hari|mūrdhajāḥ
nānā|pād'|âuṣṭha|daṃṣṭrāś ca nānā|hasta|śiro|dharāḥ
nānā|carmabhir ācchannā nānā|bhāṣāś ca Bhārata,
kuśalā deśa|bhāṣāsu jalpanto 'nyonyam īśvarāḥ
hṛṣṭāḥ paripatanti sma mahā|pāriṣadās tathā,
dīrgha|grīvā dīrgha|nakhā dīrgha|pāda|śiro|bhujāḥ
piṅg'|âkṣā nīla|kaṇṭhāś ca lamba|karṇāś ca Bhārata,
vṛk'|ôdara|nibhāś c' âiva ke cid añjana|saṃnibhāḥ
śvet'|âkṣā lohita|grīvāḥ piṅg'|âkṣāś ca tathā pare
kalmāṣā bahavo rājaṃś citra|varṇāś ca Bhārata,
cāmar'|āpīḍaka|nibhāḥ śveta|lohita|rājayaḥ
nānā|varṇāḥ sa|varṇāś ca mayūra|sa|dṛśa|prabhāḥ.

45.100 punaḥ praharaṇāny eṣāṃ kīrtyamānāni me śṛṇu.
śeṣaiḥ kṛtaḥ pāriṣadair āyudhānāṃ parigrahaḥ.

pāś'|ôdyata|karāḥ ke cid vyādit'|āsyāḥ khar'|ānanāḥ
pṛṣṭh'|âkṣā nīla|kaṇṭhāś ca tathā parigha|bāhavaḥ,
śataghnī|cakra|hastāś ca tathā musala|pāṇayaḥ
asi|mudgara|hastāś ca daṇḍa|hastāś ca Bhārata
gadā|bhuśuṇḍi|hastāś ca tathā tomara|pāṇayaḥ.
āyudhair vividhair ghorair mah"|ātmāno mahā|javāḥ

and some had four fangs. Thousands of them were terrifying and resembled elephant kings. Some had well-proportioned bodies, some were splendid, and some wore fine ornaments. Some had yellow eyes, some had pointed ears, and some had red noses, descendant of Bharata. Some had wide fangs, some had large fangs, some had huge lips, and some had green hair. Some had various different feet, lips, and teeth, and some had various different hands and heads. Some were covered in various skins, and some spoke different languages, descendant of Bharata. Skilled in provincial languages, some of the lordly great attendants gabbled to each other as they joyfully whirled around. Some had long necks, some long nails, and some long feet, heads, and arms. Some had yellow eyes, some had blue necks, and some had long ears, descendant of Bharata. Some had wolf-bellies, while others resembled lizards. Some had white eyes, some red necks, and some yellow eyes. Many were spotted and multi-colored, descendant of Bharata. Some had yak-tail head-dresses, and some had white and red streaks. Some were multi-colored, some had one color, and some had the appearance of peacocks. 45.95

Listen now to my description of the creatures' weapons. The remaining attendants took up the following weapons. 45.100

Some brandished raised nooses and had open mouths, donkey faces, eyes on their backs, blue necks, or arms like iron bars. Some brandished *shatághni* weapons and discuses, some clubs, some swords and mallets, and some sticks, descendant of Bharata. Some held maces and *bhushúndi* weapons, and some lances. Wielding various terrifying

mahā|balā mahā|vegā mahā|pāriṣadās tathā,
abhiṣekaṃ Kumārasya dṛṣṭvā hṛṣṭā raṇa|priyāḥ
ghaṇṭā|jāla|pinaddh'|âṅgā nanṛtus te mah"|âujasaḥ.

45.105 ete c' ânye ca bahavo mahā|pāriṣadā nṛpa
upatasthur mah"|ātmānaṃ Kārttikeyaṃ yaśasvinam.
divyāś c' âpy āntarikṣāś ca pārthivāś c' ânil'|ôpamāḥ
vyādiṣṭā daivataiḥ śūrāḥ Skandasy' ânucar" âbhavan*.
tādṛśānāṃ sahasrāṇi prayutāny arbudāni ca
abhiṣiktaṃ mah"|ātmānaṃ parivāry' ôpatasthire.

VAIŚAMPĀYANA uvāca:

46.1 ŚṚṆU MĀTṚ|GAṆĀN rājan Kumār'|ânucarān imān
kīrtyamānān mayā vīra sa|patna|gaṇa|sūdanān.
yaśasvinīnāṃ mātṝṇāṃ śṛṇu nāmāni Bhārata
yābhir vyāptās trayo lokāḥ kalyāṇībhiś ca bhāgaśaḥ:

Prabhāvatī Viśālākṣī Pālitā Gostanī tathā
Śrīmatī Bahulā c' âiva tath" âiva Bahuputrikā,
Apsujātā ca Gopālī Bṛhadambālikā tathā
Jayāvatī Mālatikā Dhruvaratnā Bhayaṅkarī,

46.5 Vasudāmā ca Dāmā ca Viśokā Nandinī tathā
Ekacūḍā Mahācūḍā Cakranemiś ca Bhārata,
Uttejanī Jayatsenā Kamalākṣy atha Śobhanā
Śatruñjayā tathā c' âiva Krodhanā Śalabhī Kharī,
Mādhavī Śubhavaktrā ca Tīrthaseniś ca Bhārata
Gītapriyā ca Kalyāṇī Rudraromā 'mitāśanā,
Meghasvanā Bhogavatī Subhrūś ca Kanakāvatī
Alātākṣī Vīryavatī Vidyujjihvā ca Bhārata;

ʼeapons, these great-spirited, speedy, mighty, swift and vig-
rous great attendants, who delighted in war and had nets
f bells fastened to their limbs, danced with joy when they
aw Kumára's consecration.

These and many other great attendants, Your Majesty, 45.105
tood before glorious and great-spirited Karttikéya. Some
ʼere divine, some belonged to the sky, some belonged to
he earth, and some were like the wind. Instructed by the
ods, these heroes became Skanda's attendants. Thousands,
nillions, and tens of millions of such beings surrounded
nd attended that consecrated hero.

VAISHAMPÁYANA said:

LISTEN, HEROIC king, to my description of the troops 46.1
f mothers who became Kumára's attendants and who de-
troyed hordes of enemies. Listen, descendant of Bharata,
o the names of these glorious and beautiful mothers who
ermeate the three worlds variously:*

Prabhávati, Vishalákshi, Pálita, Go·stani, Shrímati,
áhula, and Bahu·pútrika; Apsu·jata, Go·pali, Brihad·
mbálika, Jayávati, Málatika, Dhruva·ratna, and Bhayan·
ari; Vasu·dama, Dama, Vishóka, Nándini, Eka·chuda, 46.5
Maha·chuda, and Chakra·nemi, descendant of Bharata; Ut-
éjani, Jayat·sená,* Kamalákshi, Shóbhana, Shatrun·jaya,
Kródhana, Shálabhi, and Khari; Mádhavi, Shubha·vaktra,
Tirtha·seni, Gita·priya, Kalyáni, Rudra·roma, and Amitá-
hana, descendant of Bharata; Megha·svana, Bhógavati,
ubhru, Kanakávati, Alatákshi, Víryavati, and Vidyuj·jihva,
escendant of Bharata;

Padmāvatī Sunakṣatrā Kandarā Bahuyojanā
Santānikā ca Kauravya Kamalā ca Mahābalā;
46.10 Sudāmā Bahudāmā ca Suprabhā ca Yaśasvinī
Nṛtyapriyā ca rāj'|êndra Śatolūkhalamekhalā,
Śataghaṇṭā Śatānandā Bhaganandā ca Bhāvinī
Vapuṣmatī Candraśītā Bhadrakālī ca Bhārata,
Ṛkṣāmbikā Niṣkuṭikā Vāmā Catvaravāsinī
Sumaṅgalā Svastimatī Buddhikāmā Jayapriyā,
Dhanadā Suprasādā ca Bhavadā ca Jaleśvarī
Eḍī Bheḍī Sameḍī ca Vetālajananī tathā
Kaṇḍūtiḥ Kālikā c' âiva Devamitrā ca Bhārata,
Vasuśrīḥ Koṭarā c' âiva Citrasenā tath" Âcalā
Kukkuṭikā Śaṅkhalikā tathā Śakunikā nṛpa,
46.15 Kuṇḍārikā Kaukulikā Kumbhik" âtha Śatodarī
Utkrāthinī Jalelā ca Mahāvegā ca Kaṅkaṇā,
Manojavā Kaṇṭakinī Praghasā Pūtanā tathā
Keśayantrī Truṭir Vāmā Krośan" âtha Taḍitprabhā,
Mandodarī ca Muṇḍī ca Koṭarā Meghavāhinī
Subhagā Lambinī Lambā Tāmracūḍā Vikāśinī,
Ūrdhvaveṇīdharā c' âiva Piṅgākṣī Lohamekhalā
Pṛthuvaktrā Madhulikā Madhukumbhā tath" âiva ca,
Pakṣālikā Matkulikā Jarāyur Jarjarānanā
Khyātā Dahadahā c' âiva tathā Dhamadhamā nṛpa,
46.20 Khaṇḍakhaṇḍā ca rāj'|êndra Pūṣaṇā Maṇikuṭṭikā
Amoghā c' âiva Kauravya tathā Lambapayodharā,
Veṇuvīṇādharā c' âiva Piṅgākṣī Lohamekhalā
Śaśolūkamukhī Kṛṣṇā Kharajaṅghā Mahājavā,
Śiśumāramukhī Śvetā Lohitākṣī Vibhīṣaṇā
Jaṭālikā Kāmacarī Dīrghajihvā Balotkaṭā;

Padmávati, Sunakshátra, Kándara, Bahu·yójana, Santánika, Kámala, and Maha·bala, O Káurava; Sudáma, Bahu· 46.10 dama, Súprabha, Yashásvini, Nritya·priya, and Shatolúkhala·mékhala, king of kings; Shata·ghanta, Shatánanda, Bhaga·nanda, Bhávini, Vapúshmati, Chandra·shita, and Bhadra·kali, descendant of Bharata; Rikshámbika, Níshkutika, Vama, Chátvara·vásini, Sumángala, Svástimati, Buddhi·kama, Jaya·priya, Dhánada, Suprasadá,* Bhávada, Jaléshvari, Edi, Bhedi, Samédi, Vetála·jánani, Kandúti, Kaliká, and Deva·mitra, descendant of Bharata; Vasu·shri, Kótara, Chitra·sená,* Achalá,Kúkkutika, Shánkhalika, and Shákunika, Your Majesty; Kundárika, Káukulika, Kúmbhi- 46.15 ka, Shatódari, Utkráthini, Jaléla, Maha·vega, and Kánkana; Mano·java, Kántakini, Prághasa, Pútana, Kesha·yantri, Truti, Vama, Króshana, and Tadit·prabha; Mandódari, Mundi, Kótara, Megha·váhini, Súbhaga, Lámbini, Lamba, Tamra·chuda, and Vikáshini; Urdhva·veni·dhara, Pingákshi, Loha·mékhala, Prithu·vaktra, Mádhulika, and Madhu·kumbha; Pakshálika, Mátkulika, Jaráyu, Jarjaránana, Khyata, Dáhadaha, and Dhámadhama, Your Majesty; Khanda· 46.20 khanda, Púshana, Mani·kúttika, Amógha, and Lamba·payo·dhara, king of kings and descendant of Kuru; Venu·vina·dhara, Pingákshi, Loha·mékhala, Shasholúka·mukhi, Krshná,* Khara·jangha, and Maha·java; Shishu·mara·mukhi, Shvetá,* Lohitákshi, Vibhíshana, Jatálika, Kama·chari, Dirgha·jihva, and Balótkata;

Kālehikā Vāmanikā Mukuṭā c' âiva Bhārata
Lohitākṣī Mahākāyā Haripiṇḍā ca bhūmi|pa,
Ekatvacā Sukusumā Kṛṣṇakarṇī ca Bhārata
Kṣurakarṇī Catuṣkarṇī Karṇaprāvaraṇā tathā,

46.25 Catuṣpathaniketā ca Gokarṇī Mahiṣānanā
Kharakarṇī Mahākarṇī Bherīsvanamahāsvanā,
Śaṅkhakumbhaśravāś c' âiva Bhagadā ca Mahābalā
Gaṇā ca Sugaṇā c' âiva tath" Âbhīty atha Kāmadā,
Catuṣpatharatā c' âiva Bhūtitīrth" Ânyagocarī
Paśudā Vittadā c' âiva Sukhadā ca Mahāyaśāḥ,
Payodā Gomahiṣadā Suviśālā ca Bhārata
Pratiṣṭhā Supratiṣṭhā ca Rocamānā Surocanā,
Naukarṇī Mukhakarṇī ca Viśirā Manthinī tathā
Ekacandrā Meghakarṇā Meghamālā Virocanā.

46.30 etāś c' ânyāś ca bahavo mātaro Bharata'|rṣabha
Kārttikey'|ânuyāyinyo nānā|rūpāḥ sahasraśaḥ.
dīrgha|nakhyo dīrgha|dantyo dīrgha|tuṇḍyaś ca Bhārata
sa|balā madhurāś c' âiva yauvana|sthāḥ sv|alaṃkṛtāḥ,
māh"|ātmyena ca saṃyuktāḥ kāma|rūpa|dharās tathā
nirmāṃsa|gātryaḥ śvetāś ca tathā kāñcana|saṃnibhāḥ,
kṛṣṇa|megha|nibhāś c' ânyā dhūmrāś ca Bharata'|rṣabha
aruṇ'|ābhā mahā|bhogā dīrgha|keśyaḥ sit'|âmbarāḥ,
ūrdhva|veṇī|dharāś c' âiva piṅg'|âkṣyo lamba|mekhalāḥ
lamb'|ôdaryo lamba|karṇās tathā lamba|payo|dharāḥ,

46.35 tāmr'|âkṣyas tāmra|varṇāś ca hary|akṣyaś ca tathā parāḥ
vara|dāḥ kāma|cāriṇyo nityaṃ pramuditās tathā.

Kaléhika, Vámanika, Múkuta, Lohitákshi, Maha·kaya, and Hari·pinda, O descendant of Bharata and protector of the earth; Eka·tvacha, Súkusuma, Krishna·karni, Kshura·karni, Chatush·karni, and Karna·právarana, descendant of Bharata; Chatush·patha·nikéta, Go·karni, Mahishánana, Khara·karni, Maha·karni, and Bheri·svana·maha·svana; Shankha·kumbha·shravas, Bhágada, Maha·bala, Gana, Súgana, Abhíti, and Kámada; Chatush·patha·rata, Bhuti·tirtha, Anya·go·chari, Páshuda, Víttada, Súkhada, and Maha·yashas; Payóda, Go·mahíshada, Suvishála, Pratíshtha, Supratíshtha, Rochamána, and Suróchana, descendant of Bharata; Nau·karni, Mukha·karni, Víshiras, Mánthini, Eka·chandra, Megha·karna, Megha·mala, and Virochaná.* 46.25

These and many other mothers, bull of the Bharatas, attended Karttikéya in their thousands with various appearances. They had long nails, long teeth, and long mouths, descendant of Bharata. They were strong, charming, youthful, and beautifully adorned. They had majesty and could assume any appearance they desired. Their limbs were not fleshy, and they were fair and looked like gold. Some were smoke-colored and looked like dark clouds, bull of the Bharatas. Shining like dawn and enjoying great pleasures, others had long hair and white robes. Some wore their hair up in braids and had yellow eyes and long girdles. Others had hanging stomachs, long ears, or drooping breasts. Some had red eyes or were red-colored. Others had green eyes. They offered boons, could travel at will, and were always joyful. 46.30 46.35

Yāmyā Raudrās tathā Saumyāḥ
Kauberyo 'tha mahā|balāḥ
Vāruṇyo 'tha ca Māhendryas
tath" Āgneyyaḥ paran|tapa,
Vāyavyaś c' âtha Kaumāryo Brāhmyaś ca Bharata'|rṣabha
Vaiṣṇavyaś ca tathā Sauryo Vārāhyāś ca mahā|balāḥ,
rūpeṇ' âpsarasāṃ tulyā mano|hāryo mano|ramāḥ
parapuṣṭ'|ôpamā vākye tatha" rddhyā Dhanad'|ôpamāḥ,
Śakra|vīry'|ôpamā yuddhe dīptyā Vahni|samās tathā
śatrūṇāṃ vigrahe nityaṃ bhaya|dās tā bhavanty uta,
46.40 kāma|rūpa|dharāś c' âiva jave Vāyu|samās tathā
a|cintya|bala|vīryāś ca tath" â|cintya|parākramāḥ,
vṛkṣa|catvara|vāsinyaś catuṣ|patha|niketanāḥ
guhā|śmaśāna|vāsinyaḥ śaila|prasravaṇ'|ālayāḥ,
nān"|ābharaṇa|dhāriṇyo nānā|māly'|âmbarās tathā
nānā|vicitra|veṣāś ca nānā|bhāṣās tath" âiva ca.
ete c' ânye ca bahavo gaṇāḥ śatru|bhayaṅ|karāḥ
anujagmur mah"|ātmānaṃ tri|daś'|êndrasya saṃmate.
tataḥ śakty|astram adadad bhagavān Pāka|śāsanaḥ
Guhāya rāja|śārdūla vināśāya sura|dviṣām,
46.45 mahā|svanāṃ mahā|ghaṇṭāṃ dyotamānāṃ sita|prabhām
aruṇ'|āditya|varṇāṃ ca patākāṃ Bharata'|rṣabha.
dadau Paśupatis tasmai sarva|bhūta|mahā|camūm
ugrāṃ nānā|praharaṇāṃ tapo|vīrya|bal'|ânvitām,

Endowed with great power, some were associated with Yama, some with Rudra, some with Soma, some with Kubéra, some with Váruna, some with Mahéndra, and some with Agni, O scorcher of enemies. Some were associated with Vayu, some with Kumára, some with Brahma, some with Vishnu, some with Surya, and some with Varáha, bull of the Bharatas. Captivating and delighting the mind, they were equal to nymphs in their beauty. In speech they resembled the cuckoo and in prosperity they resembled wealth-giving Kubéra. In battle, their power was like Shakra's and their radiance was like that of Fire. They always terrified their enemies in war. Able to assume any appearance they desired, they were equal to Vayu in speed. Their strength and power were beyond conception, as was their prowess. They lived in trees and at crossroads and at places where four roads meet. Their dwellings were in caves, cremation grounds, mountains, and springs. They wore various ornaments, garlands, and robes. Their clothes were different and varied and they spoke various languages. 46.40

Under the instruction of Indra, that lord of the thirty gods, these and many other hosts attended great-spirited Kumára, bringing terror to their enemies.

Then, tiger-like king, Lord Indra, the chastiser of Paka, gave Guha a spear for the destruction of the gods' enemies. He also gave him a banner that was adorned with large bells and jangled loudly. Glistening, it shone with bright light and its color was like the morning sun, bull of the Bharatas. Pashu·pati also gave him a vast army made up of every type of creature. Fierce and unconquerable, the army had diverse weapons and was endowed with ascetic power 46.45

a|jeyāṃ su|guṇair yuktāṃ nāmnāṃ senāṃ Dhanañjayām
Rudra|tulya|balair yuktāṃ yodhānām ayutais tribhiḥ.
na sā vijānāti raṇāt kadā cid vinivartitum.

Viṣṇur dadau Vaijayantīṃ mālāṃ bala|vivardhinīm.
Umā dadau virajasī vāsasī ravi|sa|prabhe.
Gaṅgā kamaṇḍaluṃ divyam amṛt'|ôdbhavam uttamam
dadau prītyā Kumārāya daṇḍaṃ c' âiva Bṛhaspatiḥ.

46.50 Garuḍo dayitaṃ putraṃ mayūraṃ citra|barhiṇam
Aruṇas tāmra|cūḍaṃ ca pradadau caraṇ'|āyudham.
nāgaṃ tu Varuṇo rājā bala|vīrya|samanvitam
kṛṣṇ'|âjinaṃ tato Brahmā brahmaṇyāya dadau prabhuḥ
samareṣu jayaṃ c' âiva pradadau loka|bhāvanaḥ.

saināpatyam anuprāpya Skando deva|gaṇasya ha
śuśubhe jvalito 'rciṣmān dvitīya iva Pāvakaḥ.
tataḥ pāriṣadaiś c' âiva mātṛbhiś ca samanvitaḥ
yayau daitya|vināśāya hlādayan sura|puṅgavān.
sā senā nairṛtī bhīmā sa|ghaṇṭ"|ôcchrita|ketanā
sa|bherī|śaṅkha|murajā s'|āyudhā sa|patākinī
śāradī dyaur iv' ābhāti jyotirbhir iva śobhitā.

46.55 tato deva|nikāyās te nānā|bhūta|gaṇās tathā
vādayām āsur a|vyagrā bherīḥ śaṅkhāṃś ca puṣkalān
paṭahāñ jharjharāṃś c' âiva krakacān go|viṣāṇikān
āḍambarān gomukhāṃś ca ḍiṇḍimāṃś ca mahā|svanān.
tuṣṭuvus te Kumāraṃ tu sarve devāḥ sa|Vāsavāḥ
jaguś ca deva|gandharvā nanṛtuś c' âpsaro|gaṇāḥ.

and strength. It was invested with fine qualities and bore the name Dhanan·jayá.* It had three myriads of troops who rivaled Rudra in strength and it never knew how to flee a battlefield under any situation.

Vishnu gave Kumára the garland called Vaijayánti, which could increase strength. Uma gave him spotless clothes, which shone with the splendor of the sun. Ganga gave Kumára a fine pot, which was divine and produced from ambrosia, and Brihas·pati joyfully gave him a staff. Gáruda 46.50 gave Kumára his cherished son, a peacock adorned with beautiful feathers. Áruna gave him a red-crested cock, whose feet acted as weapons. King Váruna gave him a strong and powerful snake. Lord Brahma, the creator of the world, gave pious Kumára a dark antelope-skin and also victory in battle.

After he had received generalship over the troops of gods, Skanda shone with blazing radiance, as if he were a second Fire. Gladdening the bull-like gods, he then advanced forward with these attendants and mothers to destroy the *daityas*. With its bells, raised flags, drums, conches, tambourines, weapons and banners, that terrifying army of *náirritas* looked radiant and seemed to glisten like a fall sky gleaming with stars.

The troops of gods and hordes of various creatures then 46.55 intently played numerous drums and conches, as well as kettledrums, *jhárjhara* drums, *krákachas*, trumpets, *adámbara* drums, *go·mukhas*, and loud-sounding *díndimas*. Vásava and all the gods praised Kumára. Gods and *gandhárvas* sang, while troops of nymphs danced. Gladdened, Maha·sena gave the gods this boon: "I will slay in battle any en-

tataḥ prīto Mahāsenas tri|daśebhyo varaṃ dadau:
«ripūn hant" âsmi samare ye vo vadha|cikīrṣavaḥ.»
pratigṛhya varaṃ devās tasmād vibudha|sattamāt
prīt'|ātmāno mah"|ātmāno menire nihatān ripūn.

46.60 sarveṣāṃ bhūta|saṅghānāṃ harṣān nādaḥ samutthitaḥ
apūrayata lokāṃs trīn vare datte mah"|ātmanā.

sa niryayau Mahāseno mahatyā senayā vṛtaḥ
vadhāya yudhi daityānāṃ rakṣ"|ârthaṃ ca div'|âukasām.
Vyavasāyo Jayo Dharmaḥ Siddhir Lakṣmīr Dhṛtiḥ Smṛtiḥ
Mahāsenasya sainyānām agre jagmur nar'|âdhipa.

sa tayā bhīmayā devaḥ śūla|mudgara|hastayā
jvalit'|âlāta|dhāriṇyā citr'|ābharaṇa|varmayā
gadā|musala|nārāca|śakti|tomara|hastayā
dṛpta|siṃha|ninādinyā vinadya prayayau Guhaḥ.

46.65 taṃ dṛṣṭvā sarva|daiteyā rākṣasā dānavās tathā
vyadravanta diśaḥ sarvā bhay'|ôdvignāḥ samantataḥ.
abhyadravanta devās tān vividh'|āyudha|pāṇayaḥ.
dṛṣṭvā ca sa tataḥ kruddhaḥ Skandas tejo|bal'|ânvitaḥ
śakty|astraṃ bhagavān bhīmaṃ punaḥ punar avākirat.
ādadhac c' ātmanas tejo haviṣ" êddha iv' ânalaḥ.
abhyasyamāne śakty|astre Skanden' â|mita|tejasā
ulkā|jvālā mahā|rāja papāta vasudhā|tale.
saṃhrādayantaś ca tathā nirghātāś c' āpatan kṣitau
yath" ânta|kāla|samaye su|ghorāḥ syus tathā nṛpa.
kṣiptā hy ekā yadā śaktiḥ su|ghor'|ânala|sūnunā
tataḥ koṭyo viniṣpetuḥ śaktīnāṃ Bharata'|rṣabha.

emies that seek your slaughter." Receiving this boon from that supreme deity, the great-spirited gods felt joy and considered their enemies to be already dead. After the hero had 46.60 given this boon, all the hordes of creatures cried out a shout of joy that filled the three worlds.

Surrounded by this vast army, Maha·sena departed in order to slaughter the *daitya*s in battle and protect the gods. Vyavasáya, Jaya, Dharma, Siddhi, Lakshmi, Dhriti and Smriti advanced at the front of Maha·sena's troops, king of the people.*

Divine Guha thus advanced forward with that terrifying army. Brandishing blazing firebrands and decked with various ornaments and armor, it roared like a wild lion and wielded pikes, mallets, maces, clubs, arrows, spears, and lances. When they saw Guha, all the *daitéya*s, *rákshasa*s 46.65 and *dánava*s fled in every direction, distraught with fear on all sides. The gods ran after them, wielding various weapons. Seeing this, Lord Skanda—who possesses energy and strength—repeatedly hurled his terrifying spear in his rage. As he displayed his energy, he looked like a fire that blazes with oblations. When Skanda of immeasurable energy threw that spear, a blazing meteor fell to the ground, great king. Just as if it were the moment of death, roaring storms of great dread also fell upon the earth, Your Majesty. When the terrifying son of Fire hurled his single spear, millions of other spears also sprayed out of it, bull of the Bharatas.

46.70 tataḥ prīto Mahāseno jaghāna bhagavān prabhuḥ
daity'|êndraṃ Tārakaṃ nāma mahā|bala|parākramam
vṛtaṃ daity'|âyutair vīrair balibhir daśabhir nṛpa.
Mahiṣaṃ c' âṣṭabhiḥ padmair vṛtaṃ saṅkhye nijaghnivān
Tripādaṃ c' âyuta|śatair jaghāna daśabhir vṛtam.
Hradodaraṃ nikharvaiś ca vṛtaṃ daśabhir īśvaraḥ
jaghān' ânucaraiḥ sārdhaṃ vividh'|āyudha|pāṇibhiḥ.
tath" âkurvanta vipulaṃ nādaṃ vadhyatsu śatruṣu
Kumār'|ânucarā rājan pūrayanto diśo daśa
nanṛtuś ca vavalguś ca jahasuś ca mud"|ânvitāḥ.

śakty|astrasya tu rāj'|êndra tato 'rcirbhiḥ samantataḥ
trailokyaṃ trāsitaṃ sarvaṃ jṛmbhamāṇābhir eva ca
dagdhāḥ sahasraśo daityā nādaiḥ Skandasya c' âpare.
46.75 patākay" âvadhūtāś ca hatāḥ ke cit sura|dviṣaḥ
ke cid ghaṇṭā|rava|trastā niṣedur vasudhā|tale.
ke cit praharaṇaiś chinnā viniṣpetur gat'|āyuṣaḥ.
evaṃ sura|dviṣo 'nekān balavān ātatāyinaḥ
jaghāna samare vīraḥ Kārttikeyo mahā|balaḥ.

Bāṇo nām' âtha daiteyo Baleḥ putro mahā|balaḥ
Krauñcaṃ parvatam āśritya deva|saṅghān abādhata.
tam abhyayān Mahāsenaḥ sura|śatrum udāra|dhīḥ
sa Kārttikeyasya bhayāt Krauñcaṃ śaraṇam īyivān.
tataḥ Krauñcaṃ mahā|manyuḥ krauñca|nāda|nināditam
śaktyā bibheda bhagavān Kārttikeyo 'gni|dattayā,
46.80 sa śāla|skandha|śabalaṃ trasta|vānara|vāraṇam

Illustrious Lord Maha·sena then joyfully killed the king of the *daityas*, who was called Táraka. Endowed with great strength and prowess, Táraka was surrounded by ten myriads of heroic and mighty *daityas*, Your Majesty. Skanda also slew Máhisha in battle, who was surrounded by eight billion demons, and Tri·pada too, who was surrounded by a thousand myriads of demons. Accompanied by his attendants, who wielded diverse weapons, the Lord also killed Hradódara, who was surrounded by ten billion demons. While their enemies were being slaughtered, Kumára's followers shouted a huge roar which filled the ten directions. They danced, leaped, and laughed with joy. 46.70

Thousands of *daityas* were incinerated by the flames that issued out of Skanda's spear on all sides and that engulfed all three terrified worlds. Others were incinerated by Skanda's roars. Some of the gods' enemies were killed when fanned away by Skanda's banner and some sank to the ground, terrified by the jangling bells. Others departed after being cut down by weapons, their vitality destroyed. In this way, powerful, heroic, and mighty Karttikéya slaughtered numerous bow-drawing enemies of the gods in battle. 46.75

The *daitéya* Bana, that mighty son of Bali, then climbed onto Mount Krauncha and resisted the hosts of gods. But wise Maha·sena attacked him and, in his fear of Karttikéya, Bana took refuge in Krauncha. With the spear that he had been given by Agni, lord Karttikéya then furiously cleaved Krauncha, which echoed with the sound of curlews.* On that mountain, that was dappled with *shala* trees, the monkeys and elephants became filled with terror. Birds flew up into the sky, wheeling about, and snakes departed. The 46.80

proḍḍīn'|ôdbhrānta|vihagaṃ viniṣpatita|pannagam,
golāṅgūla'|ṛkṣa|saṅghaiś ca dravadbhir anunāditam
kuraṅgama|vinirghoṣa|ninādita|van'|ântaram.
viniṣpatadbhiḥ śarabhaiḥ siṃhaiś ca sahasā drutaiḥ
śocyām api daśāṃ prāpto rarāj' êva sa parvataḥ.
vidyādharāḥ samutpetus tasya śṛṅga|nivāsinaḥ
kinnarāś ca samudvignāḥ śakti|pāta|rav'|ôddhatāḥ.

tato daityā viniṣpetuḥ śataśo 'tha sahasraśaḥ
pradīptāt parvata|śreṣṭhād vicitr'|ābharaṇa|srajaḥ.
tān nijaghnur atikramya Kumār'|ânucarā mṛdhe.
46.85 sa c' âiva bhagavān kruddho daity'|êndrasya sutaṃ tadā
sah'|ânujaṃ jaghān' āśu Vṛtraṃ deva|patir yathā.
bibheda Krauñcaṃ śaktyā ca Pāvakiḥ para|vīra|hā
bahudhā c' âikadhā c' âiva kṛtv" ātmānaṃ mahā|balaḥ.
śaktiḥ kṣiptā raṇe tasya pāṇim eti punaḥ punaḥ.

evaṃ|prabhāvo bhagavāṃs tato bhūyaś ca Pāvakiḥ.
śauryād dvi|guṇa|yogena tejasā yaśasā śriyā
Krauñcas tena vinirbhinno daityāś ca śataśo hatāḥ.
tataḥ sa bhagavān devo nihatya vibudha|dviṣaḥ
sa bhajyamāno vibudhaiḥ paraṃ harṣam avāpa ha.
tato dundubhayo rājan neduḥ śaṅkhāś ca Bhārata
mumucur deva|yoṣāś ca puṣpa|varṣam an|uttamam
yogināṃ īśvaraṃ devaṃ śataśo 'tha sahasraśaḥ.
46.90 divya|gandham upādāya vavau puṇyaś ca mārutaḥ
gandharvās tuṣṭuvuś c' âinaṃ yajvānaś ca maha"|rṣayaḥ.

mountain rumbled with the noise of fleeing hordes of monkeys and bears and its forests resounded with the noise of antelopes. But even though the fleeing *shárabha* deer and violently charging lions gave it a pitiful aspect, the mountain still looked glorious. *Vidya·dhara*s living on the mountain peak flew up into the sky and *kínnara*s became distraught at the sound of the spear's blow.

Hundreds and thousands of *daitya*s, wearing different colored ornaments and garlands, then dispersed from that radiant and supreme mountain. The attendants of Kumára overcame them and killed them in battle. In his rage, the Lord himself swiftly slaughtered the son of the *daitya* king and his brother, just as the chief of the gods once slaughtered Vritra. The son of Fire, that mighty slayer of enemy heroes, then cleaved Krauncha with his spear and transformed himself into many aspects and again into one aspect. When he hurled his spear in battle, it repeatedly returned to his hand. 46.85

Such was the strength abundantly displayed by the illustrious son of Fire. Through his heroism, doubled zeal, power, glory and splendor, he cleaved Krauncha and destroyed hundreds of *daitya*s. After he slaughtered the enemies of the gods, the divine Lord was worshipped by deities and attained the highest joy. Kettledrums and conches then sounded, descendant of Bharata, while female deities released a shower of flowers that was beyond compare onto the divine lord of hundreds and thousands of *yogin*s. An auspicious wind began to blow, bearing divine fragrance, and the *gandhárva*s and great sacrificing seers praised him. 46.90

ke cid enaṃ vyavasyanti Pitāmaha|sutaṃ prabhum
Sanatkumāraṃ sarveṣāṃ Brahma|yoniṃ tam agra|jam.
ke cin Maheśvara|sutaṃ ke cit putraṃ Vibhāvasoḥ
Umāyāḥ Kṛttikānāṃ ca Gaṅgāyāś ca vadanty uta,
ekadhā ca dvidhā c' âiva caturdhā ca mahā|balam
yogināṃ īśvaraṃ devaṃ śataśo 'tha sahasraśaḥ.

etat te kathitaṃ rājan Kārttikey'|âbhiṣecanam
śṛṇu c' âiva Sarasvatyās tīrtha|varyasya puṇyatām.

46.95 babhūva tīrtha|pravaraṃ hateṣu sura|śatruṣu
Kumāreṇa mahā|rāja tri|viṣṭapam iv' âparam.
aiśvaryāṇi ca tatra|stho dadāv īśaḥ pṛthak pṛthak
tadā nairṛta|mukhyebhyas trailokyaṃ Pāvak'|ātma|jaḥ.

evaṃ sa bhagavāṃs tasmiṃs tīrthe daitya|kul'|ântakaḥ
abhiṣikto mahā|rāja deva|senā|patiḥ suraiḥ.
Taijasaṃ nāma tat tīrthaṃ yatra pūrvam apāṃ patiḥ
abhiṣiktaḥ sura|gaṇair Varuṇo Bharata'|rṣabha.

asmiṃs tīrtha|vare snātvā Skandaṃ c' âbhyarcya lāṅgalī
brāhmaṇebhyo dadau rukmaṃ vāsāṃsy ābharaṇāni ca.

46.100 uṣitvā rajanīṃ tatra Mādhavaḥ para|vīra|hā
pūjya tīrtha|varaṃ tac ca spṛṣṭvā toyaṃ ca lāṅgalī
hṛṣṭaḥ prīta|manāś c' âiva hy abhavan Mādhav'|ôttamaḥ.

etat te sarvam ākhyātaṃ yan māṃ tvaṃ paripṛcchasi
yath" âbhiṣikto bhagavān Skando devaiḥ samāgataiḥ.

Some describe him as Sanat·kumára,* the Grandfather's lordly son and the eldest of all Brahma's offspring. Some speak of him as the son of Mahéshvara, or the son of Vibha·vasu, or the son of Uma, the Kríttikas, or Ganga. Some speak of that mighty, divine lord of hundreds of thousands of *yogins* as the son of only one of these gods or the son of any two of them or the son of any four.

I have told you about the consecration of Kumára, Your Majesty. Listen too to the auspicious nature of the best of Sarásvati's sites.

46.95 After Kumára had slain the enemies of the gods, this eminent *tirtha* became like a second heaven, great king. Standing at this site, that Lord—the son of Fire—gave various sovereignties to eminent *náirritas*, including command over the three worlds.

In this way, great king, that Lord, who destroyed the clan of the *daityas*, was consecrated by the gods as divine general. This site, where Váruna, the lord of the waters, was also once consecrated by troops of gods, is called Táijasa, bull of the Bharatas.

Plow-bearing Bala bathed at this excellent site, worshipped Skanda, and gave gold, clothes, and ornaments to brahmins. 46.100 After spending the night there, the plow-bearing Mádhava and slayer of enemy heroes worshipped that excellent site and sipped its waters. Gladdened, that best of Mádhavas became filled with joy.

I have thus described everything that you asked me regarding the way in which Lord Skanda was consecrated by the assembled deities.

JANAMEJAYA uvāca:

47.1 ATYADBHUTAM idaṃ brahmañ śrutavān asmi tattvataḥ
abhiṣekaṃ Kumārasya vistareṇa yathā|vidhi,
yac chrutvā pūtam ātmānaṃ vijānāmi tapo|dhana
prahṛṣṭāni ca romāṇi prasannaṃ ca mano mama.
abhiṣekaṃ Kumārasya daityānāṃ ca vadhaṃ tathā
śrutvā me paramā prītir bhūyaḥ kautūhalaṃ hi me.
apāṃ patiḥ kathaṃ hy asminn abhiṣiktaḥ purā suraiḥ?
tan me brūhi mahā|prājña. kuśalo hy asi sattama.

VAIŚAMPĀYANA uvāca:

47.5 śṛṇu rājann idaṃ citraṃ pūrva|kalpe yathā|tatham
ādau Kṛta|yuge rājan vartamāne yathā|vidhi
Varuṇaṃ devatāḥ sarvāḥ samety' êdam ath' âbruvan:
«yath" âsmān sura|rāṭ Śakro bhayebhyaḥ pāti sarvadā
tathā tvam api sarvāsāṃ saritāṃ vai patir bhava!
vāsaś ca te sadā deva sāgare makar'|ālaye.
samudro 'yaṃ tava vaśe bhaviṣyati nadī|patiḥ.
Somena sārdhaṃ ca tava hāni|vṛddhī bhaviṣyataḥ.»
«evam astv iti» tān devān Varuṇo vākyam abravīt.
samāgamya tataḥ sarve Varuṇaṃ sāgar'|ālayam
apāṃ patiṃ pracakrur hi vidhi|dṛṣṭena karmaṇā.
47.10 abhiṣicya tato devā Varuṇaṃ yādasāṃ patim
jagmuḥ svāny eva sthānāni pūjayitvā jal'|ēśvaram.
abhiṣiktas tato devair Varuṇo 'pi mahā|yaśāḥ

JANAM·ÉJAYA said:

IT IS A GREAT wonder, brahmin, to have heard this true and detailed account of Kumára's consecration, which was performed with due rites. After I heard it, austerity-rich ascetic, I considered my soul to be cleansed, my hair bristled, and my mind became tranquil. When I learned of Kumára's consecration and the slaughter of the *daitya*s, I felt the highest joy and now feel even greater curiosity. How was Váruna, that lord of waters, consecrated at this site by gods in the past? Tell me, wise and excellent Vaishampáyana. For you are skilled in speaking. 47.1

VAISHAMPÁYANA said:

Listen, Your Majesty, to this wonderful description of what truly happened in a bygone eon. At the beginning of the Krita era, all the gods duly gathered before Váruna and said: 47.5

"Become the lord of all rivers, just as Shakra, the king of the gods, continuously protects us from dangers! Your dwelling place will always be the ocean, that abode of *mákara*s, O god. This ocean, the lord of the rivers, will be under your control. Your waxing and waning will be connected with the Moon."

"So be it,"Váruna replied to the gods.

The gods then all gathered together and made ocean-dwelling Váruna lord of the waters with duly prescribed rites. After they had consecrated Váruna as the ruler of sea creatures, the gods worshipped that water-lord and returned to their own abodes. Consecrated by the gods, glorious 47.10

saritaḥ sāgarāṃś c' âiva nadāṃś c' âpi sarāṃsi ca
pālayām āsa vidhinā yathā devāñ Śatakratuḥ.
tatas tatr' âpy upaspṛśya dattvā ca vividhaṃ vasu
Agnitīrthaṃ mahā|prājño jagām' âtha Pralamba|hā,
naṣṭo na dṛśyate yatra śamī|garbhe hut'|âśanaḥ
lok'|āloka|vināśe ca prādur bhūte tad" ân|agha
upatasthuḥ surā yatra sarva|loka|pitā|maham:
«Agniḥ pranaṣṭo bhagavān. kāraṇaṃ ca na vidmahe.
sarva|bhūta|kṣayo m" âbhūt. saṃpādaya vibho 'nalam.»

JANAMEJAYA uvāca:

47.15 kim|arthaṃ bhagavān Agniḥ pranaṣṭo loka|bhāvanaḥ?
vijñātaś ca kathaṃ devais? tan mam' ācakṣva tattvataḥ.

VAIŚAMPĀYANA uvāca:

Bhṛgoḥ śāpād bhṛśaṃ bhīto jāta|vedāḥ pratāpavān
śamī|garbham ath' āsādya nanāśa bhagavāṃs tataḥ.
pranaṣṭe tu tadā vahnau devāḥ sarve sa|Vāsavāḥ
anveṣanta tadā naṣṭaṃ jvalanaṃ bhṛśa|duḥkhitāḥ.
tato 'gnitīrtham āsādya śamī|garbha|stham eva hi
dadṛśur jvalanaṃ tatra vasamānaṃ yathā|vidhi.
devāḥ sarve nara|vyāghra Bṛhaspati|puro|gamāḥ
jvalanaṃ taṃ samāsādya prīt" âbhūvan sa|Vāsavāḥ
47.20 punar yath"|āgataṃ jagmuḥ. sarva|bhakṣaś ca so 'bhavat
Bhṛgoḥ śāpān mahā|bhāga yad uktaṃ brahma|vādinā.

Váruna duly protected the streams, seas, rivers, and lakes, just as Indra of a hundred sacrifices protects the gods.

After Bala had sipped the water at this site and given away diverse possessions, that wise slayer of Pralámba proceeded to the Agni·tirtha, where oblation-eating Fire once disappeared into the womb of a *shami* tree. It was at this site, faultless king, that, after the light of the world had disappeared, the gods approached the Grandfather of the entire universe and said:

"Lord Fire has disappeared. We do not know why. Do not allow the destruction of every creature. Create fire, O Lord."

JANAM·ÉJAYA said:

Why did Lord Fire, the creator of the world, disappear? How did the gods find him? Tell me this as it truly happened. 47.15

VAISHAMPÁYANA said:

After he had been cursed by Bhrigu, splendid Lord Fire felt great fear and disappeared by entering the womb of a *shami* tree. When Fire disappeared, Vásava and all the gods felt great sorrow and sought for the lost flame. Approaching the Agni·tirtha, they saw the flame duly dwelling there in the womb of a *shami* tree. On finding the flame, tiger among men, Vásava and all the gods—who were headed by Brihas·pati—became filled with joy and returned the same way they had come. As a result of Bhrigu's curse, illustrious king, Fire became an all-consumer, just as that reciter of sacred verse had said.* 47.20

tatr' âpy āplutya matimān Brahmayoniṃ jagāma ha
sasarja bhagavān yatra sarva|loka|pitā|mahaḥ.
tatr' āplutya tato Brahmā saha devaiḥ prabhuḥ purā
sasarja tīrthāni tathā devatānāṃ yathā|vidhi.

tatra snātvā ca dattvā ca vasūni vividhāni ca
Kauberaṃ prayayau tīrthaṃ tatra taptvā mahat tapaḥ
dhan'|ādhipatyaṃ saṃprāpto rājann Ailavilaḥ prabhuḥ.
tatra|stham eva taṃ rājan dhanāni nidhayas tathā
upatasthur nara|śreṣṭha. tat tīrthaṃ lāṅgalī Balaḥ
gatvā dattvā ca vidhivad brāhmaṇebhyo dhanaṃ dadau.

47.25 dadṛśe tatra tat sthānaṃ Kaubere kānan'|ôttame
purā yatra tapas taptaṃ vipulaṃ su|mah"|ātmanā
yakṣa|rājñā Kubereṇa varā labdhāś ca puṣkalāḥ,
dhan'|ādhipatyaṃ sakhyaṃ ca Rudreṇ' â|mita|tejasā
suratvaṃ loka|pālatvaṃ putraṃ ca Nalakūbaram.
yatra lebhe mahā|bāho dhan'|âdhipatir añjasā
abhiṣiktaś ca tatr' âiva samāgamya Marud|gaṇaiḥ.
vāhanaṃ c' âsya tad dattaṃ haṃsa|yuktaṃ mano|javam
vimānaṃ puṣpakaṃ divyaṃ nairṛt'|āiśvaryam eva ca.

tatr' āplutya Balo rājan dattvā dāyāṃś ca puṣkalān
jagāma tvarito Rāmas tīrthaṃ śvet'|ânulepanaḥ,

47.30 niṣevitaṃ sarva|sattvair nāmnā Badarapācanam
nāna"|rtuka|van'|ôpetaṃ sadā|puṣpa|phalaṃ śubham.

After he had bathed there, wise Bala went to Brahma·yoni, where the illustrious Grandfather of all the worlds performed his acts of creation. In the past, lord Brahma bathed with the gods at this site and, in accordance with due rites, emitted sacred sites for the deities.

After he had bathed there and given various gifts, Your Majesty, Bala proceeded to the sacred site of Kaubéra, where Lord Kubéra, the son of Ílavila, performed great austerities and attained control over wealth. Wealth and treasures came to Kubéra as he resided at that site, best of men. Plow-bearing Bala went to that *tirtha* and, after he had made proper donations, he gave wealth to brahmins. There, in the excellent forest of Kubéra, Bala saw the place where great-spirited Kubéra, that King of the *yakshas*, once performed abundant austerities and received many boons, including control over wealth, friendship with the infinitely powerful Rudra, the status of a god, the status of a world-protector, and a son called Nala·kúbara. Troops of gathered Maruts consecrated that lord of wealth at the site where he swiftly acquired these boons, mighty-armed king. In addition to sovereignty over the *náirritas*, he was also given a celestial car as a vehicle, which was divine, swift as thought, yoked with geese, and adorned with flowers. 47.25

After he had bathed at this site and given copious gifts, Bala·rama—who was smeared with white ointments—quickly proceeded to the auspicious *tirtha* of Bádara·páchana, which is frequented by every creature and has groves of various seasons as well as continual blossoms and fruits. 47.30

VAIŚAMPĀYANA uvāca:

48.1 TATAS TĪRTHA|VARAṂ Rāmo yayau Badarapācanam
tapasvi|siddha|caritaṃ yatra kanyā dhṛta|vratā
Bharadvājasya duhitā rūpeṇ' â|pratimā bhuvi
Śrutāvatī nāma vibho kumārī brahma|cāriṇī
tapaś cacāra s" âtyugraṃ niyamair bahubhir vṛtā
«bhartā me deva|rājaḥ syād iti» niścitya bhāminī.
samās tasyā vyatikrāntā bahvyaḥ Kuru|kul'|ôdvaha
carantyā niyamāṃs tāṃs tāṃs strībhis tīvrān su|duś|carān.
48.5 tasyās tu tena vṛttena tapasā ca viśāṃ pate
bhaktyā ca bhagavān prītaḥ parayā Pāka|śāsanaḥ.
ājagām' āśramaṃ tasyās tri|daś'|âdhipatiḥ prabhuḥ
āsthāya rūpaṃ vipra'|rṣer Vasiṣṭhasya mah"|ātmanaḥ.
sā taṃ dṛṣṭv" ôgra|tapasaṃ Vasiṣṭhaṃ tapatāṃ varam
ācārair munibhir dṛṣṭaiḥ pūjayām āsa Bhārata.
uvāca niyama|jñā ca kalyāṇī sā priyaṃ|vadā:
«bhagavan muni|śārdūla kim ājñāpayasi prabho?
sarvam adya yathā|śakti tava dāsyāmi su|vrata.
Śakra|bhaktyā ca te pāṇiṃ na dāsyāmi kathañ cana.
48.10 vrataiś ca niyamaiś c' âiva tapasā ca tapo|dhana
Śakras toṣayitavyo vai mayā tri|bhuvan'|ēśvaraḥ.»

VAISHAMPÁYANA said:

BALA THEN PROCEEDED to Bádara·páchana, that finest 48.1
f *tirtha*s, which is frequented by ascetics and *siddha*s. It
vas here that a radiant young woman, who practiced firm
ows and whose beauty had no parallel on earth, performed
evere austerities and followed numerous acts of discipline
fter resolving that her husband should be the king of the
ods. This chaste maiden was called Shrutávati, my lord,
nd she was the daughter of Bharad·vaja.

Many years passed as she practiced various fierce disci-
lines that are extremely difficult for women to perform,
pholder of the Kuru clan. Indra, the illustrious chastiser 48.5
f Paka, became gratified by her immense devotion and
y the asceticism that she performed, lord of the people.
hat lord, who rules over the thirty gods, then approached
er hermitage in the form of the great-spirited brahmin
eer Vasíshtha. On seeing Vasíshtha, that fine ascetic who
erforms fierce austerities, she worshipped him with obser-
ances prescribed by sages, descendant of Bharata. Knowl-
dgeable in discipline, beautiful Shrutávati spoke to him
vith fair words:

"Illustrious tiger among ascetics, what do you command,
ny lord? On this day I will give you everything I can, ascetic
f good vows. But because of my devotion to Shakra, I
annot give you my hand. I must satisfy Shakra, the lord of 48.10
he three worlds, with vows, disciplines, and asceticism, O
eer rich in austerities."

ity ukto bhagavān devaḥ smayann iva nirīkṣya tām
uvāca niyamaṃ jñātvā sāntvayann iva Bhārata:
«ugraṃ tapaś carasi vai. viditā me 'si su|vrate.
yad|artham ayam ārambhas tava kalyāṇi hṛd|gataḥ
tac ca sarvaṃ yathā|bhūtaṃ bhaviṣyati var'|ānane.
tapasā labhyate sarvaṃ yathā|bhūtaṃ bhaviṣyati.
yathā sthānāni divyāni vibudhānāṃ śubh'|ānane
tapasā tāni prāpyāni. tapo|mūlaṃ mahat sukham.
iti kṛtvā tapo ghoraṃ dehaṃ saṃnyasya mānavāḥ
devatvaṃ yānti kalyāṇi. śṛṇuṣv' âivaṃ vaco mama.
48.15 pañca c' âitāni su|bhage badarāṇi śubha|vrate
pac' êty» uktvā tu bhagavāñ jagāma Bala|sūdanaḥ.
āmantrya tāṃ tu kalyāṇīṃ tato japyaṃ jajāpa saḥ.
avidūre tatas tasmād āśramāt tīrtham uttamam
Indratīrthe 'tivikhyātaṃ triṣu lokeṣu māna|da.
tasya jijñāsan'|ârthaṃ sa bhagavān Pāka|śāsanaḥ
badarāṇām a|pacanaṃ cakāra vibudh'|âdhipaḥ.
tataḥ prataptā sā rājan vāgyatā vigata|klamā
tat|parā śuci|saṃvītā pāvake samadhiśrayat
apacad rāja|śārdūla badarāṇi mahā|vratā.
tasyāḥ pacantyāḥ su|mahān kālo 'gāt puruṣa'|rṣabha.
na ca sma tāny apacyanta dinaṃ ca kṣayam abhyagāt.
48.20 hut'|âśanena dagdhaś ca yas tasyāḥ kāṣṭha|sañcayaḥ.
a|kāṣṭham agniṃ sā dṛṣṭvā sva|śarīram ath' âdahat.
pādau prakṣipya sā pūrvaṃ pāvake cāru|darśanā

Addressed this way, the divine lord looked at her askance with a slight smile. Aware of her disciplined conduct, he then said these words as if to calm her, descendant of Bharata:

"You practice severe austerities and you have come to my notice, woman of good vows. You will fully realize the goal of your cherished undertaking, beautiful fine-faced lady. You will obtain everything that can be acquired through asceticism. The divine positions of the gods can be obtained through ascetic practice, pretty lady. Asceticism is the root of great happiness. Humans who perform gruesome austerities attain divinity after giving up their bodies, beautiful lady. Listen to these words of mine. Cook these five jujube fruits, prosperous lady of auspicious vows." Saying these words, the illustrious destroyer of Bala departed. 48.15

After he had counselled that beautiful lady, he recited some mantras. As a result, this excellent *tirtha* that lies not far from that hermitage became known throughout the three worlds as Indra·tirtha, honor-giving king.

In order to test Shrutávati, the lord of the gods—that illustrious chastiser of Paka—made the jujube fruits uncookable. Practicing heated asceticism, that virtuous woman of great vows silently, tirelessly, and devotedly placed the jujubes on a fire and tried to cook the fruits, tiger-like king. A very long time passed as she tried to cook the fruits, bull among men, But the fruits did not cook and the day began to wane. The fire consumed her bundle of firewood, and when she saw that the fire had no fuel she started to burn her own body. Placing her feet in the fire, that beautiful woman stood on her feet as they continuously burned, 48.20

dagdhau dagdhau punaḥ pādāv upāvartayat' ân|agha.
caraṇau dahyamānau ca n' âcintayad a|ninditā
kurvāṇā duṣ|karaṃ maha"|rṣi|priya|kāmyayā.
na vaimanasyaṃ tasyās tu mukha|bhedo 'thav" âbhavat.
śarīram agninā dīpya jala|madhye va* harṣitā.
tac c' âsyā vacanaṃ nityam avartadd hṛdi Bhārata:
«sarvathā badarāṇy eva paktavyān' îti» kanyakā.

48.25 sā tan manasi kṛtv" âiva maha"|rṣer vacanaṃ śubhā
apacad badarāṇy eva na c' âpacyanta Bhārata.
tasyās tu caraṇau vahnir dadāha bhagavān svayam
na ca tasyā mano duḥkhaṃ sv|alpam apy abhavat tadā.

atha tat karma dṛṣṭv" âsyāḥ prītas tri|bhuvan'|ēśvaraḥ
tataḥ saṃdarśayām āsa kanyāyai rūpam ātmanaḥ.
uvāca ca sura|śreṣṭhas tāṃ kanyāṃ su|dṛḍha|vratām:

«prīto 'smi te śubhe bhaktyā tapasā niyamena ca.
tasmād yo 'bhimataḥ kāmaḥ sa te saṃpatsyate śubhe.
dehaṃ tyaktvā mahā|bhāge tri|dive mayi vatsyasi.

48.30 idaṃ ca te tīrtha|varaṃ sthiraṃ loke bhaviṣyati
sarva|pāp'|âpahaṃ su|bhru nāmnā Badarapācanam.
vikhyātaṃ triṣu lokeṣu brahma'|rṣibhir abhiplutam.»

asmin khalu mahā|bhāge śubhe tīrtha|vare 'n|aghe
tyaktvā sapta'|rṣayo jagmur Himavantam Arundhatīm.
tatas te vai mahā|bhāgā gatvā tatra su|saṃśitāḥ
vṛtty|arthaṃ phala|mūlāni samāhartuṃ yayuḥ kila.
teṣāṃ vṛtty|arthināṃ tatra vasatāṃ Himavad|vane
an|āvṛṣṭir anuprāptā tadā dvādaśa|vārṣikī.

faultless king. In her desire to favor the great ascetic, blame-ess Shrutávati felt no concern for her burning feet as she performed that difficult task. Her mind did not falter and there was no change on her face. Even though she had set her body alight with fire, she felt joy as if immersed in water. The maiden continuously kept the ascetic's words in her heart, descendant of Bharata: "Cook the jujube fruits thoroughly." Keeping the words of the great ascetic in her mind, glorious Shrutávati continued to try to cook the ju-ubes but they did not cook, descendant of Bharata. But even though Lord Fire himself burned her feet, her mind did not feel even slight pain. 48.25

The lord of the three worlds was pleased when he saw her deed and revealed his true form to the maiden. The supreme god then said these words to that maiden of resolute vows:

"I am pleased by your devotion, asceticism, and discipline, good lady. Whatever wish you desire will be fulfilled, auspicious lady. When you give up your body, you will live with me in heaven, illustrious lady. This best of sacred sites will remain permanent in the world. Removing all sins, t will be called Bádara·páchana ('The Cooking of the Ju-ubes'), fair-browed lady. Renowned throughout the three worlds, it will be flooded with brahmin seers." 48.30

It was also at this distinguished, auspicious, pure and excellent site that the Seven Seers once left Arúndhati and departed for the Hímavat mountains.* It is said that these llustrious ascetics, who were resolute in their vows, had gone there in order to collect fruit and roots for their sus-tenance. While they were dwelling in the Hímavat forest,

te kṛtvā c' āśramaṃ tatra nyavasanta tapasvinaḥ
Arundhaty api kalyāṇī tapo|nity" âbhavat tadā.

48.35 Arundhatīṃ tato dṛṣṭvā tīvraṃ niyamam āsthitām
ath' âgamat tri|nayanaḥ su|prīto vara|das tadā.
brāhmaṃ rūpaṃ tataḥ kṛtvā Mahādevo mahā|yaśāḥ
tām abhyety' âbravīd devo: «bhikṣām icchāmy ahaṃ śubhe.»
pratyuvāca tataḥ sā taṃ brāhmaṇaṃ cāru|darśanā
«kṣīṇo 'nna|sañcayo vipra. badarāṇ' îha bhakṣaya.»
tato 'bravīn Mahādevaḥ: «pacasv' âitāni su|vrate.»

ity uktā s" âpacat tāni brāhmaṇa|priya|kāmyayā
adhiśritya samiddhe 'gnau badarāṇi yaśasvinī.
divyā mano|ramāḥ puṇyāḥ kathāḥ śuśrāva sā tadā.
atītā sā tv an|āvṛṣṭir ghorā dvādaśa|vārṣikī.

48.40 an|aśnantyāḥ pacantyāś ca śṛṇvantyāś ca kathāḥ śubhāḥ
din'|ôpamaḥ sa tasy" âtha kālo 'tītaḥ su|dāruṇaḥ.

tatas tu munayaḥ prāptāḥ phalāny ādāya parvatāt.
tataḥ sa bhagavān prītaḥ provāc' Ârundhatīṃ tataḥ:
«upasarpasva dharma|jñe yathā|pūrvam imān ṛṣīn.
prīto 'smi tava dharma|jñe tapasā niyamena ca.»
tataḥ saṃdarśayām āsa sva|rūpaṃ bhagavān Haraḥ
tato 'bravīt tadā tebhyas tasyās tac caritaṃ mahat:

«bhavadbhir Himavat|pṛṣṭhe yat tapaḥ samupārjitam
asyāś ca yat tapo viprā na samaṃ tan mataṃ mama.

48.45 anayā hi tapasvinyā tapas taptaṃ su|duś|caram.
an|aśnantyā pacantyā ca samā dvādaśa pāritāḥ.»

seeking sustenance, there was a twelve year drought. The ascetics built a hermitage to live in, while beautiful Arúndhati constantly devoted herself to her vows.

When boon-giving, three-eyed Shiva saw Arúndhati applying herself to severe discipline, he was extremely pleased and proceeded toward her. Taking on the appearance of a brahmin, glorious and divine Maha·deva approached her and said: "I seek alms, auspicious lady." Beautiful Arúndhati replied to the brahmin: "My store of food is used up, brahmin. Eat these jujube fruits." To which Maha·deva responded: "Please cook them, lady of good vows." 48.35

Addressed this way, glorious Arúndhati placed the jujube fruits on a kindled fire and cooked them in order to favor the brahmin. She then heard divine and auspicious discourses that delight the mind. The gruesome twelve-year drought then passed. Although she ate no food but only cooked and listened to auspicious discourses, that terrible period of time passed for Arúndhati as if it were a single day. 48.40

The ascetics returned, taking fruits with them from the mountain. The gratified Lord then said to Arúndhati: "Approach these seers as before, lady knowledgeable in righteousness. I am pleased by your asceticism and discipline, truth-knowing lady." Lord Hara then revealed his true form and told the ascetics about Arúndhati's great deed:

"Brahmins, this woman has achieved ascetic attainments that are, to my mind, superior to the ones that you have achieved on the ridge of the Hímavat. This ascetic woman has practiced austerities that are very difficult to perform. For twelve years she has cooked and not eaten." 48.45

tataḥ provāca bhagavāṃs tām ev' Ârundhatīṃ punaḥ:
«varaṃ vṛṇīṣva kalyāṇi yat te 'bhilaṣitaṃ hṛdi.»
s" âbravīt pṛthu|tāmr'|âkṣī devaṃ sapta'|ṛṣi|saṃsadi:

«bhagavān yadi me prītas tīrthaṃ syād idam uttamam
siddha|deva'|ṛṣi|dayitaṃ nāmnā Badarapācanam.
tath" âsmin deva|dev'|ēśa tri|rātram uṣitaḥ śuciḥ
prāpnuyād upavāsena phalaṃ dvādaśa|vārṣikam.»

«evam astv iti» tāṃ devaḥ pratyuvāca tapasvinīm.
sapta'|ṛṣibhiḥ stuto devas tato lokaṃ yayau tadā.
48.50 ṛṣayo vismayaṃ jagmus tāṃ dṛṣṭvā c' âpy Arundhatīm
a|śrāntāṃ cāvi|varṇāṃ ca kṣut|pipāsā|samāyutām.

evaṃ siddhiḥ parā prāptā Arundhatyā viśuddhayā
yathā tvayā mahā|bhāge mad|arthaṃ saṃśita|vrate.
viśeṣo hi tvayā bhadre vrate hy asmin samarpitaḥ.
tathā c' êdaṃ dadāmy adya niyamena su|toṣitaḥ.
viśeṣaṃ tava kalyāṇi prayacchāmi varaṃ vare
Arundhatyā varas tasyā yo datto vai mah"|ātmanā.
tasya c' âhaṃ prabhāvena tava kalyāṇi tejasā
pravakṣyāmi paraṃ bhūyo varam atra yathā|vidhi.
48.55 yas tv ekāṃ rajanīṃ tīrthe vatsyate su|samāhitaḥ
sa snātvā prāpsyate lokān deha|nyāsāt su|dur|labhān.»

The Lord then once again addressed Arúndhati: "Choose whatever boon your heart desires, beautiful lady." In the presence of the Seven Seers, that woman, who had wide red eyes, replied:

"If the Lord is pleased with me, then let this excellent *tirtha* be cherished by *siddha*s, gods and ascetics and bear the name Bádara·páchana. And, god of gods, if anyone dwells here virtuously for three nights, let them attain from their fast the fruit of twelve years of fasting."

"So be it," the god replied to the ascetic woman. After he had been praised by the Seven Seers, the god then returned to his realm. The seers were amazed to see that Arúndhati was unweary and had glowing skin, even though she had been subjected to hunger and thirst. 48.50

In this way, pure Arúndhati achieved the highest perfection, just as you have done for my sake, illustrious lady of resolute vows. Indeed you have achieved a superior distinction through your auspicious vow. Thoroughly satisfied by your discipline, I will today give you this boon. I will give you a boon, fine and beautiful lady, that is superior to the one that great-spirited Shiva gave Arúndhati. Through the power of this boon and through your own energy, beautiful lady, I will duly declare an even more supreme boon at this site. Whoever spends one night in deep concentration at this *tirtha* and bathes here will acquire worlds that are extremely difficult to obtain after they have given up their bodies." 48.55

ity uktvā bhagavān devaḥ sahasr'|âkṣaḥ pratāpavān
Śrutāvatīṃ tataḥ puṇyāṃ jagāma tri|divaṃ punaḥ.
gate vajra|dhare rājaṃs tatra varṣaṃ papāta ha
puṣpāṇāṃ Bharata|śreṣṭha divyānāṃ puṇya|gandhinām.
deva|dundubhayaś c' âpi nedus tatra mahā|svanāḥ
mārutaś ca vavau puṇyaḥ puṇya|gandho viśāṃ pate.
utsṛjya tu śubhā dehaṃ jagām' âsya ca bhāryatām
tapas" ôgreṇa taṃ labdhvā tena reme sah' â|cyuta.

JANAMEJAYA uvāca:

48.60 kā tasyā bhagavan mātā? kva saṃvṛddhā ca śobhanā?
śrotum icchāmy ahaṃ vipra. paraṃ kautūhalaṃ hi me.

VAIŚAMPĀYANA uvāca:

Bharadvājasya vipra'|rṣeḥ skannaṃ reto mah"|ātmanaḥ
dṛṣṭv" âpsarasam āyāntīṃ Ghṛtācīṃ pṛthu|locanām.
sa tu jagrāha tad retaḥ kareṇa japatāṃ varaḥ.
tad" āpatat parṇa|puṭe tatra sā saṃbhavat sutā.
tasyās tu jāta|karm'|ādi kṛtvā sarvaṃ tapo|dhanaḥ
nāma c' âsyāḥ sa kṛtavān Bharadvājo mahā|muniḥ
Śrutāvat" îti dharm'|ātmā deva'|rṣi|gaṇa|saṃsadi.
sve ca tām āśrame nyasya jagāma Himavad|vanam.

48.65 tatr' âpy upaspṛśya mah"|ânubhāvo
vasūni dattvā ca mahā|dvijebhyaḥ
jagāma tīrthaṃ su|samāhit'|ātmā
Śakrasya Vṛṣṇi|pravaras tadānīm.

Saying these words to pure Shrutávati, the illustrious, mighty, and thousand-eyed god returned to heaven. At the departure of the thunderbolt-wielder, a shower of divine and pure-scented flowers fell from the sky, best of Bharatas. Divine kettledrums boomed loudly and an auspicious wind of pure scent began to blow, lord of the people. When she gave up her body, virtuous Shrutávati became Indra's wife. Obtaining this status through fierce asceticism, she took pleasure with Indra, imperishable king.

JANAM·ÉJAYA said:

Who was the mother of Arúndhati, illustrious brahmin? Where was that radiant woman raised? I yearn to hear this, brahmin. For I am extremely curious. 48.60

VAISHAMPÁYANA said:

When the great-spirited brahmin seer Bharad·vaja saw the wide-eyed nymph Ghritáchi approaching him, his seed leaped out. That best of reciters caught the seed in his hand. The seed was then placed in a leaf-pot, where a daughter was born to him. After that great ascetic—who was rich in austerities—had performed her birth-ritual and other ceremonies, righteous Bharad·vaja gave her the name Shrutávati in the presence of hosts of gods and seers. The next day, he left her at his hermitage and departed for the Hímavat forest.

After he had sipped the water there, mighty Bala gave gifts to great brahmins and, with a deeply concentrated soul, that champion of the Vrishnis proceeded to the sacred site of Shakra. 48.65

VAIŚAMPĀYANA uvāca:

49.1 INDRATĪRTHAṂ tato gatvā Yadūnāṃ pravaro Balaḥ
viprebhyo dhana|ratnāni dadau snātvā yathā|vidhi.
tatra hy a|mara|rājo 'sāv īje kratu|śatena ha
Bṛhaspateś ca dev'|ēśaḥ pradadau vipulaṃ dhanam.
nirargalān sa|jārūthyān sarvān vividha|dakṣiṇān
ājahāra kratūṃs tatra yath"|ôktān veda|pāragaiḥ.
tān kratūn Bharata|śreṣṭha śata|kṛtvo mahā|dyutiḥ
pūrayām āsa vidhivat tataḥ khyātaḥ Śatakratuḥ.
49.5 tasya nāmnā ca tat tīrthaṃ śivaṃ puṇyaṃ sanātanam
Indratīrtham iti khyātaṃ sarva|pāpa|pramocanam.

upaspṛśya ca tatr' âpi vidhivan musal'|āyudhaḥ
brāhmaṇān pūjayitvā ca sadā|cchādana|bhojanaiḥ
śubhaṃ tīrtha|varaṃ tasmād Rāmatīrthaṃ jagāma ha,
yatra Rāmo mahā|bhāgo Bhārgavaḥ su|mahā|tapāḥ
a|sakṛt pṛthivīṃ jitvā hata|kṣatriya|puṅ|gavām,
upādhyāyaṃ puras|kṛtya Kaśyapaṃ muni|sattamam
ayajad vājapeyena so 'śva|medha|śatena ca
pradadau dakṣiṇāṃ c' âiva pṛthivīṃ vai sa|sāgarām.
dattvā ca dānaṃ vividhaṃ nānā|ratna|samanvitam
sa|go|hastika|dāsīkaṃ s'|âj'|âvi gatavān vanam.

VAISHAMPÁYANA said:

AFTER BALA, the champion of the Yadus, had gone to the Indra·tirtha and bathed in the proper manner, he gave wealth and jewels to brahmins. At this site, the king of the immortals—that lord of gods—had once offered up a hundred sacrifices and given large amounts of wealth to Brihas·pati. The sacrifices he offered had three kinds of stipends and various sacrificial fees; they were unimpeded and performed in the manner prescribed by experts in the Vedas. After glorious Indra had duly completed these one hundred sacrifices, best of Bharatas, he became known as Shata·kratu ("Performer of a Hundred Sacrifices"). That auspicious, pure, and everlasting site, which can dispel all sins, became known after his name as Indra·tirtha. 49.1 49.5

After he had duly sipped the water there and worshipped brahmins with perpetual clothes and food, club-weaponed Bala proceeded to the excellent and auspicious site of Rama·tirtha. There illustrious Rama, the descendant of Bhrigu, who had performed great austerities, repeatedly subjugated the earth after her bull-like warriors had been killed. Through his preceptor—the supreme ascetic Káshyapa—Rama then performed the Vajapéya ritual* with a hundred horse sacrifices and gave Káshyapa the earth and oceans as a sacrifical fee. After he had given away diverse gifts, consisting of various gems, cows, elephants, female slaves, goats and sheep, he went to the forest.*

49.10 puṇye tīrtha|vare tatra deva|brahma'|ṛṣi|sevite
munīṃś c' âiv' âbhivādy' âtha Yamunātīrtham āgamat,
yatr' ānayām āsa tadā rājasūyaṃ mahī|pate
putro 'diter mahā|bhāgo Varuṇo vai sita|prabhaḥ.
tatra nirjitya saṃgrāme mānuṣān devatās tathā
varaṃ kratuṃ samājahre Varuṇaḥ para|vīra|hā.
tasmin kratu|vare vṛtte saṃgrāmaḥ samajāyata
devānāṃ dānavānāṃ ca trailokyasya bhay'|āvahaḥ.
rājasūye kratu|śreṣṭhe nivṛtte Janamejaya
jāyate su|mahā|ghoraḥ saṃgrāmaḥ kṣatriyān prati.

49.15 tatr' âpi lāṅgalī deva ṛṣīn abhyarcya pūjayā
itarebhyo 'py adād dānam arthibhyaḥ kāma|do vibhuḥ.
vana|mālī tato hṛṣṭaḥ stūyamāno maha"|ṛṣibhiḥ
tasmād Ādityatīrthaṃ ca jagāma kamal'|ēkṣaṇaḥ,
yatr' êṣṭvā bhagavāñ jyotir bhāskaro rāja|sattama
jyotiṣām ādhipatyaṃ ca prabhāvaṃ c' âbhyapadyata.
tasyā nadyās tu tīre vai sarve devāḥ sa|Vāsavāḥ
Viśvedevāḥ sa|Maruto gandharv'|âpsarasaś ca ha,
Dvaipāyanaḥ Śukaś c' âiva Kṛṣṇaś ca Madhu|sūdanaḥ
yakṣāś ca rākṣasāś c' âiva piśācāś ca viśāṃ pate,

49.20 ete c' ânye ca bahavo yoga|siddhāḥ sahasraśaḥ
tasmiṃs tīrthe Sarasvatyāḥ śive puṇye paran|tapa.

When Bala had paid his respects to the ascetics at this excellent and auspicious *tirtha*, which was frequented by gods and brahmin seers, he proceeded to the Yámuna·tirtha. Brightly shining Váruna, the illustrious offspring of the Sun, performed a Raja·suya ritual at this site, lord of the earth. It was at this site that Váruna, that slayer of enemy heroes, offered his excellent sacrifice after he had conquered humans and gods in battle. When this excellent sacrifice had been performed, there was a battle between the gods and *dánava*s which brought terror to the three worlds. After the supreme ritual of the Raja·suya sacrifice had concluded, there was a battle of immense horror among the kshatriyas, Janam·éjaya. 49.10

Plow-bearing Bala then reverently honored the seers at this site, Your Majesty, and the desire-granting lord also gave wealth to others that asked for it. Praised by the great seers and full of joy, lotus-eyed Bala, who wears garlands of forest flowers, then proceeded to Adítya·tirtha. There, best of kings, the radiant Sun once performed a sacrifice and attained his powers and control over the stars. On the bank of that river, Vásava and all the gods, as well as the Vishve·devas, Maruts, *gandhárva*s, nymphs, Dvaipáyana, Shuka, Madhu-slaying Krishna, *yaksha*s, *rákshasa*s and *pishácha*s reside—these and many other thousands, who have been perfected by Yoga, all reside at this pure and auspicious site on the Sarásvati, O enemy-scorcher. 49.15 49.20

tatra hatvā purā Viṣṇur asurau Madhu|Kaiṭabhau
āplutya Bharata|śreṣṭha tīrtha|pravara uttame.
Dvaipāyanaś ca dharm'|ātmā tatr' âiv' āplutya Bhārata
saṃprāpya paramaṃ yogaṃ siddhiṃ ca paramāṃ gataḥ.
Asito Devalaś c' âiva tasminn eva mahā|tapāḥ
paramaṃ yogam āsthāya ṛṣir yogam avāptavān.

VAIŚAMPĀYANA uvāca:

50.1 TASMINN EVA TU dharm'|ātmā vasati sma tapo|dhanaḥ
gārhasthyaṃ dharmam āsthāya hy Asito Devalaḥ purā.
dharma|nityaḥ śucir dānto nyasta|daṇḍo mahā|tapāḥ
karmaṇā manasā vācā samaḥ sarveṣu jantuṣu.
a|krodhano mahā|rāja tulya|nind"|ātma|saṃstutiḥ
priy'|â|priye tulya|vṛttir Yamavat|sama|darśanaḥ.
kāñcane loṣṭa|bhāve ca sama|darśī mahā|tapāḥ
devān apūjayan nityam atithīṃś ca dvijaiḥ saha
brahma|carya|rato nityaṃ sadā dharma|parāyaṇaḥ.
50.5 tato 'bhyetya mahā|bhāga yogam āsthāya bhikṣukaḥ
Jaigīṣavyo munir dhīmāṃs tasmiṃs tīrthe samāhitaḥ.
Devalasy' āśrame rājan nyavasat sa mahā|dyutiḥ
yoga|nityo mahā|rāja siddhiṃ prāpto mahā|tapāḥ.
taṃ tatra vasamānaṃ tu Jaigīṣavyaṃ mahā|munim
Devalo darśayann eva n' âiv' âyuñjata dharmataḥ.

In the past, Vishnu killed the demons Madhu and Káitabha after he had bathed at this excellent and finest of *tirthas*, best of Bharatas.* Righteous Dvaipáyana also bathed at this site, descendant of Bharata, and reached the highest perfection after attaining supreme Yoga. The ascetic Ásita Dévala, a performer of great austerities, also applied himself to the highest Yoga at this site and achieved Yoga.

VAISHAMPÁYANA said:

RIGHTEOUS AND austerity-rich Ásita Dévala also used to dwell at this same site, applying himself to the householder path. Devoted to righteousness, pure, tamed, non-violent, and possessing great ascetic power, he acted equally toward all creatures in action, mind, and speech. He felt no anger, great king, and criticism and praise were equal to him. He behaved equally toward those who were dear and undear and had an impartiality similar to Yama's. This man of great austerities looked equally upon gold and clay and continuously worshipped gods, guests, and brahmins. Constantly delighting in chastity, he was always intent on righteousness. 50.1

At that time, illustrious king, a wise ascetic called Jaigishávya, who applied himself to Yoga and depended on alms, once came to this *tirtha* and meditated there. Possessing great splendor, that ascetic of great austerities dwelled at Dévala's hermitage and attained perfection through his devotion to yogic discipline. Dévala never failed in his duty in watching over that great ascetic Jaigishávya as he lived there. 50.5

evaṃ tayor mahārāja dīrgha|kālo vyatikramat;
Jaigīṣavyaṃ muni|varaṃ na dadarś' âtha Devalaḥ.
āhāra|kāle matimān parivrāḍ Janamejaya
upātiṣṭhata dharma|jño bhaikṣa|kāle sa Devalam.
50.10 sa dṛṣṭvā bhikṣu|rūpeṇa prāptaṃ tatra mahā|munim
gauravaṃ paramaṃ cakre prītiṃ ca vipulāṃ tathā.
Devalas tu yathā|śakti pūjayām āsa Bhārata
ṛṣi|dṛṣṭena vidhinā samā bahvīḥ samāhitaḥ.

kadā cit tasya nṛ|pate Devalasya mah"|ātmanaḥ
cintā su|mahatī jātā muniṃ dṛṣṭvā mahā|dyutim:
«samās tu samatikrāntā bahvyaḥ pūjayato mama.
na c' âyam alaso bhikṣur abhyabhāṣata kiñ cana!»
evaṃ vigaṇayann eva sa jagāma mah"|ôdadhim
antarikṣa|caraḥ śrīmān kalaśaṃ gṛhya Devalaḥ.
50.15 gacchann eva sa dharm'|ātmā samudraṃ saritāṃ patim
Jaigīṣavyaṃ tato 'paśyad gataṃ prāg eva Bhārata.
tataḥ sa|vismayaś cintāṃ jagām' âth' â|mita|prabhaḥ:
«kathaṃ bhikṣur ayaṃ prāptaḥ samudre snāta eva ca?»
ity evaṃ cintayām āsa maha"|rṣir Asitas tadā.

snātvā samudre vidhivac chucir japyaṃ jajāpa saḥ.
kṛta|japy'|âhnikaḥ śrīmān āśramaṃ ca jagāma ha
kalaśaṃ jala|pūrṇaṃ vai gṛhītvā Janamejaya.
tataḥ sa praviśann eva svam āśrama|padaṃ muniḥ
āsīnam āśrame tatra Jaigīṣavyam apaśyata.
50.20 na vyāharati c' âiv' âinaṃ Jaigīṣavyaḥ kathañ cana

A long time passed for the two men in this way until one lay Dévala lost sight of the supreme ascetic Jaigishávya. Iowever, when it was time to eat, the wise wanderer, who vas knowledgeable in righteousness, approached Dévala at he time for receiving alms, Janam·éjaya. When Dévala saw 50.10 he great ascetic arrive in the form of a mendicant, he felt the ighest respect and great joy. Dévala then worshipped him o his utmost ability, whereupon he practiced concentration or many years according to the injunctions prescribed by eers, descendant of Bharata.

One day, however, great-spirited King Dévala became nxious when he looked at that ascetic of great splendor, hinking: "I have spent many years worshipping him but his lazy mendicant has still not said a word to me!" Thinkng this, glorious Dévala grabbed his waterpot and travled through the air to the ocean. But as soon as righteous 50.15)évala arrived at the ocean—that lord of rivers—he saw hat Jaigishávya had already arrived before him, descendant f Bharata. Filled with wonder, Ásita, who possessed limitss splendor, had this thought: "How has this mendicant lready arrived at the ocean and bathed in it too?" Thus ondered the great seer Ásita.

When Dévala had bathed in the ocean in the proper maner and become cleansed, he recited mantras. Finishing his aily recitation, glorious Dévala returned to his hermitage, olding on to his waterpot, which was full of water, Janam·jaya. But as soon as the ascetic entered his hermitage, he saw hat Jaigishávya was already sitting there. The great ascetic 50.20 aigishávya said nothing whatsoever to Dévala but stayed in he hermitage, still as a piece of wood. Even though Dévala

kāṣṭha|bhūto ”śrama|pade* vasati sma mahā|tapāḥ.
taṃ dṛṣṭvā c' āplutaṃ toye sāgare sāgar'|ôpamam
praviṣṭam āśramaṃ c' âpi pūrvam eva dadarśa saḥ.
Asito Devalo rājaṃś cintayām āsa buddhimān
dṛṣṭvā prabhāvaṃ tapaso Jaigīṣavyasya yoga|jam.
cintayām āsa rāj'|êndra tadā sa muni|sattamaḥ:
«mayā dṛṣṭaḥ samudre ca āśrame ca kathaṃ tv ayam?»

evaṃ vigaṇayann eva sa munir mantra|pāragaḥ
utpapāt' āśramāt tasmād antarikṣaṃ viśāṃ pate
jijñās”|ârthaṃ tadā bhikṣor Jaigīṣavyasya Devalaḥ.
50.25 so 'ntarikṣa|carān siddhān samapaśyat samāhitān
Jaigīṣavyaṃ ca taiḥ siddhaiḥ pūjyamānam apaśyata.
tato 'sitaḥ su|saṃrabdho vyavasāyī dṛḍha|vrataḥ.

apaśyad vai divaṃ yāntaṃ Jaigīṣavyaṃ sa Devalaḥ.
tasmāt tu pitṛ|lokaṃ taṃ vrajantaṃ so 'nvapaśyata.
pitṛ|lokāc ca taṃ yāntaṃ Yāmyaṃ lokam apaśyata.
tasmād api samutpatya Soma|lokam abhiplutam
vrajantam anvapaśyat sa Jaigīṣavyaṃ mahā|munim,
lokān samutpatantaṃ tu śubhān ekānta|yājinām.
tato 'gni|hotriṇāṃ lokāṃs tataś c' âpy utpapāta ha
darśaṃ ca paurṇamāsaṃ ca ye yajanti tapo|dhanāḥ.
50.30 tebhyaḥ sa dadṛśe dhīmāl̃ lokebhyaḥ paśu|yājinām
vrajantaṃ lokam a|malam apaśyad deva|pūjitam.
cāturmāsyair bahu|vidhair yajante ye tapo|dhanāḥ
teṣāṃ sthānaṃ tato yātaṃ tath” âgni|ṣṭoma|yājinām.

ad earlier seen ocean-like Jaigishávya bathe in the waters of he ocean, he now saw that Jaigishávya had entered the hernitage before him. Wise Ásita Dévala then contemplated he power of the ascetic Jaigishávya, which was produced y Yoga, Your Majesty. The supreme ascetic contemplated hus, king of kings: "How can I have seen him both at the cean and in the hermitage?"

Pondering the matter in this way, the ascetic Dévala, who vas expert in mantras, flew from the hermitage up into the ky in order to learn more about the mendicant Jaigishávya, ord of the people. But when he saw *siddhas* flying through he sky in deep concentration, he also saw Jaigishávya being vorshipped by the same *siddhas*. Although full of resolve nd firm in his vows, Ásita became extremely angry at this ight. 50.25

Dévala then saw Jaigishávya traveling to heaven. He then aught sight of him going to the ancestor realm. He then saw im leaving the ancestor realm and traveling to the realm of ama. He then saw the great ascetic Jaigishávya flying from hat realm and approaching the realm of Soma. He then aw him flying to the auspicious realms of those who perorm exclusive sacrifices. From there Jaigishávya flew to the ealms of Agni·hotra sacrificers and on to the realms of those usterity-rich beings who perform the Darsha and Paurnanása sacrifices. Wise Dévala then saw him proceed from he realms of those who sacrifice animals to the pure realm hat is honored by the gods. From there he saw him travel o the realm of those austerity-rich beings who perform the haturmásya sacrifices with their many rites, and then to he realm of those who perform the Agni·shtoma sacrifice. 50.30

agniṣṭutena ca tathā ye yajanti tapo|dhanāḥ
tat sthānam anusamprāptam anvapaśyata Devalaḥ,
vājapeyaṃ kratu|varaṃ tathā bahu|suvarṇakam
āharanti mahā|prājñās teṣāṃ lokeṣv apaśyata.

yajante rājasūyena puṇḍarīkeṇa c' âiva ye
teṣāṃ lokeṣv apaśyac ca Jaigīṣavyaṃ sa Devalaḥ.
50.35 aśva|medhaṃ kratu|varaṃ nara|medhaṃ tath" âiva ca
āharanti nara|śreṣṭhās teṣāṃ lokeṣv apaśyata.
sarva|medhaṃ ca duṣ|prāpaṃ tathā sautrāmaṇiṃ ca ye
teṣāṃ lokeṣv apaśyac ca Jaigīṣavyaṃ sa Devalaḥ.
dvādaś'|âhaiś ca satraiś ca yajante vividhair nṛpa
teṣāṃ lokeṣv apaśyac ca Jaigīṣavyaṃ sa Devalaḥ.
Mitrā|Varuṇayor lokān ādityānāṃ tath" âiva ca
sa|lokatām anuprāptam apaśyata tato 'sitaḥ.
Rudrāṇāṃ ca Vasūnāṃ ca sthānaṃ yac ca Bṛhaspateḥ
tāni sarvāṇy atītāni samapaśyat tato 'sitaḥ.
50.40 āruhya ca gavāṃ lokaṃ prayāntaṃ brahma|sattriṇām
lokān apaśyad gacchantaṃ Jaigīṣavyaṃ tato 'sitaḥ.
trīl̃ lokān aparān vipram utpatantaṃ sva|tejasā
pati|vratānāṃ lokāṃś ca vrajantaṃ so 'nvapaśyata.

Dévala then saw him reach the realm of those austerity-rich beings who perform the Agni·shtuta sacrifice, and he then saw him in the realms of those wise men who perform the Vajapéya sacrifice, that fine ritual which involves much gold.*

Dévala also saw Jaigishávya in the realms of those who perform the Raja·suya and Pundaríka sacrifice,* as well as in the realms of those excellent men who perform the horse sacrifice, that supreme ritual, and the human sacrifice. Dévala also saw Jaigishávya in the realms of those who perform the Sautrámani sacrifice and of those who perform the universal sacrifice, which is so difficult to fulfill.* Dévala then saw Jaigishávya in the realms of those who perform the twelve-day sacrifices and rituals of various kinds, Your Majesty. From there Ásita saw him reside in the realms of Mitra and Váruna and also the *adítyas*. From there Ásita saw him pass through all the realms of the Rudras, Vasus, and Brihas·pati. Ásita then saw Jaigishávya ascend to the realm of cows and travel to the realms of the *brahma·sattrins*.* From there he saw the brahmin fly by means of his own power to three other realms and proceed to the realms of women who are devoted to their husbands.

50.35

50.40

tato muni|varaṃ bhūyo Jaigīṣavyam ath' Âsitaḥ
n' ânvapaśyata loka|stham antar|hitam arin|dama.
so 'cintayan mahā|bhāgo Jaigīṣavyasya Devalaḥ
prabhāvaṃ su|vratatvaṃ ca siddhiṃ yogasya c' â|tulām.
Asito 'pṛcchata tadā siddhāl lokeṣu sattamān
prayataḥ prāñjalir bhūtvā dhīras tān brahma|satriṇaḥ:

50.45 «Jaigīṣavyaṃ na paśyāmi.
tam śaṃsadhvaṃ mah"|âujasam.
etad icchāmy ahaṃ śrotuṃ.
paraṃ kautūhalaṃ hi me.»

SIDDHĀ ūcuḥ:

śṛṇu Devala bhūt'|ârthaṃ śaṃsatāṃ no dṛḍha|vrata.
Jaigīṣavyaḥ sa vai lokaṃ śāśvataṃ Brahmaṇo gataḥ.

VAIŚAMPĀYANA uvāca:

sa śrutvā vacanaṃ teṣāṃ siddhānāṃ brahma|sattriṇām
Asito Devalas tūrṇam utpapāta papāta ca.
tataḥ siddhās ta ūcur hi Devalaṃ punar eva ha:
«na Devala gatis tatra tava gantuṃ tapo|dhana
Brahmaṇaḥ sadane vipra Jaigīṣavyo yad āptavān!»

VAIŚAMPĀYANA uvāca:

teṣāṃ tad vacanaṃ śrutvā siddhānāṃ Devalaḥ punaḥ
ānupūrvyeṇa lokāṃs tān sarvān avatatāra ha.
50.50 svam āśrama|padaṃ puṇyam ājagāma patatri|vat.
praviśann eva c' âpaśyaj Jaigīṣavyaṃ sa Devalaḥ.
tato buddhyā vyagaṇayad Devalo dharma|yuktayā
dṛṣṭvā prabhāvaṃ tapaso Jaigīṣavyasya yoga|jam.

At this point Ásita lost sight of the supreme ascetic Jaigi-hávya after he disappeared in that realm, tamer of en-mies. Illustrious Dévala then contemplated Jaigishávya's ower, his excellent vows, and the unparalleled perfection f his discipline. With his hands cupped in respect, wise sita devotedly asked the *brahma·sattrins*, the highest *sid-lhas* throughout the worlds, the following question:

"I cannot see Jaigishávya. Please inform me of that pow-rful ascetic. I yearn to hear this. For I have the greatest uriosity." 50.45

THE SIDDHAS said:

Listen to the truth that we tell you, Dévala of firm vows. aigishávya has gone to the eternal realm of Brahma.

VAISHAMPÁYANA said:

Hearing the words of the *brahma·sattrin siddhas*, Ásita Dévala swiftly flew into the sky but then fell down. The *iddhas* once again addressed Dévala:

"Dévala, brahmin rich in austerities, you cannot tread the ath to the house of Brahma that Jaigishávya has reached!"

VAISHAMPÁYANA said:

Hearing the *siddhas*' words, Dévala flew down once more hrough all the realms in due order. Descending like a bird, e arrived at his hermitage. But as soon as he entered, he aw that Jaigishávya was already there. With a mind intent n righteousness, Dévala then contemplated the power of he ascetic Jaigishávya, which was produced by Yoga. 50.50

tato 'bravīn mah"|ātmānaṃ Jaigīṣavyaṃ sa Devalaḥ
vinay'|âvanato rājann upasarpya mahā|munim:
«mokṣa|dharmaṃ samāsthātum
iccheyaṃ bhagavann aham!»
tasya tad vacanaṃ śrutvā
upadeśaṃ cakāra saḥ
vidhiṃ ca yogasya paraṃ kāry'|â|kāryasya śāstrataḥ.
saṃnyāsa|kṛta|buddhiṃ taṃ tato dṛṣṭvā mahā|tapāḥ
sarvāś c' âsya kriyāś cakre vidhi|dṛṣṭena karmaṇā.

50.55 saṃnyāsa|kṛta|buddhiṃ taṃ bhūtāni pitṛbhiḥ saha
tato dṛṣṭvā praruruduḥ: «ko 'smān saṃvibhajiṣyati?»
Devalas tu vacaḥ śrutvā bhūtānāṃ karuṇaṃ tathā
diśo daśa vyāharatāṃ mokṣaṃ tyaktuṃ mano dadhe.
tatas tu phala|mūlāni pavitrāṇi ca Bhārata
puṣpāṇy oṣadhayaś c' âiva rorūyanti sahasraśaḥ:
«punar no Devalaḥ kṣudro nūnaṃ chetsyati dur|matiḥ.
a|bhayaṃ sarva|bhūtebhyo yo dattvā n' âvabudhyate!»
tato bhūyo vyagaṇayat sva|buddhyā muni|sattamaḥ
mokṣe gārhasthya|dharme vā kiṃ nu śreyas|karaṃ bhavet.

50.60 iti niścitya manasā Devalo rāja|sattama
tyaktvā gārhasthya|dharmaṃ sa mokṣa|dharmam arocayat.
evam|ādīni saṃcintya Devalo niścayāt tataḥ
prāptavān paramāṃ siddhiṃ paraṃ yogaṃ ca Bhārata.
tato devāḥ samāgamya Bṛhaspati|puro|gamāḥ
Jaigīṣavyaṃ tapaś c' âsya praśaṃsanti tapasvinaḥ.
ath' âbravīd ṛṣi|varo devān vai Nāradas tadā
«Jaigīṣavye tapo n' âsti vismāpayati yo 'sitam!»
tam evaṃ|vādinaṃ dhīraṃ pratyūcus te div'|âukasaḥ:

Bowing modestly, Your Majesty, Dévala approached the great ascetic Jaigishávya and said: "I wish to undertake the religion of liberation, my lord!" Hearing these words, Jaigishávya gave Dévala lessons and taught him the supreme ordinances of Yoga and what should and should not be done according to the Teachings. When the great ascetic saw that Dévala had resolved to become a renouncer, he performed all the rites for him with rituals prescribed by ordinance.

But on seeing that Dévala had resolved to become a renouncer, the spirits and ancestors wept, saying: "Who will now give us food?" Hearing the spirits' pitiful words proclaimed throughout the ten directions, Dévala inclined his mind toward abandoning liberation. But the sacred fruits and roots, as well as the flowers and herbs, then all cried out in their thousands, descendant of Bharata: "Now mean and wicked Dévala will surely pluck us! He who offered to protect all creatures has now become unaware!" The supreme ascetic then carefully considered whether liberation or the religion of the householder was better. After pondering this, best of kings, Dévala abandoned the religion of the householder and chose the religion of liberation.* 50.55 50.60

After contemplating the matter in this way, Dévala achieved the ultimate perfection and the highest Yoga as a result of his resolution, descendant of Bharata. The gods, who were headed by Brihas·pati, gathered together and praised Jaigishávya and his ascetic power. Then Nárada, that best of seers, addressed the gods, saying: "Jaigishávya no longer has any ascetic power because he used it to fill Ásita with wonder!" But the gods replied to wise Nárada: "Do not say such things about the great ascetic Jaigishávya! There 50.65

«n' âivam ity eva śaṃsanto Jaigīṣavyaṃ mahā|munim!
50.65 n' âtaḥ parataraṃ kiñ cit tulyam asti prabhāvataḥ
tejasas tapasaś c' âsya yogasya ca mah"|ātmanaḥ!»
evaṃ|prabhāvo dharm'|ātmā Jaigiṣavyas tath" Âsitaḥ.
tayor idaṃ sthāna|varaṃ tīrthaṃ c' âiva mah"|ātmanoḥ.
tatr' âpy upaspṛśya tato mah"|ātmā
dattvā ca vittaṃ hala|bhṛd dvijebhyaḥ
avāpya dharmaṃ param'|ârtha|karmā
jagāma Somasya mahat su|tīrtham.

VAIŚAMPĀYANA uvāca:

51.1 YATR' ĒJIVĀN uḍu|patī rājasūyena Bhārata
tasmiṃs tīrthe mahān āsīt saṃgrāmas Tārakā|mayaḥ.
tatr' âpy upaspṛśya Balo dattvā dānāni c' ātmavān
Sārasvatasya dharm'|ātmā munes tīrthaṃ jagāma ha.
tatra dvādaśa|vārṣikyām an|āvṛṣṭyāṃ dvij'|ôttamān
vedān adhyāpayām āsa purā Sārasvato muniḥ.

JANAMEJAYA uvāca:

kathaṃ dvādaśa|vārṣikyām an|āvṛṣṭyāṃ dvij'|ôttamān
ṛṣīn adhyāpayām āsa purā Sārasvato muniḥ?

VAIŚAMPĀYANA uvāca:

51.5 āsīt pūrvaṃ mahā|rāja munir dhīmān mahā|tapāḥ
Dadhīca iti vikhyāto brahma|cārī jit'|êndriyaḥ.
tasy' âtitapasaḥ Śakro bibheti satataṃ vibho.
na sa lobhayituṃ śakyaḥ phalair bahu|vidhair api.
pralobhan'|ârthaṃ tasy' âtha prāhiṇot Pāka|śāsanaḥ
divyām apsarasaṃ puṇyāṃ darśanīyām Alambuṣām.

s nothing superior or equal to this great-spirited man in ower, energy, asceticism, or Yoga!"

Such was the power of righteous Jaigishávya and of Ásita. This is the excellent site and *tirtha* of those two great-spirited nen.

After sipping the water there, the heroic plow-bearer—vhose actions have the highest purpose—gave wealth to wice-born brahmins, earned great merit, and then proeeded to the great and excellent *tirtha* of Soma.

VAISHAMPÁYANA said:

IT WAS AT this sacred site that the Moon—that lord of the tars—once offered a Raja·suya sacrifice and that there was a reat battle involving Táraka, descendant of Bharata. After e had sipped the water there, self-composed and righteous Bala gave gifts and then proceeded to the *tirtha* of the ascetic arásvata. There the ascetic Sarásvata had once taught the Vedas to excellent brahmins after a twelve-year drought. 51.1

JANAM·ÉJAYA said:

How was it that, after a twelve-year drought, the ascetic arásvata once taught these eminent brahmin seers?

VAISHAMPÁYANA said:

In the past, great king, there was a wise ascetic of great usterities known as Dadhícha, who practiced chastity and ad conquered his senses. Shakra was in constant fear of Dadhícha's extreme asceticism, my lord. It was impossible to ntice him, even though Shakra used temptations of various inds. The chastiser of Paka therefore sent a divine nymph alled Alámbusha to seduce him, who was fair and beautiful. That beautiful nymph approached great-spirited Dadhícha 51.5

tasya tarpayato devān Sarasvatyāṃ mah"|ātmanaḥ
samīpato mahā|rāja s" ôpātiṣṭhata bhāvinī.
tāṃ divya|vapuṣaṃ dṛṣṭvā tasya' rṣer bhāvit'|ātmanaḥ
retaḥ skannaṃ Sarasvatyāṃ. tat sā jagrāha nimnagā.

51.10 kukṣau c' âpy adadhadd hṛṣṭā tad retaḥ puruṣa'|rṣabha
sā dadhāra ca taṃ garbhaṃ putra|hetor mahā|nadī.
suṣuve c' âpi samaye putraṃ sā saritāṃ varā
jagāma putram ādāya tam ṛṣiṃ prati ca prabho.
ṛṣi|saṃsadi taṃ dṛṣṭvā sā nadī muni|sattamam
tataḥ provāca rāj'|êndra dadatī putram asya tam:

«brahma'|rṣe tava putro 'yaṃ tvad|bhaktyā dhārito mayā
dṛṣṭvā te 'psarasaṃ reto yat skannaṃ prāg Alambuṣām
tat kukṣiṇā vai brahma'|rṣe tvad|bhaktyā dhṛtavaty aham
‹na vināśam idaṃ gacchet tvat|teja iti› niścayāt.
pratigṛhṇīṣva putraṃ svaṃ mayā dattam a|ninditam.»

51.15 ity uktaḥ pratijagrāha
prītiṃ c' âvāpa puṣkalām
sva|sutaṃ c' âpy ajighrat taṃ
mūrdhni premṇā dvij'|ôttamaḥ.
pariṣvajya ciraṃ kālaṃ tadā Bharata|sattama
Sarasvatyai varaṃ prādāt prīyamāṇo mahā|muniḥ:

«Viśvedevāḥ sa|pitaro gandharv'|âpsarasāṃ gaṇāḥ
tṛptiṃ yāsyanti su|bhage tarpyamāṇās tav' âmbhasā.»

ity uktvā sa tu tuṣṭāva vacobhir vai mahā|nadīm
prītaḥ parama|hṛṣṭ'|ātmā. yathā|vac chṛṇu pārthiva:

while he was gratifying the gods at the Sarásvati river, great king. When the seer of purified soul saw her divine body, his seed leaped into the Sarásvati. The river held onto the seed. Indeed, the great river joyfully placed the seed in her womb (51.10) and conceived an embryo in order to produce a child, bull of the Bharatas. At the appropriate time, the supreme river gave birth to a son and, taking the child with her, went to visit the seer, my lord. Seeing that supreme ascetic in an assembly of seers, the river gave the child to him and said the following words, king of kings:

"Brahmin seer, this is your son. I have reared him out of devotion to you. Your seed leaped out when you saw the nymph Alámbusha. Led by the conviction that your vital energy could not be destroyed, I preserved the seed in my womb out of devotion to you, brahmin seer. Accept my gift of your faultless son."

Addressed this way, that supreme brahmin accepted the (51.15) child and sniffed the head of his son with affection and great joy. After embracing his son for a long time, the pleased and mighty ascetic gave Sarásvati a boon, best of Bharatas:

"The Vishve·devas, ancestors, and troops of *gandhárvas* and nymphs will be satisfied by the gratification of your waters, illustrious lady."

Saying this, the gladdened ascetic—whose soul was filled with the highest joy—praised the great river with these words. Listen to them, Your Majesty:

«prasrut" âsi mahā|bhāge saraso Brahmaṇaḥ purā.
jānanti tvāṃ saric|chreṣṭhe munayaḥ saṃśita|vratāḥ.
51.20 mama priya|karī c' âpi satataṃ priya|darśane.
tasmāt Sārasvataḥ putro mahāṃs te vara|varṇini.
tav' âiva nāmnā prathitaḥ putras te loka|bhāvanaḥ
Sārasvata iti khyāto bhaviṣyati mahā|tapāḥ!
eṣa dvādaśa|vārṣikyām an|āvṛṣṭyāṃ dvija'|rṣabhān
Sārasvato mahā|bhāge vedān adhyāpayiṣyati.
puṇyābhyaś ca saridbhyas tvaṃ sadā puṇyatamā śubhe
bhaviṣyasi mahā|bhāge mat|prasādāt Sarasvati.»

evaṃ sā saṃstut" ânena varaṃ labdhvā mahā|nadī
putram ādāya muditā jagāma Bharata'|rṣabha.

51.25 etasminn eva kāle tu virodhe deva|dānavaiḥ
Śakraḥ praharaṇ'|ânveṣī lokāṃs trīn vicacāra ha.
na c' ôpalebhe bhagavāñ Śakraḥ praharaṇaṃ tadā
yad vai teṣāṃ bhaved yogyaṃ vadhāya vibudha|dviṣām.
tato 'bravīt surāñ Śakro:

«na me śakyā mah"|âsurāḥ
ṛte 'sthibhir Dadhīcasya nihantuṃ tri|daśa|dviṣaḥ.
tasmād gatvā ṛṣi|śreṣṭho yācyatāṃ sura|sattamāḥ
‹Dadhīc'|âsthīni deh' îti› tair vadhiṣyāmahe ripūn.»

sa ca tair yācito 'sthīni yatnād ṛṣi|varas tadā
prāṇa|tyāgaṃ Kuru|śreṣṭha cakār' âiv' â|vicārayan.
sa lokān a|kṣayān prāpto deva|priya|karas tadā.
51.30 tasy' âsthibhir atho Śakraḥ saṃprahṛṣṭa|manās tadā
kārayām āsa divyāni nānā|praharaṇāni ca
gadā vajrāṇi cakrāṇi gurūn daṇḍāṃś ca puṣkalān.

"In the past, lady of great fortune, you originated from the ake of Brahma. Ascetics who keep resolute vows know you, est of rivers. You have always performed kindnesses toward ne, lady of fair appearance and fine complexion. Your great on will therefore be called Sarásvata. Your world-creating on will be known after your name and that great ascetic will e proclaimed as Sarásvata! Sarásvata will teach the Vedas o bull-like brahmins after a twelve-year drought, illustrious ady. Through my grace, auspicious and illustrious Sarásvati, ou will always remain the purest of sacred rivers." 51.20

Praised by Dadhícha in this way, the great river received he boon and joyfully departed, taking her child with her, ull of the Bharatas.

At the very same time, Shakra was scouring the three vorlds for a weapon during a conflict between the gods and he *dánavas*. When he was unable to find a weapon suitable or killing the gods' enemies, Lord Shakra addressed the ods, saying: 51.25

"I can only slaughter these mighty demons and enemies f the gods if I use the bones of Dadhícha! Go therefore and sk Dadhícha, that best of seers, to give you his bones and ve will use them to slay our enemies, eminent deities!"

When the gods vigorously entreated Dadhícha for his ones, the supreme seer gave up his life without hesitation, est of Kurus. In performing this kindness to the gods, he eached the imperishable realms. Shakra then joyfully made arious divine weapons from Dadhícha's bones, including umerous maces, thunderbolts, discuses, and heavy rods.)adhícha, that world-creator, had been fathered through evere ascetic practice by Bhrigu, the finest of seers and son 51.30

sa hi tīvreṇa tapasā saṃbhṛtaḥ parama'|ṛṣiṇā
Prajāpati|suten' âtha Bhṛguṇā loka|bhāvanaḥ.
atikāyaḥ sa tejasvī loka|sāro vinirmitaḥ.
jajñe śaila|guruḥ prāṃśur mahimnā prathitaḥ prabhuḥ.
nityam udvijate c' âsya tejasaḥ Pāka|śāsanaḥ.

tena vajreṇa bhagavān mantra|yuktena Bhārata
bhṛśaṃ krodha|visṛṣṭena Brahma|tej'|ôdbhavena ca
daitya|dānava|vīrāṇāṃ jaghāna navatīr nava.
atha kāle vyatikrānte mahaty atibhayaṅ|kare
an|āvṛṣṭir anuprāptā rājan dvādaśa|vārṣikī.
51.35 tasyāṃ dvādaśa|vārṣikyām an|āvṛṣṭyāṃ maha"|ṛṣayaḥ
vṛtty|arthaṃ prādravan rājan kṣudh"|ārtāḥ sarvato|diśam.
digbhyas tān pradrutān dṛṣṭvā muniḥ Sārasvatas tadā
gamanāya matiṃ cakre. taṃ provāca Sarasvatī:

«na gantavyam itaḥ putra. tav' āhāram ahaṃ sadā
dāsyāmi matsya|pravarān. uṣyatām iha Bhārata.»

ity uktas tarpayām āsa sa pitṝn devatās tathā
āhāram akaron nityaṃ prāṇān vedāṃś ca dhārayan.
atha tasyām an|āvṛṣṭyām atītāyām maha"|ṛṣayaḥ
anyonyaṃ paripapracchuḥ punaḥ svādhyāya|kāraṇāt.
51.40 teṣāṃ kṣudhā|parītānāṃ naṣṭā ved" âbhidhāvatām*.
sarveṣām eva rāj'|êndra na kaś cit pratibhānavān.
atha kaś cid ṛṣis teṣāṃ Sārasvatam upeyivān
kurvāṇaṃ saṃśit'|ātmānaṃ svādhyāyam ṛṣi|sattamam.
sa gatv" ācaṣṭa tebhyaś ca Sārasvatam atiprabham
svādhyāyam a|mara|prakhyaṃ kurvāṇaṃ vijane vane.

f Praja·pati. Full of energy and with an enormous body, he vas created as the essential power of the universe. Famed or his huge size, lord Dadhícha became tall and heavy as a nountain. The chastiser of Paka constantly trembled at his ower.

With his mantra-furnished thunderbolt, which arose rom the energy of Brahma and was hurled with violent nger, Lord Shakra slaughtered ninety-nine of the *daitya* and *lánava* heroes. Then, after a long and terrifying period of ime, a twelve-year drought occurred, Your Majesty. During 51.35 his twelve-year drought, the great seers were stricken with iunger and fled in every direction in order to seek sustenance. When he saw them running in all directions, the scetic Sarásvata also decided to depart. Sarásvati, however, ddressed him, saying:

"Do not leave here, my child. I will always give you food uch as fine fish. Stay here, descendant of Bharata."

Addressed this way, Sarásvata continued to satisfy the ncestors and gods. Preserving his life and the Vedas, he eceived food continuously. After the drought had passed, he great seers questioned each other once more about Vedic ecitation. But they had all lost their knowledge of the Vedas 51.40 luring their flight when they were overcome with hunger. None of the ascetics possessed this wisdom anymore, king of kings. One day, however, one of the ascetics happened ipon Sarásvata, that best of seers, as he recited the Vedas vith resolute soul. The ascetic then left and told the others bout Sarásvata's extreme splendor and how he was reciting he Vedas in the desolate forest, resembling an immortal god.

tataḥ sarve samājagmus tatra rājan maha"|rṣayaḥ
Sārasvataṃ muni|śreṣṭham idam ūcuḥ samāgatāḥ:
«asmān adhyāpayasv' êti!» tān uvāca tato muniḥ:
«śiṣyatvam upagacchadhvaṃ vidhivadd hi mam' êty» uta.
51.45 tatr' âbruvan muni|gaṇā: «bālas tvam asi putraka.»
sa tān āha: «na me dharmo naśyed iti» punar munīn.
«yo hy a|dharmeṇa vai brūyād gṛhṇīyād yo 'py a|dharmataḥ
hīyetāṃ tāv ubhau kṣipraṃ syātāṃ vā vairiṇāv ubhau.
na hāyanair na palitair na vittena na bandhubhiḥ
ṛṣayaś cakrire dharmaṃ. yo 'nūcānaḥ sa no mahān!»
etac chrutvā vacas tasya munayas te vidhānataḥ
tasmād vedān anuprāpya punar dharmaṃ pracakrire.
ṣaṣṭir muni|sahasrāṇi śiṣyatvaṃ pratipedire
Sārasvatasya vipra'|rṣer veda|svādhyāya|kāraṇāt.
51.50 muṣṭiṃ muṣṭiṃ tataḥ sarve darbhāṇāṃ te hy upāharan
tasy' āsan'|ârthaṃ vipra'|rṣer bālasy' âpi vaśe sthitāḥ.
tatr' âpi dattvā vasu Rauhiṇeyo
mahā|balaḥ Keśava|pūrva|jo 'tha
jagāma tīrthaṃ muditaḥ krameṇa
khyātaṃ mahad vṛddha|kanyā sma yatra.

JANAMEJAYA uvāca:

52.1 KATHAṂ KUMĀRĪ bhagavaṃs tapo|yuktā hy abhūt purā?
kim|arthaṃ ca tapas tepe? ko v" âsyā niyamo 'bhavat?
su|duṣ|karam idaṃ brahmaṃs tvattaḥ śrutam an|uttamam.
ākhyāhi tattvam a|khilaṃ yathā tapasi sā sthitā.

All the great seers then gathered together and, once they had assembled, they said to Sarásvata, that supreme ascetic: "Teach us!" The ascetic replied: "Become my disciples in the prescribed manner." "But you are only a child, young boy," the troops of ascetics said. Sarásvata then replied: 51.45

"May my righteousness not be destroyed! Those who teach wrongly or learn wrongly will both quickly be lost or become enemies. Seers do not practice righteousness based on years, gray hairs, wealth, or kinsmen. That man among us is great who can repeat the Vedas!"

After they had heard Sarásvata's words, the ascetics attained the Vedas in due manner and again practiced righteousness. Sixty thousand ascetics became the disciples of the brahmin seer Sarásvata in order to recite the Vedas. In 51.50 service to him, all the ascetics offered individual handfuls of *darbha* grass as a seat for the brahmin seer, even though he was only a child.

After the mighty son of Róhini, that elder brother of Késhava, had given wealth at this site, he joyfully proceeded in turn to the great *tirtha* where an old maiden used to dwell.

JANAM·ÉJAYA said:

HOW, IN OLDEN days, did that maiden come to practice 52.1 asceticism, my lord? Why did she practice austerities? What was her discipline? Your unparalleled words are extremely difficult to understand, brahmin. Tell me everything about how this woman became established in asceticism.

VAIŚAMPĀYANA uvāca:

ṛṣir āsīn mahā|vīryaḥ Kuṇir Gargo mahā|yaśāḥ
sa taptvā vipulaṃ rājaṃs tapo vai tapatāṃ varaḥ.
manas" âtha sutāṃ su|bhrūṃ samutpāditavān vibhuḥ.
tāṃ ca dṛṣṭvā muniḥ prītaḥ Kuṇir Gargo mahā|yaśāḥ
jagāma tri|divaṃ rājan saṃtyajy' êha kalevaram.

52.5 su|bhrūḥ sā hy atha kalyāṇī puṇḍarīka|nibh'|ēkṣaṇā
mahatā tapas" ôgreṇa kṛtv" āśramam a|ninditā,
upavāsaiḥ pūjayantī pitṝn devāṃś ca sā purā.
tasyās tu tapas" ôgreṇa mahān kālo 'tyagān nṛpa.
sā pitrā dīyamān" âpi tatra n' âicchad a|ninditā.
ātmanaḥ sadṛśaṃ sā tu bhartāraṃ n' ânvapaśyata.

tataḥ sā tapas" ôgreṇa pīḍayitv" ātmanas tanum
pitṛ|dev'|ârcana|ratā babhūva vijane vane.
s" ātmānaṃ manyamān" âpi kṛta|kṛtyaṃ śram'|ânvitā
vārddhakena ca rāj'|êndra tapasā c' âiva karśitā.

52.10 sā n' âśakad yadā gantuṃ padāt padam api svayam
cakāra gamane buddhiṃ para|lokāya vai tadā.
moktu|kāmāṃ tu tāṃ dṛṣṭvā śarīraṃ Nārado 'bravīt:

«a|saṃskṛtāyāḥ kanyāyāḥ kuto lokās tav' ân|aghe?
evaṃ tu śrutam asmābhir deva|loke mahā|vrate:
tapaḥ paramakaṃ prāptaṃ. na tu lokās tvayā jitāḥ.»

VAISHAMPÁYANA said:

There was once a powerful and celebrated seer called Kuni Garga, who practiced austerities in abundance and was a champion of ascetics, Your Majesty. This lordly ascetic begot a fair-browed daughter with his mind. When he saw her, the glorious ascetic Kuni Garga felt joy and departed for heaven, Your Majesty, after abandoning his body in this world.

52.5 In those days of old, that beautiful, faultless and fair-browed woman, whose eyes were like lotuses, built a hermitage, worshipping the ancestors and gods through fasts and great and severe asceticism. A long time passed as she practiced such fierce asceticism, Your Majesty. Even though her father wished to give her away in marriage, the blameless woman did not want to marry. For she could not see a husband suitable for her.

Pummeling her body with fierce asceticism, her passion lay in worshipping the ancestors and gods in the desolate forest. Despite her toil, and despite becoming emaciated through old age and austerities, she considered herself to be fulfilled. 52.10 When she was no longer able to walk even a single step by herself, she set her mind on departing for the other world. When Nárada saw her desire to give up her body, he said:

"How can you attain the heavens, faultless lady, when you are a maiden who has still not undertaken the rite of marriage? This is what I have heard in the realm of the gods, lady of great vows: you have achieved the highest asceticism but you have not won the heavens."

tan Nārada|vacaḥ śrutvā s" âbravīd ṛṣi|saṃsadi:
«tapaso 'rdhaṃ prayacchāmi pāṇi|grāhasya sattamāḥ.»
ity ukte c' âsyā jagrāha pāṇiṃ Gālava|saṃbhavaḥ
ṛṣiḥ prāk Śṛṅgavān nāma samayaṃ c' êmam abravīt:

52.15 «samayena tav' âdy' âhaṃ pāṇiṃ sprakṣyāmi śobhane
yady eka|rātraṃ vastavyaṃ tvayā saha may" êti ha.»
«tath" êti» sā pratiśrutya tasmai pāṇiṃ dadau tadā.
yathā|dṛṣṭena vidhinā hutvā c' âgniṃ vidhānataḥ
cakre ca pāṇi|grahaṇaṃ tasy" ôdvāhaṃ ca Gālaviḥ.
sā rātrāv abhavad rājaṃs taruṇī deva|varṇinī
divy'|ābharaṇa|vastrā ca divya|gandh'|ânulepanā.
tāṃ dṛṣṭvā Gālaviḥ prīto dīpayantīm iva śriyā
uvāsa ca kṣapām ekāṃ. prabhāte s" âbravīc ca tam:

«yas tvayā samayo vipra kṛto me tapatāṃ vara
ten' ôṣit" âsmi. bhadraṃ te, svasti te 'stu. vrajāmy aham.»

52.20 sā nirgat" âbravīd bhūyo: «yo 'smiṃs tīrthe samāhitaḥ
vasate rajanīm ekāṃ tarpayitvā div'|âukasaḥ,
catvāriṃśatam aṣṭau ca dvau c' âṣṭau samyag ācaret
yo brahma|caryaṃ varṣāṇi phalaṃ tasya labheta saḥ.»
evam uktvā tataḥ sādhvī dehaṃ tyaktvā divaṃ gatā.

ṛṣir apy abhavad dīnas tasyā rūpaṃ vicintayan
samayena tapo|'rdhaṃ ca kṛcchrāt pratigṛhītavān.
sādhayitvā tad" ātmānaṃ tasyāḥ sa gatim anviyāt
duḥkhito Bharata|śreṣṭha tasyā rūpa|balāt kṛtaḥ.

On hearing Nárada's words, she made this announcement in the assembly of seers: "I will give half my ascetic power to whoever takes my hand in marriage, excellent men." At her words, a seer called Shríngavat, the son of Gálava,* took her hand after first making the following pact: "Glorious lady, I will take your hand in marriage on this day on the agreement that you have to stay with me for one night." She consented to this and gave him her hand. After the son of Gálava had performed the proper fire-oblations in accordance with prescribed rites, he took her hand and married her. That night she became a young woman of divine appearance. She wore divine ornaments and clothes and divine perfumes and ointments. When he saw her almost blazing with beauty, the son of Gálava felt joy and stayed with her for one night. In the morning, she said to him: 52.15

"Brahmin and best of ascetics, I have honored the agreement you made with me by staying with you. May you have auspice and prosperity. I am leaving now."

When she departed, she spoke these further words: "Those who satisfy the gods and stay at this *tirtha* in deep concentration for one night will acquire the fruits of practicing the path of chastity for fifty-eight years." Saying this, that virtuous woman gave up her body and went to heaven. 52.20

The seer became despondent at the thought of the woman's beauty and reluctantly accepted the half portion of her ascetic power that he received from their agreement. After perfecting himself, he followed her to the place she had gone, pained by the power of her beauty, best of Bharatas.

etat te vṛddha|kanyāyā vyākhyātaṃ caritaṃ mahat
tath" âiva brahma|caryaṃ ca svargasya ca gatiḥ śubhā.
52.25 tatra|sthaś c' âpi śuśrāva hataṃ Śalyaṃ hal'|āyudhaḥ.
tatr' âpi dattvā dānāni dvi|jātibhyaḥ paran|tapaḥ
śuśrāva Śalyaṃ saṃgrāme nihataṃ Pāṇḍavais tadā.
Samantapañcaka|dvārāt tato niṣkramya Mādhavaḥ
papraccha' ṛṣi|gaṇān Rāmaḥ Kurukṣetrasya yat phalam.
te pṛṣṭā Yadu|siṃhena Kurukṣetra|phalaṃ vibho
samācakhyur mah"|ātmānas tasmai sarvaṃ yathā|tatham.

ṚṢAYA ūcuḥ:

53.1 PRAJĀPATER uttara|vedir ucyate
sanātanaṃ Rāma Samantapañcakam
samījire yatra purā div'|âukaso
vareṇa satreṇa mahā|vara|pradāḥ.
purā ca rāja'|ṛṣi|vareṇa dhīmatā
bahūni varṣāṇy a|mitena tejasā
prakṛṣṭam etat Kuruṇā mah"|ātmanā.
tataḥ «Kurukṣetram» it' îha paprathe.

RĀMA uvāca:

kim|arthaṃ Kuruṇā kṛṣṭaṃ kṣetram etan mah"|ātmanā?
etad icchāmy ahaṃ śrotuṃ kathyamānaṃ tapo|dhanāḥ.

ṚṢAYA ūcuḥ:

purā kila Kuruṃ Rāma karṣantaṃ satat'|ôtthitam
abhyetya Śakras tri|divāt paryapṛcchata kāraṇam.

I have thus explained to you the great deeds of this old maiden, her practice of the path of chastity, and her auspicious rebirth in heaven.

52.25 It was during his stay at this *tirtha* that plow-weaponed Bala heard of Shalya's death. Enemy-taming Bala learned that Shalya had been slain by the Pándavas in battle after he had given gifts to brahmins at that site. Departing from the gate of Samánta·pánchaka, Rama the Mádhava asked the groups of seers about the outcome of the battle at Kuru·kshetra. When asked by that lion of the Yadus about the outcome of the battle at Kuru·kshetra, the great-spirited ascetics told him everything as it actually occurred, my lord.

THE SEERS said:

53.1 SAMÁNTA·PÁNCHAKA is said to be the eternal northern altar of Praja·pati, O Rama. In the past, the gods—those givers of great boons—performed an excellent sacrifice here. Wise and heroic Kuru, that best of royal seers, also once plowed this area for many years with limitless energy. As a result, the area became known in the world as Kuru·kshetra ("The Field of Kuru").

RAMA said:

Why did heroic Kuru plow this field? I wish to hear this described, O seers rich in austerities.

THE SEERS said:

In the past, Rama, it is said that Shakra approached Kuru while he was continuously intent on plowing and asked him the reason for his actions.

INDRA uvāca:

53.5 kim idaṃ vartate rājan prayatnena pareṇa ca?
rāja'|rṣe kim abhipretya yen' êyaṃ kṛṣyate kṣitiḥ?

KURUR uvāca:

«iha ye puruṣāḥ kṣetre mariṣyanti, Śatakrato,
te gamiṣyanti su|kṛtāl̄ lokān pāpa|vivarjitān.»
avahasya tataḥ Śakro jagāma tri|divaṃ punaḥ.
rāja'|rṣir apy a|nirviṇṇaḥ karṣaty eva vasun|dharām.
āgamy' āgamya c' âiv' âinaṃ bhūyo bhūyo 'vahasya ca
Śatakratur a|nirviṇṇaṃ pṛṣṭvā pṛṣṭvā jagāma ha.
yadā tu tapas" ôgreṇa cakarṣa vasudhāṃ nṛpaḥ
tataḥ Śakro 'bravīd devān rāja'|rṣer yac cikīrṣitam.

53.10 etac chrutvā c' âbruvan devāḥ sahasr'|âkṣam idaṃ vacaḥ:
«vareṇa cchandyatāṃ Śakra rāja'|rṣir yadi śakyate.
yadi hy atra pramītā vai svargaṃ gacchanti mānavāḥ
asmān an|iṣṭvā kratubhir bhāgo no na bhaviṣyati!»
āgamya ca tataḥ Śakras tadā rāja'|rṣim abravīt:
«alaṃ khedena bhavataḥ! kriyatāṃ vacanaṃ mama!
mānavā ye nirāhārā dehaṃ tyakṣyanty a|tandritāḥ
yudhi vā nihatāḥ samyag api tiryag|gatā nṛpa,
te svarga|bhājo rāj'|êndra bhaviṣyanti mahā|mate.»
«tath" âstv iti» tato rājā Kuruḥ Śakram uvāca ha.

53.15 tatas tam abhyanujñāpya prahṛṣṭen' ântar|ātmanā
jagāma tri|divaṃ bhūyaḥ kṣipraṃ Bala|niṣūdanaḥ.

INDRA said:

Why such immense toil, Your Majesty? What do you seek by plowing this field, royal seer? 53.5

KURU said:

"Those who die on this field will go to the virtuous realms where sins are cleansed, O Indra of a hundred sacrifices."

Shakra laughed at this and returned to heaven. The royal seer did not, however, become despondent but continued to plow the earth. Indra of a hundred sacrifices repeatedly came back and repeatedly laughed at Kuru again and again, and after repeatedly posing the same questions to Kuru, who remained undismayed, Shakra again returned to heaven. While the king was plowing the earth with such fierce asceticism, Shakra spoke to the gods about the intentions of the royal seer. Hearing this, the gods said these words to thousand-eyed Shakra: 53.10

"Seduce the royal seer with a boon if you can, Shakra. For if humans were to go to heaven simply by dying at this site, they will not offer sacrifices to us and we will not receive our share!"

Approaching the royal seer, Shakra said:

"Enough of your toil! Follow my words! Those who give up their bodies after tirelessly living without food and those who are slaughtered in battle—whether their actions are straight or crooked—will have their share of heaven, wise king of kings."

"So be it," King Kuru replied to Shakra. Taking his leave, the slayer of Bala then quickly returned to heaven with a joyful soul. 53.15

evam etad Yadu|śreṣṭha kṛṣṭaṃ rāja'|rṣiṇā purā
Śakreṇa c' âbhyanujñātaṃ Brahm'|ādyaiś ca surais tathā.
n' âtaḥ parataraṃ puṇyaṃ bhūmeḥ sthānaṃ bhaviṣyati.
iha tapsyanti ye ke cit tapaḥ paramakaṃ narāḥ
deha|tyāgena te sarve yāsyanti Brahmaṇaḥ kṣayam.
ye punaḥ puṇya|bhājo vai dānaṃ dāsyanti mānavāḥ
teṣāṃ sahasra|guṇitaṃ bhaviṣyaty a|cireṇa vai.
ye c' êha nityaṃ manujā nivatsyanti śubh'|âiṣiṇaḥ
Yamasya viṣayaṃ te tu na drakṣyanti kadā cana.
53.20 yakṣyanti ye ca kratubhir mahadbhir manuj'|ēśvarāḥ
teṣāṃ tri|viṣṭape vāso yāvad bhūmir dhariṣyati.
api c' âtra svayaṃ Śakro jagau gāthāṃ sur'|âdhipaḥ
Kurukṣetre nibaddhāṃ vai. tāṃ śṛṇuṣva hal'|āyudha:
«pāṃsavo 'pi Kurukṣetrād vāyunā samudīritāḥ
api duṣ|kṛta|karmāṇaṃ nayanti paramāṃ gatim.
sura'|rṣabhā brāhmaṇa|sattamāś ca
tathā Nṛg'|ādyā nara|deva|mukhyāḥ
iṣṭvā mah"|ârhaiḥ kratubhir nṛ|siṃha
saṃtyajya dehān su|gatiṃ prapannāḥ.
Tarantuk'|Ârantukayor yad antaraṃ
Rāma|hradānāṃ ca Macakrukasya
etat Kurukṣetra|Samantapañcakaṃ
Prajāpater uttara|vedir ucyate.
53.25 śivaṃ mahā|puṇyam idaṃ div'|âukasāṃ
su|saṃmataṃ sarva|guṇaiḥ samanvitam.
ataś ca sarve nihatā nṛpā raṇe
yāsyanti puṇyāṃ gatim a|kṣayāṃ sadā.»
ity uvāca svayaṃ Śakraḥ saha Brahm'|ādibhis tadā.
tac c' ânumoditaṃ sarvaṃ Brahma|Viṣṇu|Maheśvaraiḥ.

In this way, best of Yadus, this field was plowed by that royal seer in days of old and became sanctioned by Shakra and the gods led by Brahma. There can be no place on earth more auspicious than here. All those who perform the highest asceticism at this site will go to the abode of Brahma when they give up their bodies. Those merit-makers who offer a gift here will soon receive it back a thousandfold. Those who continuously live here, seeking auspice, will never see the realm of Yama. Those lords among men who offer great sacrifices here will dwell in heaven as long as the earth remains. 53.20

Shakra himself, the lord of the gods, once sang a verse at this site which was composed about Kuru·kshetra. Listen to it, plow-bearing Bala:

"The very specks of dust that are borne on the wind from Kuru·kshetra will lead even evil-doers to the highest state. Bulls among gods, excellent brahmins, and eminent kings such as Nriga have all offered sacrifices of great cost and attained heaven after giving up their bodies, lion among men. The area that lies between Tarántuka and Arántuka and the lakes of Rama and Machákruka is called Kuru·kshetra or Samánta·pánchaka and is known as the northern altar of Praja·pati. This auspicious area of great merit is greatly esteemed by the gods and possesses every virtue. Every king that dies here in battle will always reach the auspicious and imperishable state."* 53.25

Such were the words that Shakra spoke, accompanied by gods such as Brahma. And all his words were approved by Brahma, Vishnu, and Mahéshvara.

VAIŚAMPĀYANA uvāca:

54.1 KURUKṢETRAṂ TATO dṛṣṭvā dattvā dāyāṃś ca Sātvataḥ
āśramaṃ su|mahad divyam agamaj Janamejaya
madhūk'|āmra|vaṇ'|ôpetaṃ plakṣa|nyagrodha|saṃkulam
cirabilva|yutaṃ puṇyaṃ panas'|ârjuna|saṃkulam.
taṃ dṛṣṭvā Yādava|śreṣṭhaḥ pravaraṃ puṇya|lakṣaṇam
papraccha tān ṛṣīn sarvān kasy' āśrama|varas tv ayam.
te tu sarve mah"|ātmānam ūcū rājan hal'|āyudham:
«śṛṇu vistaraśo Rāma yasy' âyaṃ pūrvam āśramaḥ.
54.5 atra Viṣṇuḥ purā devas taptavāṃs tapa uttamam.
atr' âsya vidhivad yajñāḥ sarve vṛttāḥ sanātanāḥ.
atr' âiva brāhmaṇī siddhā kaumāra|brahma|cāriṇī
yoga|yuktā divaṃ yātā tapaḥ|siddhā tapasvinī.
babhūva śrīmatī rājañ Śāṇḍilyasya mah"|ātmanaḥ
sutā dhṛta|vratā sādhvī niyatā brahma|cāriṇī.
sā tu taptvā tapo ghoraṃ duś|caraṃ strī|janena ha
gatā svargaṃ mahā|bhāgā deva|brāhmaṇa|pūjitā.»
śrutvā ṛṣīṇāṃ vacanam āśramaṃ taṃ jagāma ha.
ṛṣīṃs tān abhivādy' âtha pārśve Himavato 'cyutaḥ
sandhyā|kāryāṇi sarvāṇi nirvarty' āruruhe '|calam.
54.10 n' âtidūraṃ tato gatvā nagaṃ tāla|dhvajo balī
puṇyaṃ tīrtha|varaṃ dṛṣṭvā vismayaṃ paramaṃ gataḥ.
prabhāvaṃ ca Sarasvatyāḥ Plakṣaprasravaṇaṃ Balaḥ

VAISHAMPÁYANA said:

AFTER HE HAD seen Kuru·kshetra, the Sátvata gave gifts and then went to an enormous heavenly hermitage, Janam·éjaya. This auspicious hermitage had *chira·bilva* trees and groves of *madhúka* and mango trees, and abounded with *plaksha* and *nyagródha* fig trees, as well as jackfruit and *árjuna* trees. When that supreme Yádava saw this excellent and pure hermitage, he asked all the seers whom it belonged to. They all answered the plow-weaponed hero thus: 54.1

"Listen, Rama, to a detailed account of who owned this hermitage in the past.

In the past, the god Vishnu practiced the highest asceticism at this site. It was here that he duly offered all the eternal sacrifices. Here too a brahmin female ascetic practiced chastity from her youth and attained perfection. Applying herself to Yoga, she attained perfection in asceticism and went to heaven. Virtuous, disciplined, and firm in her vows, this chaste ascetic was the glorious daughter of great-spirited Shandílya. After practicing gruesome austerities that are difficult for women to perform, this woman of great prosperity went to heaven, honored by gods and brahmins." 54.5

On hearing the seers' words, Bala proceeded to the hermitage. Saying his farewells to the seers, Áchyuta performed all the twilight rituals on the slopes of the Hímavat mountain and then began to climb the peak. After proceeding not very far up the mountain, mighty palm-bannered Bala became filled with immense wonder when he saw a sacred and excellent *tirtha*. After he had seen Sarásvati's power and the site of Plaksha·prásravana, Bala arrived at the excellent 54.10

samprāptaḥ Kārapavanaṃ pravaram tīrtham uttamam.
hal'|āyudhas tatra c' âpi dattvā dānaṃ mahā|balaḥ
āplutaḥ salile puṇye su|śīte vimale śucau
saṃtarpayām āsa pitṝn devāṃś ca raṇa|dur|madaḥ.
tatr' ôṣy' âikāṃ tu rajanīṃ yatibhir brāhmaṇaiḥ saha
Mitrā|Varuṇayoḥ puṇyaṃ jagām' āśramam Acyutaḥ.
Indro 'gnir Aryamā c' âiva yatra prāk prītim āpnuvan
taṃ deśaṃ Kārapavanād Yamunāyāṃ jagāma ha.

54.15 snātvā tatra ca dharm'|ātmā parāṃ prītim avāpya ca
ṛṣibhiś c' âiva siddhaiś ca sahito vai mahā|balaḥ
upaviṣṭaḥ kathāḥ śubhrāḥ śuśrāva Yadu|puṅ|gavaḥ.

tathā tu tiṣṭhatāṃ teṣāṃ Nārado bhagavān ṛṣiḥ
ājagām' âtha taṃ deśaṃ yatra Rāmo vyavasthitaḥ.
jaṭā|maṇḍala|saṃvītaḥ svarṇa|cīro mahā|tapāḥ
hema|daṇḍa|dharo rājan kamaṇḍalu|dharas tathā,
kacchapīṃ sukha|śabdāṃ tāṃ gṛhya vīṇāṃ mano|ramām
nṛtye gīte ca kuśalo deva|brāhmaṇa|pūjitaḥ.
prakartā kalahānāṃ ca nityaṃ ca kalaha|priyaḥ
taṃ deśam agamad yatra śrīmān Rāmo vyavasthitaḥ.

54.20 pratyutthāya ca taṃ samyak pūjayitvā yata|vratam
deva'|rṣiṃ paryapṛcchat sa yathā|vṛttaṃ Kurūn prati.
tato 'sy' âkathayad rājan Nāradaḥ sarva|dharma|vit
sarvam eva yathā|vṛttam atīva Kuru|saṃkṣayam.
tato 'bravīd Rauhiṇeyo Nāradaṃ dīnayā girā:

and supreme *tirtha* of Kara·pávana. When mighty, plow-weaponed Bala—who is difficult to defeat in battle—had given gifts at this site, he bathed in the sacred, clear, clean and pure water and satisfied ancestors and gods. After spending one night there with brahmin ascetics, Áchyuta proceeded to the sacred hermitage of Mitra and Váruna. From Kara·pávana he traveled along the Yámuna to the site where Indra, Agni and Áryaman once acquired joy. After bathing there, righteous Bala obtained the highest happiness. Sitting in the company of seers and *siddhas*, that mighty bull of the Yadus listened to their auspicious discourses. 54.15

While the ascetics were thus engaged, the illustrious seer Nárada arrived at the spot where Rama was resting. Carrying a gourd and a gold staff, that great ascetic had a mop of matted hair and wore golden rags. Skilled in dance and song and honored by gods and brahmins, he had with him a lute made of tortoise-shell, which delighted the mind with its pleasing sounds. A creator of quarrels and ever fond of quarrels, Nárada arrived at the site where glorious Rama was staying. After standing up and duly honoring that ascetic of disciplined vows, Rama asked the divine seer to describe what had happened to the Kurus. Nárada, who knows all that is right, then told him everything about the terrible destruction of the Kurus in exact detail. The son of Róhini then addressed Nárada with melancholic words: 54.20

«kim|avastham tu tat kṣatraṃ ye tu tatr' âbhavan nṛpāḥ?
śrutam etan mayā pūrvaṃ sarvam eva tapo|dhana.
vistara|śravaṇe jātaṃ kautūhalam atīva me.»

NĀRADA uvāca:

pūrvam eva hato Bhīṣmo Droṇaḥ Sindhu|patis tathā
hato Vaikartanaḥ Karṇaḥ putrāś c' âsya mahā|rathāḥ,
54.25 Bhūriśravā Rauhiṇeya Madra|rājaś ca vīryavān
ete c' ânye ca bahavas tatra tatra mahā|balāḥ,
priyān prāṇān parityajya jay'|ârthaṃ Kauravasya vai
rājāno rāja|putrāś ca samareṣv a|nivartinaḥ.
a|hatāṃs tu mahā|bāho śṛṇu me tatra Mādhava.
Dhārtarāṣṭra|bale śeṣās trayaḥ samiti|mardanāḥ:
Kṛpaś ca Kṛtavarmā ca Droṇa|putraś ca vīryavān
te 'pi vai vidrutā Rāma diśo daśa bhayāt tadā.
Duryodhano hate Śalye vidruteṣu Kṛp'|ādiṣu
hradaṃ Dvaipāyanaṃ nāma viveśa bhṛśa|duḥkhitaḥ.
54.30 śayānaṃ Dhārtarāṣṭraṃ tu salile stambhite tadā
Pāṇḍavāḥ saha Kṛṣṇena vāgbhir ugrābhir ārdayan.
sa tudyamāno balavān vāgbhī Rāma samantataḥ
utthitaḥ sa hradād vīraḥ pragṛhya mahatīṃ gadām.
sa c' âpy upagato yoddhuṃ Bhīmena saha sāṃpratam.
bhaviṣyati tayor adya yuddhaṃ Rāma su|dāruṇam.
yadi kautūhalaṃ te 'sti vraja Mādhava mā|ciram.
paśya yuddhaṃ mahā|ghoraṃ śiṣyayor yadi manyase.

"What is the state of the kshatriya kings who were there? I have heard all this before, ascetic rich in austerities. But I am extremely curious to hear it in detail."

NÁRADA said:

Bhishma, Drona, and Jayad·ratha, the lord of the Sindhus, are already dead. Karna, the Sun's offspring, is also dead, as are Karna's sons, those great warriors. Bhuri·shravas and the mighty king of the Madras have also been killed, son of Róhini. These and many other mighty men—kings and princes who never fled in battle—have all died here and there, giving up their dear lives for the sake of the Káurava's victory. 54.25

Hear now, mighty-armed Mádhava, of those who have not died in this war. Three assembly-crushers have survived from the army of Dhrita·rashtra's son: Kripa, Krita·varman, and the powerful son of Drona. They have fled out of fear in all ten directions, Rama. When Shalya was killed, and when Kripa and the others had fled, Dur·yódhana was filled with great distress and entered a lake called Dvaipáyana. Krishna and the Pándavas tormented Dhrita·rashtra's son with harsh words as he lay in frozen water. Goaded by these words that came at him from all sides, the mighty hero emerged from the lake, grasping hold of his huge mace. He has presently undertaken to fight Bhima. There will be a terrible battle between these two men, Rama. Go there quickly, Mádhava, if you are interested. Watch the awful battle between your disciples, if you so desire. 54.30

VAIŚAMPĀYANA uvāca:

Nāradasya vacaḥ śrutvā tān abhyarcya dvija'|rṣabhān
sarvān visarjayām āsa ye ten' âbhyāgatāḥ saha.

54.35 «gamyatāṃ Dvārakāṃ c' êti» so 'nvaśād anuyāyinaḥ
so 'vatīry' â|cala|śreṣṭhāt Plakṣaprasravaṇāc chubhāt.
tataḥ prīta|manā Rāmaḥ śrutvā tīrtha|phalaṃ mahat
viprāṇāṃ saṃnidhau ślokam agāyad imam a|cyutaḥ:

«Sarasvatī|vāsa|samā kuto ratiḥ?
Sarasvatī|vāsa|samāḥ kuto guṇāḥ?
Sarasvatīṃ prāpya divaṃ gatā janāḥ
sadā smariṣyanti nadīṃ Sarasvatīm.
Sarasvatī sarva|nadīṣu puṇyā.
Sarasvatī loka|śubh'|āvahā sadā.
Sarasvatīṃ prāpya janāḥ su|duṣ|kṛtaṃ
sadā na śocanti paratra c' êha ca.»

tato muhur muhuḥ prītyā prekṣamāṇaḥ Sarasvatīm
hayair yuktaṃ rathaṃ śubhram ātiṣṭhata paran|tapaḥ.

54.40 sa śīghra|gāminā tena rathena Yadu|puṅ|gavaḥ
didṛkṣur abhisaṃprāptaḥ śiṣya|yuddham upasthitam.

VAISHAMPÁYANA said:

Hearing Nárada's words, Bala worshipped the bull-like brahmins and dismissed all those who had come with him. Descending from that supreme mountain and from auspicious Plaksha·prásravana, he instructed his attendants to go to Dváraka. Filled with joy at hearing the great fruits of the *tirthas*, unshakeable Rama sang this verse in front of the brahmins: 54.35

"Where is there joy equal to living by Sarásvati? Where are there virtues equal to living by Sarásvati? People who have come to Sarásvati and reached heaven will always remember the river Sarásvati. Sarásvati is the most sacred of all rivers. Sarásvati always brings auspice to the world. When people arrive at Sarásvati, they never grieve over their bad deeds, whether in this world or the next."

After repeatedly gazing at Sarásvati with joy, the enemy-tamer ascended his glorious, horse-yoked chariot. Eager to see the battle that was commencing between his disciples, that bull of the Yadus then reached his destination on that swift chariot. 54.40

55–57
THE DUEL

VAIŚAMPĀYANA uvāca:

55.1 EVAM TAD ABHAVAD yuddhaṃ tumulaṃ Janamejaya
yatra duḥkh'|ânvito rājā Dhṛtarāṣṭro 'bravīd idam.

DHṚTARĀṢṬRA uvāca:

Rāmaṃ saṃnihitaṃ dṛṣṭvā gadā|yuddha upasthite
mama putraḥ kathaṃ Bhīmaṃ pratyayudhyata Sañjaya?

SAÑJAYA uvāca:

Rāma|sāṃnidhyam āsādya putro Duryodhanas tava
yuddha|kāmo mahā|bāhuḥ samahṛṣyata vīryavān.
dṛṣṭvā lāṅgalinaṃ rājā pratyutthāya ca Bhārata
prītyā paramayā yuktaḥ samabhyarcya yathā|vidhi
āsanaṃ ca dadau tasmai paryapṛcchad an|āmayam.
55.5 tato Yudhiṣṭhiraṃ Rāmo vākyam etad uvāca ha
madhuraṃ dharma|saṃyuktaṃ śūrāṇāṃ hitam eva ca:
«mayā śrutaṃ kathayatām ṛṣīṇāṃ rāja|sattama
Kurukṣetraṃ paraṃ puṇyaṃ pāvanaṃ svargyam eva ca
daivatair ṛṣibhir juṣṭaṃ brāhmaṇaiś ca mah"|ātmabhiḥ.
tatra vai yotsyamānā ye dehaṃ tyakṣyanti mānavāḥ
teṣāṃ svarge dhruvo vāsaḥ Śakreṇa saha māriṣa.
tasmāt Samantapañcakam ito yāma drutaṃ nṛpa.
prathit" ôttara|vedī sā deva|loke Prajāpateḥ.
tasmin mahā|puṇyatame trailokyasya sanātane
saṃgrāme nidhanaṃ prāpya dhruvaṃ svargo bhaviṣyati.»
55.10 «tath" êty» uktvā mahā|rāja Kuntī|putro Yudhiṣṭhiraḥ
Samantapañcakaṃ vīraḥ prāyād abhimukhaḥ prabhuḥ.
tato Duryodhano rājā pragṛhya mahatīṃ gadām
padbhyām a|marṣī dyutimān agacchat Pāṇḍavaiḥ saha.

VAISHAMPÁYANA said:

THIS WAS HOW that tumultuous battle came about, Janam·éjaya. Regarding it King Dhrita·rashtra said this in his sorrow. 55.1

DHRITA·RASHTRA said:

When my son saw Rama arrive just as the mace battle was imminent, how did he fight against Bhima, Sánjaya?

SÁNJAYA said:

At Rama's arrival, Dur·yódhana—your powerful and mighty-armed son—became eager for battle and was joyful. When King Yudhi·shthira saw the plow-bearer, he got up and duly worshipped him with great joy, descendant of Bharata. He then gave Rama a seat and asked after his health. Rama then said these words to Yudhi·shthira, which were pleasant, righteous, and beneficial to heroes: 55.5

"Best of kings, I have heard seers say that Kuru·kshetra is an extremely sacred and pure place that leads to heaven and is frequented by gods, seers and great-spirited brahmins. Those who give up their bodies in battle there will forever live with Shakra in heaven, my lord. Let us therefore quickly go to Samánta·pánchaka, Your Majesty. In the realm of the gods, Samánta·pánchaka is famed as the northern altar of Praja·pati. Those who die in battle in that eternal and most sacred place in the three worlds will certainly reach heaven."

Agreeing, lord Yudhi·shthira, the heroic son of Kunti, proceeded straight for Samánta·pánchaka. Full of wrath and splendor, King Dur·yódhana also took up his huge mace and walked on foot together with the Pándavas. The gods that flew in the sky honored him with shouts of approval as 55.10

tathā yāntaṃ gadā|hastaṃ varmaṇā c' âpi daṃśitam
antarikṣa|carā devāḥ «sādhu sādhv ity» apūjayan.
vātikāś cāraṇā ye tu dṛṣṭvā te harṣam āgatāḥ.
sa Pāṇḍavaiḥ parivṛtaḥ Kuru|rājas tav' ātma|jaḥ
mattasy' êva gaj'|êndrasya gatim āsthāya so 'vrajat.
tataḥ śaṅkha|ninādena bherīṇāṃ ca mahā|svanaiḥ
siṃha|nādaiś ca śūrāṇāṃ diśaḥ sarvāḥ prapūritāḥ.

55.15 tatas te tu Kurukṣetraṃ prāptā nara|var'|ôttamāḥ
pratīcy|abhimukhaṃ deśaṃ yath"|ôddiṣṭaṃ sutena te
dakṣiṇena Sarasvatyāḥ sv|ayanaṃ tīrtham uttamam.
tasmin deśe tv an|iriṇe te tu yuddham arocayan.

tato Bhīmo mahā|koṭiṃ gadāṃ gṛhy' âtha varma|bhṛt
bibhrad rūpaṃ mahā|rāja sadṛśaṃ hi Garutmataḥ.
avabaddha|śiras|trāṇaḥ saṅkhye kāñcana|varma|bhṛt
rarāja rājan putras te kāñcanaḥ śaila|rāḍ iva.
varmabhyāṃ saṃyatau vīrau Bhīma|Duryodhanāv ubhau
saṃyuge ca prakāśete saṃrabdhāv iva kuñjarau.

55.20 raṇa|maṇḍala|madhya|sthau bhrātarau tau nara'|rṣabhau
aśobhetāṃ mahā|rāja candra|sūryāv iv' ôditau.
tāv anyonyaṃ nirīkṣetāṃ kruddhāv iva mahā|dvipau
dahantau locanai rājan paras|para|vadh'|âiṣiṇau.

he proceeded mace in hand and clad in armor. The wind-traveling *chāranas* were filled with joy when they saw him. Although surrounded by the Pándavas, your son, the king of the Kurus, walked with the gait of a raging king of elephants. All the directions then filled with the blare of conches, the din of drums, and the lion-roars of heroes.

Those supreme champions then arrived at Kuru·kshetra and proceeded to a place situated westwards that was designated by your son. Lying to the south of the Sarásvati, it was an excellent *tirtha* that was easy to move about on. It was in this unbarren place that they chose to fight. 55.15

Armor-clad Bhima then took hold of his large-tipped mace and assumed an appearance similar to Gáruda, great king. Wearing gold armor and strapping on his protective head-gear in battle, your son looked radiant, Your Majesty, like the golden king of the mountains. Clad in armor, the heroes Bhima and Dur·yódhana both looked glorious in battle, just like two enraged elephants. Standing in the center of the battle-circle, the two brothers and bull-like men shone radiantly, great king, resembling a risen moon and sun. Burning each other with their eyes and eager to kill each other, they looked at one another askance like two great elephants filled with fury, Your Majesty. 55.20

saṃprahṛṣṭa|manā rājan gadām ādāya Kauravaḥ
sṛkkiṇī saṃlihan rājan krodha|rakt'|ēkṣaṇaḥ śvasan.
tato Duryodhano rājan gadām ādāya vīryavān
Bhīmasenam abhiprekṣya gajo gajam iv' āhvayat.
adri|sāra|mayīṃ Bhīmas tath" âiv' ādāya vīryavān
āhvayām āsa nṛ|patiṃ siṃhaṃ siṃho yathā vane.

55.25 tāv udyata|gadā|pāṇī Duryodhana|Vṛkodarau
saṃyuge sma prakāśetāṃ girī sa|śikharāv iva.
tāv ubhau samatikruddhāv ubhau bhīma|parākramau
ubhau śiṣyau gadā|yuddhe Rauhiṇeyasya dhīmataḥ.
ubhau sadṛśa|karmāṇau Yama|Vāsavayor iva
tathā sadṛśa|karmāṇau Varuṇasya mahā|balau.
Vāsudevasya Rāmasya tathā Vaiśravaṇasya ca
sadṛśau tau mahā|rāja Madhu|Kaiṭabhayor yudhi.
ubhau sadṛśa|karmāṇau tathā Sund'|ôpasundayoḥ
Rāma|Rāvaṇayoś c' âiva Vāli|Sugrīvayos tathā
tath" âiva Kālasya samau Mṛtyoś c' âiva paran|tapau.

55.30 anyonyam abhidhāvantau mattāv iva mahā|dvipau
vāsitā|saṃgame dṛptau śarad' îva mad'|ôtkaṭau.
ubhau krodha|viṣaṃ dīptaṃ vamantāv uragāv iva
anyonyam abhisaṃrabdhau prekṣamāṇāv arin|damau
ubhau Bharata|śārdūlau vikrameṇa samanvitau.
siṃhāv iva dur|ādharṣau gadā|yuddha|viśāradau
nakha|daṃṣṭr'|āyudhau vīrau vyāghrāv iva dur|utsahau.
prajā|saṃharaṇe kṣubdhau samudrāv iva dus|tarau
lohit'|âṅgāv iva kruddhau pratapantau mahā|rathau.
pūrva|paścima|jau meghau prekṣamāṇāv arin|damau

Joyfully taking up his mace, the Káurava licked the corners of his mouth as he breathed heavily, his eyes red with rage. Mighty Dur·yódhana then took up his mace and glared at Bhima·sena, challenging him like one elephant challenging another, Your Majesty. In the same way, mighty Bhima took up his iron mace and challenged that lord of men, just like one lion challenging another in a forest. Wielding their raised maces, Dur·yódhana and Vrikódara looked glorious in battle, like two peaked mountains. Both were filled with extreme rage, both had terrifying prowess, and both had been disciples in mace-fighting under the wise son of Róhini. Both were similar to Yama or Vásava in their actions and both were men of great power, whose deeds resembled Váruna's. In battle they were like Vasudéva, Rama, Váishravana,* Madhu or Káitabha, Your Majesty. Both performed deeds that were similar to Sunda and Upasúnda, Rama and Rávana, or Valin and Sugríva, and both were enemy-scorchers who resembled Time and Death. 55.25

Charging against each other, they were like two enormous frenzied elephants mad with passion in the fall season and wild with desire to mate with a cow on heat. As they glared at each other in their rage, the enemy-tamers were like two snakes that spit out fiery poison born of wrath. Both were tigers among Bharatas and both were valorous. Skilled in mace combat, the heroes were as dangerous as lions and as difficult to quell as tigers that use claws and teeth as weapons. They were like two uncrossable oceans that swell up to destroy creatures. In their fury, the great warriors blazed as if they were the planet Mars. Those enemy-tamers looked like two clouds that rise in the east and west, thundering 55.30

garjamānau su|viṣamaṃ kṣarantau prāvṛṣ' îva hi.
55.35 raśmi|yuktau mah"|ātmānau dīptimantau mahā|balau
dadṛśāte Kuru|śreṣṭhau kāla|sūryāv iv' ôditau.
vyāghrāv iva su|saṃrabdhau garjantāv iva toyadau
jahṛṣāte mahā|bāhū siṃhau kesariṇāv iva
gajāv iva su|saṃrabdhau jvalitāv iva pāvakau
dadṛśāte mah"|ātmānau sa|śṛṅgāv iva parvatau.

roṣāt prasphuramāṇ'|ôṣṭhau nirīkṣantau paras|param
tau sametau mah"|ātmānau gadā|hastau nar'|ôttamau.
ubhau parama|saṃhṛṣṭāv ubhau parama|saṃmatau
sad|aśvāv iva heṣantau bṛṃhantāv iva kuñjarau.
55.40 vṛṣabhāv iva garjantau Duryodhana|Vṛkodarau
daityāv iva bal'|ônmattau rejatus tau nar'|ôttamau.

tato Duryodhano rājann idam āha Yudhiṣṭhiram
bhrātṛbhiḥ sahitaṃ c' âiva Kṛṣṇena ca mah"|ātmanā
Rāmeṇ' â|mita|vīryeṇa vākyaṃ śauṭīrya|saṃmatam
Kekayaiḥ Sṛñjayair dṛptaṃ Pañcālaiś ca mah"|ātmabhiḥ:

«idaṃ vyavasitaṃ yuddhaṃ mama Bhīmasya c' ôbhayoḥ
upopaviṣṭāḥ paśyadhvaṃ sahitair nṛpa|puṅ|gavaiḥ!»

śrutvā Duryodhana|vacaḥ pratyapadyanta tat tathā.
tataḥ samupaviṣṭaṃ tat su|mahad rāja|maṇḍalam
virājamānaṃ dadṛśe div' îv' āditya|maṇḍalam.
55.45 teṣāṃ madhye mahā|bāhuḥ śrīmān Keśava|pūrva|jaḥ
upaviṣṭo mahā|rāja pūjyamānaḥ samantataḥ.
śuśubhe rāja|madhya|stho nīla|vāsāḥ sita|prabhaḥ
nakṣatrair iva saṃpūrṇo vṛto niśi niśā|karaḥ.

terribly and pouring down rain in the monsoon season. In their radiance and splendor, the mighty and great-spirited champions of the Kurus looked like two suns that rise when the world is destroyed. Resembling two enraged tigers or thundering clouds, the mighty-armed men bristled with joy like maned lions. The heroes were like two enraged elephants or two burning fires and they resembled peaked mountains. 55.35

Glaring at each other, their lips quivering with fury, the two great-spirited and excellent men encountered one another, wielding their maces. Greatly esteemed, they both experienced the highest joy as they neighed like fine horses and trumpeted like elephants. Bellowing like bulls, Dur·yódhana and Vrikódara—those best of men—looked as glorious as two power-intoxicated *daityas*. 55.40

Dur·yódhana then said these proud and haughty words to Yudhi·shthira, Your Majesty, who was accompanied by his brothers, heroic Krishna, infinitely powerful Rama, the Kékayas, Srínjayas, and great-spirited Panchálas:

"Sit with these assembled bull-like kings and watch the battle that has been arranged between me and Bhima!"

Hearing Dur·yódhana's words, they all acted accordingly and the huge circle of kings sat down, radiant as a circle of *adítya* deities in heaven. The glorious and mighty-armed elder brother of Késhava sat down in their midst, honored on all sides, great king. As he sat in the middle of those kings with his blue robes and bright complexion, he resembled the full moon at night when surrounded by stars. 55.45

tau tathā tu mahā|rāja gadā|hastau su|duḥ|sahau
anyonyaṃ vāgbhir ugrābhis takṣamāṇau vyavasthitau.
a|priyāṇi tato 'nyonyam uktvā tau Kuru|sattamau
udīkṣantau sthitau vīrau Vṛtra|Śakrau yath" āhave.

VAIŚAMPĀYANA uvāca:

56.1 TATO VĀG|YUDDHAM abhavat tumulaṃ Janamejaya
yatra duḥkh'|ânvito rājā Dhṛtarāṣṭro 'bravīd idam:
«dhig astu khalu mānuṣyaṃ yasya niṣṭh" êyam īdṛśī
ekādaśa|camū|bhartā yatra putro mam' ân|agha
ājñāpya sarvān nṛ|patīn bhuktvā c' êmāṃ vasun|dharām
gadām ādāya vegena padātiḥ prasthito raṇe.
bhūtvā hi jagato nātho hy a|nātha iva me sutaḥ.
gadām udyamya yo yāti kim anyad bhāgadheyataḥ?
56.5 aho duḥkhaṃ mahat prāptaṃ putreṇa mama Sañjaya!»
evam uktvā sa duḥkh'|ārto virarāma jan'|âdhipaḥ.

SAÑJAYA uvāca:

sa megha|ninado harṣān ninadann iva go|vṛṣaḥ
ājuhāva tadā Pārthaṃ yuddhāya yudhi vīryavān.
Bhīmam āhvayamāne tu Kuru|rāje mah"|ātmani
prādur āsan su|ghorāṇi rūpāṇi vividhāny uta.
vavur vātāḥ sa|nirghātāḥ pāṃsu|varṣaṃ papāta ca
babhūvuś ca diśaḥ sarvās timireṇa samāvṛtāḥ.

Wielding their maces and extremely difficult to quell, the two warriors then took up position as they cut into each other with fierce words. Saying harsh words to one another, those heroes and best of Kurus stood there glaring at each other, just as Vritra and Shakra once did in their battle.

VAISHAMPÁYANA said:

THERE WAS THEN a tumultuous contest of words, Janam·éjaya, regarding which King Dhrita·rashtra said this in his sorrow: 56.1

"How terrible that humans should have the type of end my son has had! Once the leader of eleven armies, Dur·yódhana used to command every king and enjoy this earth, faultless Sánjaya. But he now sets off on foot for the battlefield, swiftly taking up his mace. Once the lord of the world, my son now resembles someone lordless. When he has departed in this way, wielding his mace, what else can this be but fate? Alas Sánjaya! My son has been afflicted by great suffering!" 56.5

Saying these words, that lord of the people fell silent, tormented by suffering.

SÁNJAYA said:

With the rumble of a thundercloud, mighty Dur·yódhana roared joyfully like a bull as he challenged Pritha's son to fight in battle. Various terrifying visions appeared when the heroic king of the Kurus challenged Bhima. Winds and hurricanes blew. A shower of dust fell from the sky and all the directions became covered with darkness. Huge storms thundered loudly, bringing confusion and making

mahā|svanāḥ su|nirvātās tumulā loma|harṣaṇāḥ
petus tath" ôlkāḥ śataśaḥ sphoṭayantyo nabhas|talān.

56.10 Rāhuś c' âgrasad ādityam a|parvaṇi viśāṃ pate
cakampe ca mahā|kampaṃ pṛthivī sa|vana|drumā.
dīptāś ca vātāḥ pravavur nīcaiḥ śarkara|karṣiṇaḥ
girīṇāṃ śikharāṇy eva nyapatanta mahī|tale.
mṛgā bahu|vidh'|ākārāḥ saṃpatanti diśo daśa
dīptāḥ śivāś c' âpy anadan ghora|rūpāḥ su|dāruṇāḥ.
nirghātāś ca mahā|ghorā babhūvur loma|harṣaṇāḥ.
dīptāyāṃ diśi rāj'|êndra mṛgāś c' â|śubha|vedinaḥ.
udapāna|gatāś c' āpo vyavardhanta samantataḥ
a|śarīrā mahā|nādāḥ śrūyante sma tadā nṛpa.

56.15 evam|ādīni dṛṣṭv" âtha nimittāni Vṛkodaraḥ
uvāca bhrātaraṃ jyeṣṭhaṃ Dharma|rājaṃ Yudhiṣṭhiram:

«n' âiṣa śakto raṇe jetuṃ mand'|ātmā māṃ Suyodhanaḥ.
adya krodhaṃ vimokṣyāmi vigūḍhaṃ hṛdaye ciram
Suyodhane Kaurav'|êndre Khāṇḍave Pāvako yathā.
śalyam ady' ôddhariṣyāmi tava Pāṇḍava hṛc|chayam
nihatya gadayā pāpam imaṃ Kuru|kul'|âdhamam.
adya kīrti|mayīṃ mālāṃ pratimokṣyāmy ahaṃ tvayi
hatv" êmaṃ pāpa|karmāṇaṃ gadayā raṇa|mūrdhani.
ady' âsya śatadhā dehaṃ bhinadmi gaday" ânayā.
n' âyaṃ praveṣṭā nagaraṃ punar vāraṇa|sāhvayam.

one's hair stand on end. Hundreds of meteors fell to the ground, bursting through the firmament. Rahu swallowed the sun at an irregular moment and the earth trembled violently, along with its forest and trees, lord of the people. Blazing winds began to blow, pouring down gravel, and mountain peaks fell to the ground. Wild animals with various forms charged about in all ten directions. Terrifying, blazing jackals roared with gruesome appearances. Hideous whirlwinds arose, making one's hair stand on end. The directions blazed brightly and wild beasts heralded ill fortune. The water in the wells swelled on all sides, Your Majesty, and one could hear huge roars that had no physical body as their source. 56.10

Seeing such signs, Vrikódara said these words to his elder brother Yudhi·shthira, the King of Righteousness: 56.15

"It is impossible for dim-witted Su·yódhana to conquer me in battle today. Against Su·yódhana, the king of the Káuravas, I will today release the anger that has long remained hidden in my heart, just as Fire once released his anger onto the Khándava forest. Today I will extract the dart that lies in your heart, Pándava, and with my mace I will kill this sinner, the lowest of the Kuru clan. Slaughtering this evil-doer with my mace at the front of the battlefield, I will today place a garland of glory around your neck. With this mace, I will today split Dur·yódhana's body into a hundred pieces. He will never again enter the elephant-named city of Hástina·pura.

56.20 sarp'|ôtsargasya śayane viṣa|dānasya bhojane
Pramāṇakoṭyāṃ pātasya dāhasya jatu|veśmani,
sabhāyām avahāsasya sarva|sva|haraṇasya ca
varṣam a|jñāta|vāsasya vana|vāsasya c' ân|agha,
ady' ântam eṣāṃ duḥkhānāṃ gant" âhaṃ Bharata'|rṣabha.
ek'|âhnā vinihaty" êmaṃ bhaviṣyāmy ātmano 'n|ṛṇaḥ.
ady' āyur Dhārtarāṣṭrasya dur|mater a|kṛt'|ātmanaḥ
samāptaṃ Bharata|śreṣṭha mātā|pitroś ca darśanam.
adya saukhyaṃ tu rāj'|êndra Kuru|rājasya dur|mateḥ
samāptaṃ ca mahā|rāja nārīṇāṃ darśanaṃ punaḥ.
56.25 ady' âyaṃ Kuru|rājasya Śāntanoḥ kula|pāṃsanaḥ
prāṇāñ śriyaṃ ca rājyaṃ ca tyaktvā śeṣyati bhū|tale.
rājā ca Dhṛtarāṣṭro 'dya śrutvā putraṃ nipātitam
smariṣyaty a|śubhaṃ karma yat tac Chakuni|buddhi|jam.»
ity uktvā rāja|śārdūla gadām ādāya vīryavān
abhyatiṣṭhata yuddhāya Śakro Vṛtram iv' āhvayan.
tam udyata|gadaṃ dṛṣṭvā Kailāsam iva śṛṅgiṇam
Bhīmasenaḥ punaḥ kruddho Duryodhanam uvāca ha:
«rājñaś ca Dhṛtarāṣṭrasya tathā tvam api c' ātmanaḥ
smara tad duṣ|kṛtaṃ karma yad vṛttaṃ Vāraṇāvate.
56.30 Draupadī ca parikliṣṭā sabhā|madhye rajasvalā.
dyūte ca vañcito rājā yat tvayā Saubalena ca.
vane duḥkhaṃ ca yat prāptam asmābhis tvat|kṛtaṃ mahat
Virāṭa|nagare c' âiva yony|antara|gatair iva

Dur·yódhana dispatched snakes against me in my sleep. He laced my food with poison. He threw me into the river at Pramána·koti. He set fire to the lac house. He laughed at us in the assembly hall. He stole all our possessions. We endured a life of disguise for a year and a life in the forest, faultless Yudhi·shthira.* Today I will end these sufferings, bull of the Bharatas. By slaughtering this man, I will erase my debts in a single day. 56.20

On this day the life of Dhrita·rashtra's foolish and corrupt son will come to an end. He will never again see his mother and father, best of Bharatas. On this day, king of kings, the villainous monarch of the Kurus will cease to be happy and will never again look upon women. On this day he will give up his life, glory and kingdom and will lie on the ground, having defiled the family of Shántanu's son, that king of the Kurus. On this day King Dhrita·rashtra will learn that his son has fallen and remember the evil deeds that sprang from Shákuni's mind." 56.25

Saying these words, tiger-like king, mighty Bhima took up his mace and stood ready to fight, like Shakra challenging Vritra. When he saw Dur·yódhana wielding his mace and looking like the peaked mountain Kailása, Bhima·sena once again became filled with rage and said to Dur·yódhana:

"Remember the evil deeds that you and king Dhrita·rashtra performed at Varanávata. Dráupadi was wronged in the assembly hall while she was menstruating. Both you and Súbala's son deceived King Yudhi·shthira in a game of dice. Today I will avenge the great suffering that you caused us, both when we were in the forest and when we were living 56.30

tat sarvaṃ pātayāmy adya. diṣṭyā dṛṣṭo 'si dur|mate!
tvat|kṛte 'sau hataḥ śete śara|talpe pratāpavān
Gāṅgeyo rathināṃ śreṣṭho nihato Yājñaseninā.
hato Droṇaś ca Karṇaś ca tathā Śalyaḥ pratāpavān
vair'|âgner ādi|kart" âsau Śakuniḥ Saubalo hataḥ.
prātikāmī tataḥ pāpo Draupadyāḥ kleśa|kṛdd hataḥ
bhrātaras te hatāḥ sarve śūrā vikrānta|yodhinaḥ.

56.35 ete c' ânye ca bahavo nihatās tvat|kṛte nṛpāḥ.
tvām adya nihaniṣyāmi gadayā. n' âtra saṃśayaḥ.»

ity evam uccai rāj'|êndra bhāṣamāṇaṃ Vṛkodaram
uvāca gata|bhī rājan putras te satya|vikramaḥ:

«kiṃ katthanena bahunā? yudhyasva tvaṃ Vṛkodara!
adya te 'haṃ vineṣyāmi yuddha|śraddhāṃ kul'|âdhama!
na hi Duryodhanaḥ kṣudra kena cit tvad|vidhena vai
śakyas trāsayituṃ vācā yath" ânyaḥ prākṛto naraḥ.

cira|kāl'|ēpsitaṃ diṣṭyā hṛdaya|stham idaṃ mama.
tvayā saha gadā|yuddhaṃ tri|daśair upapāditam.

56.40 kiṃ vācā bahun" ôktena katthitena ca dur|mate?
vāṇī saṃpadyatām eṣā karmaṇā! mā ciraṃ kṛthāḥ!»

tasya tad vacanaṃ śrutvā sarva ev' âbhyapūjayan
rājānaḥ Somakāś c' âiva ye tatr' āsan samāgatāḥ.
tataḥ saṃpūjitaḥ sarvaiḥ saṃprahṛṣṭa|tanū|ruhaḥ
bhūyo dhīrāṃ matiṃ cakre yuddhāya Kuru|nandanaḥ.
unmattam iva mātaṅgaṃ tala|śabdair nar'|âdhipāḥ
bhūyaḥ saṃharṣayāṃ cakrur Duryodhanam a|marṣaṇam.

n Viráta's city, pretending to be men with altered births. How splendid it is to see you, you villain!

It is because of you that Bhishma, that mighty son of Ganga and best of chariot-warriors, lies dead on a bed of arrows, slaughtered by Yajna·sena's son.* Drona has been killed, as have Karna and mighty Shalya. Shákuni, the son of Súbala—the initiator of this blazing feud—has also been lain. The evil usher who wronged Dráupadi is also dead, and all your heroic and courageous brothers have been laughtered. These and many other kings have died for your ake. Today I will kill you with my mace. I have no doubt about that." 56.35

While Vrikódara bellowed in this way, your fearless and ruly valiant son replied with these words, king of kings:

"Why all this talk? You should fight, Vrikódara! Today I will dispel your faith in battle, lowest of the Pándava family! Measly wretch, Dur·yódhana is not some ordinary person hat can be terrified by the words of a man such as you.

How fortunate I am! This has long been my heart's desire. The gods must have arranged this mace battle with you. What is the use of words and longwinded speeches, you fool? Fulfill your words with action! Cease your delaying!" 56.40

On hearing his words, the kings and the Sómakas who had gathered there all honored Dur·yódhana. Honored by ll these men, that delight of the Kurus felt his hair bristle nd once again firmly set his heart on battle. By clapping heir hands, those lords of men cheered on wrathful Dur·yódhana still further, like men stirring a frenzied elephant.

taṃ mah”|ātmā mah”|ātmānaṃ
gadām udyamya Pāṇḍavaḥ
abhidudrāva vegena
Dhārtarāṣṭraṃ Vṛkodaraḥ.

56.45 bṛṃhanti kuñjarās tatra hayā hreṣanti c' â|sakṛt
śastrāṇi c' âpy adīpyanta Pāṇḍavānāṃ jay'|âiṣiṇām.

SAÑJAYA uvāca:

57.1 TATO DURYODHANO dṛṣṭvā Bhīmasenaṃ tathā|gatam
pratyudyayāv a|dīn'|ātmā vegena mahatā nadan.
samāpetatur anyonyaṃ śṛṅgiṇau vṛṣabhāv iva
mahā|nirghāta|ghoṣaś ca prahārāṇām ajāyata.
abhavac ca tayor yuddhaṃ tumulaṃ loma|harṣaṇam
jigīṣator yath” ânyonyam Indra|Prahlādayor iva.
rudhir'|ôkṣita|sarv'|âṅgau gadā|hastau manasvinau
dadṛśāte mah”|ātmānau puṣpitāv iva kiṃśukau.

57.5 tathā tasmin mahā|yuddhe vartamāne su|dāruṇe
kha|dyota|saṅghair iva khaṃ darśanīyaṃ vyarocata.
tathā tasmin vartamāne saṃkule tumule bhṛśam
ubhāv api pariśrāntau yudhyamānāv arin|damau.
tau muhūrtaṃ samāśvasya punar eva paran|tapau
abhyahārayat' ânyonyaṃ saṃpragṛhya gade śubhe.

tau tu dṛṣṭvā mahā|vīryau samāśvastau nara'|rṣabhau
balinau vāraṇau yadvad vāsit”|ârthe mad'|ôtkaṭau,
samāna|vīryau saṃprekṣya pragṛhīta|gadāv ubhau
vismayaṃ paramaṃ jagmur deva|gandharva|mānavāḥ.

57.10 pragṛhīta|gadau dṛṣṭvā Duryodhana|Vṛkodarau
saṃśayaḥ sarva|bhūtānāṃ vijaye samapadyata.
samāgamya tato bhūyo bhrātarau balināṃ varau
anyonyasy' ântara|prepsū pracakrāte 'ntaraṃ prati.

Raising his mace, Vrikódara, the heroic son of Pandu, then swiftly charged against the heroic son of Dhrita·rashtra. Elephants trumpeted, horses neighed repeatedly, and the weapons of the Pándavas blazed in their desire for victory. 56.45

SÁNJAYA said:

WHEN DUR·YÓDHANA saw Bhima·sena charging forward in this way, he counter-attacked him with great speed, roaring passionately. The two men clashed together like horned bulls and the noise of their blows boomed like a huge thunderstorm. The battle between them was tumultuous and hair-raising—like the battle between Indra and Prahláda—with both men eager to conquer the other. Wielding their maces, the spirited heroes looked like flowering *kínshuka* trees as all their limbs became drenched in blood.* During that great and horrific battle, the sky glistened beautifully as if with swarms of fireflies. During that extremely chaotic and tumultuous battle, both enemy-tamers became exhausted from their fighting. But after they had rested a while, the enemy-scorchers once again took up their splendid maces and attacked one another. 57.1 57.5

Equal in strength, the powerful bull-like men were like mighty elephants intoxicated with passion for a cow on heat. Gods, *gandhárvas*, and humans all felt extreme wonder as they gazed at the rested men and watched them brandishing their maces. When they saw Dur·yódhana and Vrikódara wielding their maces, every living creature felt unsure as to who would win. Clashing together once more, the two brothers and champions among powerful men attacked each other, eager to find their opponent's weaknesses. 57.10

Yama|daṇḍ'|ôpamāṃ gurvīm Indr'|âśanim iv' ôdyatām
dadṛśuḥ prekṣakā rājan raudrīṃ viśasanīṃ gadām.
āvidhyato gadāṃ tasya Bhīmasenasya saṃyuge
śabdaḥ su|tumulo ghoro muhūrtaṃ samapadyata.
āvidhyantam ariṃ prekṣya Dhārtarāṣṭro 'tha Pāṇḍavam
gadām a|tula|vegāṃ tāṃ vismitaḥ saṃbabhūva ha.

57.15 caraṃś ca vividhān mārgān maṇḍalāni ca Bhārata
aśobhata tadā vīro bhūya eva Vṛkodaraḥ.
tau paras|param āsādya yat tāv anyonya|rakṣaṇe
mārjārāv iva bhakṣ'|ârthe tatakṣāte muhur muhuḥ.
acarad Bhīmasenas tu mārgān bahu|vidhāṃs tathā
maṇḍalāni vicitrāṇi gata|pratyāgatāni ca.

astra|yantrāṇi citrāṇi sthānāni vividhāni ca
parimokṣaṃ prahārāṇāṃ varjanaṃ paridhāvanam,
abhidravaṇam ākṣepam avasthānaṃ sa|vigraham
parivartana|saṃvartam avaplutam upaplutam
upanyastam apanyastaṃ: gadā|yuddha|viśāradau.

57.20 evaṃ tau vicarantau tu nyaghnatāṃ vai paras|param.
vañcayānau punaś c' âiva ceratuḥ Kuru|sattamau.
vikrīḍantau su|balinau maṇḍalāni viceratuḥ
tau darśayantau samare yuddha|krīḍāṃ samantataḥ.

The spectators gazed at Bhima's mace, Your Majesty, which was terrifying and destructive. As heavy as Yama's staff, it was wielded like Indra's thunderbolt. As Bhima·sena wielded this mace in battle, there was a horrific noise for a while that created great confusion. The son of Dhrita·rashtra became filled with wonder when he saw his enemy, the Pándava, brandishing that mace of unrivaled force.

Heroic Vrikódara looked still more glorious as he moved around in various tracks and circles, descendant of Bharata. As they attacked one another and protected themselves, the two heroes repeatedly mangled each other like cats fighting over food. Bhima·sena careered around in different tracks and circles, back and forth. 57.15

Both men were skilled in mace-combat. Displaying various methods of striking and avoiding blows, they assumed diverse positions. Sometimes they delivered blows and other times they avoided and escaped them. Sometimes they attacked their opponent and other times they drew them in. Sometimes they stood still and other times they took advantage of their enemy's attacks. On the one hand they moved around their enemy, on the other hand they prevented their enemy from moving around them. By bending down or jumping up, they foiled their enemy's blows. Sometimes they struck their enemy face-to-face and other times they struck them in the back.*

Both men thus careered around and struck one another. Deceiving each other, the supreme Kurus maneuvered in this way. Moving around in circles, the mighty men sported and displayed every type of battle ploy in their combat. The enemy-tamers struck each other violently with their maces, 57.20

gadābhyāṃ sahas" ânyonyam ājaghnatur arin|damau
paras|paraṃ samāsādya daṃṣṭrābhyāṃ dviradau yathā.
aśobhetāṃ mahā|rāja śoṇitena pariplutau.

evaṃ tad abhavad yuddhaṃ ghora|rūpaṃ paran|tapa
parivṛtte 'hani krūraṃ Vṛtra|Vāsavayor iva.

gadā|hastau tatas tau tu maṇḍal'|âvasthitau balī.
dakṣiṇaṃ maṇḍalaṃ rājan Dhārtarāṣṭro 'bhyavartata.
savyaṃ tu maṇḍalaṃ tatra Bhīmaseno 'bhyavartata.

57.25 tathā tu caratas tasya Bhīmasya raṇa|mūrdhani
Duryodhano mahā|rāja pārśva|deśe 'bhyatāḍayat.
āhatas tu tato Bhīmaḥ putreṇa tava Bhārata
āvidhyata gadāṃ gurvīṃ prahāraṃ tam a|cintayan
Indr'|âśani|samāṃ ghorāṃ Yama|daṇḍam iv' ôdyatām
dadṛśus te mahārāja Bhīmasenasya tāṃ gadām.
āvidhyantaṃ gadāṃ dṛṣṭvā Bhīmasenaṃ tav' ātma|jaḥ
samudyamya gadāṃ ghorāṃ pratyavidhyat paran|tapaḥ.
gadā|māruta|vegena tava putrasya Bhārata
śabda āsīt su|tumulas tejaś ca samajāyata.

57.30 sa caran vividhān mārgān maṇḍalāni ca bhāgaśaḥ
samaśobhata tejasvī bhūyo Bhīmāt Suyodhanaḥ.
āviddhā sarva|vegena Bhīmena mahatī gadā
sa|dhūmaṃ s'|ârciṣaṃ c' âgniṃ mumoc' ôgra|mahā|svanā.
ādhūtāṃ Bhīmasenena gadāṃ dṛṣṭvā Suyodhanaḥ
adri|sāra|mayīṃ gurvīm āvidhyan bahv aśobhata.
gadā|māruta|vegaṃ hi dṛṣṭvā tasya mah"|âtmanaḥ
bhayaṃ viveśa Pāṇḍūṃs tu sarvān eva sa|Somakān.
tau darśayantau samare yuddha|krīḍāṃ samantataḥ
gadābhyāṃ sahas" ânyonyam ājaghnatur arin|damau.

attacking one another like elephants with tusks. Drenched in blood, they looked radiant, great king.

In this way, that horrific and fierce battle occurred at the day's close, enemy-scorcher. It was like the battle between Vritra and Vásava.

The mighty men took up positions in different circles as they wielded their maces. The son of Dhrita·rashtra moved in a right circle while Bhima·sena moved in a left. Dur·yódhana then hit Bhima on a section of his flanks as he moved around at the front of the battlefield, great king. But although struck by your son, Bhima did not give the blow a thought and instead wielded his heavy mace, descendant of Bharata. The spectators gazed at Bhima·sena's mace, great king, which was dreadful as Indra's thunderbolt and raised like Yama's staff. When your son saw Bhima·sena wielding his mace, the enemy-scorcher lifted his own terrifying mace and struck him again. Creating a huge noise and a flash of light, the force of your son's mace was like the wind. 57.25

Powerful Su·yódhana looked even more glorious than Bhima as he careered around in various tracks and circles, one after the other. Bhima whirled his huge mace with all his strength. Making a loud and violent noise, the mace released a flame that smoked and blazed. When he saw Bhima·sena brandishing his mace, Su·yódhana looked extremely glorious as he wielded his own heavy mace made of iron. All the Pandus and Sómakas became fearful when they saw the wind-like velocity of the hero's mace. The two enemy-tamers violently struck one another with their maces as they revealed in battle every type of strategy. Attacking 57.30 57.35

57.35 tau paras|param āsādya daṃṣṭrābhyāṃ dviradau yathā
aśobhetāṃ mahā|rāja śoṇitena pariplutau.
evaṃ tad abhavad yuddhaṃ ghora|rūpam a|saṃvṛtam
parivṛtte 'hani krūraṃ Vṛtra|Vāsavayor iva.
dṛṣṭvā vyavasthitaṃ Bhīmaṃ tava putro mahā|balaḥ
caraṃś citratarān mārgān Kaunteyam abhidudruve.
tasya Bhīmo mahā|vegāṃ jāmbūnada|pariṣkṛtām
atikruddhasya kruddhas tu tāḍayām āsa tāṃ gadām.
sa|visphuliṅgo nirhrādas tayos tatr' âbhighāta|jaḥ
prādur āsīn mahā|rāja sṛṣṭayor vajrayor iva.
57.40 vegavatyā tayā tatra Bhīmasena|pramuktayā
nipatantyā mahā|rāja pṛthivī samakampata.
tāṃ n' âmṛṣyata Kauravyo gadāṃ pratihatāṃ raṇe
matto dvipa iva kruddhaḥ pratikuñjara|darśanāt.
sa savyaṃ maṇḍalaṃ rājā udbhrāmya kṛta|niścayaḥ
ājaghne mūrdhni Kaunteyaṃ gadayā bhīma|vegayā.
tayā tv abhihato Bhīmaḥ putreṇa tava Pāṇḍavaḥ
n' âkampata mahā|rāja. tad adbhutam iv' âbhavat.
āścaryaṃ c' âpi tad rājan sarva|sainyāny apūjayan
yad gad"|âbhihato Bhīmo n' âkampata padāt padam.
57.45 tato gurutarāṃ dīptāṃ gadāṃ hema|pariṣkṛtām
Duryodhanāya vyasṛjad Bhīmo bhīma|parākramaḥ.
taṃ prahāram a|saṃbhrānto lāghavena mahā|balaḥ
moghaṃ Duryodhanaś cakre; tatr' âbhūd vismayo mahān.
sā tu moghā gadā rājan patantī Bhīma|coditā
cālayām āsa pṛthivīṃ mahā|nirghāta|niḥsvanā.

each other like elephants with their tusks, the two men looked radiant as they were drenched in blood, great king.

In this way, that horrific, vicious, and unrestrained battle continued at the day's close. It was like the battle between Vritra and Vásava.

When he saw Bhima positioned on the battlefield, your powerful son charged against the offspring of Kunti, making even more elaborate movements. Enraged, Bhima struck the powerful, gold-covered mace of furious Dur·yódhana. At the maces' collision, there was a crash accompanied by sparks, just as if two thunderbolts had been hurled against each other, great king. The force of the mace thrown by Bhima·sena made the earth shake as it fell to the ground, Your Majesty. 57.40

Just as a frenzied elephant becomes enraged at the sight of his rival, so the Káurava could not endure to see his mace being struck in battle. Full of resolve, King Dur·yódhana wheeled around in a left circle and then applied terrifying force to hit the son of Kunti on the head with his mace. But although struck by your son with his mace, Bhima, the son of Pandu, did not falter, Your Majesty. It was like a miracle. All the troops praised this wondrous feat as Bhima did not even shift his feet when struck by Dur·yódhana's mace.

Bhima, who possessed terrifying prowess, then hurled a heavier mace at Dur·yódhana, which blazed and was covered with gold. Without flinching, mighty Dur·yódhana foiled the blow through his agility, creating great amazement among the spectators. The earth shook and there was the noise of a huge earthquake as the foiled mace that had been hurled by Bhima fell to the ground. Using the *káushika* 57.45

āsthāya kauśikān mārgān utpatan sa punaḥ punaḥ
gadā|nipātaṃ prajñāya Bhīmasenam avañcayat.
vañcayitvā tadā Bhīmaṃ gadayā Kuru|sattamaḥ
tāḍayām āsa saṃkruddho vakṣo|deśe mahā|balaḥ.
57.50 gadayā nihato Bhīmo muhyamāno mahā|raṇe
n' âbhyamanyata kartavyaṃ putreṇ' âbhyāhatas tava.
tasmiṃs tathā vartamāne rājan Somaka|Pāṇḍavāḥ
bhṛś'|ôpahata|saṃkalpā na hṛṣṭa|manaso 'bhavan.
sa tu tena prahāreṇa mātaṅga iva roṣitaḥ
hastivadd hasti|saṃkāśam abhidudrāva te sutam.
tatas tu tarasā Bhīmo gadayā tanayaṃ tava
abhidudrāva vegena siṃho vana|gajaṃ yathā.
upasṛtya tu rājānaṃ gadā|mokṣa|viśāradaḥ
āvidhyata gadāṃ rājan samuddiśya sutaṃ tava.
57.55 atāḍayad Bhīmasenaḥ pārśve Duryodhanaṃ tadā.
sa vihvalaḥ prahāreṇa jānubhyām agaman mahīm.
tasmin Kuru|kula|śreṣṭhe jānubhyām avanīṃ gate
udatiṣṭhat tato nādaḥ Sṛñjayānāṃ jagat|pate.
teṣāṃ tu ninadaṃ śrutvā Sṛñjayānāṃ nara'|rṣabhaḥ
a|marṣād Bharata|śreṣṭha putras te samakupyata.
utthāya tu mahā|bāhur mahān nāga iva śvasan
didhakṣann iva netrābhyāṃ Bhīmasenam avaikṣata.
tataḥ sa Bharata|śreṣṭho gadā|pāṇir abhidravat
pramathiṣyann iva śiro Bhīmasenasya saṃyuge.
57.60 sa mah"|ātmā mah"|ātmānaṃ Bhīmaṃ bhīma|parākramaḥ
atāḍayac chaṅkha|deśe. na cacāl' â|cal'|ôpamaḥ.
sa bhūyaḥ śuśubhe Pārthas tāḍito gadayā raṇe

move and leaping up repeatedly, Dur·yódhana observed the descent of his opponent's mace and tricked Bhima·sena. After tricking Bhima, the enraged and mighty champion of the Kurus then struck him in the chest with his mace. Struck by Dur·yódhana's mace, Bhima became stunned in that great battle and was at a loss after receiving this blow from your son. 57.50

At this event, the Sómakas and Pándavas became despondent, Your Majesty, their hopes severely dashed. In response to the blow, however, Bhima became as furious as an elephant and charged against your son like one elephant charging against another. With swift force, Bhima attacked your son with his mace, like a lion attacking a forest elephant. Skilled at hurling maces, he approached the king and wielded his weapon, aiming it at your son. Bhima·sena then struck Dur·yódhana on his side. Stunned by the blow, Dur·yódhana fell on his knees to the ground. 57.55

The Srínjayas roared when that champion of the Kuru clan fell on his knees to the ground, lord of the world. But your son, that bull among men, became filled with intolerant rage when he heard the Srínjayas' roar, best of Bharatas. Raising himself up like a huge hissing snake, mighty-armed Dur·yódhana glared at Bhima·sena as if desiring to incinerate him with his eyes. That best of Bharatas then charged forward, wielding his mace and eager to crush Bhima·sena's head in battle. With terrifying prowess, great-spirited Dur·yódhana struck heroic Bhima on the temple. But, like an unshakeable mountain, Bhima did not falter. Indeed, although struck by Dur·yódhana's mace in battle, the Partha 57.60

udbhinna|rudhiro rājan prabhinna iva kuñjaraḥ.
tato gadāṃ vīra|haṇīm ayo|mayīṃ
pragṛhya vajr'|âśani|tulya|niḥsvanām
atāḍayac chatrum a|mitra|karṣano
balena vikramya Dhanañjay'|âgra|jaḥ.
sa Bhīmasen'|âbhihatas tav' ātma|jaḥ
papāta saṃkampita|deha|bandhanaḥ
su|puṣpito māruta|vega|tāḍito
vane yathā śāla iv' âvaghūrṇitaḥ.
tataḥ praṇedur jahṛṣuś ca Pāṇḍavāḥ
samīkṣya putraṃ patitaṃ kṣitau tava.
tataḥ sutas te pratilabhya cetanāṃ
samutpapāta dvirado yathā hradāt.
57.65 sa pārthivo nityam a|marṣitas tadā
mahā|rathaḥ śikṣitavat paribhraman
atāḍayat Pāṇḍavam agrataḥ sthitaṃ.
sa vihval'|âṅgo jagatīm upāspṛśat.
sa siṃha|nādaṃ vinanāda Kauravo
nipātya bhūmau yudhi Bhīmam ojasā
bibheda c' âiv' âśani|tulya|tejasā
gadā|nipātena śarīra|rakṣaṇam.
tato 'ntarikṣe ninado mahān abhūd
div'|âukasām apsarasāṃ ca neduṣām
papāta c' ôccair a|mara|praveritaṃ
vicitra|puṣp'|ôtkara|varṣam uttamam.
tataḥ parān āviśad uttamaṃ bhayaṃ
samīkṣya bhūmau patitaṃ nar'|ôttamam
a|hīyamānaṃ ca balena Kauravaṃ
niśamya bhedaṃ su|dṛḍhasya varmaṇaḥ.

looked even more glorious as blood flowed from his head, just as an elephant secretes juices when its temple is cleft.

Taking up his hero-destroying mace, which was made of iron and boomed like a thunderbolt, the elder brother of Dhanan·jaya—that bane of his enemies—attacked his opponent and struck him with force. Hit by Bhima·sena, your son fell down, his muscles quivering, and shook like a blossoming *shala* tree that has been struck by a gust of wind in the forest. The Pándavas roared and were delighted when they saw your son fall to the ground. But, like an elephant emerging from a lake, your son regained his senses and raised himself up. Wheeling around with expertise, that great warrior and ever-furious king then struck the Pándava as he stood before him. His limbs quivering, Bhima fell to the ground. After violently striking Bhima to the ground in battle, the Káurava roared a lion-roar. He then split open Bhima's body armor with a blow from his mace that was as powerful as a thunderbolt. 57.65

There was then a huge roar in the sky from cheering deities and nymphs and the gods rained down an exquisite shower of diverse and abundant flowers. Your enemies were overcome by intense fear when they saw that champion among men fall to the ground and witnessed how Bhima's strong armor had been breached and how the Káurava was not inferior in strength.

tato muhūrtād upalabhya cetanāṃ
pramṛjya vaktraṃ rudhir'|âktam ātmanaḥ
dhṛtiṃ samālambya vivṛtya locane
balena saṃstabhya Vṛkodaraḥ sthitaḥ.

After a while, however, Bhima recovered his senses. Wip-
ng his blood-stained face and gathering his resolve, Vrikó-
lara rolled his eyes and stood up, vigorously steadying
imself.

58
DUR·YÓDHANA DEFEATED

SAÑJAYA uvāca:

58.1 SAMUDĪRṆAṂ TATO dṛṣṭvā
saṃgrāmaṃ Kuru|mukhyayoḥ
ath' âbravīd Arjunas tu
Vāsudevaṃ yaśasvinam:
«anayor vīrayor yuddhe ko jyāyān bhavato mataḥ?
kasya vā ko guṇo bhūyān? etad vada Janārdana.»

VĀSUDEVA uvāca:

«upadeśo 'nayos tulyo. Bhīmas tu balavattaraḥ
kṛtī yatna|paras tv eṣa Dhārtarāṣṭro Vṛkodarāt.
Bhīmasenas tu dharmeṇa yudhyamāno na jeṣyati.
anyāyena tu yudhyan vai hanyād eva Suyodhanam.
māyayā nirjitā devair asurā iti naḥ śrutam.
58.5 Virocanas tu Śakreṇa māyayā nirjitaḥ sa vai
māyayā c' ākṣipat tejo Vṛtrasya Bala|sūdanaḥ.
tasmān māyā|mayaṃ Bhīma ātiṣṭhatu parākramam.
pratijñātaṃ ca Bhīmena dyūta|kāle Dhanañjaya
‹ūrū bhetsyāmi te saṅkhye gaday" êti› Suyodhanam.
so 'yaṃ pratijñāṃ tāṃ c' âpi pālayatv ari|karṣaṇaḥ!
māyāvinaṃ tu rājānaṃ māyay" âiva nikṛntatu!
yady eṣa balam āsthāya nyāyena prahariṣyati
viṣama|sthas tato rājā bhaviṣyati Yudhiṣṭhiraḥ.
punar eva tu vakṣyāmi. Pāṇḍaveya nibodha me.
Dharmarāj'|âparādhena bhayaṃ naḥ punar āgatam.
58.10 kṛtvā hi su|mahat karma hatvā Bhīṣma|mukhān Kurūn
jayaḥ prāpto yaśaḥ prāgryaṃ vairaṃ ca pratiyātitam.
tad evaṃ vijayaḥ prāptaḥ punaḥ saṃśayitaḥ kṛtaḥ.
a|buddhir eṣā mahatī Dharmarājasya Pāṇḍava:

SÁNJAYA said:

WHEN ÁRJUNA SAW the battle raging between the two eminent Kurus, he said these words to glorious Vasudéva: 58.1

"Which of these heroes do you think will be victorious in battle? Who has what quality? Tell me this, Janárdana."

VASUDÉVA said:

"Their training is equal. But Bhima is stronger whereas the son of Dhrita·rashtra is more skillful and persevering than Vrikódara. Bhima·sena will not win if he fights justly. He will only kill Su·yódhana if he fights by unlawful means. We are told that the gods conquered the demons through deceit. Shakra used deceit to defeat Viróchana and it was through deceit that the slayer of Bala removed Vritra's power. Bhima should therefore employ a form of attack that uses deceit. 58.5

In the gambling-match, Dhanan·jaya, Bhima vowed that he would break Su·yódhana's thighs with his mace in battle. That enemy-tormentor should keep his vow! Let him use deceit to cut down this king who is himself deceitful! King Yudhi·shthira will be in a perilous situation if Bhima relies on his strength and fights morally.

I will tell you something more. Listen to me, Pándava. Danger has once again come upon us due to the fault of the King of Righteousness. The King of Righteousness has performed enormous feats and destroyed the Kurus led by Bhishma. He has attained victory and the highest glory and achieved his revenge. But even though such victory has been achieved, it is now again jeopardized. The great folly of the 58.10

yad eka|vijaye yuddhaṃ paṇitaṃ ghoram īdṛśam.
Suyodhanaḥ kṛtī vīra ek'|âyana|gatas tathā.

api c' Ôśanasā gītaḥ śrūyate 'yaṃ purātanaḥ
ślokas tattv'|ârtha|sahitas. tan me nigadataḥ śṛṇu:
‹punar āvartamānānāṃ bhagnānāṃ jīvit'|âiṣiṇām
bhetavyam ari|śeṣāṇām. ek'|âyana|gatā hi te.›

58.15 sāhas'|ôtpatitānāṃ ca nirāśānāṃ ca jīvite
na śakyam agrataḥ sthātuṃ Śakreṇ' âpi Dhanañjaya.

Suyodhanam imaṃ bhagnaṃ
hata|sainyaṃ hradaṃ gatam
parājitaṃ vana|prepsuṃ
nirāśaṃ rājya|lambhane
ko nv eṣa saṃyuge prājñaḥ punar dvandve samāhvayet?
api no nirjitaṃ rājyaṃ na hareta Suyodhanaḥ!
yas trayodaśa|varṣāṇi gadayā kṛta|niśramaḥ
caraty ūrdhvaṃ ca tiryak ca Bhīmasena|jighāṃsayā,
enaṃ cen na mahā|bāhur a|nyāyena haniṣyati
eṣa vaḥ Kauravo rājā Dhārtarāṣṭro bhaviṣyati!»

58.20 Dhanañjayas tu śrutv" âitat Keśavasya mah"|ātmanaḥ
prekṣato Bhīmasenasya savyam ūrum atāḍayat.
gṛhya saṃjñāṃ tato Bhīmo gadayā vyacarad raṇe
maṇḍalāni vicitrāṇi yamakān' îtarāṇi ca.
dakṣiṇaṃ maṇḍalaṃ savyaṃ gomūtrakam ath' âpi ca
vyacarat Pāṇḍavo rājann ariṃ saṃmohayann iva.
tath" âiva tava putro 'pi gadā|mārga|viśāradaḥ

King of Righteousness lies in this, Pándava: that he risks such a magnificent and horrific battle on a single contest. Su·yódhana is a skilled hero who follows a path of single focus.

I have heard an ancient verse sung by Úshanas that is invested with truth and benefit. Listen to my recitation of it: 'One should fear enemies who survive war out of desire for life and who return to battle after being crushed. For such men follow a path of single focus.' Even Shakra cannot stand before those who rise up rashly without any hope for life, Dhanan·jaya. 58.15

Su·yódhana was crushed and then fled to a lake after his army had been destroyed. In his defeat, he desired to enter the forest. He had no hope of keeping his kingdom. Who that is wise in matters of war would challenge him to a duel? Su·yódhana may even steal the kingdom that we have won! For thirteen years he has practiced with his mace. And now, in his desire to kill Bhima·sena, he careers around, jumping upwards and sideways. If mighty-armed Bhima does not kill him through unlawful means, then this Káurava son of Dhrita·rashtra will become your king!"

When Dhanan·jaya heard heroic Késhava's words, he slapped his left thigh before Bhima·sena's eyes. Understanding the sign, Bhima wheeled around with his mace on the battlefield, moving in various circles and making double-moves and other maneuvers. Seeming to confound his enemy, the Pándava careered around in a right circle and then a left one and then zigzagged, Your Majesty. In the same 58.20

vyacaral laghu citraṃ ca Bhīmasena|jighāṃsayā.
ādhunvantau gade ghore candan'|âgaru|rūṣite
vairasy' ântaṃ parīpsantau raṇe kruddhāv iv' ântakau.

58.25 anyonyaṃ tau jighāṃsantau pravīrau puruṣa'|rṣabhau
yuyudhāte garutmantau yathā nāg'|āmiṣ'|âiṣiṇau.

maṇḍalāni vicitrāṇi carator nṛpa|Bhīmayoḥ
gadā|saṃpāta|jās tatra prajajñuḥ pāvak'|ârciṣaḥ.
samaṃ praharatos tatra śūrayor balinor mṛdhe
kṣubdhayor vāyunā rājan dvayor iva samudrayoḥ,
tayoḥ praharatos tulyaṃ matta|kuñjarayor iva
gadā|nirghāta|saṃhrādaḥ prahārāṇām ajāyata.

tasmiṃs tadā saṃprahāre dāruṇe saṃkule bhṛśam
ubhāv api pariśrāntau yudhyamānāv arin|damau

58.30 tau muhūrtaṃ samāśvasya punar eva paran|tapa
abhyahārayatāṃ kruddhau pragṛhya mahatī gade.

tayoḥ samabhavad yuddhaṃ ghora|rūpam a|saṃvṛtam
gadā|nipātai rāj'|êndra takṣator vai paras|param.
samare pradrutau tau tu vṛṣabh'|âkṣau tarasvinau
anyonyaṃ jaghnatur vīrau paṅka|sthau mahiṣāv iva.
jarjarī|kṛta|sarv'|âṅgau rudhireṇ' âbhisaṃplutau
dadṛśāte Himavati puṣpitāv iva kiṃśukau.

Duryodhanas tu Pārthena vivare saṃpradarśite
īṣad unmiṣamāṇas tu sahasā prasasāra ha.

58.35 tam abhyāśa|gataṃ prājño raṇe prekṣya Vṛkodaraḥ
avākṣipad gadāṃ tasmin vegena mahatā balī.

way, your son, who was skilled in mace maneuvers, also careered around with agility and variety, eager to kill Bhima·sena. Shaking their terrifying maces, which were smeared with aloe and sandalwood, the men looked like two battle-enraged Deaths as they sought to conclude their feud. In their desire to kill each other, the heroic bull-like men fought like two *gárudas* that covet the flesh of a snake. 58.25

As King Dur·yódhana and Bhima careered around in various circles, sparks of fire could be seen flying from the collision of their maces. The mighty heroes struck each other with equal force in battle and resembled a pair of oceans whipped up by the wind. The two warriors resembled frenzied elephants as they attacked each other in equal measure and the blows of their maces boomed like a thunderstorm.

During this horrific and extremely turbulent battle, both enemy-tamers became exhausted from fighting. But after resting a while, they once again took up their huge maces and furiously assailed each other, enemy-scorcher. 58.30

Lacerating each other with blows from their maces, the two men fought an unrestrained battle that was horrific to see, king of kings. Like bulls wading in mud, the violent bull-eyed heroes charged forward in battle and struck one another. Drenched in blood, their limbs all mangled, they looked like two blossoming *kínshuka* trees on the Hímavat mountain.

The Partha then exposed an opening, whereupon Dur·yódhana violently rushed forward, smiling slightly. But when wise Vrikódara saw Dur·yódhana approaching him on the battlefield, the mighty hero hurled his mace at him with great force. Your son, however, shifted his position on 58.35

ākṣipantaṃ tu taṃ dṛṣṭvā putras tava viśāṃ pate
avāsarpat tataḥ sthānāt. sā moghā nyapatad bhuvi.
mokṣayitvā prahāraṃ taṃ sutas tava su|saṃbhramāt
Bhīmasenaṃ ca gadayā prāharat Kuru|sattama.
tasya visyandamānena rudhireṇ' â|mit'|âujasaḥ
prahāra|guru|pātāc ca mūrch" êva samajāyata.
Duryodhano na taṃ veda pīḍitaṃ Pāṇḍavaṃ raṇe
dhārayām āsa Bhīmo 'pi śarīram atipīḍitam.
58.40 amanyata sthitaṃ hy enaṃ prahariṣyantam āhave
ato na prāharat tasmai punar eva tav' ātma|jaḥ.

tato muhūrtam āśvasya Duryodhanam upasthitam
vegen' âbhyapatad rājan Bhīmasenaḥ pratāpavān.
tam āpatantaṃ saṃprekṣya saṃrabdham a|mit'|âujasam
mogham asya prahāraṃ taṃ cikīrṣur Bharata'|rṣabha,
avasthāne matiṃ kṛtvā putras tava mahā|manāḥ
iyeṣ' ôtpatituṃ rājaṃś chalayiṣyan Vṛkodaram.
abuddhyad Bhīmasenas tu rājñas tasya cikīrṣitam
ath' âsya samabhidrutya samutkruśya ca siṃhavat,
58.45 sṛtyā vañcayato rājan punar ev' ôtpatiṣyataḥ
ūrubhyāṃ prāhiṇod rājan gadāṃ vegena Pāṇḍavaḥ.
sā vajra|niṣpeṣa|samā prahitā bhīma|karmaṇā
ūrū Duryodhanasy' âtha babhañja priya|darśanau.
sa papāta nara|vyāghro vasudhām anunādayan
bhagn'|ōrur Bhīmasenena putras tava mahī|pate.

seeing Bhima's throw and the mace fell to the ground, foiled. After avoiding this blow, your son zealously attacked Bhima·sena with his mace, best of Kurus. Although he possessed infinite power, Bhima seemed stunned by the violence of the blow and by the blood that poured from his body. But Dur·yódhana did not realize that the Pándava had been subdued in battle, even though Bhima was trying to stabilize his body. Your son thought that Bhima was stable and about 58.40 to attack in battle and therefore did not assail him again.

After recuperating a while, mighty Bhima·sena rushed with speed against Dur·yódhana, who was standing nearby, Your Majesty. Seeing that hero of limitless power furiously charging toward him, Dur·yódhana sought to foil his attack, bull of the Bharatas. Deciding on the *avasthána* move, your proud son aimed to jump into the air in order to trick Vrikódara.* But Bhima·sena guessed the king's intention. Charging at him and roaring like a lion, the Pándava 58.45 violently hurled his mace at Dur·yódhana's thighs as his opponent leaped in the air once more in order to deceive his enemy, Your Majesty. With the crash of a thunderbolt, the mace hurled by that warrior of terrifying deeds broke Dur·yódhana's handsome thighs. His thighs smashed, your son, that tiger among men, fell to the ground, making the earth resound, Your Majesty.

vavur vātāḥ sa|nirghātāḥ pāṃśu|varṣaṃ papāta ca
cacāla pṛthivī c' âpi sa|vṛkṣa|kṣupa|parvatā.
tasmin nipatite vīre patyau sarva|mahī|kṣitām
mahā|svanā punar dīptā sa|nirghātā bhayaṅ|karī
papāta c' ôlkā mahatī patite pṛthivī|patau.

58.50 tathā śoṇita|varṣaṃ ca pāṃśu|varṣaṃ ca Bhārata
vavarṣa Maghavāṃs tatra tava putre nipātite.
yakṣāṇāṃ rākṣasānāṃ ca piśācānāṃ tath" âiva ca
antarikṣe mahā|nādaḥ śrūyate Bharata'|rṣabha.
tena śabdena ghoreṇa mṛgāṇām atha pakṣiṇām
jajñe ghorataraḥ śabdo bahūnāṃ sarvato|diśam.
ye tatra vājinaḥ śeṣā gajāś ca manujaiḥ saha
mumucus te mahā|nādaṃ tava putre nipātite.

bherī|śaṅkha|mṛdaṅgānām abhavac ca svano mahān
antar|bhūmi|gataś c' âiva tava putre nipātite.

58.55 bahu|pādair bahu|bhujaiḥ kabandhair ghora|darśanaiḥ
nṛtyadbhir bhaya|dair vyāptā diśas tatr' âbhavan nṛpa.
dhvajavanto 'stravantaś ca śastravantas tath" âiva ca
prākampanta tato rājaṃs tava putre nipātite.
hradāḥ kūpāś ca rudhiram udvemur nṛpa|sattama
nadyaś ca su|mahā|vegāḥ pratisroto|vah" âbhavan.
pul|liṅgā iva nāryas tu strī|liṅgāḥ puruṣ" âbhavan*
Duryodhane tadā rājan patite tanaye tava.

Stormy winds then blew and a shower of dust fell from the sky. The earth quaked, along with its trees, shrubs, and mountains. A huge and terrifying meteor also descended from the sky when that heroic monarch and lord of all kings collapsed and fell to the ground. Making a vast noise, the meteor blazed with fire and was accompanied by whirlwinds. At the fall of your son in battle, Mághavat rained down a shower of blood and a shower of dust, descendant of Bharata. *Yakshas*, *rákshasas*, and *pisháchas* roared loudly in the sky, bull of the Bharatas. At that terrible noise, hordes of wild beasts and birds began to make an even more horrific sound in every direction. The surviving horses, elephants, and men also let out a huge roar at your son's fall. 58.50

At the fall of your son, there was a huge noise of kettle-drums, conches, and tabors that penetrated the earth's innards. The directions became pervaded by horrendous looking torsoes. With their many feet and many arms, they danced and aroused fear, Your Majesty. Men bearing standards, arrows, or weapons trembled when your son was felled, Your Majesty. Lakes and wells vomited blood, best of kings, and rivers began to flow upstream with strong currents. Women took on the characteristics of men and men took on the characteristics of women when your son Dur·yódhana fell, O king. 58.55

dṛṣṭvā tān adbhut'|ôtpātān Pañcālāḥ Pāṇḍavaiḥ saha
āvigna|manasaḥ sarve babhūvur Bharata'|rṣabha.

58.60 yayur devā yathā|kāmam gandharv'|âpsarasas tathā
kathayanto 'dbhutaṃ yuddhaṃ sutayos tava Bhārata.
tath" âiva siddhā rāj'|êndra tathā vātika|cāraṇāḥ
nara|siṃhau praśaṃsantau viprajagmur yath"|āgatam.

All the Panchálas and Pándavas became bewildered when they saw these incredible portents, bull of the Bharatas. The gods, *gandhárvas*, and nymphs then departed at will, discussing the wondrous battle between your sons, descendant of Bharata. In the same way, the *siddhas* and wind-traveling *cháranas* left the same way they had come, praising the two lion-like men.

58.60

59–61
INSULTS AND REBUKES

SAÑJAYA uvāca:

59.1 TAM PĀTITAM tato dṛṣṭvā mahā|śālam iv' ôdgatam
prahṛṣṭa|manasaḥ sarve dadṛśus tatra Pāṇḍavāḥ.
unmattam iva mātaṅgaṃ siṃhena vinipātitam
dadṛśur hṛṣṭa|romāṇaḥ sarve te c' âpi Somakāḥ.
tato Duryodhanaṃ hatvā Bhīmasenaḥ pratāpavān
pātitaṃ Kaurav'|êndraṃ tam upagamy' êdam abravīt:

«‹gaur gaur iti› purā manda Draupadīm eka|vāsasam
yat sabhāyāṃ hasann asmāṃs tadā vadasi dur|mate
tasy' âvahāsasya phalam adya tvaṃ samavāpnuhi!»

59.5 evam uktvā sa vāmena padā maulim upāspṛśat
śiraś ca rāja|siṃhasya pādena samaloḍayat.
tath" âiva krodha|saṃrakto Bhīmaḥ para|bal'|ârdanaḥ
punar ev' âbravīd vākyaṃ yat tac chṛṇu nar'|âdhipa:

«ye 'smān puro 'panṛtyanta mūḍhā ‹gaur iti› ‹gaur iti›
tān vayaṃ pratinṛtyāmaḥ punar ‹gaur iti› ‹gaur iti.›
n' âsmākaṃ nikṛtir vahnir n' âkṣa|dyūtaṃ na vañcanā.
sva|bāhu|balam āśritya prabādhāmo vayaṃ ripūn!»

so 'vāpya vairasya parasya pāraṃ
Vṛkodaraḥ prāha śanaiḥ prahasya
Yudhiṣṭhiraṃ Keśava|Sṛñjayāṃś ca
Dhanañjayaṃ Mādravatī|sutau ca:

Sánjaya said:

The Pándavas were all delighted when they saw Dur·yódhana collapse like a tall uprooted *shala* tree and all the Sómakas felt their hair bristle when they saw Dur·yódhana struck down like a crazed elephant toppled by a lion. After he had struck down Dur·yódhana, mighty Bhima·sena approached the fallen king of the Káuravas and said: 59.1

"Previously, you dim-witted fool, you laughed at Dráupadi in the assembly hall when she was clothed only in a single garment and you said to me: 'Ox! Ox!'* Attain on this day the fruit of your scorn!"

Saying this, he placed his left foot on Dur·yódhana's head and rubbed the head of the lion-like king with his sole. Red with anger, Bhima—that destroyer of enemy armies—then addressed Dur·yódhana once more. Hear the words he spoke, lord of men. 59.5

"Repeatedly shouting 'Ox! Ox!' we will dance around the fools who danced around us in the past and cried out: 'Ox! Ox!' We have used no dishonesty, fire, dice-game, or deceit. We have suppressed our enemies by relying on the strength of our arms!"

Vrikódara—who had reached the further shore of his greatest enmity—then spoke slowly and with a laugh to Yudhi·shthira, Késhava, the Srínjayas, Dhanan·jaya and the two sons of Mádravati, saying:

59.10 «rajasvalāṃ Draupadīm ānayan ye
ye c' âpy akurvanta sadasy a|vastrām
tān paśyadhvaṃ Pāṇḍavair Dhārtarāṣṭrān
raṇe hatāṃs tapasā Yājñasenyāḥ!
ye naḥ purā ṣaṇḍha|tilān avocan
krūrā rājño Dhṛtarāṣṭrasya putrāḥ
te no hatāḥ sa|gaṇāḥ s'|ânubandhāḥ.
kāmaṃ svargaṃ narakaṃ vā patāmaḥ!»
punaś ca rājñaḥ patitasya bhūmau
sa tāṃ gadāṃ skandha|gatāṃ pragṛhya
vāmena pādena śiraḥ pramṛdya
Duryodhanaṃ naikṛtikaṃ nyavocat.
hṛṣṭena rājan Kuru|sattamasya
kṣudr'|ātmanā Bhīmasenena pādam
dṛṣṭvā kṛtaṃ mūrdhani n' âbhyanandan
dharm'|ātmānaḥ Somakānāṃ prabarhāḥ.
tava putraṃ tathā hatvā
katthamānaṃ Vṛkodaram
nṛtyamānaṃ ca bahuśo
Dharmarājo 'bravīd idam:

59.15 «gato 'si vairasy' ānṛṇyaṃ. pratijñā pūritā tvayā—
śubhen' âth' â|śubhen' âiva karmaṇā. viram' âdhunā.
mā śiro 'sya padā mardīr. mā dharmas te 'tigo bhavet.
rājā jñātir hataś c' âyaṃ. n' âitan nyāyyaṃ tav' ân|agha!
ekādaśa|camū|nāthaṃ Kurūṇām adhipaṃ tathā
mā sprākṣīr Bhīma pādena rājānaṃ jñātim eva ca.
hata|bandhur hat'|āmātyo bhraṣṭa|sainyo hato mṛdhe.
sarv'|ākāreṇa śocyo 'yaṃ. n' âvahāsyo 'yam īśvaraḥ.
vidhvasto 'yaṃ hat'|āmātyo hata|bhrātā hata|prajaḥ
utsanna|piṇḍo bhrātā ca. n' âitan nyāyyaṃ kṛtaṃ tvayā.

"The sons of Dhrita·rashtra once led Dráupadi into the assembly hall and disrobed her while she was menstruating. Look now at how these men have been slaughtered by the Pándavas in battle through the ascetic power of Yajna·sena's daughter!* They once called us barren sesame seeds*—but we have now killed the vicious sons of King Dhrita·rashtra along with their troops and relatives! We can now go to heaven or hell as we like!" 59.10

Picking up the mace that rested on his shoulder, he once again rubbed the head of the fallen king with his left foot and abused vile Dur·yódhana. But the righteous champions of the Sómakas were not pleased when they saw mean-spirited Bhima·sena gleefully place his foot on the head of that supreme Kuru. The King of Righteousness then addressed Vrikódara as he bragged and danced wildly after slaying your son:

"You have paid off the debt of your enmity. You have fulfilled your vow—whether by good or bad deed. Stop now. Do not rub his head with your foot. Do not transgress morality. The king is a relative and has been struck down. You are not acting lawfully, faultless Bhima! Do not touch this lord of eleven armies and ruler of Kurus with your foot, Bhima. He is a king and a relative. His kinsmen and counsellors have been slaughtered. His army has been crushed and he has been slain in battle. He is pitiable in every way. This lord should not be insulted. He has been ruined. He has lost his counsellors, brothers, and people. He has no ancestor-offerings and he is our brother. Your conduct is improper. People previously used to call you 'Righteous 59.15

‹dhārmiko Bhīmaseno 'sāv ity› āhus tvāṃ purā janāḥ.
sa kasmād Bhīmasena tvaṃ rājānam adhitiṣṭhasi?»

59.20 ity uktvā Bhīmasenaṃ tu s'|âśru|kaṇṭho Yudhiṣṭhiraḥ
upasṛty' âbravīd dīno Duryodhanam arin|damam:

«tāta manyur na te kāryo. n' ātmā śocyas tvayā tathā.
nūnaṃ pūrva|kṛtaṃ karma su|ghoram anubhūyate.
Dhātr" ôpadiṣṭaṃ viṣamaṃ nūnaṃ phalam a|saṃskṛtam
yad vayaṃ tvāṃ jighāṃsāmas tvaṃ c' âsmān Kuru|sattama.
ātmano hy aparādhena mahad vyasanam īdṛśam
prāptavān asi yal lobhān madād bālyāc ca Bhārata.
ghātayitvā vayasyāṃś ca bhrātṝn atha pitṝṃs tathā
putrān pautrāṃs tathā c' ânyāṃs tato 'si nidhanaṃ gataḥ.

59.25 tav' âparādhād asmābhir bhrātaras te nipātitāḥ
nihatā jñātayaś c' âpi. diṣṭaṃ manye dur|atyayam.
ātmā na śocanīyas te. ślāghyo mṛtyus tav' ân|agha!
vayam ev' âdhunā śocyāḥ sarv'|âvasthāsu Kaurava.
kṛpaṇaṃ vartayiṣyāmas tair hīnā bandhubhiḥ priyaiḥ
bhrātṝṇāṃ c' âiva putrāṇāṃ tathā vai śoka|vihvalāḥ.
kathaṃ drakṣyāmi vidhavā vadhūḥ śoka|pariplutāḥ?
tvam ekaḥ su|sthito rājan. svarge te nilayo dhruvaḥ.
vayaṃ naraka|saṃjñaṃ vai duḥkhaṃ prāpyāma dāruṇam.
snuṣāś ca prasnuṣāś c' âiva Dhṛtarāṣṭrasya vihvalāḥ
garhayiṣyanti no nūnaṃ vidhavāḥ śoka|karśitāḥ.»

Bhima·sena.' So why, Bhima·sena, do you now humiliate the king?"

Saying these words to Bhima·sena, Yudhi·shthira, who was distressed and choked with tears, approached enemy-taming Dur·yódhana and said: 59.20

"Do not be angry, my friend. And do not feel sorry for yourself. You are surely experiencing the fruit of terrible deeds committed in the past. The fact that we desire to kill you and you desire to kill us shows that Dhatri has surely determined this cruel and harsh outcome, best of Kurus. It is because of your own wrongdoing—your greed, madness and stupidity—that you suffer this terrible misfortune, descendant of Bharata. You have arrived at your own destruction after causing the deaths of your friends, brothers, fathers, sons, grandchildren and others.

It is because of your transgressions that we have slaughtered your brothers and killed your relatives. Fate is, I believe, unsurpassable. You are not to be pitied. Your death is to be praised, faultless Dur·yódhana! We are the ones who now ought to be pitied in every way, Káurava. We will live a wretched life, bereft of our dear kinsmen and distraught with grief for our brothers and sons. How can I look at the widows who are overwhelmed with grief? You alone are in a good situation, O king. For your place in heaven is secure. But we will endure that terrible suffering called hell. Distraught and emaciated with grief, Dhrita·rashtra's widowed daughters-in-law and granddaughters-in-law will surely censure us." 59.25

SAÑJAYA uvāca:

59.30 evam uktvā su|duḥkh'|ārto niśaśvāsa sa pārthivaḥ
vilalāpa ciraṃ c' âpi Dharma|putro Yudhiṣṭhiraḥ.

DHṚTARĀṢṬRA uvāca:

60.1 A|DHARMEṆA HATAṂ dṛṣṭvā rājānaṃ Mādhav'|ôttamaḥ
kim abravīt tadā sūta Baladevo mahā|balaḥ?
gadā|yuddha|viśeṣa|jño gadā|yuddha|viśāradaḥ
kṛtavān Rauhiṇeyo yat tan mam' ācakṣva Sañjaya.

SAÑJAYA uvāca:

śirasy abhihataṃ dṛṣṭvā Bhīmasenena te sutam
Rāmaḥ praharatāṃ śreṣṭhaś cukrodha balavad balī.
tato madhye nar'|êndrāṇām
ūrdhva|bāhur hal'|āyudhaḥ
kurvann ārta|svaraṃ ghoraṃ:
«dhig dhig Bhīm' êty» uvāca ha.
60.5 «aho dhig yad adho nābheḥ prahṛtaṃ dharma|vigrahe
n' âitad dṛṣṭaṃ gadā|yuddhe kṛtavān yad Vṛkodaraḥ.
‹adho nābhyā na hantavyam iti› śāstrasya niścayaḥ.
ayaṃ tv a|śāstra|vin mūḍhaḥ sva|cchandāt saṃpravartate!»
tasya tat tad bruvāṇasya roṣaḥ samabhavan mahān.
tato rājānam ālokya roṣa|saṃrakta|locanaḥ
Baladevo mahā|rāja tato vacanam abravīt:
«na c' âiṣa patitaḥ Kṛṣṇa! kevalaṃ mat|samo '|samaḥ.
āśritya tu daurbalyād āśrayaḥ paribhartsyate.»

SÁNJAYA said:

59.30 Saying these words and afflicted with great sorrow, King Yudhi·shthira, the son of Righteousness, sighed and lamented a long while.

DHRITA·RASHTRA said:

60.1 WHAT DID MIGHTY Bala·deva, that champion of the Mádhavas, say when he saw the king unjustly slain, charioteer? Bala knows the specifics of mace fighting and is skilled in mace combat. So tell me what the son of Róhini did, Sánjaya.

SÁNJAYA said:

When mighty Rama saw Bhima·sena strike your son on the head, that best of warriors became filled with immense anger. Raising his arms in the middle of those kings, plow-weaponed Rama made a terrible noise of distress, shouting:

60.5 "Shame on you, Bhima! Shame on you! It is shameful to strike an opponent below the navel in honorable combat. I have never seen an action like Vrikódara's before in a mace contest. The Teachings state that one should never strike below the navel. This fool does not know the Teachings and acts according to his own will!"

Great anger arose in Rama as he spoke these words. Bala·deva looked at the king and then said these words, Your Majesty, his eyes red with fury:

"This man has not fallen, Krishna! He has no rival and is only equal to me. The one whom you foolishly relied on will be chastized."*

tato lāṅgalam udyamya Bhīmam abhyadravad balī.
tasy' ōrdhva|bāhoḥ sadṛśaṃ rūpam āsīn mah"|ātmanaḥ
bahudhā tu vicitrasya śvetasy' êva mahā|gireḥ.

60.10 tam utpatantaṃ jagrāha Keśavo vinay'|ânvitaḥ
bāhubhyāṃ pīna|vṛttābhyāṃ prayatnād balavad balī.
sit'|â|sitau Yadu|varau śuśubhāte 'dhikaṃ tadā
nabho|gatau yathā rājaṃś candra|sūryau dina|kṣaye.
uvāca c' âinaṃ saṃrabdhaṃ śamayann iva Keśavaḥ:

«ātma|vṛddhir mitra|vṛddhir mitra|mitr'|ôdayas tathā
viparītaṃ dviṣatsv etat ṣaḍ|vidhā vṛddhir ātmanaḥ.
ātmany api ca mitre ca viparītaṃ yadā bhavet
tadā vidyān mano|glānim āśu śānti|karo bhavet.
asmākaṃ saha|jaṃ mitraṃ Pāṇḍavāḥ śuddha|pauruṣāḥ
svakāḥ pitṛ|ṣvasuḥ putrās te parair nikṛtā bhṛśam.

60.15 pratijñā|pālaṇaṃ dharmaḥ kṣatriyasy' êha: ‹vedmy aham:
Suyodhanasya gadayā bhaṅkt" âsmy ūrū mah"|āhave›
iti pūrvaṃ pratijñātaṃ Bhīmena hi sabhā|tale.
Maitreyeṇ' âbhiśaptaś ca pūrvam eva maha"|rṣiṇā
‹ūrū te bhetsyate Bhīmo gaday" êti› paran|tapa.
ato doṣaṃ na paśyāmi. mā kruddhyasva Pralamba|han.
yaunaḥ svaiḥ sukha|hārdaiś ca saṃbandhaḥ saha Pāṇḍavaiḥ.
teṣāṃ vṛddhyā hi vṛddhir no. mā krudhaḥ puruṣa'|rṣabha!»

Wielding his plow, mighty Rama then charged against Bhima. Raising his arms high, the hero looked like a huge white mountain mottled with various colors. With a mighty effort, however, powerful and self-composed Késhava used his thick, rounded arms to seize hold of Rama as he charged forward. With their fair and dark colors, the two excellent Yadus looked extremely glorious and resembled the moon and sun in the sky at the day's close, Your Majesty. Késhava then addressed furious Bala·deva in order to calm him: 60.10

"There are six kinds of prosperity: the prosperity of oneself; the prosperity of one's friends; the progress of one's friends' friends; and the opposite for one's enemies. When misfortune falls on oneself or one's friends, one should understand this decline and quickly act to solve it. The Pándavas are pure in their bravery and are our friends by blood. They are the sons of our father's sister and have been severely wronged by their enemies.*

It is the duty of a warrior to keep his vows in this world. Bhima previously made the following vow in the assembly-hall: 'This I know: I will break Su·yódhana's thighs with my mace in a great battle!' The great seer Maitréya also once cursed Dur·yódhana, O enemy-scorcher, saying: 'Bhima will break your thighs with a mace.'* I therefore see no fault in this act. Do not be angry, slayer of Pralámba. We have a blood connection with the Pándavas and they are our friends. Our prosperity derives from their prosperity. Do not be angry, bull among men!" 60.15

Vāsudeva|vacaḥ śrutvā sīra|bhṛt prāha dharma|vit:
«dharmaḥ su|caritaḥ sadbhiḥ sa ca dvābhyāṃ niyacchati:
arthaś c' âtyartha|lubdhasya kāmaś c' âtiprasaṅginaḥ.
dharm'|ârthau dharma|kāmau ca
kām'|ârthau c' âpy a|pīḍayan
dharm'|ârtha|kāmān yo 'bhyeti
so 'tyantaṃ sukham aśnute.

60.20 tad idaṃ vyākulaṃ sarvaṃ kṛtaṃ dharmasya pīḍanāt
Bhīmasenena Govinda. kāmaṃ tvaṃ tu yath" āttha mām.»

KṚṢṆA uvāca:

a|roṣaṇo hi dharm'|ātmā satataṃ dharma|vatsalaḥ
bhavān prakhyāyate loke. tasmāt saṃśāmya mā krudhaḥ.
prāptaṃ Kali|yugaṃ viddhi pratijñāṃ Pāṇḍavasya ca
ānṛṇyaṃ yātu vairasya pratijñāyāś ca Pāṇḍavaḥ.

SAÑJAYA uvāca:

dharma|cchalam api śrutvā Keśavāt sa viśāṃ pate
n' âiva prīta|manā Rāmo vacanaṃ prāha saṃsadi:
«hatv" â|dharmeṇa rājānaṃ
dharm'|ātmānaṃ Suyodhanam
jihma|yodh" îti loke 'smin
khyātiṃ yāsyati Pāṇḍavaḥ.

60.25 Duryodhano 'pi dharm'|ātmā gatiṃ yāsyati śāśvatīm
ṛju|yodhī hato rājā Dhārtarāṣṭro nar'|âdhipaḥ.
yuddha|dīkṣāṃ praviśy' ājau raṇa|yajñaṃ vitatya ca

When he heard Vasudéva's words, plow-bearing Rama, who is knowledgeable in righteousness, said:

"Righteousness is properly practiced by the good. But it is limited by two factors: when people are excessively greedy for profit, it is limited by profit, and when people have excessive attachments, it is limited by desire. That man attains great happiness who does not suppress righteousness and profit, or righteousness and desire, or desire and profit, but practices righteousness, profit and desire together. This entire turmoil has arisen because Bhima·sena suppressed righteousness, Go·vinda. You can tell me what you like." 60.20

KRISHNA said:

You have been hailed in the world as one devoid of anger and as one who is righteous and always devoted to morality. Be calm, therefore, and cease your anger. Be aware that the Kali era is at hand.* And be aware too of the Pándava's vow. Let the Pándava pay off the debts of his enmity and his vow.

SÁNJAYA said:

Displeased at hearing Késhava speak this fraudulent morality, Rama said these words in the assembly, lord of the people:

"The Pándava will be known in the world as a crooked fighter because he has slain righteous King Su·yódhana through unjust means. But righteous Dur·yódhana—the royal son of Dhrita·rashtra and lord of men—will attain the eternal realm because he was killed as a fair fighter. On being initiated into the sacrifice of war, Dur·yódhana prepared the sacrificial arena of the battlefield and offered 60.25

hutv” ātmānam a|mitr’|âgnau prāpa c’ âvabhṛthaṃ yaśaḥ!»

ity uktvā ratham āsthāya Rauhiṇeyaḥ pratāpavān
śvet’|âbhra|śikhar’|ākāraḥ prayayau Dvārakāṃ prati.
Pañcālāś ca sa|Vārṣṇeyāḥ Pāṇḍavāś ca viśāṃ pate
Rāme Dvāravatīṃ yāte n’ âtipramanaso ’bhavan.
tato Yudhiṣṭhiraṃ dīnaṃ cintā|param adho|mukham
śok’|ôpahata|saṃkalpaṃ Vāsudevo ’bravīd idam:

VĀSUDEVA uvāca:

60.30 Dharmarāja kim|arthaṃ tvam a|dharmam anumanyase
hata|bandhor yad etasya patitasya vicetasaḥ
Duryodhanasya Bhīmena mṛdyamānaṃ śiraḥ padā?
upaprekṣasi kasmāt tvaṃ dharma|jñaḥ san nar’|âdhipa?

YUDHIṢṬHIRA uvāca:

na mam’ âitat priyaṃ Kṛṣṇa yad rājānaṃ Vṛkodaraḥ
padā mūrdhny aspṛśat krodhān. na ca hṛṣye kula|kṣaye.
nikṛtyā nikṛtā nityaṃ Dhṛtarāṣṭra|sutair vayam.
bahūni paruṣāṇy uktvā vanaṃ prasthāpitāḥ sma ha.
Bhīmasenasya tad duḥkham atīva hṛdi vartate
iti saṃcintya Vārṣṇeya may” âitat samupekṣitam.
60.35 tasmādd hatv” â|kṛta|prajñaṃ lubdhaṃ kāma|vaś’|ânugam
labhatāṃ Pāṇḍavaḥ kāmaṃ dharme ’|dharme ca vā kṛte!

himself up as an oblation into the fire of his enemy. For his sacrificial purification he has now attained glory!"

Saying these words, the mighty son of Róhini—who resembled the crest of a white cloud—climbed his chariot and left for Dváraka. The Panchálas, Vrishnis, and Pándavas became despondent when Rama departed for Dváravati, lord of the people. Vasudéva then said these words to Yudhi·shthira, who was wretched and anxious and whose face was hanging low, his convictions stricken with grief.

VASUDÉVA said:

King of Righteousness, why do you allow Bhima to committ the immoral act of rubbing Dur·yódhana's head with his foot, especially when Dur·yódhana has lost his kinsmen and is fallen, bereft of his wits? Why do you overlook this, Your Majesty, if you know what is right? 60.30

YUDHI·SHTHIRA said:

I am not pleased, Krishna, that in his rage Vrikódara has touched the king's head with his foot. Nor do I feel joy at the destruction of my clan. We were constantly wronged by the wickedness of Dhrita·rashtra's sons. They abused us greatly and exiled us into the forest. I overlooked Bhima·sena's conduct when I considered the extreme suffering that he feels in his heart, Varshnéya. Since he has slain foolish and greedy Dur·yódhana, who is ruled by desire, let the Pándava do as he likes, whether right or wrong be done! 60.35

SAÑJAYA uvāca:

ity ukte Dharmarājena Vāsudevo 'bravīd idam:
«kāmam astv etad iti» vai kṛcchrād Yadu|kul'|ôdvahaḥ.
ity ukto Vāsudevena Bhīma|priya|hit'|âiṣiṇā
anvamodata tat sarvaṃ yad Bhīmena kṛtaṃ yudhi.

Bhīmaseno 'pi hatv" ājau tava putram a|marṣaṇaḥ
abhivādy' âgrataḥ sthitvā saṃprahṛṣṭaḥ kṛt'|âñjaliḥ,
provāca su|mahā|tejā Dharmarājaṃ Yudhiṣṭhiram
harṣād utphulla|nayano jita|kāśī viśāṃ pate

60.40 «tav' âdya pṛthivī sarvā kṣemā nihata|kaṇṭakā.
tāṃ praśādhi mahā|rāja sva|dharmam anupālaya.
yas tu kart" âsya vairasya nikṛtyā nikṛti|priyaḥ
so 'yaṃ vinihataḥ śete pṛthivyāṃ pṛthivī|pate.
Duḥśāsana|prabhṛtayaḥ sarve te c' ôgra|vādinaḥ
Rādheyaḥ Śakuniś c' âiva hatāś ca tava śatravaḥ.
s" êyaṃ ratna|samākīrṇā mahī sa|vana|parvatā
upāvṛttā mahā|rāja tvām adya nihata|dviṣam.»

YUDHIṢṬHIRA uvāca:

gato vairasya nidhanaṃ hato rājā Suyodhanaḥ!
Kṛṣṇasya matam āsthāya vijit" êyaṃ vasun|dharā!

60.45 diṣṭyā gatas tvam ānṛṇyaṃ mātuḥ kopasya c' ôbhayoḥ!
diṣṭyā jayasi dur|dharṣa! diṣṭyā śatrur nipātitaḥ!

SÁNJAYA said:

In response to the words of the King of Righteousness, Vasudéva, that upholder of Yadu's clan, reluctantly replied: "Let it be as you wish." Addressed this way by Vasudéva, who desired to benefit and favor Bhima, Yudhi·shthira approved of everything that Bhima had done in battle.

After slaying your son in battle, intolerant Bhima·sena stood in front of Yudhi·shthira and joyfully paid his respects, his hands cupped together. His eyes wide open with joy, that powerful conqueror then addressed Yudhi·shthira, the King of Righteousness, with these words, lord of the people:

60.40 "The entire earth is today yours. She is safe and her thorns have been removed. Rule over her, great king, and preserve your duty. The man who caused this feud through his wickedness and fondness for base behavior now lies on the earth, struck down, Your Majesty. Duhshásana and all your other harsh-tongued enemies are dead, as are Radha's son and Shákuni. Your enemies have been slaughtered and the earth—with its forests, mountains, and abundance of gems—has returned to you this day, great king."

YUDHI·SHTHIRA said:

King Su·yódhana has ceased his hostility and has been slain! We have conquered the earth by following Krishna's advice! 60.45 How marvellous that you have paid off your debt, to both your mother and your anger! How marvellous that you have been victorious, unassailable Bhima! How marvellous that our enemy has been felled!

DHṚTARĀṢṬRA uvāca:

61.1 HATAṂ DURYODHANAṂ dṛṣṭvā Bhīmasenena saṃyuge
Pāṇḍavāḥ Sṛñjayāś c' âiva kim akurvata Sañjaya?

SAÑJAYA uvāca:

hataṃ Duryodhanaṃ dṛṣṭvā Bhīmasenena saṃyuge
siṃhen' êva mahā|rāja mattaṃ vana|gajaṃ yathā
prahṛṣṭa|manasas tatra Kṛṣṇena saha Pāṇḍavāḥ
Pañcālāḥ Sṛñjayāś c' âiva nihate Kuru|nandane.
āvidhyann uttarīyāṇi siṃha|nādāṃś ca nedire.
n' âitān harṣa|samāviṣṭān iyaṃ sehe vasun|dharā.

61.5 dhanūṃṣy anye vyākṣipanta jyāś c' âpy anye tath" ākṣipan
dadhmur anye mahā|śaṅkhān anye jaghnuś ca dundubhīn.
cikrīḍuś ca tath" âiv' ânye jahasuś ca tav' â|hitāḥ
abruvaṃś c' â|sakṛd vīrā Bhīmasenam idaṃ vacaḥ:
«duṣ|karaṃ bhavatā karma raṇe 'dya su|mahat kṛtam
Kaurav'|êndraṃ raṇe hatvā gaday" âtikṛta|śramam.
Indreṇ' êva hi Vṛtrasya vadhaṃ parama|saṃyuge
tvayā kṛtam amanyanta śatror vadham imaṃ janāḥ.
carantaṃ vividhān mārgān maṇḍalāni ca sarvaśaḥ
Duryodhanam imaṃ śūraṃ ko 'nyo hanyād Vṛkodarāt?

61.10 vairasya ca gataḥ pāraṃ tvam ih' ânyaiḥ su|dur|gamam.
a|śakyam etad anyena saṃpādayitum īdṛśam.
kuñjareṇ' êva mattena vīra saṃgrāma|mūrdhani
Duryodhana|śiro diṣṭyā pādena mṛditaṃ tvayā!
siṃhena mahiṣasy' êva kṛtvā saṃgaram uttamam
Duḥśāsanasya rudhiraṃ diṣṭyā pītaṃ tvay" ân|agha!

DHRITA·RASHTRA said:

WHEN THE PÁNDAVAS and Srínjayas saw that Bhima·sena had slain Dur·yódhana in battle, what did they do, Sánjaya? 61.1

SÁNJAYA said:

When they saw that Dur·yódhana had been slain by Bhima·sena in battle, like a crazed forest elephant vanquished by a lion, the Pándavas, Panchálas, Srínjayas, and Krishna felt joy at the slaughter of the delight of the Kurus, Your Majesty. Waving their outer garments, they roared lion-roars. The earth was unable to sustain them, so overwhelmed were they with joy. Some stretched their bows 61.5 while others drew their bow-strings. Some blew huge conches while others banged on drums. In their hostility toward you, some of the heroes sported around, laughing, and repeatedly said these words to Bhima·sena:

"On this day you have performed a huge and difficult deed in battle. You have slain the king of the Káuravas with your mace in battle, even though he exerted himself greatly. The people compare your slaughter of this enemy to Indra's slaughter of Vritra in that supreme battle. Who else apart from Vrikódara could have slain heroic Dur·yódhana as he careered everywhere in various tracks and circles? You have 61.10 reached the further shore of your enmity, a feat that others in this world have found extremely difficult to attain. No-one else could perform such a deed.

How splendid that you have rubbed Dur·yódhana's head with your foot at the front of the battle like a frenzied elephant, O hero! How splendid that you have waged a great battle and drunk the blood of Duhshásana, like a

ye viprakurvan rājānaṃ dharm'|ātmānaṃ Yudhiṣṭhiram
mūrdhni teṣāṃ kṛtaḥ pādo diṣṭyā te svena karmaṇā!
a|mitrāṇām adhiṣṭhānād vadhād Duryodhanasya ca
Bhīma diṣṭyā pṛthivyāṃ te prathitaṃ su|mahad yaśaḥ!

61.15 evaṃ nūnaṃ hate Vṛtre Śakraṃ nandanti bandinaḥ
tathā tvāṃ nihat'|â|mitraṃ vayaṃ nandāma Bhārata!
Duryodhana|vadhe yāni romāṇi hṛṣitāni naḥ
ady' âpi na vikṛṣyante tāni tad viddhi Bhārata!»
ity abruvan Bhīmasenaṃ vātikās tatra saṃgatāḥ.

tān hṛṣṭān puruṣa|vyāghrān Pañcālān Pāṇḍavaiḥ saha
bruvato '|sadṛśaṃ tatra provāca Madhu|sūdanaḥ:

«na nyāyyaṃ nihataṃ śatruṃ bhūyo hantuṃ jan'|âdhipā
a|sakṛd vāgbhir ugrābhir. nihato hy eṣa manda|dhīḥ.
tad" âiv' âiṣa hataḥ pāpo yad" âiva nirapatrapaḥ
lubdhaḥ pāpa|sahāyaś ca suhṛdāṃ śāsan'|âtigaḥ.

61.20 bahuśo Vidura|Droṇa|Kṛpa|Gāṅgeya|Sṛñjayaiḥ
Pāṇḍubhyaḥ prārthyamāno 'pi pitryam aṃśaṃ na dattavān.
n' âiṣa yogyo 'dya mitraṃ vā śatrur vā puruṣ'|âdhamaḥ.
kim anen' âtibhugnena vāgbhiḥ kāṣṭha|sa|dharmaṇā?

ratheṣv ārohata kṣipraṃ gacchāmo vasudh"|âdhipāḥ!
diṣṭyā hato 'yaṃ pāp'|ātmā s'|āmātya|jñāti|bāndhavaḥ!»

lion drinking the blood of a buffalo, faultless Bhima.* How splendid that, through your own actions, you have placed your foot on the heads of men who wronged righteous King Yudhi·shthira! How splendid, Bhima, that your huge fame has spread across the earth as a result of standing above your enemies and slaying Dur·yódhana! Just as bards praise Shakra for slaughtering Vritra, so we praise you, descendant of Bharata, upon your slaughter of your enemies! Know this, descendant of Bharata: our hairs bristled when you slew Dur·yódhana and they will not stop bristling today!" These were the words spoken to Bhima·sena by the eulogisers gathered there. 61.15

The slayer of Madhu then addressed the Pándavas and tiger-like Panchálas as they gleefully spoke these unseemly words:

"O kings, it is not right to slay a felled enemy once more by repeatedly uttering such vicious words. This foolish man has already been struck down. This sinner was already dead when—shameless, greedy, and a companion of villains—he transgressed his friends' advice. Even though he was entreated several times by Vídura, Drona, Kripa, the son of Ganga, and the Srínjayas, Dur·yódhana still did not give the Pandus their ancestral share. This lowest of men is today unfit to be either a friend or an enemy. What is the use of speaking to someone so crooked and now like a piece of wood? 61.20

Climb onto your chariots, lords of the earth, and let us leave quickly! How splendid that this villain has been slain, along with his counsellors, relatives, and kinsmen!"

iti śrutvā tv adhikṣepaṃ Kṛṣṇād Duryodhano nṛpaḥ
a|marṣa|vaśam āpanna udatiṣṭhad viśāṃ pate.
sphig|deśen' ôpaviṣṭaḥ sa dorbhyāṃ viṣṭabhya medinīm
dṛṣṭiṃ bhrū|saṃkaṭāṃ kṛtvā Vāsudeve nyapātayat.

61.25 ardh'|ônnata|śarīrasya rūpam āsīn nṛpasya tu
kruddhasy' āśī|viṣasy' êva cchinna|pucchasya Bhārata.
prāṇ'|ânta|karaṇīṃ ghorāṃ vedanām apy a|cintayan
Duryodhano Vāsudevaṃ vāgbhir ugrābhir ārdayat:

«Kaṃsa|dāsasya dāy'|āda na te lajj" âsty anena vai
a|dharmeṇa gadā|yuddhe yad ahaṃ vinipātitaḥ
‹ūrū bhindh' îti› Bhīmasya smṛtiṃ mithyā prayacchatā.
kiṃ na vijñātam etan me yad Arjunam avocathāḥ?
ghātayitvā mahī|pālān ṛju|yuddhān sahasraśaḥ
jihmair upāyair bahubhir na te lajjā na te ghṛṇā.

61.30 ahany ahani śūrāṇāṃ kurvāṇaḥ kadanaṃ mahat
Śikhaṇḍinaṃ puras|kṛtya ghātitas te* pitā|mahaḥ.
Aśvatthāmnaḥ sa|nāmānaṃ hatvā nāgaṃ su|dur|mate
ācāryo nyāsitaḥ śastraṃ. kiṃ tan na viditaṃ mayā?
sa c' ânena nṛ|śaṃsena Dhṛṣṭadyumnena vīryavān
pātyamānas tvayā dṛṣṭo na c' âinaṃ tvam a|vārayaḥ.
vadh'|ârthaṃ Pāṇḍu|putrasya yācitāṃ śaktim eva ca
Ghaṭotkace vyaṃsayataḥ. kas tvattaḥ pāpa|kṛttamaḥ?

chinna|hastaḥ prāya|gatas tathā Bhūriśravā balī
tvay" âbhisṛṣṭena hataḥ Śaineyena mah"|ātmanā.

61.35 kurvāṇaś c' ôttamaṃ karma Karṇaḥ Pārtha|jigīṣayā
vyaṃsanen' Âśvasenasya pannag'|êndra|sutasya vai

When King Dur·yódhana heard Krishna's rebuke, he became overwhelmed by intolerant fury and tried to stand up, lord of the people. Sitting on his buttocks and propping himself up on the ground with his arms, he contracted his eyebrows and glared at Vasudéva. In his fury, the king, with his body half-raised, resembled a poisonous snake that has had its tail lopped off, descendant of Bharata. Ignoring the terrible and fatal pain he suffered, Dur·yódhana attacked Vasudéva with fierce words: 61.25

"Son of Kansa's slave, you show no shame at the fact that I was unjustly felled in this mace battle after you deceitfully reminded Bhima to break my thighs. Did I not notice you speaking to Árjuna? You show no shame or compassion at the fact that you used numerous crooked ploys to kill thousands of kings who themselves fought uprightly.

Even as you caused a huge massacre of heroes day after day, you then had our grandfather killed by placing Shikhándin in front of Árjuna.* Then, you villain, you killed an elephant that bore the same name as Ashva·tthaman and caused the teacher Drona to lay aside his weapons. Do I not know this? You watched as cruel Dhrishta·dyumna struck down that mighty hero and you did not restrain him.* You used Ghatótkacha to foil the spear that Karna requested from Shakra in order to kill the son of Pandu.* Who has acted more wickedly than you? 61.30

You also sent Sátyaki, the great-spirited descendant of Shini, to kill mighty Bhuri·shravas when his hand had been lopped off and when he was renouncing his life through the *praya* vow.* You destroyed Ashva·sena, that prince of snakes, when Karna was performing supreme feats in his desire to 61.35

punaś ca patite cakre vyasan'|ārtaḥ parājitaḥ
pātitaḥ samare Karṇaś cakra|vyagro 'gra|ṇīr nṛṇām!
yadi māṃ c' âpi Karṇaṃ ca Bhīṣma|Droṇau ca saṃyutau
ṛjunā pratiyudhyethā na te syād vijayo dhruvam.
tvayā punar an|āryeṇa jihma|mārgeṇa pārthivāḥ
sva|dharmam anutiṣṭhanto vayaṃ c' ânye ca ghātitāḥ.»

VĀSUDEVA uvāca:

hatas tvam asi Gāndhāre sa|bhrātṛ|suta|bāndhavaḥ
sa|gaṇaḥ sa|suhṛc c' âiva pāpa|mārgam anuṣṭhitaḥ.
61.40 tav' âiva duṣ|kṛtair vīrau Bhīṣma|Droṇau nipātitau.
Karṇaś ca nihataḥ saṅkhye tava śīl'|ânuvartakaḥ.
yācyamānaṃ mayā mūḍha pitryam aṃśaṃ na ditsasi
Pāṇḍavebhyaḥ sva|rājyaṃ ca lobhāc Chakuni|niścayāt.
viṣaṃ te Bhīmasenāya dattaṃ sarve ca Pāṇḍavāḥ
pradīpitā jatu|gṛhe mātrā saha su|dur|mate.
sabhāyāṃ Yājñasenī ca kṛṣṭā dyūte rajasvalā.
tad" âiva tāvad duṣṭ'|ātman vadhyas tvaṃ nirapatrapa.
an|akṣa|jñaṃ ca dharma|jñaṃ Saubalen' âkṣa|vedinā
nikṛtyā yat parājaiṣīs tasmād asi hato raṇe.
61.45 Jayadrathena pāpena yat Kṛṣṇā kleśitā vane
yāteṣu mṛgayāṃ c' âiva Tṛṇabindor ath' āśramam

conquer the Partha Árjuna. And you had Karna killed in battle when, distraught and defeated, that champion among men was preoccupied with his wheel after it had sunk into the ground!*

You would certainly never have been victorious if you had fought me, Karna, Bhishma or Drona in an upright manner. Instead, by following an ignoble and crooked path, you have killed kings who practiced their moral duty—not only us but others too."

VASUDÉVA said:

Son of Gandhári, it is because you practiced an evil path that you and your brothers, sons, kinsmen, followers and friends have been killed. It is because of your wrongdoings (61.40) that heroic Bhishma and Drona were slaughtered. Karna too was slain because he followed your moral practices. Foolish man, it is due to your greed and Shákuni's advice that you were unwilling to give the Pándavas their ancestral share and kingdom when I asked for it.

You tried to poison Bhima·sena and you tried to burn all the Pándavas and their mother in the lac house, evil-minded man. During the gambling match, the daughter of Yajna·sena was dragged in the assembly hall while she was menstruating. That is why, shameless sinner, it is right for you to be killed in this way.

Through Súbala's son, that expert in dice, you dishonestly defeated a man who was untrained in dice and only knew righteousness. That is why you have been slain in battle. Evil Jayad·ratha wronged Krishná in the forest while (61.45) the Pándavas were hunting near Trina·bindu's hermitage.*

Abhimanyuś ca yad bāla eko bahubhir āhave
tvad|doṣair nihataḥ pāpa tasmād asi hato raṇe.
yāny a|kāryāṇi c' âsmākaṃ kṛtān' îti prabhāṣase
vaiguṇyena tav' âtyarthaṃ sarvaṃ hi tad anuṣṭhitam.
Bṛhaspater Uśanaso n' ôpadeśaḥ śrutas tvayā.
vṛddhā n' ôpāsitāś c' âiva hitaṃ vākyaṃ na te śrutam.
lobhen' âtibalena tvaṃ tṛṣṇayā ca vaśī|kṛtaḥ
kṛtavān asy a|kāryāṇi. vipākas tasya bhujyatām!

DURYODHANA uvāca:

61.50 adhītaṃ. vidhivad dattaṃ. bhūḥ praśāstā sa|sāgarā.
mūrdhni sthitam a|mitrāṇāṃ. ko nu sv|antataro mayā?
yad iṣṭaṃ kṣatra|bandhūnāṃ sva|dharmam anupaśyatām
tad idaṃ nidhanaṃ prāptaṃ. ko nu sv|antataro mayā?
dev'|ârhā mānuṣā bhogāḥ prāptā a|su|labhā nṛpaiḥ
aiśvaryaṃ c' ôttamaṃ prāptaṃ. ko nu sv|antataro mayā?
sa|suhṛt s'|ânugaś ca svargaṃ gant" âham Acyuta.
yūyaṃ nihata|saṃkalpāḥ śocanto vartayiṣyatha.

SAÑJAYA uvāca:

asya vākyasya nidhane Kuru|rājasya dhīmataḥ
apatat su|mahad varṣaṃ puṣpāṇāṃ puṇya|gandhinām.
61.55 avādayanta gandharvā vāditraṃ su|mano|haram
jaguś c' âpsaraso rājño yaśaḥ saṃbaddham eva ca,
siddhāś ca mumucur vācaḥ «sādhu sādhv iti» pārthiva
vavau ca su|rabhir vāyuḥ puṇya|gandho mṛduḥ sukhaḥ
vyarājaṃś ca diśaḥ sarvā nabho vaiḍūrya|saṃnibham.

Because of your criminal actions, you villain, Abhimányu—a mere boy—was also slaughtered, one against many. That is why you have been slain in battle.

Through your lack of virtue, you have committed in excess all the wrongdoings that you accuse us of committing. You never listened to the teachings of Brihas·pati and Úshanas. You never honored the elderly or listened to beneficial words. A slave to desire, you committed evil deeds because of excessive greed. Enjoy the fruit of your actions!

DUR·YÓDHANA said:

I have studied the Vedas and I have given due gifts. I have ruled over the earth with its oceans. I have stood on the heads of my enemies. Who has a better end than I? I have attained the death that is desired by warriors who practice the moral code of their class. Who has a better end than I? I have attained human pleasures that are worthy of the gods and that are difficult for kings to acquire. I have achieved the highest sovereignty. Who has a better end than I? I will go to heaven alongside my friends and followers, Áchyuta. You will live here in grief, your wills destroyed. 61.50

SÁNJAYA said:

When the wise king of the Kurus had finished speaking, an enormous shower of pure-scented flowers fell from the sky. *Gandhárvas* played instruments that captivated the mind and nymphs sang in unison about the king's glory. *siddhas* uttered words of approval, Your Majesty. A mild, fragrant and soothing wind began to blow with auspicious scents and the sky gleamed in every direction like lapis lazuli. 61.55

atyadbhutāni te dṛṣṭvā Vāsudeva|puro|gamāḥ
Duryodhanasya pūjāṃ tu dṛṣṭvā vrīḍām upāgaman.
hatāṃś c' â|dharmataḥ śrutvā śok'|ārtāḥ śuśucur hi te
Bhīṣmaṃ Droṇaṃ tathā Karṇaṃ Bhūriśravasam eva ca.
tāṃs tu cintā|parān dṛṣṭvā Pāṇḍavān dīna|cetasaḥ
provāc' êdaṃ vacaḥ Kṛṣṇo megha|dundubhi|niḥsvanaḥ:

61.60 «n' âiṣa śakyo 'tiśīghr'|âstras te ca sarve mahā|rathāḥ
ṛju|yuddhena vikrāntā hantuṃ yuṣmābhir āhave.
n' âiṣa śakyaḥ kadā cit tu hantuṃ dharmeṇa pārthivaḥ
te vā Bhīṣma|mukhāḥ sarve mah"|êṣv|āsā mahā|rathāḥ.
may" ânekair upāyais tu māyā|yogena c' â|sakṛt
hatās te sarva ev' ājau bhavatāṃ hitam icchatā.
yadi n' âivaṃ|vidhaṃ jātu kuryāṃ jihmaṃ ahaṃ raṇe
kuto vo vijayo bhūyaḥ? kuto rājyaṃ? kuto dhanaṃ?
te hi sarve mah"|ātmānaś catvāro 'tirathā bhuvi
na śakyā dharmato hantuṃ loka|pālair api svayam.

61.65 tath" âiv' âyaṃ gadā|pāṇir Dhārtarāṣṭro gata|klamaḥ
na śakyo dharmato hantuṃ Kālen' âp' îha daṇḍinā.

na ca vo hṛdi kartavyaṃ yad ayaṃ ghātito ripuḥ.
mithyā vadhyās tath" ôpāyair bahavaḥ śatravo 'dhikāḥ.
pūrvair anugato mārgo devair a|sura|ghātibhiḥ.
sadbhiś c' ânugataḥ panthāḥ sa sarvair anugamyate.
kṛta|kṛtyāś ca sāy'|âhne nivāsaṃ rocayāmahe.
s'|âśva|nāga|rathāḥ sarve viśramāmo nar'|âdhipāḥ.»

When they saw these miracles and witnessed the honor being done to Dur·yódhana, the men who were headed by Vasudéva were ashamed. When they heard how Bhishma, Drona, Karna and Bhuri·shravas had been immorally killed, they were sorrowful and stricken with grief. But on seeing the Pándavas anxious and downcast, Krishna spoke these words with a voice that boomed like a cloud or kettledrum:

"If you had fought fairly in battle, you could never have killed swift-weaponed Dur·yódhana or all these great and courageous warriors. This king could never have been killed through just means, nor could all the great archers and great warriors that were led by Bhishma. In my desire to benefit you, I have killed every one of these men in battle by using various ploys and repeated deception. How could you have your victory if I had not performed such crooked acts in battle? How could you have your kingdom? How your wealth? Even the world-protectors themselves could not have lawfully killed all four of these heroic and superior warriors on earth.* Nor even could staff-wielding Time have lawfully killed this tireless, mace-bearing son of Dhrita·rashtra. 61.60 61.65

Do not bear it in your hearts that this foe has been killed in this way. When enemies are numerous and too many, they should be killed through deception and ploys. Gods in the past followed this path when they slew demons. If the path has been followed by the good, then it can be followed by everyone. Our purposes have been achieved and it is evening time. Let us retire. Let us rest, lords of men, along with our horses, elephants, and chariots."

Vāsudeva|vacaḥ śrutvā tadānīṃ Pāṇḍavaiḥ saha
Pañcālā bhṛśa|saṃhṛṣṭā vineduḥ siṃha|saṅgha|vat.
61.70 tataḥ prādhmāpayañ śaṅkhān Pāñcajanyaṃ ca Mādhavaḥ
hṛṣṭā Duryodhanaṃ dṛṣṭvā nihataṃ puruṣa'|rṣabha.

When they heard Vasudéva's words, the Panchálas and Pándavas roared with great joy like a pride of lions. Delighted at witnessing Dur·yódhana's death, they blew their conches together with the Mádhava, who also blew his Panchajánya conch, bull among men. 61.70

62–63
KRISHNA AIDS

SAÑJAYA uvāca:

62.1 TATAS TE PRAYAYUḤ sarve nivāsāya mahī|kṣitaḥ
śaṅkhān pradhmāpayanto vai hṛṣṭāḥ parigha|bāhavaḥ.
Pāṇḍavān gacchataś c' âpi śibiraṃ no viśāṃ pate
mah"|êṣv|āso 'nvagāt paścād Yuyutsuḥ Sātyakis tathā.
Dhṛṣṭadyumnaḥ Śikhaṇḍī ca Draupadeyāś ca sarvaśaḥ
sarve c' ânye mah"|êṣv|āsā yayuḥ sva|śibirāṇy uta.
tatas te prāviśan Pārthā hata|tviṭkaṃ hat'|ēśvaram
Duryodhanasya śibiraṃ raṅgavad visṛte jane.
62.5 gat'|ôtsavaṃ puram iva hṛta|nāgam iva hradam.
strī|varṣa|vara|bhūyiṣṭhaṃ vṛddh'|āmātyair adhiṣṭhitam.
tatr' âitān paryupātiṣṭhan Duryodhana|puraḥsarāḥ
kṛt'|âñjali|puṭā rājan kāṣāya|malin'|âmbarāḥ.
śibiraṃ samanuprāpya Kuru|rājasya Pāṇḍavāḥ
avaterur mahā|rāja rathebhyo ratha|sattamāḥ.
tato Gāṇḍīva|dhanvānam abhyabhāṣata Keśavaḥ
sthitaḥ priya|hite nityam atīva Bharata'|rṣabha:
«avaropaya Gāṇḍīvam a|kṣayyau ca mah"|êṣu|dhī.
ath' âham avarokṣyāmi paścād Bharata|sattama.
62.10 svayaṃ c' âiv' âvaroha tvam. etac chreyas tav' ân|agha.»
tac c' âkarot tathā vīraḥ Pāṇḍu|putro Dhanañjayaḥ.
atha paścāt tataḥ Kṛṣṇo raśmīn utsṛjya vājinām
avārohata medhāvī rathād Gāṇḍīva|dhanvanaḥ.
ath' âvatīrṇe bhūtānām īśvare su|mah"|ātmani
kapir antar|dadhe divyo dhvajo Gāṇḍīva|dhanvanaḥ:
sa dagdho Droṇa|Karṇābhyāṃ divyair astrair mahā|rathaḥ

SÁNJAYA said:

JOYFULLY BLOWING their conches, those kings, who had arms like iron-bars, all retired for the night. Sátyaki and the great archer Yuyútsu followed behind the Pándavas, who proceeded to our camp, Your Majesty, while Dhrishta·dyumna, Shikhándin, the five sons of Dráupadi, and all the other great archers went to their own tents. 62.1

The Parthas then entered Dur·yódhana's tent. Deprived of its lord and bereft of splendor, the tent looked like a theater empty of people. It was like a city devoid of festivals or like a lake bereft of its elephant. Previously abounding with women and eunuchs, it was once overseen by elderly counsellors. Wearing dark-red garments and with palms cupped in respect, Dur·yódhana's attendants used to serve these old men, Your Majesty. 62.5

Arriving at the tent of the Kuru king, the Pándavas, those best of warriors, descended from their chariots, great king. Késhava, who was always concerned for the welfare of his dear ones, then addressed Árjuna, the wielder of the Gandíva bow, O bull of the Bharatas:

"Bring the Gandíva and two inexhausitble quivers. I will descend after you, best of Bharatas. You should get down. This is best for you, faultless Árjuna." 62.10

Dhanan·jaya, the heroic son of Pandu, did as Krishna said. Releasing the horses' reins, wise Krishna then followed after him and dismounted from the chariot of the Gandíva-wielder. As soon as the great-spirited lord of creatures had descended, the divine monkey-standard of the Gandíva-wielder disappeared: for Drona and Karna had earlier set alight the great chariot with their divine weapons and it

ath' ādīpto 'gninā hy āśu prajajvāla mahī|pate.
s'|ôpāsaṅgaḥ sa|raśmiś ca s'|âśvaḥ sa|yuga|bandhuraḥ
bhasmī|bhūto 'patad bhūmau ratho Gāṇḍīva|dhanvanaḥ.

62.15 taṃ tathā bhasma|bhūtaṃ tu dṛṣṭvā Pāṇḍu|sutāḥ prabho
abhavan vismitā rājann Arjunaś c' êdam abravīt
kṛt'|âñjaliḥ sa|praṇayaṃ praṇipaty' âbhivādya ha:
«Govinda kasmād bhagavan ratho dagdho 'yam agninā?
kim etan mahad āścaryam abhavad Yadu|nandana?
tan me brūhi mahā|bāho śrotavyaṃ yadi manyase.»

VĀSUDEVA uvāca:

«astrair bahu|vidhair dagdhaḥ pūrvam ev' âyam Arjuna
mad|adhiṣṭhitatvāt samare na viśīrṇaḥ paran|tapa.
idānīṃ tu viśīrṇo 'yaṃ dagdho brahm'|âstra|tejasā
mayā vimuktaḥ Kaunteya tvayy adya kṛta|karmaṇi.»

62.20 īṣad utsmayamānas tu bhagavān Keśavo 'ri|hā
pariṣvajya ca rājānaṃ Yudhiṣṭhiram abhāṣata:
«diṣṭyā jayasi Kaunteya! diṣṭyā te śatravo jitāḥ!
diṣṭyā Gāṇḍīva|dhanvā ca Bhīmasenaś ca Pāṇḍavaḥ
tvaṃ c' âpi kuśalī rājan Mādrī|putrau ca Pāṇḍavau
muktā vīra|kṣayād asmāt saṃgrāmān nihata|dviṣaḥ!
kṣipram uttara|kālāni kuru kāryāṇi Bhārata.

now blazed with fire, smoldering swiftly, lord of the earth. The chariot of the Gandíva-wielder collapsed to the ground, reduced to ashes, along with its quivers, reins, horses, yoke, and driver's box.

62.15 Pandu's sons were amazed when they saw the chariot reduced to ashes, my lord. Árjuna then bowed reverently to Krishna and, with hands cupped in respect, he asked:

"Why has my chariot been consumed by fire, Lord Go·vinda? What is this great wonder that has occurred, delight of the Yadus? Tell me this, mighty-armed Go·vinda, if you think it is worthy of report."

VASUDÉVA said:

"This chariot was earlier set alight by various weapons, Árjuna. But because I attended it, it did not fall apart in battle, enemy-scorcher. The chariot has now fallen apart from being incinerated by the blaze of a *brahmástra* weapon.* I abandoned it after you performed your feats this day, son of Kunti."

62.20 With a slight smile, enemy-slaying Lord Késhava then embraced King Yudhi·shthira and said:

"How marvellous that you have attained victory, son of Kunti! How marvellous that your enemies have been conquered! How marvellous that Árjuna the Gandíva-wielder, Bhima·sena the son of Pandu, your prosperous self, and the two Pándava sons of Madri have survived this hero-destroying battle and slaughtered their enemies, Your Majesty! Quickly perform the things that need to be done, descendant of Bharata.

upāyātam Upaplavyaṃ saha Gāṇḍīva|dhanvanā
ānīya madhu|parkaṃ māṃ yat purā tvam avocathāḥ:
‹eṣa bhrātā sakhā c' âiva tava Kṛṣṇa Dhanañjayaḥ
rakṣitavyo mahā|bāho sarvāsv āpatsv iti prabho.›
62.25 tava c' âivaṃ bruvāṇasya ‹tath" êty› ev' âham abruvam.
sa Savyasācī guptas te vijayī ca jan'|ēśvara.
bhrātṛbhiḥ saha rāj'|êndra śūraḥ satya|parākramaḥ
mukto vīra|kṣayād asmāt saṃgrāmāl loma|harṣaṇāt.»
evam uktas tu Kṛṣṇena Dharma|rājo Yudhiṣṭhiraḥ
hṛṣṭa|romā mahā|rāja pratyuvāca Janārdanam.

YUDHIṢṬHIRA uvāca:

«pramuktaṃ Droṇa|Karṇābhyāṃ
brahm'|âstram ari|mardana
kas tvad|anyaḥ sahet s'|âkṣād
api vajrī Purandaraḥ?
bhavatas tu prasādena Saṃśaptaka|gaṇā jitāḥ
mahā|raṇa|gataḥ Pārtho yac ca n' āsīt parāṅ|mukhaḥ.
62.30 tath" âiva ca mahā|bāho paryāyair bahubhir mayā
karmaṇām anusantānaṃ tejasaś ca gatīḥ śubhāḥ.
Upaplavye maha"|rṣir me Kṛṣṇa|Dvaipāyano 'bravīt:
‹yato dharmas tataḥ Kṛṣṇo yataḥ Kṛṣṇas tato jayaḥ.›»
ity evam ukte te vīrāḥ śibiraṃ tava Bhārata
praviśya pratyapadyanta kośa|ratna'|rddhi|sañcayān
rajataṃ jātarūpaṃ ca maṇīn atha ca mauktikān
bhūṣaṇāny atha mukhyāni kambalāny ajināni ca

In the past, when I arrived at Upaplávya, you once brought me a honey-offering together with the Gandíva-wielder and said: 'Krishna, this is my brother and friend Dhanan·jaya. You should protect him in every dangerous situation, mighty-armed lord.' I agreed to your request. I have protected Savya·sachin for you and you have achieved victory, lord of the people. This hero of true prowess has, along with his brothers, survived this hair-bristling war in which brave men were massacred, king of kings." 62.25

Addressed this way by Krishna, Yudhi·shthira, the King of Righteousness, felt his hair bristle with joy and replied to Janárdana with these words, great king.

YUDHI·SHTHIRA said:

"Who else but you, enemy-crusher, including even thunderbolt-wielding Puran·dara himself, could have resisted the *brahmástra* weapon that was hurled by Drona and Karna? It is through your grace that the Sansháptaka hordes have been conquered and that the Partha did not turn his back when engaged in the great battle. It is also because of you, mighty-armed Krishna, that I have performed a series of deeds through various means and acquired the auspicious goal of radiant power. 62.30

At Upaplávya, the great seer Krishna Dvaipáyana once said to me: 'Krishna exists wherever righteousness is found, and victory exists wherever Krishna is found.'"

After Yudhi·shthira's speech, the heroes entered your camp, descendant of Bharata, and took hold of piles of treasure, jewels, and riches, including silver, gold, gems, pearls, fine ornaments, blankets, skins, countless male and

dāsī|dāsam a|saṅkhyeyaṃ rājy'|ôpakaraṇāni ca.
te prāpya dhanam a|kṣayyaṃ tvadīyaṃ Bharata'|rṣabha
udakrośan mahā|bhāgā nar'|êndra vijit'|ârayaḥ.

62.35 te tu vīrāḥ samāśvasya vāhanāny avamucya ca
atiṣṭhanta muhuḥ sarve Pāṇḍavāḥ Sātyakis tathā.
ath' âbravīn mahā|rāja Vāsudevo mahā|yaśāḥ:
«asmābhir maṅgal'|ârthāya vastavyaṃ śibirād bahiḥ.»
«tath" êty» uktvā hi te sarve Pāṇḍavāḥ Sātyakis tathā
Vāsudevena sahitā maṅgal'|ârthaṃ bahir yayuḥ.

te samāsādya saritaṃ puṇyām Oghavatīṃ nṛpa
nyavasann atha tāṃ rātriṃ Pāṇḍavā hata|śatravaḥ.
tataḥ saṃpreṣayām āsur Yādavaṃ nāga|sāhvayam.
sa ca prāyāj javen' āśu Vāsudevaḥ pratāpavān
Dārukaṃ ratham āropya yena rāj'|Âmbikā|sutaḥ.

62.40 tam ūcuḥ saṃprayāsyantaṃ Śaibya|Sugrīva|vāhanam:
«pratyāśvāsaya Gāndhārīṃ hata|putrāṃ yaśasvinīm.»
sa prāyāt Pāṇḍavair uktas tat puraṃ Sātvatāṃ varaḥ
āsasāda tataḥ kṣipraṃ Gāndhārīṃ nihat'|ātma|jām.

JANAMEJAYA uvāca:

63.1 KIM|ARTHAṂ dvija|śārdūla Dharma|rājo Yudhiṣṭhiraḥ
Gāndhāryāḥ preṣayām āsa Vāsudevaṃ paran|tapam?
yadā pūrvaṃ gataḥ Kṛṣṇaḥ śam'|ârthaṃ Kauravān prati
na ca taṃ labdhavān kāmaṃ. tato yuddham abhūd idam.
nihateṣu tu yodheṣu hate Duryodhane tadā
pṛthivyāṃ Pāṇḍaveyasya niḥ|sapatne kṛte yudhi,
vidrute śibire śūnye prāpte yaśasi c' ôttame

female slaves, and various royal furnishings. Their enemies vanquished, those men of great fortune cheered loudly after they had taken possession of your inexhaustible wealth, bull of the Bharatas.

Unyoking their animals, those heroic men—the Pándavas and Sátyaki—all rested and stayed in that place a while. Glorious Vasudéva then spoke these words, great king: "It would be auspicious if we were to spend the night outside the camp." The Pándavas and Sátyaki all agreed and, for reasons of auspice, departed from the camp with Vasudéva. 62.35

Their enemies slaughtered, the Pándavas proceeded to the sacred river of Óghavati and spent the night there. They then sent the Yádava to elephant-named Hástina·pura. Taking Dáruka onto his chariot, mighty Vasudéva set off with great speed for the royal son of Ámbika. When Krishna was about to leave, driven by the horses Shaibya and Sugríva, the Pándavas said to him: "Comfort glorious Gandhári, for she has lost all her sons." Addressed this way, that best of Sátvatas left for the city and swiftly approached Gandhári, whose sons had all been killed. 62.40

JANAM·ÉJAYA said:

WHY DID Yudhi·shthira, the King of Righteousness, send enemy-scorching Vasudéva to Gandhári, tiger among brahmins? Krishna had previously gone to make peace with the Káuravas, but he could not achieve his desire and the war had subsequently started. So why did Krishna return again, brahmin, when the warriors had already been slaughtered, Dur·yódhana had already been killed, the war had already divested the Pándava's earth of any rivals, the abandoned 63.1

kiṃ nu tat kāraṇaṃ brahman yena Kṛṣṇo gataḥ punaḥ?
63.5 na c' âitat kāraṇaṃ brahmann alpaṃ vipratibhāti me
yatr' âgamad a|mey'|ātmā svayam eva Janārdanaḥ.
tattvato vai samācakṣva sarvam adhvaryu|sattama
yac c' âtra kāraṇaṃ brahman kāryasy' âsya viniścaye.

VAIŚAMPĀYANA uvāca:

tvad|yukto 'yam anupraśno yan māṃ pṛcchasi pārthiva!
tat te 'haṃ saṃpravakṣyāmi yathāvad Bharata'|rṣabha.
hataṃ Duryodhanaṃ dṛṣṭvā Bhīmasenena saṃyuge
vyutkramya samayaṃ rājan Dhārtarāṣṭraṃ mahā|balam
a|nyāyena hataṃ dṛṣṭvā gadā|yuddhena Bhārata
Yudhiṣṭhiraṃ mahā|rāja mahad bhayam ath' āviśat
63.10 cintayāno mahā|bhāgāṃ Gāndhārīṃ tapas" ânvitām
ghoreṇa tapasā yuktāṃ «trai|lokyam api sā dahet.»
tasya cintayamānasya
buddhiḥ samabhavat tadā:
«Gāndhāryāḥ krodha|dīptāyāḥ
pūrvaṃ praśamanaṃ bhavet.
sā hi putra|vadhaṃ śrutvā kṛtam asmābhir īdṛśam
mānasen' âgninā kruddhā bhasmasān naḥ kariṣyati.
kathaṃ duḥkham idaṃ tīvraṃ Gāndhārī saṃpraśakṣyati
śrutvā vinihataṃ putraṃ chalen' â|jihma|yodhinam?»
evaṃ vicintya bahudhā bhaya|śoka|samanvitaḥ
Vāsudevam idaṃ vākyaṃ Dharma|rājo 'bhyabhāṣata:

camp had already been deserted, and the highest glory had already been obtained? It seems the reason cannot be trivial, brahmin, if Janárdana of limitless spirit himself went there. Tell me truly, best of *adhváryu* priests, the full reason for deciding upon this action. 63.5

VAISHAMPÁYANA said:

Your question is worthy of you, Your Majesty! I will explain it to you as it really is, bull of the Bharatas.

When Yudhi·shthira saw Bhima·sena slay mighty Dur·yódhana in battle by violating the rules of combat and when he witnessed how Dhrita·rashtra's son had been unfairly struck down in that mace contest, he became overwhelmed by great fear as he considered how illustrious Gandhári might incinerate the very three worlds, invested as she was with ascetic power and furnished with gruesome austerities, descendant of Bharata. Contemplating the matter, he had this thought: 63.10

"Gandhári, who blazes with anger, should first be pacified. For when she hears how we have slaughtered her son, she will, in her rage, turn us into ash through the fire of her mind. How will Gandhári be able to endure this bitter pain when she learns that her son, who fought honorably, was slain by means of deceit?"

After contemplating the matter at length, the King of Righteousness said these words to Vasudéva, filled as he was with fear and grief:

63.15 «tava prasādād Govinda rājyaṃ nihata|kaṇṭakam.
a|prāpyaṃ manas" âp' îdaṃ prāptam asmābhir Acyuta.
pratyakṣaṃ me mahā|bāho saṃgrāme loma|harṣaṇe
vimardaḥ su|mahān prāptas tvayā Yādava|nandana.
tvayā dev'|âsure yuddhe vadh'|ârtham a|mara|dviṣām
yathā sāhyaṃ purā dattaṃ hatāś ca vibudha|dviṣaḥ,
sāhyaṃ tathā mahā|bāho dattam asmākam Acyuta
sārathyena ca Vārṣṇeya bhavatā hi dhṛtā vayam.
yadi na tvaṃ bhaven nāthaḥ Phālgunasya mahā|raṇe
kathaṃ śakyo raṇe jetuṃ bhaved eṣa bal'|ârṇavaḥ?

63.20 gadā|prahārā vipulāḥ parighaiś c' âpi tāḍanam
śaktibhir bhindipālaiś ca tomaraiḥ sa|paraśvadhaiḥ,
asmat|kṛte tvayā Kṛṣṇa vācaḥ su|paruṣāḥ śrutāḥ
śastrāṇāṃ ca nipātā vai vajra|sparś'|ôpamā raṇe.
te ca te sa|phalā jātā hate Duryodhane 'cyuta.
tat sarvaṃ na yathā naśyet punaḥ Kṛṣṇa tathā kuru!
saṃdeha|dolāṃ prāptaṃ naś cetaḥ Kṛṣṇa jaye sati.

Gāndhāryā hi mahā|bāho krodhaṃ budhyasva Mādhava!
sā hi nityaṃ mahā|bhāgā tapas" ôgreṇa karśitā.
putra|pautra|vadhaṃ śrutvā dhruvaṃ naḥ saṃpradhakṣyati!
tasyāḥ prasādanaṃ vīra prāpta|kālaṃ mataṃ mama.

63.25 kaś ca tāṃ krodha|tāmr'|âkṣīṃ putra|vyasana|karśitām
vīkṣituṃ puruṣaḥ śaktas tvām ṛte puruṣ'|ôttama?

"Through your grace, Go·vinda, the kingdom has had its thorns removed. We have obtained what we could not even imagine obtaining, Áchyuta. Before my very eyes, mighty-armed delight of the Yádavas, you have engaged in a huge conflict in this hair-raising battle. In the past you offered yourself as an ally in order to kill the gods' enemies in the war between the gods and demons, and the gods' enemies were killed. In the same way, mighty-armed Áchyuta, you have offered yourself as an ally to us and supported us with your chariotship, Varshnéya. If you had not protected Phálguna in this great battle, how could we have conquered that ocean of troops in war? 63.15

You have endured numerous blows from maces and borne the pounding of clubs, spears, javelins, lances and axes. For our sake you have heard vicious words, Krishna, and suffered the blows of weapons that crash like thunderbolts in battle. The fruit of these afflictions has been realized at Dur·yódhana's slaughter, Áchyuta. Act once more so that all this is not lost, Krishna! Even though we are victorious, my mind sways with doubt, Krishna. 63.20

Take note of Gandhári's anger, mighty-armed Mádhava! For that illustrious woman constantly emaciates herself with fierce austerities. She will surely incinerate us when she hears of the slaughter of her sons and grandchildren! I think the time has come to calm her, hero. Who other than you, best of men, can look at her when her eyes are red with anger, tormented by her son's misfortune? 63.25

tatra me gamanaṃ prāptaṃ rocate tava Mādhava
Gāndhāryāḥ krodha|dīptāyāḥ praśam'|ârtham arin|dama.
tvaṃ hi kartā vikartā ca lokānāṃ prabhav'|â|vyayaḥ.
hetu|kāraṇa|saṃyuktair vākyaiḥ kāla|samīritaiḥ
kṣipram eva mahā|bāho Gāndhārīṃ śamayiṣyasi.
pitā|mahaś ca bhagavān Kṛṣṇas tatra bhaviṣyati.
sarvathā te mahā|bāho Gāndhāryāḥ krodha|nāśanam
kartavyaṃ Sātvata|śreṣṭha Pāṇḍavānāṃ hit'|ârthinā.»

Dharma|rājasya vacanaṃ śrutvā Yadu|kul'|ôdvahaḥ
āmantrya Dārukaṃ prāha: «rathaḥ sajjo vidhīyatām!»

63.30 Keśavasya vacaḥ śrutvā tvaramāṇo 'tha Dārukaḥ
nyavedayad rathaṃ sajjaṃ Keśavāya mah"|ātmane.
taṃ rathaṃ Yādava|śreṣṭhaḥ samāruhya paran|tapaḥ
jagāma Hāstinapuraṃ tvaritaḥ Keśavo vibhuḥ.
tataḥ prāyān mahā|rāja Mādhavo bhagavān rathī
nāga|sāhvayam āsādya praviveśa ca vīryavān.
praviśya nagaraṃ vīro ratha|ghoṣeṇa nādayan
vidito Dhṛtarāṣṭrasya so 'vatīrya rath'|ôttamāt
abhyagacchad a|dīn'|ātmā Dhṛtarāṣṭra|niveśanam.
pūrvaṃ c' âbhigataṃ tatra so 'paśyad ṛṣi|sattamam.

63.35 pādau prapīḍya Kṛṣṇasya rājñaś c' âpi Janārdanaḥ
abhyavādayad a|vyagro Gāndhārīṃ c' âpi Keśavaḥ.
tatas tu Yādava|śreṣṭho Dhṛtarāṣṭram Adhokṣajaḥ
pāṇim ālambya rāj'|êndra su|svaraṃ praruroda ha.
sa muhūrtād iv' ôtsṛjya bāṣpaṃ śoka|samudbhavam

It would please me, enemy-taming Mádhava, if you could go to Hástina·pura and pacify Gandhári in her blazing fury. For, imperishable in your power, you are the creator and transformer of the worlds. Using words that are reasoned and appropriate, you will quickly pacify Gandhári, mighty-armed Krishna. The illustrious grandfather, Krishna Dvaipáyana, will also be there. May you completely destroy Gandhári's anger in order to benefit the Pándavas, mighty-armed champion of the Sátvatas."

Hearing the words of the King of Righteousness, the perpetuator of Yadu's clan then summoned Dáruka and said: "Equip my chariot!" Hearing his words, Dáruka swiftly informed great-spirited Késhava that his chariot was ready. Lord Késhava, that enemy-scorcher and best of Yádavas, then climbed onto his chariot and quickly proceeded to Hástina·pura. The illustrious and powerful Mádhava traveled to Hástina·pura on his chariot and, after arriving at the elephant-named city, he entered it, great king. The hero made the city rumble with the sound of his chariot as he entered it and when his presence had been announced to Dhrita·rashtra, he got down from his fine vehicle and proceeded into Dhrita·rashtra's palace with vigorous spirits. There he saw Krishna Dvaipáyana, that supreme seer, who had arrived before him. 63.30

After Janárdana had embraced the feet of Krishna Dvaipáyana and King Dhrita·rashtra, Késhava calmly greeted Gandhári. Adhókshaja, that best of Yádavas, then held onto Dhrita·rashtra's hand and wept with soft tones. After shedding tears of grief for some time, the enemy-tamer washed 63.35

prakṣālya vāriṇā netre hy ācamya ca yathā|vidhi
uvāca prastutaṃ vākyaṃ Dhṛtarāṣṭram arin|damaḥ:

«na te 'sty a|viditaṃ kiṃ cid vṛddhasya tava, Bhārata
kālasya ca yathā vṛttaṃ tat te su|viditaṃ prabho,
yad idaṃ Pāṇḍavaiḥ sarvais tava citt'|ânurodhibhiḥ
kathaṃ kula|kṣayo na syāt tathā kṣatrasya Bhārata.

63.40 bhrātṛbhiḥ samayaṃ kṛtvā kṣāntavān dharma|vatsalaḥ
dyūta|cchala|jitaiḥ śuddhair vana|vāso hy upāgataḥ,
a|jñāta|vāsa|caryā ca nānā|veṣa|samāvṛtaiḥ
anye ca bahavaḥ kleśās tv a|śaktair iva sarvadā.
mayā ca svayam āgamya yuddha|kāla upasthite
sarva|lokasya sāṃnidhye grāmāṃs tvaṃ pañca yācitaḥ.
tvayā kāl'|ôpasṛṣṭena lobhato n' âpavarjitāḥ.
tav' âparādhān nṛ|pate sarvaṃ kṣatraṃ kṣayaṃ gatam.

Bhīṣmeṇa Somadattena Bāhlīkena Kṛpeṇa ca
Droṇena ca sa|putreṇa Vidureṇa ca dhīmatā
yācitas tvaṃ śamaṃ nityaṃ na ca tat kṛtavān asi.

63.45 kāl'|ôpahata|cittā hi sarve muhyanti Bhārata
yathā mūḍho bhavān pūrvam asminn arthe samudyate.

kim anyat kāla|yogādd hi? diṣṭam eva parāyaṇam!
mā ca doṣān mahā|prājña Pāṇḍaveṣu niveśaya.
alpo 'py atikramo n' âsti Pāṇḍavānāṃ mah"|ātmanām
dharmato nyāyataś c' âiva snehataś ca paran|tapa.
etat sarvaṃ tu vijñāya hy ātma|doṣa|kṛtaṃ phalam

his eyes with water, sipped water from his hand in the prescribed manner, and then said the following words of praise to Dhrita·rashtra:

"There is nothing unknown to you in your old age, descendant of Bharata. You know the events of time thoroughly, my lord—how, out of respect for you, all the Pándavas would not destroy their clan and the kshatriya race, Bhárata. Yudhi·shthira, who is ever fond of righteousness, made a pact with his brothers and lived patiently in the forest with those pure men after they had been deceitfully beaten in gambling. Assuming various disguises, they lived a life of anonymity and suffered many other injuries too, like men that were utterly powerless. When the war was imminent, I myself approached you and asked for five villages in the presence of the entire world. But you did not give them up because you were greedy and plagued by Time. The entire kshatriya race has been destroyed because of your wrongdoing, Your Majesty. 63.40

Even though Bhishma, Soma·datta, Bahlíka, Kripa, Drona, Drona's son, and wise Vídura all constantly entreated you to make peace, you did not follow their advice. Everyone becomes stupefied when their minds are afflicted by Time, and you too became stupefied when this event occurred. 63.45

What else can this be but the ordinance of Time? Destiny is surely supreme! Do not blame the Pándavas, wise Dhrita·rashtra. The heroic Pándavas have not committed even a slight transgression, enemy-scorcher—whether in morality, propriety, or affection. When you consider that all this is the fruit of your own fault, you should not feel any spite toward

asūyāṃ Pāṇḍu|putreṣu na bhavān kartum arhati.
kulaṃ vaṃśaś ca piṇḍāś ca yac ca putra|kṛtaṃ phalam
Gāndhāryās tava vai nātha Pāṇḍaveṣu pratiṣṭhitam.
63.50 tvaṃ c' âiva Kuru|śārdūla Gāndhārī ca yaśasvinī
mā śuco nara|śārdūla Pāṇḍavān prati kilbiṣam.
etat sarvam anudhyāya ātmanaś ca vyatikramam
śivena Pāṇḍavān pāhi. namas te Bharata'|rṣabha!

jānāsi ca mahā|bāho Dharma|rājasya yā tvayi
bhaktir Bharata|śārdūla snehaś c' âpi svabhāvataḥ.
etac ca kadanaṃ kṛtvā śatrūṇām apakāriṇām
dahyate sa divā rātrau na ca śarm' âdhigacchati.
tvāṃ c' âiva nara|śārdūla Gāndhārīṃ ca yaśasvinīm
sa śocan nara|śārdūlaḥ śāntim n' âiv' âdhigacchati.
63.55 hriyā ca paray" āviṣṭo bhavantaṃ n' âdhigacchati
putra|śok'|âbhisaṃtaptaṃ buddhi|vyākulit'|êndriyam.»

evam uktvā mahā|rāja Dhṛtarāṣṭraṃ Yad'|ûttamaḥ
uvāca paramaṃ vākyaṃ Gāndhārīṃ śoka|karśitām:

«Saubaleyi nibodha tvaṃ! yat tvāṃ vakṣyāmi tac chṛṇu!
tvat|samā n' âsti loke 'sminn adya sīmantinī śubhe.
jānāsi ca yathā rājñi sabhāyāṃ mama saṃnidhau
dharm'|ârtha|sahitaṃ vākyam ubhayoḥ pakṣayor hitam
uktavaty asi kalyāṇi na ca te tanayaiḥ kṛtam.
Duryodhanas tvayā c' ôkto jay'|ârthī paruṣaṃ vacaḥ:
63.60 ‹śṛṇu mūḍha vaco mahyaṃ! yato dharmas tato jayaḥ!›
tad idaṃ samanuprāptaṃ tava vākyaṃ nṛp'|ātma|je.

Pandu's sons. For both you and Gandhári, clan, lineage and ancestor-offerings—and whatever other benefit one may receive from one's sons—now depend on the Pándavas, my lord. Neither you, tiger-like Kuru, nor glorious Gandhári should complain that the Pándavas have wronged you. Considering all these things, as well as your own wrongdoings, protect the Pándavas favorably. I pay homage to you, bull of the Bharatas! 63.50

You are well aware of how the King of Righteousness is devoted to you and feels natural affection for you, mighty-armed tiger of the Bharatas. After slaughtering the enemies that wronged him, he burns with sorrow day and night and cannot find any happiness. That tiger-like man cannot find peace as he grieves for both you and glorious Gandhári, tiger among men. Overcome by utter shame, he has not come to you himself because you are tormented by grief for your sons and your mind is troubled." 63.55

Saying this to Dhrita·rashtra, that best of Yadus spoke the following fine words to Gandhári, who was emaciated with grief, great king:

"Take note, daughter of Súbala! Listen to what I have to say! On this day there is no woman who rivals you in the world, glorious lady. You are well aware of how, in the assembly hall and in my presence, you spoke words that were righteous, profitable, and beneficial to both sides, lovely queen—but your sons did not follow your advice. You spoke the following harsh words to Dur·yódhana when he sought victory: 'Listen to my words, you fool! Victory exists wherever there is righteousness!' Your words have become realized, royal lady. 63.60

evaṃ viditvā kalyāṇi mā sma śoke manaḥ kṛthāḥ.
Pāṇḍavānāṃ vināśāya mā te buddhiḥ kadā cana.
śaktā c' âsi mahā|bhāge pṛthivīṃ sa|car'|â|carām
cakṣuṣā krodha|dīptena nirdagdhuṃ tapaso balāt.»

Vāsudeva|vacaḥ śrutvā Gāndhārī vākyam abravīt:
«evam etan mahā|bāho yathā vadasi Keśava.
ādhibhir dahyamānāyā matiḥ saṃcalitā mama
sā me vyavasthitā śrutvā tava vākyaṃ Janārdana.

63.65 rājñas tv andhasya vṛddhasya hata|putrasya Keśava
tvaṃ gatiḥ saha tair vīraiḥ Pāṇḍavair dvi|padāṃ vara.»

etāvad uktvā vacanaṃ mukhaṃ pracchādya vāsasā
putra|śok'|âbhisaṃtaptā Gāndhārī praruroda ha.
tata enāṃ mahā|bāhuḥ Keśavaḥ śoka|karśitām
hetu|kāraṇa|saṃyuktair vākyair āśvāsayat prabhuḥ.
samāśvāsya ca Gāndhārīṃ Dhṛtarāṣṭraṃ ca Mādhavaḥ
Drauṇi|saṃkalpitaṃ bhāvam anvabuddhyata Keśavaḥ.
tatas tvarita utthāya pādau mūrdhnā praṇamya ca
Dvaipāyanasya rāj'|êndra tataḥ Kauravam abravīt:

63.70 «āpṛcche tvāṃ Kuru|śreṣṭha. mā ca śoke manaḥ kṛthāḥ.
Drauṇeḥ pāpo 'sty abhiprāyas ten' âsmi sahas" ôtthitaḥ.
Pāṇḍavānāṃ vadhe rātrau buddhis tena pradarśitā.»

etac chrutvā tu vacanaṃ Gāndhāryā sahito 'bravīt
Dhṛtarāṣṭro mahā|bāhuḥ Keśavaṃ Keśi|sūdanam:

Knowing this to be true, do not lend your heart to grief, lovely lady. Never set your mind on the Pándavas' destruction. By using your eye that blazes with fury, you could incinerate the earth with all its moving and unmoving creatures through the power of your asceticism, illustrious lady."

Hearing Vasudéva's speech, Gandhári said these words:

"What you say is true, mighty-armed Késhava. My mind was unstable as it burned with distress, but it has now become steady after hearing your words, Janárdana. You and the heroic sons of Pandu are the refuge of this blind old king who has lost his sons, best of men." 63.65

Saying these words, Gandhári covered her face with her robe and wept, tormented by grief for her sons. Using reasoned words, mighty-armed Lord Késhava then consoled Gandhári, who was emaciated with sorrow. After comforting Gandhári and Dhrita·rashtra, Késhava, the descendant of Madhu, became aware of the mental state of Drona's son. Rising quickly, king of kings, he lowered his head to Dvaipáyana's feet and then addressed Dhrita·rashtra the Káurava, saying:

"Let me take my leave, best of Kurus, Do not lend your heart to grief. The son of Drona has evil intentions—that is why I have risen so suddenly. His plan to kill the Pándavas at night has been revealed to me." 63.70

Hearing these words, mighty-armed Dhrita·rashtra and Gandhári both replied to Késhava, the destroyer of Keshin, thus:

«śīghraṃ gaccha mahā|bāho. Pāṇḍavān paripālaya.
bhūyas tvayā sameṣyāmi kṣipram eva Janārdana.»
prāyāt tatas tu tvarito Dārukeṇa sah' Âcyutaḥ.
Vāsudeve gate rājan Dhṛtarāṣṭraṃ jan'|ēśvaram
āśvāsayad a|mey'|ātmā Vyāso loka|namas|kṛtaḥ.
Vāsudevo 'pi dharm'|ātmā kṛta|kṛtyo jagāma ha
śibiraṃ Hāstinapurād didṛkṣuḥ Pāṇḍavān nṛpa.
63.75 āgamya śibiraṃ rātrau so 'bhyagacchata Pāṇḍavān.
tac ca tebhyaḥ samākhyāya sahitas taiḥ samāhitaḥ.

"Go quickly, mighty-armed Krishna. Protect the Pándavas. I will meet you again soon, Janárdana."

Áchyuta then swiftly left with Dáruka. After Vasudéva had departed, Your Majesty, infinite-spirited Vyasa, who is revered in the world, consoled King Dhrita·rashtra. His task achieved, righteous Vasudéva traveled from Hástina·pura to the camp, eager to see the Pándavas, O king. Arriving at 63.75 the camp at night, he went to the Pándavas and in their company zealously told them his news.

64–65
DUR·YÓDHANA DEFIANT

DHṚTARĀṢṬRA uvāca:

64.1 ADHIṢṬHITAḤ PADĀ mūrdhni
bhagna|saktho mahīṃ gataḥ
śauṭīrya|mānī putro me
kim abhāṣata Sañjaya?
atyarthaṃ kopano rājā jāta|vairaś ca Pāṇḍuṣu.
vyasanaṃ paramaṃ prāptaḥ kim āha param'|āhave?

SAÑJAYA uvāca:

śṛṇu rājan pravakṣyāmi yathā|vṛttaṃ nar'|âdhipa
rājñā yad uktaṃ bhagnena tasmin vyasana āgate.
bhagna|saktho nṛpo rājan pāṃsunā so 'vaguṇṭhitaḥ
yamayan mūrdha|jāṃs tatra vīkṣya c' âiva diśo daśa,
64.5 keśān niyamya yatnena niḥśvasann urago yathā
saṃrambh'|âśru|parītābhyāṃ netrābhyām abhivīkṣya mām,
bāhū dharaṇyāṃ niṣpiṣya su|dur|matta iva dvipaḥ
prakīrṇān mūrdha|jān dhunvan dantair dantān upaspṛśan,
garhayan Pāṇḍavaṃ jyeṣṭhaṃ niḥśvasy' êdam ath' âbravīt:
«Bhīṣme Śāntanave nāthe Karṇe śastra|bhṛtāṃ vare
Gautame Śakunau c' âpi Droṇe c' âstra|bhṛtāṃ vare
Aśvatthāmni tathā Śalye śūre ca Kṛtavarmaṇi
imām avasthāṃ prāpto 'smi. kālo hi dur|atikramaḥ.
ekādaśa|camū|bhartā so 'ham etāṃ daśāṃ gataḥ.
kālaṃ prāpya mahā|bāho na kaś cid ativartate.

DHRITA·RASHTRA said:

WHAT DID MY haughty son say, Sánjaya, when his head was rubbed by Bhima's foot as he lay on the ground, his thighs shattered? The king is prone to extreme anger and is hostile toward the Pandus. What did he say when he suffered such terrible misfortune in that supreme battle? 64.1

SÁNJAYA said:

Listen, Your Majesty, as I tell you precisely what the broken king said when disaster fell upon him. Covered in dust, his thighs shattered, the king stared in all ten directions as he tied back his hair. After tying back his hair with effort, he glared at me with eyes filled with tears of rage, hissing like a snake. Pounding his arms on the ground and grinding his teeth together, he resembled an extremely frenzied elephant as he shook his straggling locks. Breathing heavily, he then berated the eldest of the Pándavas with these words: 64.5

"I have reached this state even though I was protected by Bhishma the son of Shántanu, Karna that best of weapon-bearers, Shákuni the descendant of Gótama, Drona that champion of weapon-wielders, as well as Ashva·tthaman, Shalya, and heroic Krita·varman. Time cannot be transgressed if I, the leader of eleven armies, suffer this plight. No-one can surpass Time when they encounter it, mighty-armed Yudhi·shthira.

64.10 ākhyātavyaṃ madīyānāṃ ye 'smiñ jīvanti saṃyuge
yath" âhaṃ Bhīmasenena vyutkramya samayaṃ hataḥ.
bahūni su|nṛśaṃsāni kṛtāni khalu Pāṇḍavaiḥ
Bhūriśravasi Karṇe ca Bhīṣme Droṇe ca śrīmati.
idaṃ c' â|kīrti|jaṃ karma nṛśaṃsaiḥ Pāṇḍavaiḥ kṛtam
yena te satsu nirvedaṃ gamiṣyanti hi me matiḥ.

kā prītiḥ sattva|yuktasya kṛtv" ôpādhi|kṛtaṃ jayam?
ko vā samaya|bhettāraṃ budhaḥ saṃmantum arhati?
a|dharmeṇa jayaṃ labdhvā ko nu hṛṣyeta paṇḍitaḥ
yathā saṃhṛṣyate pāpaḥ Pāṇḍu|putro Vṛkodaraḥ?
64.15 kin nu citram itas tv adya bhagna|sakthasya yan mama
kruddhena Bhīmasenena pādena mṛditaṃ śiraḥ?
pratapantaṃ śriyā juṣṭaṃ vartamānaṃ ca bandhuṣu
evaṃ kuryān naro yo hi sa vai Sañjaya pūjitaḥ?

abhijñau yuddha|dharmasya mama mātā pitā ca me
tau hi Sañjaya duḥkh'|ārtau vijñāpyau vacanādd hi me:

‹iṣṭaṃ. bhṛtyā bhṛtāḥ samyag. bhūḥ praśāstā sa|sāgarā.
mūrdhni sthitam a|mitrāṇāṃ jīvatām eva Sañjaya.
dattā dāyā yathā|śakti. mitrāṇāṃ ca priyaṃ kṛtam.
a|mitrā bādhitāḥ sarve. ko nu sv|antataro mayā?
64.20 mānitā bāndhavāḥ sarve. vaśyaḥ saṃpūjito janaḥ.
tritayaṃ sevitaṃ sarvaṃ. ko nu sv|antataro mayā?
ājñaptaṃ nṛpa|mukhyeṣu. mānaḥ prāptaḥ su|dur|labhaḥ.
ājāneyais tathā yātaṃ. ko nu svantataro mayā?
yātāni para|rāṣṭrāṇi nṛpā bhuktāś ca dāsa|vat.

If any of my troops still survive this war, they should be told how Bhima·sena killed me by violating the rules of combat. The Pándavas have committed numerous wicked deeds against Bhuri·shravas, Karna, Bhishma, and glorious Drona. This too is an infamous act committed by the wicked Pándavas—it will, I believe, be abhorred by the good. 64.10

What joy can there be for a pure man in gaining victory from deceit? What intelligent man would condone someone that breaks pacts? What wise man, after winning victory through unjust means, would rejoice in the way that Vrikódara, the evil son of Pandu, rejoices? What is more astounding than that today Bhima·sena has furiously ground my head with his foot after my thighs have been shattered? Should one honor a man when he behaves like this toward someone who gleams with glory and who is cherished among his companions, Sánjaya? 64.15

My mother and father are well acquainted with the code of battle. Tell them the following words as they suffer in sorrow, Sánjaya:

'I have performed sacrifices. I have properly supported my dependents. I have ruled over the earth with its oceans. I have stood on the heads of my enemies, even while they were alive, Sánjaya. I have given gifts to my utmost ability. I have performed kindnesses for my friends. I have repelled all my enemies. Who has a better end than I? I have venerated all my kinsmen. I have honored my subjects. I have followed all of the three pursuits.* Who has a better end than I? I have commanded eminent kings. I have earned an esteem that is extremely difficult to acquire. I have ridden on thoroughbred horses. Who has a better end than I? I 64.20

priyebhyaḥ prakṛtaṃ sādhu. ko nu sv|antataro mayā?
adhītaṃ. vidhivad dattaṃ. prāptam āyur nirāmayam.
sva|dharmeṇa jitā lokāḥ. ko nu sv|antataro mayā?
 diṣṭyā n' âhaṃ jitaḥ saṅkhye parān preṣyavad āśritaḥ!
diṣṭyā me vipulā lakṣmīr mṛte tv anya|gatā vibho!
64.25 yad iṣṭaṃ kṣatra|bandhūnāṃ sva|dharmam anutiṣṭhatām
nidhanaṃ tan mayā prāptaṃ. ko nu sv|antataro mayā?
diṣṭyā n' âhaṃ parāvṛtto vairāt prākṛta|vaj jitaḥ!
diṣṭyā na vimatiṃ kāñ cid bhajitvā tu parājitaḥ!
suptaṃ v" âtha pramattaṃ vā yathā hanyād viṣeṇa vā
evaṃ vyutkrānta|dharmeṇa vyutkramya samayaṃ hataḥ.›
 Aśvatthāmā mahā|bhāgaḥ Kṛtavarmā ca Sātvataḥ
Kṛpaḥ Śāradvataś c' âiva vaktavyā vacanān mama:
‹a|dharmeṇa pravṛttānāṃ Pāṇḍavānām anekaśaḥ
viśvāsaṃ samaya|ghnānāṃ na yūyaṃ gantum arhatha.›»
64.30 vārtikāṃś c' âbravīd rājā putras te satya|vikramaḥ:
 «a|dharmād Bhīmasenena nihato 'haṃ yathā raṇe.
so 'haṃ Droṇaṃ svarga|gataṃ Karṇa|Śalyāv ubhau tathā
Vṛṣasenaṃ mahā|vīryaṃ Śakuniṃ c' âpi Saubalam
Jalasandhaṃ mahā|vīryaṃ Bhagadattaṃ ca pārthivam
Somadattaṃ mah"|êṣv|āsaṃ Saindhavaṃ ca Jayadratham
Duḥśāsana|puro|gāṃś ca bhrātṝn ātma|samāṃs tathā

have entered enemy kingdoms and enjoyed kings as slaves. I have treated my loved ones well. Who has a better end than I? I have studied the Vedas. I have given due gifts. I have had a life without illness. I have won the heavenly realms by practicing the moral code of my class. Who has a better end than I?

How fortunate that I was never conquered in battle or made to rely on my enemies like a slave! How fortunate, my lord, that my vast wealth only belongs to another at my death! I have attained the death that is desired by warriors who follow the duty of their class. Who has a better end than I? How fortunate that I was not turned from my enmity and conquered like a common man! How fortunate that I was not defeated because of succumbing to doubt. I have been killed through a violation of morality and a violation of a code—just like killing someone with poison or slaying someone who is asleep or unaware.' 64.25

Illustrious Ashva·tthaman, Krita·varman the Sátvata, and Kripa the son of Sharádvat should be told the following: 'Never trust the Pándavas: they break pacts and have committed many immoral deeds.'"

Your son, that truly valiant king, then said these words to some messengers: 64.30

"I have been unjustly slain by Bhima·sena in battle. Like a traveller who has lost his caravan, so I will follow Drona, who is now in heaven, and Karna, Shalya, mighty Vrisha·sena, Shákuni the son of Súbala, powerful Jala·sandha, King Bhaga·datta, the great archer Soma·datta, Jayad·ratha of the Sindhus, my brothers who were led by Duhshásana and who were equal to myself, the brave son of Duhshásana and

Dauḥśāsanim̩ ca vikrāntam̩ Lakṣmaṇam̩ c' ātma|jāv ubhau
etām̩ś c' ânyām̩ś ca su|bahūn madīyām̩ś ca sahasraśaḥ
pr̩ṣṭhato 'nugamiṣyāmi sārtha|hīno yath" âdhva|gaḥ.

64.35 katham̩ bhrātr̩̄n hatāñ śrutvā bhartāram̩ ca svasā mama
rorūyamāṇā duḥkh'|ārtā Duḥśalā sā bhaviṣyati?
snuṣābhiḥ prasnuṣābhiś ca vr̩ddho rājā pitā mama
Gāndhārī|sahitaś c' âiva kām̩ gatim̩ pratipatsyati?
nūnam̩ Lakṣmaṇa|māt" âpi hata|putrā hat'|ēśvarā
vināśam̩ yāsyati kṣipram̩ kalyāṇī pr̩thu|locanā.
yadi jānāti Cārvākaḥ parivrāḍ vāg|viśāradaḥ
kariṣyati mahā|bhāgo dhruvam̩ c' âpacitim̩ mama.
Samantapañcake puṇye triṣu lokeṣu viśrute
aham̩ nidhanam āsādya lokān prāpsyāmi śāśvatān.»

64.40 tato jana|sahasrāṇi bāṣpa|pūrṇāni māriṣa
pralāpam̩ nr̩|pateḥ śrutvā vyadravanta diśo daśa.
sa|sāgara|vanā ghorā pr̩thivī sa|car'|â|carā
cacāl' âtha sa|nirhrādā diśaś c' âiv' āvil" âbhavan.

te Droṇa|putram āsādya yathā|vr̩ttam̩ nyavedayan
vyavahāram̩ gadā|yuddhe pārthivasya ca pātanam.
tad ākhyāya tataḥ sarve Droṇa|putrasya Bhārata
dhyātvā ca su|ciram̩ kālam̩ jagmur ārtā yath"|āgatam.

SAÑJAYA UVĀCA:

65.1 VĀRTIKĀNĀM̩ SA|KĀŚĀT tu śrutvā Duryodhanam̩ hatam
hata|śiṣṭās tato rājan Kauravāṇām̩ mahā|rathāḥ
vinirbhinnāḥ śitair bāṇair gadā|tomara|śaktibhiḥ
Aśvatthāmā Kr̩paś c' âiva Kr̩tavarmā ca Sātvataḥ

my own son Lákshmana—these and many other thousands of my allies.

64.35 What will become of my sister Dúhshala when she weeps, stricken with grief on hearing that her brothers and husband have been killed? What will be the fate of my father, that old king, who now only has the company of Gandhári, his daughters-in-law and granddaughters-in-law? The beautiful, wide-eyed mother of Lákshmana will surely soon die now that she has lost both her son and her lord. If Charváka, that illustrious and eloquent wanderer, learns of this, he will certainly avenge me. I will meet my death at sacred Samánta·pánchaka, which is renowned throughout the three worlds, and attain the eternal realms."

64.40 Hearing the king's lament, thousands of people tearfully ran in all ten directions, my lord. The earth—with its oceans, forests, and both moving and unmoving creatures—quaked and rumbled dreadfully and the directions became murky.

The messengers then approached the son of Drona and informed him of the exact events of the mace battle and the slaying of the king. After narrating their message to Drona's son, they all brooded for a long while and sorrowfully departed the same way they had come, descendant of Bharata.

SÁNJAYA said:

65.1 WHEN THEY HEARD the messengers report that Dur·yódhana had been slain, Your Majesty, the surviving great warriors of the Káuravas—Ashva·tthaman, Kripa, and Krita·varman the Sátvata—all hastily returned to the battlefield

tvaritā javanair aśvair āyodhanam upāgaman.
tatr' âpaśyan mah"|ātmānaṃ Dhārtarāṣṭraṃ nipātitam
prabhagnaṃ vāyu|vegena mahā|śālaṃ yathā vane,
bhūmau viceṣṭamānaṃ taṃ rudhireṇa samukṣitam
mahā|gajam iv' āraṇye vyādhena vinipātitam,
65.5 vivartamānaṃ bahuśo rudhir'|âugha|pariplutam
yad|ṛcchayā nipatitaṃ cakram āditya|go|caram,
mahā|vāta|samutthena saṃśuṣkam iva sāgaram
pūrṇa|candram iva vyomni tuṣār'|āvṛta|maṇḍalam,
reṇu|dhvastaṃ dīrgha|bhujaṃ mātaṅgam iva vikrame
vṛtaṃ bhūta|gaṇair ghoraiḥ kravy'|âdaiś ca samantataḥ
yathā dhanaṃ lipsamānair bhṛtyair nṛ|pati|sattamam,
bhru|kuṭī|kṛta|vaktr'|ântaṃ krodhād udvṛtta|cakṣuṣam
s'|â|marṣaṃ taṃ nara|vyāghraṃ vyāghraṃ nipatitaṃ yathā,

te taṃ dṛṣṭvā mah"|êṣv|āsaṃ bhū|tale patitaṃ nṛpam
moham abhyāgaman sarve Kṛpa|prabhṛtayo rathāḥ.
65.10 avatīrya rathebhyaś ca prādravan rāja|saṃnidhau.
Duryodhanaṃ ca saṃprekṣya sarve bhūmāv upāviśan.
tato Drauṇir mahā|rāja bāṣpa|pūrṇ'|ēkṣaṇaḥ śvasan
uvāca Bharata|śreṣṭhaṃ sarva|lok'|ēśvar'|ēśvaram:

«na nūnaṃ vidyate satyaṃ mānuṣe kiñ cid eva hi
yatra tvaṃ puruṣa|vyāghra śeṣe pāṃsuṣu rūṣitaḥ.
bhūtvā hi nṛ|patiḥ pūrvaṃ samājñāpya ca medinīm
katham eko 'dya rāj'|êndra tiṣṭhase nirjane vane?
Duḥśāsanaṃ na paśyāmi n' âpi Karṇaṃ mahā|ratham

on their swift horses, even though they were wounded by sharp arrows, maces, lances, and spears. There they saw the heroic son of Dhrita·rashtra, crushed and fallen to the ground, like a great *shala* tree in a forest that has been shattered by a gust of wind. Writhing on the ground, he was drenched in blood and resembled a mighty elephant slain by a hunter in a forest. Quivering violently, he was bathed 65.5 in pools of blood, having unexpectedly fallen to the ground, as if he were the orb of the sun. He was like an ocean that had been dried up by the gust of a great wind or like the full moon when its disc is covered by mist. Strewn with dust, and like an elephant in his bravery, the long-armed hero was surrounded on all sides by terrifying hordes of spirits who feed off flesh—just as an eminent king is surrounded by dependents who covet wealth. The brows on his forehead were drawn together and his eyes rolled with anger. That enraged tiger among men looked like a fallen tiger.

When they saw that this king and great archer had fallen to the ground, Kripa and the other warriors all became bewildered. Descending from their chariots, they ran to 65.10 their king. Seeing Dur·yódhana, they all sat on the ground beside him. Sighing, and with eyes full of tears, the son of Drona then addressed that best of Bharatas and lord over every ruler in the world, Your Majesty:

"There can surely be no truth whatsoever in the human world if you lie here soiled with dust, tiger among men. How is it, king of kings, that today you lie here alone in this peopleless forest, when previously you ruled over men and commanded the earth? I cannot see Duhshásana, or the great warrior Karna, or any of our friends. Why is this, bull

n' âpi tān suhṛdaḥ sarvān. kim idaṃ Bharata'|rṣabha?

65.15 duḥkhaṃ nūnaṃ Kṛtāntasya gatiṃ jñātuṃ kathañ cana
lokānāṃ ca bhavān yatra śete pāṃsuṣu rūṣitaḥ.

eṣa mūrdh'|âvasiktānām agre gatvā paran|tapaḥ
sa|tṛṇaṃ grasate pāṃsuṃ. paśya Kālasya paryayam!
kva te tad a|malaṃ chatraṃ vyajanaṃ kva ca pārthiva?
sā ca te mahatī senā kva gatā pārthiv'|ôttama?
dur|vijñeyā gatir nūnaṃ kāryāṇāṃ kāraṇ'|ântare
yad vai loka|gurur bhūtvā bhavān etāṃ daśāṃ gataḥ.
a|dhruvā sarva|martyeṣu śrīr upālakṣyate bhṛśam
bhavato vyasanaṃ dṛṣṭvā Śakra|vispardhino bhṛśam!»

65.20 tasya tad vacanaṃ śrutvā duḥkhitasya viśeṣataḥ
uvāca rājan putras te prāpta|kālam idaṃ vacaḥ
vimṛjya netre pāṇibhyāṃ śoka|jaṃ bāṣpam utsṛjan
Kṛp'|ādīn sa tadā vīrān sarvān eva nar'|âdhipaḥ:

«īdṛśo loka|dharmo 'yaṃ Dhātrā nirdiṣṭa ucyate:
vināśaḥ sarva|bhūtānāṃ Kāla|paryāyam āgataḥ.
so 'yaṃ māṃ samanuprāptaḥ pratyakṣaṃ bhavatāṃ hi yaḥ.
pṛthivīṃ pālayitv" âham etāṃ niṣṭhām upāgataḥ.

diṣṭyā n' âhaṃ parāvṛtto yuddhe kasyāñ cid āpadi!
diṣṭy" âhaṃ nihataḥ pāpaiś chalen' âiva viśeṣataḥ!

65.25 utsāhaś ca kṛto nityaṃ mayā diṣṭyā yuyutsatā!
diṣṭyā c' âsmin hato yuddhe nihata|jñāti|bāndhavaḥ!
diṣṭyā ca vo 'haṃ paśyāmi muktān asmāj jana|kṣayāt
svasti|yuktāṃś ca kalyāṃś ca. tan me priyam an|uttamam.

of the Bharatas? It is indeed difficult to understand suffering and the course of Death and the worlds if you lie here, soiled with dust. 65.15

This enemy-scorcher, who used to walk at the head of consecrated kings, now eats dust and grass. Observe the changes of Time! Where is your spotless parasol, Your Majesty, and where is your fan? Where has that great army of yours gone, supreme king? It is surely hard to understand the role of destiny among the causes of actions if you have reached this condition after once being guru of the world. Seeing you in this terrible plight shows the great instability of glory for all mortals—for you were once a rival to Shakra himself!"

After hearing the speech of Ashva·tthaman, who was filled with intense sorrow, your son replied with these fitting words, Your Majesty. Wiping his eyes with his hands and shedding tears of grief, that lord of men addressed Kripa and all the other heroes, saying: 65.20

"Such is the nature of the world, said to be ordained by Dhatri himself: that the death of every being must contend with Time's vagaries. You yourselves have witnessed how I have arrived at this state. After protecting the earth, I now suffer this plight.

How fortunate that I was not put to flight in battle during some disaster! How fortunate that I have been killed by sinners and especially through deceit! How fortunate that I always persevered in my desire to fight in battle! How fortunate that, when my relatives and kinsmen have been slaughtered, I too have been slain in this war! How fortunate 65.25

mā bhavanto 'tra tapyantāṃ sauhṛdān nidhanena me.
yadi vedāḥ pramāṇaṃ vo jitā lokā may" â|kṣayāḥ.
manyamānaḥ prabhāvaṃ ca Kṛṣṇasy' â|mita|tejasaḥ
tena na cyāvitaś c' âhaṃ kṣatra|dharmāt sv|anuṣṭhitāt.
sa mayā samanuprāpto. n' âsmi śocyaḥ kathañ cana.
kṛtaṃ bhavadbhiḥ sadṛśam anurūpam iv' ātmanaḥ.
yatitaṃ vijaye nityaṃ. daivaṃ tu dur|atikramam.»

65.30 etāvad uktvā vacanaṃ bāṣpa|vyākula|locanaḥ
tūṣṇīṃ babhūva rāj'|êndra ruj" âsau vihvalo bhṛśam.
tathā dṛṣṭvā tu rājānaṃ bāṣpa|śoka|samanvitam
Drauṇiḥ krodhena jajvāla yathā vahnir jagat|kṣaye.
sa ca krodha|samāviṣṭaḥ pāṇau pāṇiṃ nipīḍya ca
bāṣpa|vihvalayā vācā rājānam idam abravīt:

«pitā me nihataḥ kṣudraiḥ su|nṛśaṃsena karmaṇā.
na tathā tena tapyāmi yathā rājaṃs tvay" âdya vai.
śṛṇu c' êdaṃ vaco mahyaṃ satyena vadataḥ prabho
iṣṭ'|âpūrtena dānena dharmeṇa su|kṛtena ca.

65.35 ady' âhaṃ sarva|Pañcālān Vāsudevasya paśyataḥ
sarv'|ôpāyair hi neṣyāmi preta|rāja|niveśanam.
anujñāṃ tu mahā|rāja bhavān me dātum arhati.»

iti śrutvā tu vacanaṃ Droṇa|putrasya Kauravaḥ
manasaḥ prīti|jananaṃ Kṛpaṃ vacanam abravīt:
«ācārya śīghraṃ kalaśaṃ jala|pūrṇaṃ samānaya.»
sa tad vacanam ājñāya rājño brāhmaṇa|sattamaḥ

to see that you have escaped from this slaughter of men and that you are well and healthy. This above all is dear to me.

Do not be pained by my death because of your feelings of friendship. If the Vedas are your authority, then I have won the imperishable realms. Although I am aware of the might of infinitely powerful Krishna, he has not toppled me from practicing the kshatriya law properly. I have fulfilled that law. I am not at all to be mourned. You have acted in ways that become you. You have constantly striven for victory. But fate is hard to overcome."

65.30 With these words, Dur·yódhana became silent, extremely distraught and his eyes full of tears, king of kings. When the son of Drona saw the king so overwhelmed by tears and grief, he blazed with anger, like the fire that arises when the universe is destroyed. Possessed by fury and clasping his hands together, he said these words to the king with a voice quivering with tears:

"These base men slaughtered my father through a despicable deed. But that does not pain me as much as what has happened to you today, Your Majesty. Listen to these words of mine, my lord. I speak them by the truth, by my sacrificial store, and by my gifts, merit, and good deeds. Before 65.35 Vasudéva's very eyes, I will today use every means to send all the Panchálas to the abode of the king of the dead. But you have to give me your permission, great king."

When the Káurava heard the son of Drona say these words, which filled his mind with joy, he said to Kripa: "Quickly bring me a pot full of water, teacher." At the king's command, that best of brahmins brought a filled pot and

kalaśaṃ pūrṇam ādāya rājño 'ntikam upāgamat.
tam abravīn mahā|rāja putras tava viśāṃ pate:
«mam' ājñayā dvija|śreṣṭha Droṇa|putro 'bhiṣicyatām
saināpatyena—bhadraṃ te—mama ced icchasi priyam.
rājño niyogād yoddhavyaṃ brāhmaṇena viśeṣataḥ
vartatā kṣatra|dharmeṇa hy. evaṃ dharma|vido viduḥ.»

65.40 rājñas tu vacanaṃ śrutvā Kṛpaḥ Śāradvatas tataḥ
Drauṇiṃ rājño niyogena saināpatye 'bhyaṣecayat.
so 'bhiṣikto mahā|rāja pariṣvajya nṛp'|ôttamam
prayayau siṃha|nādena diśaḥ sarvā vinādayan.
Duryodhano 'pi rāj'|êndra śoṇitena pariplutaḥ
tāṃ niśāṃ pratipede 'tha sarva|bhūta|bhay'|āvahām.
apakramya tu te tūrṇaṃ tasmād āyodhanān nṛpa
śoka|saṃvigna|manasaś cintā|dhyāna|par" âbhavan.*

approached the king. Your son then said these words, lord of the people:

"Fortune be with you, best of brahmins. If you wish to favor me, then follow my command and consecrate the son of Drona as general. Even a brahmin can fight on the order of a king, especially if he practices the kshatriya law. So understand those who know what is right."*

When he heard the king's words, Kripa, the son of Sharád-vat, consecrated the son of Drona as general on the order of the king. After he had been consecrated, Ashva·tthaman embraced that supreme king and departed with a lion roar, filling every direction with his shout, Your Majesty. Dur·yódhana then stayed there for the night, drenched in blood, king of kings—it was a night that would bring terror to every living creature.* Anxious and brooding, the other heroes quickly departed from the battlefield, Your Majesty, their minds troubled by grief. 65.40

NOTES

Bold *references are to the English text;* ***bold italic*** *references are to the Sanskrit text. An asterisk (*) in the body of the text marks the word or passage being annotated.*

30.2 **King Dur·yódhana**: following the convention in 'Shalya,' Volume One, I have chosen to mark the prefixes *dur-* and *su-* for Dur·yódhana and Su·yódhana in order to highlight the different meanings of the man's two names: "he who is difficult to fight" and "good fighter" respectively.

30.3 **kshatriya**: a member of the warrior class. There are four classes in Brahmanical thought: brahmins (the priestly class), kshatriyas (the warrior class), vaishyas (the agricultural class), and shudras (the servile class).

30.4 **Lake**: the previous volume ('Shalya,' Volume One) concluded with Dur·yódhana fleeing and taking refuge in a lake called Dvaipáyana.

30.18 **Sacrificial store**: the concept is of an accumulation of merit from performing sacrificial ritual.

30.26 ***vyādh" âbhyajānan***: for this type of double sandhi, see OBERLIES §1.8.7.

30.63 **O king**: the use of the singular form ***rājan*** is slightly awkward, since the conversation involves three men. A few manuscripts in the apparatus of the Critical Edition read *vīrāḥ*, which would make better sense, but this is not attested in Nīlakaṇṭha manuscripts. One could argue that the singular form expresses the idea that the heroes are addressing each other individually as "king."

31.8 **Daityas** and **dánavas** are classes of demon. **Vishnu** tricks Bali in his incarnation as a dwarf by gaining the demon's agreement that he will give him as much territory as can be covered in three strides, whereupon Vishnu strides across all three worlds. See also MBh CE III.100.21 for Vishnu's defeat of Bali.

31.9 In MBh CE XII.326.72f. we are told that Vishnu slays **Hiranyáksha** in his incarnation as a boar. For **Hiránya·káshipu**, see MBh CE III.100.20, which states that Vishnu killed this demon in his man-lion incarnation (*nara/siṃha*). For Indra's slaughter of **Vritra**, see MBh CE/CSL V.10. Indra makes a pact with Vritra that he will not kill him with any weapon, nor with anything wet or dry, and neither by day nor by night. He finds a solution to the problem by killing Vritra with foam at twilight.

31.10 For Rama's defeat of Rávana (the central topic of the great epic the 'Ramáyana'), see MBh CSL III.273–292.

31.11 **Táraka and Vipra·chitti**: in other passages, both of these demons are said to be slain by Indra; e.g. MBh CE VI.90.28f., VI.91.17.

31.12 For a story on Ílvala and Vatápi, see MBh CE III.94ff. For Indra's slaughter of Tri·shiras, see MBh CE/CSL V.9. The story of how the gods connived to make Sunda and Upasúnda kill each other through jealousy is described in MBh CE I.201ff.

31.14 **Rákshasas** are a class of demon.

31.54 In Brahmanical thought, it is primarily a brahmin's duty to accept gifts.

31.57 For Krishna's attempt to sue for peace, see MBh CE V.87ff.

31.66 For the burning of the lac house, see MBh CE I.132ff. For the snakes, poison, and attempted drowning events, see MBh CE I.119.

31.69 **Pándava heroes**: the use of the plural jars slightly since only Yudhi·shthira has spoken so far. Verse 7 in the next canto (32.7) also refers to Dur·yódhana being reviled by Yudhi·shthira and his brothers and so it seems that the text is loosely including Yudhi·shthira's brothers through association (and in fact Bhima also criticizes Dur·yódhana later).

32.3 ***s' âivaṃ***: for this type of double sandhi, see OBERLIES §1.8.6.

32.42 **Slapped each other's hands**: I follow MONIER-WILLIAMS' interpretation, although in MBh CE III.227.24, VAN BUITENEN translates as "offered their palms."

32.56 **Abhimányu**: for Abhimányu's death, see MBh CSL VII.33–49.

32.61 **King of the mountains**: Mount Hímavat.

33.5 **Compassion**: this is not the first time that compassion or pity, in the wrong context, is described as a flaw. In addition to the famous episode of Krishna's advice to Árjuna in the *Bhagavad/gītā*, see MBh CSL IX.7.36, where Yudhi·shthira is told not to feel compassion for Shalya.

33.7 **The gambling match**, in which Yudhi·shthira loses his kingdom to the Káuravas, is the main event of Book II, 'The Great Hall' (*Sabhā/parvan*).

33.25 **Husband of Shachi**: Indra. See MBh CE/CSL V.10 for this event.

33.31 **Fire in the Khándava forest**: for this event, see MBh CE I.214ff. Bhima's words in this canto are closely paralled by his speech in Canto 56 (verses 16ff.) of the *Śalya/parvan*.

33.34 **Impure deed**: namely, Shákuni's role in devising the gambling match.

33.41 **Varanávata**: it is at Varanávata that Dur·yódhana attempts to burn the Pándavas in a lac house; see MBh CE I.132ff.

33.42 For Dráupadi's humiliation and Yudhi·shthira's loss of his kingdom in the gambling match, see 'The Great Hall' (*Sabhā/parvan*).

33.47 **Usher**: this refers to the usher who was sent to bring Dráupadi to the assembly hall: MBh CSL II.67.1ff.

35.4 See MBh CE V.87ff. for Krishna's unsuccessful attempt to sue for peace. **Madhu** is a demon slain by Krishna. See MBh CE III.194.

35.11 **Tirtha**: see Introduction, note 13 for this word. For Rama's departure on his pilgrimage of the Sarásvati, see MBh CE V.154.

35.40 *t" âbhavan*: for this type of double sandhi, see OBERLIES §1.8.7.

35.46 According to Indian tradition, the moon became marked with a hare-sign to commemorate the act of a hare that offered itself up into a fire in order to provide food for a brahmin.

36.2 **Twice-born**: Brahmins are said to have a second birth when they undergo the ceremony of the sacred thread (*upanayana*). Although all of the first three classes undergo this ritual, the term "twice-born" is often specifically used for brahmins.

36.3 **Soma**: a juice of debatable origin that is central to several Vedic rituals.

36.7 One could convey the lightheartedness of the brothers' names by translating as "Brothers One, Two and Three."

36.12 **The Vedas** are the most authoritative texts in Brahmanical thought, said to be direct hearings (*śruti*) of sacred truth. The four Vedas are: the *Ṛg Veda*, *Sāma Veda*, *Yajur Veda*, and *Atharva Veda*.

36.31 **Hotri priest**: a priest of the *Ṛg Veda*.

36.32 **The Rich, Yajush, and Saman verses** are derived from three of the four Vedas.

37.1 **Shudras** are the lowest of the four classes in Brahmanism. The Abhíras tend to be deprecated in the 'Maha·bhárata' and are often associated with shudras. In MBh CE III.130.4, Sarásvati is said to disappear out of her hatred for the Nishádas.

37.9 **Gandhárvas** are celestial musicians.

37.21 **Yakshas** are a class of demon or semi-divine being. **Vidya·dharas** are deities that wield magic powers. **Pisháchas** are a type of demon or goblin. A **siddha** is a semi-divine being of great perfection.

37.36 **Adhváryu priests**: priests of the *Yajur Veda*.

37.38 **The Krita era** is the first of the four eras of the cosmos and is described as a type of golden age. **Sattra**: a sacrificial session of varying periods of time, ranging from twelve days to several years.

37.43 **Agni·hotra**: a Vedic ritual involving a twice daily offering into fire.

37.44 **Valakhílyas**: in MBh CE I.27, the Valakhílyas are said to be so tiny (because of their austerities) that a group of them are seen carrying a single leaf.

38.22 There is some confusion here, as in one verse the text states that the son or descendant of Uddálaka (Auddálaki) is performing a sacrifice and in the next verse it states that Uddálaka is performing a sacrifice. It may be that in the latter verse Uddálaka is being used as a name for Uddálaka's son.

38.41 **Brahmin**: the mention of a brahmin implies that the god has disguised himself in order to further his plans, a common motif in Indian literature.

39.4 **Release**: the "release" is primarily from the polluting head that attaches itself to Mahódara, but on another level there is an implication of the ascetic's achievement of spiritual release.

39.10 **Jana·sthana**: according to MBh CE III.147.30, it was at Jana·sthana that the demon Rávana kidnapped Rama's wife, Sitá.

39.32 **Future death**: contrary to VAN BUITENEN's translation of ***śvo/maraṇa*** as "imminent death" in the almost identical verse at MBh CE III.81.126, I translate as "future death" because an imminent death seems to make little sense if the devotee has already given up his body (unless the meaning is that he will not have an imminent death once he has attained heaven). Nīlakaṇṭha glosses ***śvo/maranaṃ tapet*** as: *a/kṣayaṃ svargam āpnot' îti* ("he attains the imperishable heaven").

39.36 **Devápi**: in MBh CE V.147.16ff., Devápi is not allowed to be consecrated as king because he has a skin disease.

40.19 *Vasiṣṭho "śramam*: see OBERLIES §1.2.4 for this sandhi.

40.18 **Vishva·mitra and Vasíshtha**: for other passages describing the hostility between Vishva·mitra and Vasíshtha, see MBh CE I.65f. and I.164ff.

41.1 **Brahma·yoni**: in MBh CE III.81.121, we are told that bathing at Brahma·yoni results in attaining the Brahma world. **Dhrita·rashtra** is in fact the biological son of Krishna Dvaipáyana (Vyasa), who begets Dhrita·rashtra through Vichítra·virya's wife, Ámbika, after Vichítra·virya has died.

41.3 **Víshvajit**: a Vedic ritual. Part of the *Gavām/ayana* sacrifice.

41.31 **Yayáti**: for the story of Yayáti and his fall from divine status, see MBh CE I.70–88.

42.29 **The Grandfather's lake**: the lake of Brahma is called Mánasa.

42.31 Except for Uma, the wife of Shiva, several of these goddesses are personifications of various qualities or virtues. Thus Pushti means "Growth," Dyuti "Splendor," Kirti "Fame," Siddhi "Success," Buddhi "Intelligence," Vani "Speech" and Svaha is a ritual exclamation used in Vedic sacrifice.

43.19 **Brahmin rákshasas** are a type of demon of the brahmin class, as demons also have classes.

43.27 I accent **Aruná** (*Aruṇā*) this way to differentiate it from the masculine name Áruna (*Aruṇa*).

43.34 This event is closely related to Indra's slaughter of Vritra in MBh CE/CSL V.10.

43.45 **Raja·suya**: a Vedic ritual for the consecration of a king.

44.10 **The Kríttikas** are a type of nymph.

44.20 **The fourfold Veda**: the *Ṛg Veda*, *Yajur Veda*, *Sāma Veda*, and *Atharva Veda*.

44.21 **Dhanur·veda**: a treatise on archery. **Sángraha**: name of a treatise (meaning "compendium" or "summary").

44.24 **Mákara**: a type of sea creature.

44.25 **Porcupines**: the Sanskrit (***śvā/vic/chalyaka***) literally means "having quills that pierce dogs."

44.30 I accent **Yáma** (*Yāma*) this way to differentiate it from Yama, the king of the dead.

45.5 ***ca Aṃśena***: on such lack of sandhi, see OBERLIES §1.1.1.

45.5 All seven of those accompanying Rudra are *ādiyas*.

45.13 I accent **Kalá** (*kalā*) this way to distinguish the word from Kala (*kāla*) meaning "time." A *kalā* and a *kāṣṭhā* are measurements of time.

45.51 The following list of names contains many words that could be either proper nouns or epithets. In this context, it is often impossible to determine which is which; for example *priya/darśanaḥ* could either be a proper noun or an epithet meaning "of pleasing appearance." I have usually opted to write the words as proper nouns.

45.64 **Kratha and Krátha**: I have accented the words this way to distinguish the short vowel in *Kratha* from the long vowel in *Krātha*.

45.106 ***ânucar" âbhavan***: for this type of double sandhi, see OBERLIES §1.8.7.

46.2 In this list too it is often impossible to determine whether a word is a name or an epithet and I have usually opted to write the words as names. Some of the names are repeated in the list.

46.6 I accent **Jayat·sená** (*Jayatsenā*) this way to differentiate it from the masculine name Jayat·sena (*Jayatsena*).

46.13 I accent **Suprasadá** (*Suprasādā*) this way to differentiate it from the masculine name Suprasáda (*Suprasāda*). I also accent **Kaliká** (*Kālikā*) this way to differentiate it from the masculine name Kálika (*Kālika*).

46.14 I accent **Chitra·sená** (*Citrasenā*) this way to differentiate it from the masculine name Chitra·sena (*Citrasena*). I also accent **Achalá** (*Acalā*) this way to differentiate it from the masculine name Áchala (*Acala*).

46.21 I accent **Krishná** (*Kṛṣṇā*, feminine) this way to differentiate it from the masculine name Krishna (*Kṛṣṇa*).

46.22 I accent **Shvetá** (*Śvetā*) this way to differentiate it from the masculine name Shveta (*Śveta*).

46.29 I accent **Virochaná** (*Virocanā*) this way to differentiate it from the masculine name Viróchana (*Virocana*).

46.47 I accent **Dhanan·jayá** (*Dhanañjayā*) this way to differentiate it from the masculine name Dhanan·jaya (*Dhanañjaya*).

46.62 These gods are all personifications: Effort, Victory, Righteousness, Success, Fortune, Steadfastness, and Tradition.

46.79 **Krauncha**: the Sanskrit word for curlew is ***krauñca***. The verse is thus giving an explanation for the mountain's name.

46.91 **Sanat·kumára**: "ever young."

47.20 **Bhrigu's curse**: an account of this curse is given in MBh CE I.6.

48.23 ***jala/madhye va***: this may be a case of double sandhi (*jalamadhyeva* from *jalamadhye* and *iva*), for which see Oberlies §1.8.12, or it may simply be a case of *va* being used for *iva* (see Monier-Willliams).

48.31 **The Seven Seers** are: Atri, Bharad·vaja, Gáutama, Jamad·agni, Káshyapa, Vasíshtha and Vishva·mitra.

49.8 **Vajapéya**: an elaborate *soma* ritual.

49.9 This refers to Párashu·rama, the son of Jamad·agni. For his extermination of the kshatriya race, see MBh CE I.98. On Rama's sacrifice and his gift of the earth to Káshyapa, see MBh CE I.117.10ff.

49.21 For Vishnu's slaughter of Madhu and Káitabha, see MBh CE III.194.

50.20 ***kāṣṭha/bhūto "śrama/pade***: for this type of sandhi, see Oberlies §1.2.4.

50.33 Several Vedic rituals are mentioned in this section. The **Agni·hotra** is a twice daily offering into fire. The **Darsha** and **Paurnamása** sacrifices are often grouped together and occur on new and full moon days. **Chaturmásya** sacrifices are "four-monthly" or seasonal sacrifces. The **Agni·shtoma** sacrifice is a one-day soma sacrifice; it serves as a model for all *soma* sacrifices. The **Agni·shtuta** is connected to the Agni·shtoma ritual and the **Vajapéya** ritual is an elaborate *soma* sacrifice.

50.34 The **Raja·suya** sacrifice is a Vedic ritual used for the consecration of kings. The **Pundaríka** is another Vedic ritual.

50.36 The **Sautrámani** ritual is a sacrifice involving the oblation of wine (*surā*).

50.40 **Brahma·sattrin**: in *Manu* 2.106, the *Brahma/sattra* ritual is a daily Vedic recitation, "in which the Veda is used as the oblation in the place of the burned offering" (DONIGER AND SMITH 1991: 100).

50.60 This tension between the householder path and renouncer path is a central theme of several Brahmanical texts.

51.40 ***ved" âbhidhāvatām***: for this type of double sandhi, see OBERLIES §1.8.7.

52.14 **Gálava**: for an account of this ascetic, see MBh CE V.104–21.

53.25 **Kuru·kshetra**: for other passages on the auspicious nature of Kuru·kshetra, see MBh CE III.181.1ff. and III.181.173ff.

55.28 **Váishravana** means "son of Víshravas" and could refer to either Kubéra or Rávana, although it seems to be used more often of the former.

56.21 The Pándavas' life in the forest for twelve years and in disguise for one year is described in Book III, 'The Forest' (*Vana/parvan*), and Book IV, 'Viráta' (*Virāṭa/parvan*), respectively.

56.32 **Yajna·sena's son**: Shikhándin.

57.4 The **kínshuka** flower is red.

57.19 My translation uses Nīlakaṇṭha's interpretation of these terms.

58.43 **Avasthána**: the fact that Dur·yódhana jumps into the air seems to contradict Nīlakaṇṭha's interpretation of *avasthāna* in 57.19, where he explains it as "remaining steady" (*a/cāñcalyam*).

58.58 ***puruṣ" âbhavan*** and ***pratisroto/vah" âbhavan*** in the previous verse are examples of double sandhi, for which see OBERLIES §1.8.7.

59.4 **"Ox! Ox!"**: see MBh CSL II.77.19, although there the words are spoken by Duhshásana.

59.10 **Yajna·sena's daughter**: Dráupadi.

59.11 **Sesame seeds**: This refers to Duhshásana's words of abuse in MBh CSL II.77.14.

60.8 Verses 60.7–8 are only found in editions B and K and are not attested in any other manuscript in the apparatus of the Critical Edition. The elliptical nature of the verses also suggests that they are suspect.

60.14 **Our father's sister**: Vasu·deva's sister is Kunti.

60.16 **Maitréya**: for Maitréya's curse, see MBh CE III.11.

60.22 **The Kali era** is the last of the four eras and is characterized by degeneracy.

61.12 **Drunk the blood of Duhshásana**: for this event see MBh CSL VIII.84.

61.30 I read *te* as performing an instrumental function here. See 61.42 for a similar occurrence and also OBERLIES §4.1.3, 4.2.4.

61.30 **Grandfather killed**: see MBh CE VI.104ff. for Bhishma's defeat. Following Bhishma's own counsel, Árjuna overcomes the general of the Káuravas by firing arrows at him from behind Shikhándin. Bhishma had vowed never to fight a woman, and because Shikhándin was previously a woman, Bhishma is unable to attack him.

61.32 **Drona's death** occurs in MBh CE VII.159ff. After the death of an elephant called Ashva·tthaman, Drona is told by Yudhi·shthira that Ashva·tthaman has been slain. Believing this to be his son, Drona gives up his will to live and is killed by Dhrishta·dyumna.

61.33 Karna is given a **divine spear** by Indra, with which he intends to kill Árjuna. However, Karna is instead compelled to use the spear against Ghatótkacha, the son of Bhima, thus damaging his chances of slaying Árjuna. See MBh CE VII.148ff.

61.34 **Bhuri·shravas** is killed in MBh CE VII.116ff. Árjuna cuts off Bhuri·shravas' arm with an arrow from a concealed position, whereupon Bhuri·shravas undertakes **praya**, a type of meditative act involving the giving up of one's life. Sátyaki takes advantage of the situation to lop off Bhuri·shravas' head.

61.36 **Ashva·sena** is a snake that enters one of Karna's arrows and attacks Árjuna. Árjuna slays **Karna** while he is trying to extract his chariot-wheel from the ground. See MBh CSL VIII.90–91.

61.45 **Evil Jayad·ratha**: see MBh CE III.248ff. for Jayad·ratha's attempted abduction of Dráupadi.

61.64 **These heroic and superior warriors**: this refers to the four generals who have been slain: Bhishma, Drona, Karna, and Shalya.

62.19 **Brahmástra**: a type of celestial weapon.

64.20 **The three pursuits** are (in ascending order of importance): *kāma* (desire or pleasure), *artha* (benefit or profit) and *dharma* (righteousness or morality).

65.39 **Even a brahmin**: the reason for Dur·yódhana's comment about brahmins is that Ashva·tthaman is a brahmin and war is usually considered the preserve of the kshatriya.

65.43 ***cintā/dhyāna/par" âbhavan***: for this type of double sandhi, see OBERLIES §1.8.7.

65.42 **A night that would bring terror**: this comment looks forward to the next book, in which Ashva·tthaman slaughters the Pándava army at night in a gruesome massacre.

PROPER NAMES AND EPITHETS

ABHIMÁNYU Son of Árjuna and Subhádra.

ABHÍRA Name of a people. Often associated with shudras.

ÁCHYUTA Name for many characters in the epic, including Bala·rama, Krishna, and Yudhi·shthira. Literally, "unfallen," "imperishable."

ADÁMBARA An attendant of Skanda, given by Dhatri.

ADHÓKSHAJA A name for Krishna. Literally, "born under an axle-tree."

ÁDITI Daughter of Daksha. Wife of Káshyapa. Mother of the *adítyas*.

ADÍTYA A class of god. Sons of Áditi and Káshyapa. They are: Dhatri, Mitra, Áryaman, Indra, Váruna, Ansha, Bhaga, Vivásvat, Pushan, Savítri, Tvashtri, and Vishnu.

ADÍTYA·TIRTHA A *tirtha* on the Sarásvati.

AGNI The god of fire. Also known as Vibha·vasu.

AGNI·TIRTHA A *tirtha* on the Sarásvati.

AIRÁVANA/AIRÁVATA Elephant of Indra.

AJÁTA·SHATRU Name for Yudhi·shthira. Literally, "one without enemies."

ÁMBIKA Mother of Dhrita·rashtra.

AMSHA An *adítya*.

ÁNDHAKA Name of a people. Also the name of a demon killed by Rudra.

ÁNGIRAS An ascetic. One of the mind-born sons of Brahma.

ANUCHÁKRA An attendant of Skanda, given by Tvashtri.

ÁNUMATI A goddess.

ARÁNTUKA A location marking the boundary of Kuru·kshetra.

ÁRJUNA The third of the five Pándava brothers. Son of Pandu and Kunti. Also known as: Dhanan·jaya, Pándava, Partha, Phálguna, Savya·sachin.

ARSHTISHÉNA An ascetic who attains brahminhood.

ARTÁYANI Name for Shalya.

ÁRUNA Dawn. Charioteer of the sun and brother of Gáruda.

ARUNÁ A sacred river.

ARÚNDHATI An ascetic. Wife of Vasíshtha.

ASHMA·KUTTA A type of ascetic.

ASHVA·SENA A snake.

ASHVA·TTHAMAN Son of Drona and Kripi. Fights for the Káuravas.

ASHVINS Divine twins skilled in medicine.

ÁSITA DÉVALA An ascetic. Also known as Dévala.

ÁTIBALA An attendant of Skanda, given by Vayu.

ATISHRÍNGA An attendant of Skanda, given by Vindhya.

ATÍSTHIRA An attendant of Skanda, given by Meru.

ATIVÁRCHASA An attendant of Skanda, given by Hímavat.

ATRI One of the mind-born sons of Brahma and one of the Seven Seers, along with Bharad·vaja, Gáutama, Jamad·agni, Káshyapa, Vasíshtha and Vishva·mitra.

AUDDÁLAKI Son or descendant of Uddálaka. Often used for Shveta·ketu.

AUSHÁNASA A *tirtha* on the Sarásvati. Also known as Kapála·móchana. Literally, "related to Úshanas."

AVAKÍRNA A *tirtha* on the Sarásvati.

BÁDARA·PÁCHANA A *tirtha* on the Sarásvati.

BAHLÍKA Father of Soma·datta. Brother of Shántanu. Fights for the Káuravas.

BAKA An ascetic, also known as Baka Dalbhya.

BAKA DALBHYA An ascetic. Also known as Baka.

BALA A name for Bala·rama. Also the name of a demon (sometimes known as Vala) slain by Indra. Also the name of an attendant of Skanda, given by Vayu.

BALA·BHADRA A name for Bala·rama.

BALA·DEVA A name for Bala·rama.

BALA·RAMA Elder brother of Krishna. Son of Róhini. Also known as:

Áchyuta, Bala, Bala·bhadra, Bala·deva, Rama.

BALI A demon that was defeated by Vishnu in his incarnation as a dwarf. Son of Viróchana. Father of Bana.

BANA A demon slain by Skanda. Son of Bali. Also the name of one of Skanda's troops.

BHAGA·DATTA King of Prag·jyótisha. Fights for the Káuravas.

BHARAD·VAJA An ancient seer. Father of Drona. Grandfather of Ashva·tthaman. One of the Seven Seers along with Atri, Gáutama, Jamad·agni, Káshyapa, Vasíshtha and Vishva·mitra. Father of Shrutávati.

BHARATA Prototypical ruler of North India; ancestor of most of the characters in the 'Maha·bhárata.'

BHÁRATA Descendant of Bharata. Used of numerous people in the epic.

BHÁSKARA An attendant of Skanda, given by Surya.

BHIMA The second of the five Pándava brothers. Son of Pandu and Kunti. Also known as Bhima·sena, Pándava, Partha, Vrikódara. Literally, "terrifying." Also the name of an attendant of Skanda, given by Ansha.

BHIMA·SENA Name for Bhima. Literally, "he who has a terrifying army."

BHISHMA Son of Shántanu and Ganga. Fights for the Káuravas. Sometimes referred to as "grandfather."

BHOJA Name of a people. Connected with the Vrishnis and Ándhakas.

BHRIGU An ascetic.

BHURI·BALA A son of Dhrita·rashtra.

BIBHÁTSU A name for Árjuna. Literally, "the tormentor."

BHURI·SHRAVAS A warrior that fights for the Káuravas.

BOWER OF SARÁSVATI Name of a *tirtha* on the Sarásvati where the river meets with Aruná.

BRAHMA A god. Creator of the universe, also known as Grandfather. In his neuter form as Brahman, he represents the impersonal absolute of the universe.

Brahman The absolute essence of the universe. Also the sacred speech of the immortal Vedas.

Brahma·yoni A *tirtha* on the Sarásvati. Literally, "womb of Brahma."

Brihas·pati The chief priest of the gods.

Buddhi A goddess ("Intelligence"). Daughter of Daksha and wife of Dharma.

Chakra An attendant of Skanda, given by Vishnu. Also the name of an attendant of Skanda, given by Tvashtri.

Chamasódbheda A *tirtha* on the Sarásvati.

Chárana A class of deity.

Charváka A demon. A friend of Dur·yódhana.

Chedi Name of a people.

Chitra·sena A son of Karna. Fights for the Káuravas.

Dadhícha An ascetic.

Dáhana An attendant of Skanda, given by Ansha.

Dáhati An attendant of Skanda, given by Ansha.

Daitya A class of demon.

Daksha A Praja·pati (lord of creatures). Also a name for Shiva.

Dámbara An attendant of Skanda, given by Dhatri.

Dánava A class of demon.

Dándaka Name of a forest.

Dantolúkhalin A type of ascetic.

Dáruka Charioteer of Krishna.

Dashárha Name of a people. Krishna is a chief of the Dashárhas.

Dévaki Daughter of Dévaka. Wife of Vasu·deva. Mother of Krishna.

Dévala Ásita Dévala.

Deväpi A kshatriya who becomes an ascetic and attains brahminhood. Son of Pratípa.

DHANAN·JAYA A name for Árjuna. Literally, "wealth-winner."

DHANAN·JAYÁ Name of an army given by Shiva to Skanda.

DHARMA God of Righteousness. Begets Yudhi·shthira through Kunti.

DHATRI The Orderer/Creator. Often identical with Brahma.

DHÍSHANA A goddess.

DHRISHTA·DYUMNA Son of the Panchála king Drúpada, brother of Dráupadi. Born from a sacrificial fire. Fights for the Pándavas.

DHRITA·RASHTRA King of the Kurus. Son of Vichítra·virya and Ámbika (though biological son of Krishna Dvaipáyana). Father of Dur·yódhana and 99 other sons.

DHRITI A goddess ("Steadfastness").

DRÁUPADI Daughter of Drúpada. Wife of the five Pándava brothers. Also known as Krishná. She has five sons: Prativíndhya, Suta·soma, Shruta·kirti, Shataníka, Shruta·sena.

DRONA Son of Bharad·vaja. Husband of Kripi. Father of Ashva·tthaman. Preceptor of the sons of Pandu and the sons of Dhrita·rashtra. Fights for the Káuravas.

DRÚPADA Panchála king. Father of Dhrishta·dyumna, Dráupadi, and Shikhándin. Also known as Yajna·sena.

DÚHSHALA Daughter of Dhrita·rashtra and Gandhári.

DUHSHÁSANA A son of Dhrita·rashtra.

DUR·YÓDHANA Eldest son of Dhrita·rashtra and Gandhári. Also known as Su·yódhana. Literally, "he who is difficult to fight."

DVAIPÁYANA Krishna Dvaipáyana (Vyasa). Also the name of a lake.

DVAITA·VANA A *tirtha* on the Sarásvati.

DVÁRAKA Capital of the Vrishnis. Same as Dváravati.

DVITA An ascetic. Brother of Ékata and Trita.

DYUTI A goddess ("Splendor").

ÉKATA An ascetic. Brother of Dvita and Trita.

GADHI A king who becomes an ascetic. Father of Vishva·mitra. Son of

Kúshika.

GÁLAVA An ascetic. Father of Shríngavat.

GANDHÁRA A name of a people.

GANDHÁRI Wife of Dhrita·rashtra. Mother of Dur·yódhana and ninety-nine other sons. Literally, "princess of Gandhára." Daughter of Gandhára king Súbala.

GANDHÁRVA A type of celestial musician.

GANDÍVA The bow of Árjuna.

GANGA Name of a river and goddess. Mother of Bhishma.

GANGÉYA A name for Skanda.

GARGA An ascetic. Also known as Kuni Garga.

GARGA·SROTAS A *tirtha* on the Sarásvati.

GÁRUDA A divine bird. Son of Káshyapa and Vínata. Brother of Áruna.

GÁUTAMA Name of various ascetics. Means "descendant of Gótama."

GAVÁLGANA The father of Sánjaya.

GAYA Name of an ancient king. In the plural (the Gayas), name of the people in Gaya's kingdom.

GHANTÁKARNA An attendant of Skanda, given by Brahma.

GHATÓTKACHA Son of Bhima and Hidímba. A *rákshasa* (demon). Fights for the Pándavas.

GÓTAMA An ancient seer. Father of Sharádvat. Grandfather of Kripa.

GO·VINDA A name for Krishna.

GRANDFATHER Brahma.

GRITÁCHI A nymph.

GUHA A name for Skanda.

HARA A name for Shiva. Literally, "seizer."

HÁSTINA·PURA Capital of the Kurus.

HÍMAVAT The Himálaya mountains. Father of Uma, the wife of Shiva.

HIRANYA·KÁSHIPU A demon slain by Vishnu in his man-lion incarnation. Son of Diti.

HIRANYÁKSHA A demon slain by Vishnu in his boar incarnation.

HRADÓDARA A demon slain by Skanda.

HRI A goddess ("Shame").

HRÍDIKA Father of Krita·varman.

HRISHI·KESHA A name for Krishna.

ÍLAVILA Mother of Kubéra.

ÍLVALA A demon. Elder brother of Vatápi.

INDRA King of the gods (*devas*). Also known as: Mághavat, Puran·dara, Shakra, Shata·kratu, Vásava.

INDRA·TIRTHA A *tirtha* on the Sarásvati.

ISHÁNA A name for Rudra/Shiva.

JAIGISHÁVYA An ascetic.

JALA·SANDHA A Mágadha king. Fights for the Káuravas.

JAMAD·AGNI A seer. Father of Párashu·rama.

JAMBHA A demon conquered by Indra.

JANAM·ÉJAYA son of Paríkshit and Mádravati. At his snake sacrifice, Vaishampáyana recited the 'Maha·bhárata' for the first time. Literally, "people-trembler."

JANÁRDANA A name for Krishna. Literally, "people-agitator."

JANA·STHANA An area in the Dándaka forest.

JAYA An attendant of Skanda, given by Vásuki. Also Victory personified.

JAYAD·RATHA King of the Sindhus. Fights for the Káuravas.

JAYAT·SENA A son of Dhrita·rashtra.

JIHVA An attendant of Skanda, given by Fire.

JVALA An attendant of Skanda, given by Fire.

KAILÁSA A mountain; abode of Kubéra.

KÁITABHA A demon slain by Vishnu.

KALA Time personified. Often identical to Death.

KALÁ A small measure of time.

KÁLIKA An attendant of Skanda, given by Pushan.

KALÍNGA One of Skanda's troops. In the plural, name of a people.

KAMBÓJA Name of a people. The king of the Kambójas (who is himself often called Kambója) is Sudákshina.

KANSA King of Máthura. Killed by Krishna.

KÁNCHANA An attendant of Skanda, given by Meru.

KANCHANÁKSHI One of the seven Sarásvati rivers.

KAPÁLA·MÓCHANA A *tirtha* on the Sarásvati. Also known as Áushanasa. Literally, "release from the skull."

KARA·PÁVANA A *tirtha* on the Sarásvati.

KARNA Son of Surya (the Sun) and Kunti. Adopted by the charioteer Ádhiratha and his wife Radha. Often known as "the charioteer"s son'. Fights for the Káuravas.

KARTTIKÉYA A name for Skanda.

KASHTHA A measure of time.

KÁSHYAPA One of the Seven Seers, along with Atri, Bharad·vaja, Gáutama, Jamad·agni, Vasíshtha and Vishva·mitra.

KAUBÉRA A *tirtha* on the Sarásvati.

KÁURAVA Descendant of Kuru. Often refers to Dhrita·rashtra's sons and their followers but the Pándavas are also sometimes called Káurava (since they too are descendants of Kuru).

KAVI An ascetic. Son of Bhrigu and father of Úshanas.

KÉKAYA Name of a people. Also refers to five princes of the Kékayas that joined Yudhi·shthira.

KÉSHAVA A name for Krishna.

KESHIN A demon slain by Krishna.

KIN·KARA The rod of Yama.

KÍNNARA A type of being, half-man and half-horse.

KING OF RIGHTEOUSNESS Yudhi·shthira.

KIRTI A goddess ("fame"). Daughter of Daksha and wife of Dharma.

KRATU An ascetic. One of the mind-born sons of Brahma.

KRAUNCHA A mountain.

KRIPA Son of Sharádvat. Grandson of Gótama. Brother of Kripi. Fights for the Káuravas.

KRISHNA Son of Vasu·deva and Dévaki. Also identified as Vishnu/Naráyana, the supreme God. Also known as: Áchyuta, Adhókshaja, Go·vinda, Janárdana, Késhava, Mádhava, Varshnéya, Vasudéva. The "two Krishnas" are Árjuna and Krishna. Krishna is also the name of one of Skanda's troops.

KRISHNA DVAIPÁYANA Son of Sátyavati and the seer Paráshara. Father of Dhrita·rashtra, Pandu, and Vídura. Also known as Vyasa. His name derives from the fact that he was abandoned on an island (*dvipa*). Sometimes referred to as "grandfather."

KRISHNÁ A name for Dráupadi. Also one of the mothers attending Skanda.

KRITA·VARMAN A Vrishni ruler. Son of Hrídika. Fights for the Káuravas.

KSHATTRI A name for Vídura. A term referring to the fact that he was born from a low-caste shudra woman; also meaning "steward."

KUBÉRA King of the *gúhyakas*, *rákshasas* and *yakshas*. Known for his riches.

KUHU A goddess. The new moon. Daughter of Ángiras.

KUMÁRA A name for Skanda.

KÚMUDA An attendant of Skanda, given by Dhatri. Also one of Skanda's troops.

KÚMUDA·MALIN An attendant of Skanda, given by Brahma.

KUNDA An attendant of Skanda, given by Dhatri.

KUNI GARGA An ascetic. Also known as Garga.

KUNTI Wife of Pandu. Mother of Karna by the god Surya, and mother of Yudhi·shthira, Bhima and Árjuna by Pandu (through the gods Dharma, Vayu, and Indra respectively). Also known as Pritha.

KUNTI·BHOJA Adoptive father of Kunti. Fights for the Pándavas.

KURU An ancient king. Ancestor of the Bháratas. "The Kurus" are the descendants of Kuru and include both the Káuravas and Pándavas, although the term often refers only to Dhrita·rashtra's sons and their followers.

KURU·KSHETRA "Field of the Kurus." The area of the great battle between the Káuravas and Pándavas. Those who die in battle there are said to attain heaven.

KÚSHIKA An ancient king. Father of Gadhin. Grandfather of Vishva·mitra.

KÚSUMA An attendant of Skanda, given by Dhatri.

LÁKSHMANA Son of Dur·yódhana.

LAKSHMI A goddess ("Fortune").

LOHITÁKSHA An attendant of Skanda, given by Brahma.

MACHAKRÚKA A lake.

MÁDHAVA A name of a people. Descendant of Madhu. A name for Krishna Vasudéva, Sátyaki, and Krita·varman.

MADHU A demon slain by Krishna. Also the name of an ancient king who is the ancestor of the Mádhavas.

MADRA/MADRAKA A name of a people. Shalya is the king of the Madras.

MÁDRAVATI Madri.

MADRI Second wife of Pandu. A princess of the Madras. Sister of Shalya. Mother of the twins Nákula and Saha·deva by the two Ashvin gods. Also known as Mádravati.

MÁGADHA A name of a people.

MÁGHAVAT A name for Indra. Literally, "bountiful."

MAHA·DEVA A name for Shiva (although used for other gods too). Literally, "great god."

MAHA·JAYA An attendant of Skanda, given by Vásuki.

MAHA·SENA A name for Skanda. Literally, "possessing a mighty army."

MAHÉNDRA A name for Indra. Literally, "great Indra."

MAHÉSHVARA A name for Shiva. Literally, "great lord."

MAHÍSHA A demon slain by Skanda.

MAHÓDARA An ascetic.

MAITRÁVARUNI A name for Vasíshtha, meaning "son of Mitra and Váruna."

MAITRÉYA An ascetic.

MANI An attendant of Skanda, given by Soma.

MÁNKANAKA An ascetic.

MANO·RAMA One of the seven Sarásvati rivers.

MANU Father of the human race.

MARÍCHI An ascetic. One of the mind-born sons of Brahma and father of Káshyapa.

MARUT A class of god associated with the wind.

MATARÍSHVAN Variously identified as Agni (Fire), Vayu (Wind), or a son of Gáruda. Father of Mánkanaka.

MEGHA·MALIN An attendant of Skanda, given by Meru.

MERU A mountain at the center of the cosmos.

MITRA An *adítya* deity. Often linked with Váruna.

NAGA·DHÁNVANA A *tirtha* on the Sarásvati.

NÁHUSHA An ancient king. Father of Yayáti. Temporarily king of the gods.

NAIGAMÉYA An aspect of Skanda.

NAIMÍSHA A sacred forest.

NAIMISHÍYA An area on the Sarásvati where there is a group of *tirthas*.

NÁIRRITA A type of deity. Connected to Nírriti.

NÁKULA One of the Pándava brothers (twin of Saha·deva). Son of Pandu and Madri (by one of the Ashvin gods).

NALA·KÚBARA A son of Kubéra.

NÁMUCHI A demon killed by Indra.

NÁNDANA An attendant of Skanda, given by the Ashvins. Also one of Skanda's troops.

NANDI·SENA An attendant of Skanda, given by Brahma.

NARA Primeval Man. Often considered a god and coupled with Naráyana. Identified with Árjuna.

NÁRADA A divine seer. Often acts as messenger between gods and men.

NARÁYANA Name of the god Vishnu. Often coupled with Nara. Identified with Krishna. Also the name of a people.

NRIGA A king.

ÓGHAVATI One of the seven Sarásvati rivers.

PAKA A demon slain by Indra.

PANCHAJÁNYA The conch of Krishna.

PÁNCHAKA An attendant of Skanda, given by Indra.

PANCHÁLA Name of a people who fight on the side of the Pándavas. The king of the Panchálas is Drúpada.

PÁNDAVA Son of Pandu = Yudhi·shthira, Bhima, Árjuna, Nákula and Saha·deva. Often also refers to the followers of the sons of Pandu.

PANDU Son of Krishna Dvaipáyana and Ambálika. Half-brother of Dhrita·rashtra and Vídura. Father of the Pándavas. Husband of Kunti and Madri.

PANÍTAKA An attendant of Skanda, given by Pushan.

PARÍKSHIT son of Abhimányu and Úttara. Father of Janam·éjaya.

PÁRIGHA An attendant of Skanda, given by Ansha.

PARJÁNYA God of rain, often identified with Indra.

PARTHA Son of Pritha = Yudhi·shthira, Bhima·sena, Árjuna. Often refers to the followers of the sons of Pritha.

PÁRVATI A name for Uma.

PASHU·PATI Lord of animals. Often identified with Shiva.

PÁURAVA Descendant of Puru. Name of a people.

PHÁLGUNA A name for Árjuna.

PISHÁCHA A type of goblin or demon.

PLAKSHA·PRÁSRAVANA A *tirtha* on the Sarásvati.

PRABHÁDRAKA A division of the Panchálas.

PRABHÁSA A *tirtha* on the Sarásvati. Also the name of one of Skanda's troops.

PRACHÉTAS An ascetic.

PRAHLÁDA A demon.

PRAJA·PATI A name used for various deities or creator beings. Literally, "lord of creatures."

PRALÁMBA A demon.

PRAMÁNA·KOTI A location on the river Ganga.

PRÁMATHA An attendant of Skanda, given by Yama.

PRASANKHÁYANA A type of ascetic.

PRÍSHATA Father of Drúpada, grandfather of Dhrishta·dyumna.

PRITHA A name for Kunti.

PRITHÚDAKA A *tirtha* on the Sarásvati. Literally, "having deep water."

PÚLAHA An ascetic. One of the mind-born sons of Brahma.

PULASTYA Another name for Víshravas. An ascetic. Father of Kubéra (Váishravana) and Rávana. One of the mind-born sons of Brahma.

PURAN·DARA A name for Indra. Literally, "destroyer of cities."

PURU An ancient king.

PÚSHKARA Name of a group of *tirthas*.

PUSHPA·DANTA An attendant of Skanda, given by Párvati.

PUSHTI A goddess ("Growth"). Daughter of Daksha and wife of

Dharma.

RADHA Adoptive mother of Karna. Wife of the charioteer Ádhiratha.

RAKA A goddess. The full moon.

RÁKSHASA A type of demon.

RAHU A demon that swallows the sun and the moon and creates an eclipse.

RAMA Used for three main characters: Bala·rama, Rama the son of Dasha·ratha (who slays Rávana), and Rama the son of Jamad·agni (also known as Párashu·rama). Also the name of a lake.

RAMA·TIRTHA A *tirtha* on the Sarásvati.

RÁVANA King of *rákshasas* in Lanka. Slain by Rama (son of Dasha·ratha).

RÓHINI Daughter of Daksha and wife of Soma. Also the name of the wife of Vasu·deva, who is the mother of Bala·rama.

RUDRA A god. Associations with Shiva.

RUDRAS A class of gods, followers of Shiva.

RUSHÁNGU A brahmin ascetic.

SADHYA A class of gods.

SAHA·DEVA One of the Pándava brothers. Twin brother of Nákula. Son of Madri and Pandu (by one of the Ashvin gods).

SAMÁNTA·PÁNCHAKA Name of a *tirtha* and of the area of Kuru·kshetra.

SANSHÁPTAKA A group of Káurava warriors.

SANAT·KUMÁRA A name for Skanda. Literally, "ever young."

SÁNGRAHA An attendant of Skanda, given by the Ocean. Also the name of a treatise.

SÁNKRAMA An attendant of Skanda, given by Vishnu.

SÁNJAYA Son of Gaválgana. Narrates the events of the great battle to Dhrita·rashtra.

SAPTA·SARÁSVATA A *tirtha* where the seven Sarásvatis meet.

SARÁSVATA An ascetic. Son of Dadhícha and Sarásvati.

SARÁSVATI Name of a river and goddess. The goddess is often associated with speech and learning.

SÁTVATA Name of a people belonging to the Yádavas. Used of Krishna, Krita·varman, and Sátyaki.

SATYA·KARMAN A Tri·garta prince.

SATYA·SANDHA An attendant of Skanda, given by Mitra.

SÁTYAKI A Vrishni. Also called Yuyudhána. Means "son of Sátyaka." Grandson of Shini. Fights for the Pándavas.

SAVYA·SACHIN A name for Árjuna. Literally, "he who draws (a bow) with his left hand."

SHÁBARA A wild mountaineer tribe.

SHACHI Wife of Indra.

SHAIBYA A horse driving Krishna's chariot.

SHAKA Name of a people.

SHAKHA An aspect of Skanda.

SHÁKUNI Son the Gandhára king Súbala. Father of Ulúka.

SHALYA King of the Madras. Brother of Madri. Also known as Artáyani.

SHÁMBARA A demon slain by Indra.

SHANDÍLYA An ascetic.

SHANKHA A *tirtha* on the Sarásvati. Named after a *shankha* tree.

SHANKU·KARNA An attendant of Skanda, given by Párvati. Also the name of one of Skanda's troops.

SHÁNTANU A king. Son of Pratípa. Father of Bhishma by Ganga. Father of Vichítra·virya and Chitrángada by Sátyavati.

SHARÁDVAT Father of Kripa.

SHATA·KRATU A name for Indra ("performer of a hundred sacrifices").

SHIKHÁNDIN Son (originally daughter) of Drúpada. Fights for the Pándavas and is pivotal in Árjuna's slaughter of Bhishma.

SHINI Father of Sátyaka. Grandfather of Sátyaki.

SHIVA A god. Also known as Hara, Ishána, Maha·deva, Mahéshvara,

Pashu·pati and Sthanu.

SHRI A goddess ("Prosperity").

SHRÍNGAVAT An ascetic.

SHRUTÁVATI A female ascetic. Daughter of Bharad·vaja.

SHUBHA·KARMAN An attendant of Skanda, given by Vidhátri.

SHUKA Son of Vyasa.

SIDDHA Semi-divine being of great perfection.

SIDDHI A goddess ("Success").

SINDHU·DVIPA A king who becomes an ascetic and attains brahminhood.

SINIVÁLI A goddess. Daughter of Ángiras.

SITÁ Wife of Rama, the son of Dasha·ratha.

SKANDA General of the gods. Son of Agni (Fire) and Svaha. Also known as Gangéya, Guha, Karttikéya, Kumára, Maha·sena, Sanat·kumára.

SMRITI A goddess. Personification of the *smriti* scriptures (texts that are "remembered" by seers).

SOMA The moon. Often described as "hare-marked" or "night-maker."

SOMA·DATTA Father of Bhuri·shravas. Fights for the Káuravas.

SÓMAKA Name of a people. Often grouped with the Panchálas.

SON OF RIGHTEOUSNESS (DHARMA) Yudhi·shthira.

SRÍNJAYA Name of a people. Often grouped with the Panchálas.

STHANU A name for Shiva and a Rudra deity. Also an attendant of Skanda, given by Brahma.

STHANU·TIRTHA A *tirtha* on the Sarásvati.

STHIRA An attendant of Skanda, given by Meru.

SÚBALA Father of Shákuni.

SÚBHRAJA An attendant of Skanda, given by Surya.

SUBHÚMIKA A *tirtha* on the Sarásvati.

SUGRÍVA A monkey chief. Brother of Valin. Also the name of a horse driving Krishna's chariot.

SUKÁNYA Mother of Mánkanaka.

SÚMANI An attendant of Skanda, given by Soma.

SUNDA A demon. Brother of Upasúnda.

SÚPRABHA One of the seven Sarásvati rivers. Also one of the mothers attending Skanda.

SURÉNU One of the seven Sarásvati rivers.

SURYA The sun.

SUVÁRCHASA An attendant of Skanda, given by Hímavat.

SÚVRATA An attendant of Skanda, given by Mitra. Also the name of an attendant of Skanda, given by Vidhátri.

SU·YÓDHANA A name for Dur·yódhana. Literally, "good fighter."

SVAHA A goddess. Originally a ritual exclamation in Vedic sacrifice.

TÁIJASA A *tirtha* on the Sarásvati.

TÁRAKA A demon slain by Vishnu or Skanda.

TARÁNTUKA A location marking the boundary of Kuru·kshetra.

TIRTHA OF SOMA A *tirtha* on the Sarásvati.

TIRTHA OF THE GANDHÁRVAS A *tirtha* on the Sarásvati.

TRINA·BINDU An ascetic.

TRI·PADA A demon slain by Skanda.

TRI·SHIRAS A name for Vishva·rupa. Three-headed ascetic slain by Indra. Son of Tvashtri.

TRITA an ascetic. Brother of the ascetics Ékata and Dvita.

TVASHTRI A god. One of the *adítyas*. Divine craftsman of weapons such as the thunderbolt.

UCCHAIH·SHRAVAS A divine horse, created from nectar when the ocean was churned by gods and demons.

UCCHRÍNGA An attendant of Skanda, given by Vindhya.

UDÁPANA A *tirtha* on the Sarásvati.

UDDÁLAKA An ascetic. Father of Shveta·ketu.

UMA A goddess. Daughter of Hímavat and wife of Shiva. Also known as Párvati.

UNMÁDA An attendant of Skanda, given by Párvati.

ÚNMATHA An attendant of Skanda, given by Yama.

UPAPLÁVYA A city near the capital of the Matsya king Viráta.

UPASÚNDA A demon. Brother of Sunda.

UPÉNDRA A name for Vishnu.

ÚSHANAS An ancient seer. Also known as Shukra.

UTKRÓSHA An attendant of Skanda, given by Indra.

UTTAMÁUJAS A Panchála warrior fighting for the Pándavas. Brother of Yudha·manyu.

VAIJAYÁNTI A garland given by Vishnu to Skanda.

VAIKHÁNASA A group of ascetics.

VAISHAMPÁYANA Disciple of Krishna Dvaipáyana. Recited the 'Maha·bhárata' at Janam·éjaya's snake sacrifice.

VÁISHRAVANA Son of Víshravas.

VALAKHÍLYA A group of ascetics, said to be of minute size.

VALIN A monkey chief. Brother of Sugríva.

VANÉYA A type of ascetic.

VANI A goddess ("Speech").

VARÁHA Vishnu in his incarnation as a boar.

VARANÁVATA The location of Dur·yódhana's attempt to kill the Pándavas in a fire.

VÁRDHANA An attendant of Skanda, given by the Ashvins.

VARSHNÉYA Another name for a Vrishni.

VÁRUNA A god. One of the *adítyas*. Lord of the waters.

VÁSAVA Name of Indra.

VASÍSHTHA A brahmin ascetic. Son of Váruna (or Mitra and Váruna).

Also known as Maitrávaruni. One of the Seven Seers along with Atri, Bharad·vaja, Gáutama, Jamad·agni, Káshyapa, and Vishva·mitra.

VASISHTHÁPAVAHA A *tirtha* on the Sarásvati. Literally, "the channel (or carrying-off) of Vasíshtha."

VASU A class of gods.

VASU·DEVA Father of Krishna and Bala·rama.

VASUDÉVA Name of Krishna. Means "son of Vasu·deva."

VÁSUKI King of the snakes.

VATA An attendant of Skanda, given by Ansha.

VATÁPI A demon. Younger brother of Ílvala.

VAYU God of the wind.

VAYU·BALA A Marut (wind-god).

VAYU·CHAKRA A Marut (wind-god).

VAYU·JVALA A Marut (wind-god).

VÁYUHAN A Marut (wind-god).

VAYU·MÁNDALA A Marut (wind-god).

VAYU·RETAS A Marut (wind-god).

VAYU·VEGA A Marut (wind-god).

VIBHA·VASU A name for Agni.

VICHÍTRA·VIRYA A king. Son of Shántanu and Sátyavati. Brother of Chitrángada and half-brother of Bhishma.

VIDHÁTRI The Ordainer/Creator. Often coupled with Dhatri.

VÍDURA Son of Krishna Dvaipáyana and a low-caste shudra woman. Uncle of the Pándavas and sons of Dhrita·rashtra.

VIDYA·DHARA A type of deity wielding magical power.

VÍGRAHA An attendant of Skanda, given by the Ocean.

VÍJAYA A name for Árjuna. Literally, "victory."

VIKÁRNA A son of Dhrita·rashtra.

VÍKRAMAKA An attendant of Skanda, given by Vishnu.

VIMALÓDAKA One of the seven Sarásvati rivers.

VÍNASHANA A *tirtha* on the Sarásvati.

VINDHYA A mountain.

VIPRA·CHITTI A demon slain by Vishnu.

VIRÁTA King of the Matsyas.

VIRÓCHANA A demon slain by Indra.

VISHÁKHA An aspect of Skanda.

VISHÁLA One of the seven Sarásvati rivers.

VISHNU A god. Often identified with Krishna. Also known as Upéndra.

VÍSHRAVAS Pulástya.

VISHVA·MITRA A king who becomes an ascetic and attains brahminhood. Son of Gadhin. One of the Seven Seers along with Atri, Bharad·vaja, Gáutama, Jamad·agni, Káshyapa, and Vasíshtha.

VISHVA Same as Vishve·deva. A class of god.

VISHVÁSU A *gandhárva* king.

VISHVE·DEVA A class of god. Same as Vishvas.

VIVÁSVAT Father of Yama. One of the *adítya*s and often identical to Surya (the sun).

VRIKÓDARA A name for Bhima. Literally, "wolf-bellied."

VRISHA·SENA A son of Karna.

VRISHNI Name of a Yádava people. Connected with the Ándhakas and Bhojas. Krishna, Sátyaki, and Krita·varman belong to this clan.

VRITRA A demon slain by Indra.

VYASA Krishna Dvaipáyana.

VYAVASÁYA A god ("Effort").

YÁDAVA Name of a people. Descendant of Yadu. Used of Krishna.

YADU Son of Yayáti, ancestor of the Yadus (= Yádavas). The Yadus are often synonymous with the Vrishnis.

YAJNA·SENA Drúpada.

YAKSHA A type of demon or powerful semi-divine being.

YAMA The god of the dead. Son of Vivásvat.

YÁMA A class of god.

YÁMUNA·TIRTHA A *tirtha* on the Sarásvati.

YATI A group of ascetics, the word itself meaning "ascetic."

YÁVANA Name of a people. Connected with Greeks.

YAYÁTA A *tirtha* on the Sarásvati. Connected with Yayáti.

YAYÁTI An ancient king. Son of Náhusha.

YUDHA·MANYU A Panchála warrior fighting for the Pándavas. Brother of Uttamáujas.

YUDHI·SHTHIRA Eldest of the Pándava brothers. Son of Pandu and Kunti (by the god Dharma). Also known as Áchyuta, the Son of Righteousness (Dharma), and the King of Righteousness.

YUYUDHÁNA Sátyaki's proper name.

YUYÚTSU Son of Dhrita·rashtra and a vaishya woman. Joins the Pándavas.

INDEX

Sanskrit words are given in the English alphabetical order, according to the accented CSL pronuncuation aid. They are followed by the conventional diacritics in brackets.

Permitted finals: (Except āḥ/aḥ)

k	ṭ	t	p	ṅ	n	m	ḥ/r	āḥ	aḥ	*Initial letters:*
k	ṭ	t	p	ṅ	n	ṃ	ḥ	āḥ	aḥ	k/kh
g	ḍ	d	b	ṅ	n	ṃ	r	ā	o	g/gh
k	ṭ	c	p	ṅ	ṃś	ṃ	ś	āś	aś	c/ch
g	ḍ	j	b	ṅ	ñ	ṃ	r	ā	o	j/jh
k	ṭ	ṭ	p	ṅ	ṃṣ	ṃ	ṣ	āṣ	aṣ	ṭ/ṭh
g	ḍ	ḍ	b	ṅ	ṇ	ṃ	r	ā	o	ḍ/ḍh
k	ṭ	t	p	ṅ	ṃs	ṃ	s	ās	as	t/th
g	ḍ	d	b	ṅ	n	ṃ	r	ā	o	d/dh
k	ṭ	t	p	ṅ	n	ṃ	ḥ	ā	aḥ	p/ph
g	ḍ	d	b	ṅ	n	ṃ	r	ā	o	b/bh
ṅ	ṇ	n	m	ṅ	n	ṃ	r	ā	o	*nasals* (n/m)
g	ḍ	d	b	ṅ	n	ṃ	r	ā	o	y/v
g	ḍ	d	b	ṅ	n	ṃ	*zero*[1]	ā	o	r
g	ḍ	l	b	ṅ	l̃[2]	ṃ	r	ā	o	l
k	ṭ	c ch	p	ṅ	ñ ś/ch	ṃ	ḥ	āḥ	aḥ	ś
k	ṭ	t	p	ṅ	n	ṃ	ḥ	āḥ	aḥ	ṣ/s
gg h	ḍḍ h	dd h	bb h	ṅ	n	ṃ	r	ā	o	h
g	ḍ	d	b	ṅ/ṅṅ[3]	n/nn[3]	m	r	ā	a[4]	*vowels*
k	ṭ	t	p	ṅ	n	m	ḥ	āḥ	aḥ	*zero*

[1]ḥ or r disappears, and if a/i/u precedes, this lengthens to ā/ī/ū. [2]e.g. tān+lokān=tāl̃ lokān.
[3]The doubling occurs if the preceding vowel is short. [4]Except: aḥ+a=o '.

Final vowels:

a	ā	i	ī	u	ū	ṛ	e	ai	o	au	*Initial vowels:*
' â	" â	y a	y a	v a	v a	r a	e '	ā a	o '	āv a	a
' ā	" ā	y ā	y ā	v ā	v ā	r ā	a ā	ā ā	a ā	āv ā	ā
' ê	" ê	' î	" î	v i	v i	r i	a i	ā i	a i	āv i	i
' ē	" ē	' ī	" ī	v ī	v ī	r ī	a ī	ā ī	a ī	āv ī	ī
' ô	" ô	y u	y u	' û	" û	r u	a u	ā u	a u	āv u	u
' ō	" ō	y ū	y ū	' ū	" ū	r ū	a ū	ā ū	a ū	āv ū	ū
a' r	a" r	y ṛ	y ṛ	v ṛ	v ṛ	' ṝ	a ṛ	ā ṛ	a ṛ	āv ṛ	ṛ
' âi	" âi	y e	y e	v e	v e	r e	a e	ā e	a e	āv e	e
' āi	" āi	y ai	y ai	v ai	v ai	r ai	a ai	ā ai	a ai	āv ai	ai
' âu	" âu	y o	y o	v o	v o	r o	a o	ā o	a o	āv o	o
' āu	" āu	y au	y au	v au	v au	r au	a au	ā au	a au	āv au	au

THE CLAY SANSKRIT LIBRARY

Current Volumes

For more details please consult the CSL website.

1. The Emperor of the Sorcerers (*Bṛhatkathāślokasaṃgraha*) (vol. 1 of 2) by *Budhasvāmin*. Sir James Mallinson
2. Heavenly Exploits (*Divyāvadāna*) Joel Tatelman
3. Maha·bhárata III: The Forest (*Vanaparvan*) (vol. 4 of 4) William J. Johnson
4. Much Ado about Religion (*Āgamaḍambara*) by *Bhaṭṭa Jayanta*. Csaba Dezső
5. The Birth of Kumára (*Kumārasaṃbhava*) by *Kālidāsa*. David Smith
6. Ramáyana I: Boyhood (*Bālakāṇḍa*) by *Vālmīki*. Robert P. Goldman
7. The Epitome of Queen Lilávati (*Līlāvatīsāra*) (vol. 1 of 2) by *Jinaratna*. R.C.C. Feynes
8. Ramáyana II: Ayódhya (*Ayodhyākāṇḍa*) by *Vālmīki*. Sheldon I. Pollock
9. Love Lyrics (*Amaruśataka, Śatakatraya & Caurapañcāśikā*) by *Amaru, Bhartṛhari & Bilhaṇa*. Greg Bailey & Richard Gombrich
10. What Ten Young Men Did (*Daśakumāracarita*) by *Daṇḍin*. Isabelle Onians
11. Three Satires (*Kaliviḍambana, Kalāvilāsa & Bhallaṭaśataka*) by *Nīlakaṇṭha, Kṣemendra & Bhallaṭa* Somadeva Vasudeva
12. Ramáyana IV: Kishkíndha (*Kiṣkindhākāṇḍa*) by *Vālmīki*. Rosalind Lefeber

13. The Emperor of the Sorcerers (*Bṛhatkathāślokasaṃgraha*) (vol. 2 of 2) by *Budhasvāmin*. Sir James Mallinson
14. Maha·bhárata IX: Shalya (*Śalyaparvan*) (vol. 1 of 2) Justin Meiland
15. Rákshasa's Ring (*Mudrārākṣasa*) by *Viśākhadatta*. Michael Coulson
16. Messenger Poems (*Meghadūta, Pavanadūta & Haṃsadūta*) by *Kālidāsa, Dhoyī & Rūpa Gosvāmin*. Sir James Mallinson
17. Ramáyana III: The Forest (*Araṇyakāṇḍa*) by *Vālmīki*. Sheldon I. Pollock
18. The Epitome of Queen Lilávati (*Līlāvatīsāra*) (vol. 2 of 2) by *Jinaratna*. R.C.C. Feynes
19. Five Discourses on Worldly Wisdom (*Pañcatantra*) by *Viṣṇuśarman*. Patrick Olivelle
20. Ramáyana V: Súndara (*Sundarakāṇḍa*) by *Vālmīki*. Robert P. Goldman & Sally J. Sutherland Goldman
21. Maha·bhárata II: The Great Hall (*Sabhāparvan*) Paul Wilmot
22. The Recognition of Shakúntala (*Abhijñānaśākuntala*) (Kashmir Recension) by *Kālidāsa*. Somadeva Vasudeva
23. Maha·bhárata VII: Drona (*Droṇaparvan*) (vol. 1 of 4) Vaughan Pilikian
24. Rama Beyond Price (*Anargharāghava*) by *Murāri*. Judit Törzsök
25. Maha·bhárata IV: Viráta (*Virāṭaparvan*) Kathleen Garbutt
26. Maha·bhárata VIII: Karna (*Karṇaparvan*) (vol. 1 of 2) Adam Bowles
27. "The Lady of the Jewel Necklace" and "The Lady who Shows her Love" (*Ratnāvalī & Priyadarśikā*) by *Harṣa*. Wendy Doniger
28. The Ocean of the Rivers of Story (*Kathāsaritsāgara*) (vol. 1 of 9) by *Somadeva*. Sir James Mallinson
29. Handsome Nanda (*Saundarananda*) by *Aśvaghoṣa*. Linda Covill

To Appear in 2007

"Friendly Advice" (*Hitopadeśa*) by *Nārāyaṇa* &
"King Víkrama's Adventures" (*Vikramacarita*). JUDIT TÖRZSÖK

Rama's Last Act (*Uttararāmacarita*)
by *Bhavabhūti*. SHELDON I. POLLOCK

"How the Nagas were Pleased" (*Nāgānanda*) by *Harṣa* &
"The Shattered Thighs" (*Ūrubhaṅga*) by *Bhāsa*
ANDREW SKILTON

The Life of the Buddha (*Buddhacarita*) by *Aśvaghoṣa*
PATRICK OLIVELLE

Maha·bhárata V: Preparations for War (*Udyogaparvan*) (vol. 1 of 2)
KATHLEEN GARBUTT

Maha·bhárata VI: Bhishma (*Bhīṣmaparvan*) (vol. 1 of 2)
ALEX CHERNIAK

Maha·bhárata VIII: Karna (*Karṇaparvan*) (vol. 2 of 2)
ADAM BOWLES

The Ocean of the Rivers of Story (*Kathāsaritsāgara*) (vol. 2 of 9)
by *Somadeva*. SIR JAMES MALLINSON